Empire of Blood and Darkness

BOOK 1

Written by Travis Yardley

Inspired Forever Books
Dallas, Texas

Inspired Forever Books™
"Words with Lasting Impact"
Dallas, Texas
(888) 403-2727
https://inspiredforeverbooks.com

Library of Congress Control Number: 2021916720

Paperback ISBN 13: 978-1-948903-43-1

Printed in the United States of America

Thank You

Reader, this page is a thank you note and an explanation of the naming occurring within this book. Now some character names are purely made up, due to how I started writing this. I then began to base them on actual name meanings. There are a few that follow these criteria. The names for words are also pronounced a certain way. There are four in-universe writing systems used. The main one is Onglikae (On-gla-kay), which is the in-world version of English. Magic is written using this system as well as standard writing. Three of the countries use the Onglikae script as their standard writing system with the other three using it for trade. Onglikae is also solely spoken in three countries. The other three countries will have their own languages, with certain individuals being fluent in Onglikae. Now some words are pronounced a certain way due to me intentionally setting them up that way. However, some pronunciation comes from Onglikae's origins. Onglikae evolved from Nillequoaon (Nee-el-a-kwa-an), the language used by the Nillequoa (Nee-el-a-kwa). For example, this book is called *Blood of Thaemell*. Thaemell is pronounced fay-mell. Any time a th- is used regarding either magic or place names, it is pronounced like f-. Another is xaen- X in front of words is always pronounced like a z. Ae is always pronounced long, such as fate or bait. Single j- at the start of words is pronounced as h-. Double i, ie-, and y- are all pronounced as long e, as in heat or beet. I- by itself is pronounced like hit. Uu- is pronounced long, as in you. Oo- is pronounced as dew. Single o is pronounced like hot. Ooo- is pronounced as one o. This is actually going to be transcribed with the symbol Ɵ or ϴ. This can be used interchangeably in Latin script. Ei- is pronounced like eye. Ith- is pronounced like the long e and f sound in beef. Yba- is pronounced long e- then short a- like bat. C- at the beginning of words is pronounced like s. G- is pronounced hard like the sound in joule. De- is pronounced as a hard d- followed by an -a sound, as in saying a book for example. R- at the beginning of a word is pronounced normally, as in English words like rock. R- at the end of a word is pronounced like fur. –P, -k, and t- are all pronounced the same way as in English. E- is pronounced short, like bet, but with an l behind it is always pronounced like the letter l-. This is the criteria for words that have their origins in Niellequaon, which was an older language spoken on the continent of Thaemell many, many, many years before the story. This is to help you with the pronunciation of words such as various magic or place names of countries or landmarks because it all stems from that language. So, for the countries in the story, they are pronounced as follows Eltheneae (el-fen-a-a-ay), Ciimerii (see-mer-ee), Xythuu (zeef-you), Geroooith (ger-o-eef), Hyybeth (he-bef), and Mooelae (moo-el-ay). The next few pages will include the Ongikae script, which is a calligraphy form of writing, meaning all the letters connect closely to each other. This is to give you the idea I had imagined certain magic taking over the years I have written this. Now there is also a timeline and calendar. Now the months are the same due to this being a creation. However, the timeline is different. This timeline does not use our standard B.C. (Before Christ) or A.D. (Anno Domini). It also does not utilize the B.C.E (Before Common Era) or C.E (Common Era) method either. Instead, it uses ANF. Specifically, the story starts at 1000 ANF. Now I won't quite reveal just yet what that stands for. Lastly, I want to thank you for buying this book and hopefully reading it all. If not, I totally understand. My dream has always been to be a published writer and I have been working on that now for eight long years. I greatly appreciate your buying my work because without the support of my readers, I won't get anywhere. So read on and enjoy.

Prologue

On the continent of Thaemell there once existed a race of people called the Niellequa. The Niellequa were known for their wisdom and societal advancement. Long ago in a different age, they arrived from a land far away. Upon arrival to the new world, they made the place their home and spread across the continent. They lived relatively peaceful lives and had an abundance of knowledge. The Niellequa documented the phenomenon known in the world as *magic*. Unfortunately, much of their knowledge has been lost with their disappearance. It is not known what happened to most of the Niellequa. Scholars argue that they faced some sort of cataclysm or possibly fought intense wars over fierce debates. Many know that with the destruction of the Niellequaon society, those who remained formed tribes and changed over time. The descendants of these survivors would go on to shape the modern world in Thaemell.

Close to one hundred years after the fall of the Niellequa, hundreds of tribes, each comprising thousands of people, settled around the Escali Forest and down the Escali River. Three tribes banded together and founded a city-state. Eventually, two of the three tribe leaders died, and the last was declared the city-state's king. This was how the Kingdom of Eltheneae was founded.

As time drew on, more tribes assimilated into the kingdom, many out of a desire to become part of a larger unity. Some were defeated when they foolishly attacked the kingdom, and Eltheneae took control of their land to ensure no more threats could arise. This was how Eltheneae came to its current size. To the south of the kingdom's territory, many separate tribes banded together with others and established city-states around a river they named Regalian for its regality. This first city-state sought to expand their territory, seek resources, and bring glory to their state. They assimilated the other city-states into their own and began to aggressively attack all in their way until they spread across the land and stretched to the mountains and the sea. This was the birth of the Kingdom of Xythuu.

Many tribes leaving Eltheneae and Xythuu migrated until they reached the sea. Those brave souls then sailed across the sea, taking a northern sea route that led them to a northern island. They then established a city and spread across the island. Those new nationals favored a democratic style of government and established the Republic of Hyybeth. Many of the island's inhabitants were not fully satisfied with this style of government—particularly, there was a group of five influential members who had many followers. They wanted to run the government the way they thought best, with the five members making decisions and sharing all the authority. This was denied by the new republic, and a brief civil war started. The supporters of the five lost and fled the island to avoid persecution. They sailed farther west and discovered another island that was larger and covered in lush rainforest. They encountered unknown people there. The local population clashed with the newcomers but were then made part of the new nation. The new members established their home, and the five began to make the decisions of the fledgling nation. This was how the Oligarchy of Mooelae was born. Many descendants of the five still rule the island nation.

There were many tribes that had settled next to a river named Kaethan. Eventually these tribes faced confrontation with the Kingdom of Xythuu and abandoned the location and traveled west. They settled there and eventually spread south to the mountains. This tribe had developed a religion and brought their beliefs with them. This faith helped give birth to their new nation in their new settled lands, which became known as the Theocracy of Ciimerii. Their ruler was established by a selection of priests who elected a priest whom they believed held the light incarnate.

According to legend, when the Kingdom of Xythuu had attacked their lands, one man had led the people to the west, where the light had been shining. This was how the first Rex Legis came to be. Rex Legis was the name given to the ruler of Ciimerii, who was responsible for administering the country and ensuring its faith.

Many people disagreed with the theocracy's combined zeal and rule. One man openly spoke out against it early in the nation's history and inspired people to follow him. A threat of war ensued, and the man departed with his followers before a war could tear apart the young nation. They were given supplies and made their way to the sea. They sailed west and landed on an island with red beaches and rugged and mountainous terrain. They established their own cities there, and the man who led them was crowned the first king of Geroooith.

This was how the modern nations were established. Unfortunately, during this time of disaster and the founding of tribal states and nations, the survivors did not write much down, and their oral histories began to change with time. Their descendants live on, however, in their own tales of strife and hope.

Map and Alphabet

Map notes

*(capital)

<u>Top left</u>

Mooelae

Tarakeina*, next to mountains known as the Tarakeina Mts

Ahistowaha, at the end of the Tarakeina River entering ocean

Black Rainforest

<u>Lower Left</u>

Geroooith

Horanostin*, center of Geroooith between Horanostin River and Atbrɘxi River

Horanotrexni, next to Horanotrexni River in west Geroooith

Atrexi, on coast of east Geroooith between Horanostin and Atrexi Rivers

Rekami, on southeast coast between the Rekami and Horanostin Rivers

The island of Geren is in the middle of the sea

Kosecha island lies north

Top middle

Hyybeth

Faraeth* lies in the middle northern coast

Faraeth Plains compose most of the island

Lower middle

Ciimerii

Linwae* in the center, next to Linwae River

Lein on Ydaeriin River, across from Fort Ydaeriin

Riiwae on western North coast

Nuuwae on western southern coast

Ciimerii mts on eastern border, with Ciimerii River wrapping around and makes border with Xythuu

Top Right

Eltheneae

Fort Ydaeriin across from Lein

Ydaeriin Plains north of Fort Ydaeriin

Port Ivory on western lower coast

Ilgeth on western top coast

Escali River forms in the plains and branches of into the eastern branch into Escali Forest

Escali Forest is east of the river

Jylinae*, North of the forest

Adaexo Plains east of the forest

Fort Escali South next to Escali River

Regalian south on the River west of Regalian Forest

Regalian River comprises border with Xythuu

Pearl River west of the Adaexo Plains

Bottom right

Xythuu

Asterae, southwestern Xythuu on Ciimerii River

Fort Kaethan on Kaethan River

Kaethan River flows from Kaethan Mts that compose the border with Eltheneae

Lake Kaethan is slightly southeast of the river

Upper Kaethan is the northernmost city on the lake

Kaethan* lies southeast of there

Middle Kaethan lies south of Kaethan

Lower Kaethan lies at the south of the lake

Regalia lies at the north on the Regalian River

Port Regalia lies east on the coast

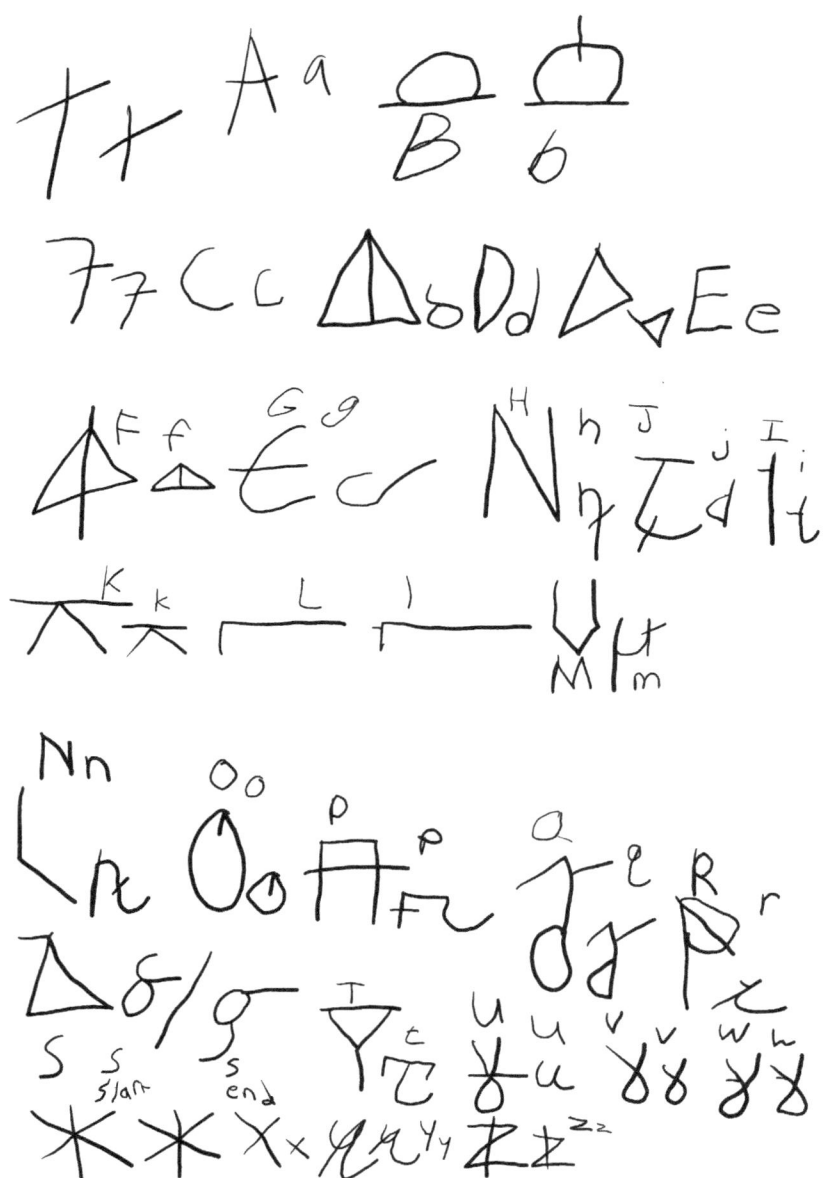

Chapter 1

Alexander felt the sun shining upon his face from the top-right sliver of his window. He slowly sat up and rubbed the sleep from his eyes, and afterward he stumbled wearily to his bathroom. The cold stone underneath his feet sent chills up his spine. Inside his bathroom was a wooden stool with an enclosed side and a medium-sized bronze urn placed on the floor next to the stool. He moved the urn to reveal a hole in the floor that connected to the plumbing system underneath. He began to relieve himself into the hole and then moved the urn back into place. Once finished, he proceeded back into his room and reached for a brush and mirror from a side table attached to his bed frame. He brushed his tousled brown hair until it lay neatly, the front sweeping across his eyebrows. He then reached into a large potter urn and removed a flowing, slightly shiny brown robe. He slipped on a pair of long sandals and laced them together tightly.

Alexander walked with grace down the stairs of his house. His family lived in the middle of the three sections of Jylinae, the capital of Eltheneae. His parents had bought the house during their engagement. His mother, Eirene, stopped and looked at him with admiration.

Her red-brown hair flowed freely down her shoulders, over her light-blue robe, perfectly suiting her natural artistic persona. "You look wonderful," she said. "I wish your father were still alive to see to this, though." He could see a sadness in her eyes.

"So do I, Mother," Alexander said, trying to comfort his mother. His father, Patrick, had been a Loxeias—or middle-ranking military member—in the Kingdom of Eltheneae. Patrick had been part of a garrison that had been assigned to protect cargo ships carrying supplies into the kingdom from Hyybeth. The ship, unfortunately, had been attacked by pirates, and Patrick had been killed in the defense of the ships. That was six years ago, shortly after Alexander had turned twelve years old. He still remembered the day he had received the news and how he had repeatedly cried into his bed. Alexander still always thought of his father and was honored to be his son.

"I know he would be just as proud of you as I am," his mother said. With that, he and his mother walked out the door, fully embracing the future. They made their way down a busy street with marble buildings lining both sides of it. Many people dressed in robes were moving in the same direction as them. After about fifteen minutes of walking, they reached the Grand Courtyard of Jylinae. The Grand Courtyard was a massive open circle of grass with a wooden stage in the center of it. Many wooden chairs were set up around the stage. His mother left his side to go take a seat.

After a brief walk, Alexander joined his friends Camilla, Urien, Cadfan, Tesni, Dysan, Aeronwen, and Delyth, and they all took their seats close to the stage. His friends were suited in similar flowing brown robes. They had each decided to join the military. Ceremonies were usually done all across Eltheneae to celebrate the new members of their military.

"Hi, everybody," Tesni said warmly. "Is anybody as excited as I am?"

"Yes. This is my calling in life," Camilla stated.

Alexander and his childhood friends had each decided on joining for their own reasons. Alexander had wanted to follow in his father's footsteps. Cadfan and Urien, too, were joining because of their fathers' tales. Cadfan had once said he thought it would personally bring him glory. Tesni and Aeronwen hoped to provide help to those who needed it, while Camilla wanted to experience other places. Delyth was joining so that she one day could be an instructor in Jylinae, and Dysan had a goal of becoming a general. More people gathered into seats near them and began to crowd the area around the chairs. Alexander could see a huge group of troops gathering toward the opening of the Grand Courtyard, and three figures stood in the middle, which meant that the king, queen, and prince of Eltheneae were now in attendance.

A man on the stage stepped forward and spoke into a horn to project his voice. The man was named Hector and was an orator; he regularly gave speeches or made announcements at Jylinae events.

Hector stepped forward at the podium. Hector was thirty years old and had very short hair and thin facial hair on his narrow, slightly tanned face. "Good morning, Jylinae! I trust you are all nervous and excited? From this day on, you will step on the base of the mountains that will be your lives. As you all know, this is a tradition that has been passed on through the ages. This is the Apprentice Ceremony, where we publicly announce those who have elected to join our military and announce which guild they will train in before being assigned their duty. When you leave today, many of you will leave as apprentices in the military guilds of Eltheneae! Know this—you are always meant for something. With that in mind, let us proceed to naming the apprentices."

Hector removed a piece of papyrus from his pocket. "Now as many know, if you are skilled with a bow, you can join the Bowman guild among other things. This list is of those who opted to join the ranks of Eltheneae in this role." Hector then began to read off names on his list.

Camilla was seated next to Alexander, and he could see a slight sad smile on her face. Her father, Geoffrey, had been a Bowman and had been part of the same garrison as Alexander's father. He had also been killed by the same pirates. He had taught her well before he had died.

Two more names were called; then Hector said, "Camilla Ridgeson."

In total, Hector read off one hundred names. He then removed another list from his pocket. "Our next category is our newest future

Dynamis. These are our members with the brown affinity for magic, making them capable of increasing their physical strength for short durations. They usually wield axes as their choice of weapon and are one of the many cogs of our military." Hector read off his list of names one by one. A few minutes had passed by the time he called Dysan's name. He soon finished the list. A thunderous applause followed.

The applause died down, and Hector continued on. "This next list is one of our most important," Hector said as he paced with the horn in his hand. "Our next list is often the most vulnerable. They are in charge of gathering intelligence of any potential adversaries of the kingdom. A majority of them even command the gray affinity, allowing them to harness their energy to hide them and others from sight. Rogue criminals are tracked down and captured by them. This puts these brave men and women in danger constantly. For this reason, we celebrate them, and this list has the names of the newest Nightcloaks-to-be." Hector removed another list from within his robe. He called one name, then followed with more. Hector called the name of Urien's rival, Michael. Michael turned from his seat at the end of the row in front of Alexander and his friends. He shot a smug look toward Urien. After a few more names had been called, Hector shouted out Urien's name in a masterful display of charisma.

After the subsequent applause had died down, Hector paused his pacing. "Our next list is another important cog in our armies. These members are known for their mastery of long, slender, and elegant swords. They also possess and master the hazel affinity, making them capable of extremely fast body movements and reactions. Due to the nature of their skills, many are often used as personal guards, such as those of the Royal Guard behind us. Our own King Aldric and Crown Prince Ethan were trained as Lepides. We will now announce the new Lepides of Eltheneae!" Hector began rattling off his list of names. He shouted off Cadfan Arvil shortly into his list.

Cadfan leaned back in his chair, tilting slightly, and smirked.

"Obviously. Who wouldn't want me?" Cadfan said.

"Stop being so arrogant," Aeronwen chided.

"No society functions without its members who provide care for the sick and injured," Hector stated boisterously. "This next list is our members who possess the white affinity, making them capable of healing various mechanical wounds to the body. They also practice many herbal remedies for sickness, administering them to the population. Once sufficiently advanced in their magical prowess, they can bring those recent victims of unnatural death back from the brink with exchange of their own life force, shortening their own lives. Many have walked the path of martyrs before. We now honor the new members who have the capability and have elected to be Vivicanterns." Hector began to sound off names, with applause following after each. "Aeronwen Eirylis," he shouted elegantly.

"Good job," said Tesni as she hugged Aeronwen.

"Now our next list is a second list of those who have the white affinity and practice healing. However, these are the only known people to have two types of affinities—white and blue. This enables them to not only practice the healing arts but also gives them the capability of strengthening natural properties through blessings. These members are sufficient lance-and-shield warriors and form the bulk of our garrisons. This list, of course, refers to our newest Oracles," Hector said with a cheerful bellow. Hector read off a list of names in rapid succession. In the middle, he shouted Tesni Glenice. Alexander saw her smile from ear to ear. He finished that list, and then the applause died down.

"Our next list makes up a majority of our armies. The most special thing about this list is that, like myself and many of you, those in this path primarily have no affinity for any magic. Those with magic affinities who undertake this training go into specialized corps. Those without, however, are still capable and experienced after undergoing rigorous lance-and-shield training. I now announce our newest Ascalons!" Hector exclaimed, his voice echoing into the courtyard. He shouted off name after name. Hector carried on for a few long minutes and was nearing the end of his list. The final name he called was with a thunderous bellow as he shouted out Delyth Vaughn.

Tesni hugged her other friend sitting next to her.

The crowd once again quieted down. Alexander eyed Hector as he slowly paced on stage. "Our next list is of those with the black affinity, who are capable of managing the various aspects of dark magic. They study omens and curses as a means to fight against them. Our next list is of our newest Skotadi." Hector methodically went over his list. He was met with the same applause as before. The applause died down, and he carried on.

"Now our final list is one of our most important. This list contains those members with the green affinity. This makes them capable of generating and mastering the various forms of the elements. They utilize fire, wind, water, and lightning to augment our forces. Those members of this affinity are also extremely vital to powering our methods of transport. This is our list of Illustratum!" There was a thunderous applause that followed. Once the crowd quieted down, Hector read off his list of names. Somewhere in the middle, Hector shouted at Alexander Kai, and Alexander smiled widely.

"Apprentices, you start your training Monday morning. Everyone, congratulate Eltheneae's newest. Remember—you are always meant for something. This concludes our ceremony."

Afterward, people began to clear out of the Grand Courtyard. Alexander and his friends walked to where their parents were seated. His mother hugged him tight and exclaimed with great joy in her voice, "I'm so proud of you! You're going to be an Illustratum! Your father would be just as proud." Her smile fell for just a moment, and Alexander wished that his father could still be alive to see him in this moment. He wondered what he would say or how he would act.

Dysan's parents hugged their son. His father was about the same size as him, but Dysan had to bend so as to hug his mother. Many often wondered how she had given birth to him.

Tesni's eight-year-old sister, Sophie, bounded up to her. She had the same auburn hair as Tesni. "Tesni, one day I want to be an Oracle too."

"Then I'm more than positive that one day you will," Tesni said, bending over to be at eye level with her sister.

Alexander watched as the rest of his friends celebrated with their parents, all hugging each other and talking eagerly about the training to come.

* * *

Later in the evening, Alexander and his friends went to the wall in the first section, as they had numerous times before, to bask in the beautiful setting rays of the sun as they were cast upon the Escali Forest.

"It's hard to believe how much our lives will soon change. We'll be making our way into the world," Camilla said as she leaned on the wall.

Aeronwen, who stood next to her, said, "Yes, we are. One day we will be something more than what we are now."

Tesni remarked, "Yeah, but it is a bit scary. Being assigned away from you all makes me nervous. But at least we can learn magic now." Everyone laughed.

Cadfan, sitting on the wall with his feet dangling, said, "One day they will erect statues of all of us, and people will gasp at their magnificence!"

Aeronwen scolded him slightly. "You're being arrogant again. We shouldn't expect to be carved in stone," she said.

"You know you want a statue of yourself," Cadfan said to her.

Tesni stuck her hand into the middle of their circle of friends. Alexander and the rest of them knew from experience that this meant she wanted her friends to make and keep a promise, so they all placed their hands upon hers.

"Let's promise that no matter what happens to any of us, we will always remain friends." They all promised at the same time. As the sun dipped under the horizon and the darkness began to settle, Alexander and his friends returned to their homes, eager to begin the next chapters in their lives.

Chapter 2

It was shortly after dawn when Alexander and his friends met in the Grand Courtyard before leaving for their training. Instead of the simple brown robes they had all worn yesterday, they each wore clothing that suited their individual styles. Alexander had his father's cloak pinned over his shirt. Once they started their training, they would be required to wear the training gear that their guilds required in green, the color of apprenticeship.

Camilla was sitting on the edge of the fountain and sighed. "First day," she said.

"Don't be nervous," Aeronwen encouraged.

"It will be fine," Tesni said with her usual warm cheer. "I wonder what I'll learn first."

Alexander laughed. "They'll probably make us decipher surviving Niellequaon artifacts." He would enjoy that. He, Tesni, and Aeronwen regularly studied artifacts at the museum.

Cadfan chuckled and said, "Maybe for the three of you. I will be spending the day with a sword."

"We need to go soon," said Delyth quietly. There was a silence briefly and then shuffling as they all began to stand. The sun was a bit higher in the sky, which signaled that it was time for them to leave.

"Well, good luck," said Tesni. At that, they all walked their separate ways to their schools.

Alexander walked into the marble Illustratum building. It was four stories high, as were most of the buildings in Jylinae, and spread sixty feet from end to end. Silver banners emblazoned with the Illustratum glyph hung freely from the pillars. Alexander pushed through the doors to find the other Illustratum apprentices standing together in the middle of the front room. Alexander, followed by three more apprentices, joined the mass. The noise of multiple people speaking at once ceased as an older Illustratum walked through the door.

"Quiet, everyone," he instructed. He appeared to be in his early thirties, had brown hair tied behind his head, and had a neatly trimmed beard on his chin and under his nose. He had the glyph of Panoloxeias, a rank that was above Loxeias, marked on his robe—a diamond surrounded by the same depictions of the four basic elements that other Illustratum wore. "My name is Regnor Streng. First, we'll start by getting you your robes. You must wear your robes every day. If you show up not in your robes, I will deduct points, and you'll be given tedious things to do." At his command, the apprentices walked one by one to a table where the cloaks were laid out. Alexander removed his father's cloak and placed it in a satchel he was carrying. He then lifted the green apprentice robe over his head and draped it over himself. It crossed over his right shoulder, hung to his knees, and fit snugly on him.

"Second, attendance is mandatory. You are now part of the army and have to be where you are assigned. If you don't show up, I can administer various punishments at my level in command," said Regnor. That was standard policy in the kingdom. Most apprenticeships were strict on attendance. At this point, all the students had their apprentice robes draped over their regular clothing.

"You have all signed on to be Illustratum and will thus be taught magic use. You will learn to harness energy in Lapideases, use magic offensively, and defend against it. We will not be studying Niellequaon. What artifacts survive remain in the museum, and they will not allow them to leave. Not only are you learning magic, but you are learning tactics. You will learn to analyze situations and not just go about swinging an axe like a madman. We will also learn swordplay with short swords but not the intense training our Lepides brothers and sisters do. All apprentices learn tactics, as you know, but we want ours to be in the best condition possible. Now, everyone, follow me into your classroom." Regnor led his students from the main room down the hall and entered a room four doors down. "Your seat has a paper with your name etched on it. Take your seats."

The apprentices began looking for their seats. Alexander found his in the middle of the third row. Three books were waiting for him—one red, one blue, and one green.

"I'll explain the rules," said Regnor. "You are to bring these books *every* day. Failure to bring a book will result in you losing a point. Do *not* lose them because they are expensive to replace, and you probably do not want to spend any money you might make on new books. You are to be in this room and in your seat precisely at eight. Do whatever you need to do before class," Regnor said very adamantly.

"We have daily points that will be averaged for every day in a six-week period. You start with ten a day, but you will lose one point for every book that you do not bring, one point for being tardy, and five for not wearing your robe. The passing score at the end of this course will be two thousand and ninety. Meaning if you lose more than ten points, you will be washed into a newer class and start over. If you lose more than ten on your second go, you are then dropped from the entire apprenticeship and discharged from the army, and you forfeit all entitlements. Before you leave here, you will see a financier and start your pay. You will report alphabetically on the fifth of every month to receive your pay. From eight to ten, we will be studying swordplay, mechanics, and anatomy. From ten to twelve, we will work on magic, starting with harnessing energy from Lapideases and eventually from your own body, and once you can do that, we will move on to offensive magic. From twelve to one, you get lunch. You can eat food here. It's very cheap and good. Or you can leave here and go wherever it is you want to eat. I don't care, just as long as you are in this room and in your seat by one.

"From one to two, we will practice defensive magic, fortifications, and breaking fortifications. Once you get proficiently skilled, you will do combat against each other. From two to three, you will be studying tactics. Pull out your blue books, and open to the table of contents." Alexander and the other students put their green and red books in the wooden slots under their desks and opened the blue books. The title was *Sword Mechanics and Human Anatomy.* Alexander took in a breath and smiled. It was going to be difficult, but it was what he wanted.

* * *

Camilla walked past the blue Bowman banners of the Bowman building and into the main room. The noise of the room soon filled her ears. All the young apprentices were talking about how excited they were to be in archery or what they would amount to. Moments later, a female Bowman, no older than twenty, with a single long black braid walked through a door on the far side of the room.

"Hello, everyone. My name is Jennifer Kelthin, and I'm going to be your primary teacher for this apprenticeship," she said warmly. Camilla overheard some of the male apprentices whisper about her attractiveness, and she tried to brush off her own irritation about the comments. "First off," said Jennifer, "come grab your jackets."

Camilla followed several other students to a table nearby and grabbed a Bowman jacket in her size. Like other apprentice clothes, it was green. "Next, if you will all follow me, we'll discuss the class expectations," Jennifer said, leading her students into the room she had walked out of. "Now find your seats." Camilla took her seat in the back. Placed atop the desk were three books.

"First of all," Jennifer said, still cheerily, "you are to wear your jackets every day. If you do not, you lose a point. Ladies today is okay, but afterward you need to wear pants. You are expected to be in your seat at eight, and if you are late, you lose a point. Bring your books every day, because you lose a point for each one that you do not bring. In this class you will learn about archery. You will learn how to shoot a bow. You will make your own bow. You will learn how to track and hunt. The training for this class is to instill precision in your shooting capabilities. First, we will start you off with training bows with arrow notches.

"However, after three weeks have passed and you have made your own bow, you will be expected to know how to shoot a bow without the notches. Your bow, whether the training one or your personal one, is required every day. If you have one at home that meets the standards of use upon inspection by me or someone else, by all means bring it. A bow is required every day, or you lose a point." Jennifer continued to explain how the point system worked as Camilla listened attentively, trying to grasp every detail.

Jennifer moved on to the daily schedule. "You are to be seated at eight. From eight to ten, we study the anatomy of humans and other creatures to ensure fatal shots. You get a ten-minute break at nine. From nine to twelve, we practice your shooting skills. From twelve to one, you get your lunch. You must be back in your seat by one. From one to three, you will practice your tracking abilities as well as sword fighting with practice swords. You will be assigned your first project today.

"Due in four weeks, you are to craft your very own bow. You can make it as decorative as you want, provided you have the time to do it. And you will show each step of crafting the bow. It must have your name on it so that we know you didn't buy one. Do not attempt to buy a bow," she said with emphasis, "because I will be able to tell, and you will automatically fail. Now get out your green books." The students opened their green books and proceeded into their training.

* * *

Urien approached the Nightcloak training building and stepped inside, where he followed the noise of conversation until he found the group of apprentices in a classroom. As his gaze swept the room, he made eye contact with Michael, who snorted and turned away.

After looking over the names on the remaining desks, Urien took his seat. Four books and a green cloak sat in front of him. He glanced around to see if his fellow apprentices were wearing their cloaks yet, and the two women to his right hastily acted as though they had not just been caught staring at him and started whispering between themselves.

An instructor walked into the room. He had scruffy brown hair and a brown beard. "Good morning. My name is Victor Ariti. I will be your instructor. We start class at eight sharp, so that is when you need to be in your seats. You are to wear your cloaks every day. You will lose points and possibly have to do some tedious assignment if you do not bring them. You also lose a point if you do not bring your books when needed. Our schedule is as follows. Eight to ten, we study human anatomy. From ten to ten fifteen, you get a break. You must be back in your seats or in the assigned training area on time or you lose points.

"Attendance is mandatory. You all chose this field, and so as future Nightcloaks, you represent this guild, and you will not sully it. Being a Nightcloak is also serious business, for which I will train you to become the best spies, infiltrators, thieves, and assassins of this kingdom. Know this job involves highly clandestine operations, most of which can be very dangerous. You can choose to leave and be put into another apprenticeship, but I can't guarantee where you'll go. More than likely something boring with no affinity requirement."

No one left their seat. "Good, then. That's what I like to see. From ten fifteen to eleven, we will practice your stealth skills. From eleven to eleven fifteen, you get a second break. From then on until twelve, we practice various combat skills. From twelve to one, you get your lunch. No matter where you go to eat, as with other breaks, you must be in your seat or the assigned training area by one. From one to three, we practice counter stealth operations. Now put on your cloaks and open your *Human Anatomy* books." Urien and the rest of the students did as instructed.

* * *

In the middle of the Vivicantern building was a serene fountain with water gently flowing out of the top. Aeronwen slowly walked past it, admiring its aesthetic. After a few moments, she veered to a room on her right, where she could see other apprentices gathering. Two of them walked over when she entered the room.

"Hi. I'm Marcus, and this is Malcolm," said the man with short brown hair, gesturing toward the one with neat, flowing blond hair. "We've seen you before and wanted to know if you would like to join us for lunch so we can get to know you," Marcus asked.

"Today I'm joining my friends for lunch. Perhaps some other time?" Aeronwen said.

"Very well. No issues there," Marcus replied, a lackluster expression on his face.

At that moment, a young woman in a flowing white robe, blue gloves, and a blue sash walked in from the doors at the back of the room.

"Congratulations on making it to the apprenticeship level. If you do well, you will pass this apprenticeship and become Vivicanterns. I am Eurwen, and I will be instructing you." As Eurwen spoke, she motioned toward the room she had just come from, and they all began to file in. Aeronwen found her seat near the door, which was marked with her name. At this point she looked to the front of the class. Her instructor was most likely in her mid twenties, with vermillion hair that flowed past her shoulders and hung above her eyes.

"Hopefully I will have all of your names memorized in a week and you can remove that awful tag on your seat," Eurwen commented. "First, take out your robe, and put it on; then drape your sash over your shoulder." The apprentices did as instructed, draping themselves in their white robes and hanging their green sashes over their shoulders.

"We serve the light in this class. We dedicate ourselves to helping others, no matter the situation. You will learn light magic here as well as medicine. You will learn to harness energy from a Lapideas. You will be healers and heal all manners of injuries and illnesses. Here is our schedule. From eight to ten, we study medicine. You get a fifteen-minute break here. And then from ten fifteen to eleven, we will be learning to use

Lapideases. You get a five-minute break here. From eleven to twelve, we practice hands-on first aid without magic use. Then from twelve to one, you get lunch. Yay, right? That's what you all want right now—not to hear me talk," Eurwen said. Some students laughed. "Be back on time or you will lose a point. You guys can eat here or leave, but either way, be back in your seat by one. Then we spend the last hours of our day in nap time."

"Really?" asked a male student.

"No. If I don't get to sleep, you guys don't get to sleep. Our last hours focus on combat use of light magic once you are able to harness energy. I have just a few rules for this class. I'm not as strict as the older Vivicanterns. I ask that you come to class. Obviously, attendance is mandatory. But no one wants us knocking on your door. You represent the Vivicanterns of this building always, and you will not sully our name. I also ask that you treat me, your classmates, and others with respect. But that is also obvious. You are apprentices and know not to disrespect a Loxeias or other ranking members.

"It will make your duty in this class much easier. We can have fun while learning. However, if you disrespect me or your classmates, this class will turn into a living hell. I don't always like to do that, but if I have to, I will. But I like things to be fun sometimes, so don't lose that privilege. Okay, so now open that pretty blue book on your desk that says *Medicinal Applications*."

* * *

Cadfan looked around at his fellow apprentices with a smug smile slung across his face. *Time to weigh the competition and outshine them,* he thought wryly. The one to his right appeared to be a merchant's son. *Easy competition.*

A man with short brown hair and a pointed beard stood at the front of the room. "All right, settle down, everybody," he said. "My name is Price Vason, and I am your primary instructor. In this course you will be trained to become Lepides. You will learn swordplay. You will learn maneuverings, disarming techniques, reflex training, and eventually physical manipulation. Your uniforms are on your desks. Open them now and put them on." The students scrambled to put on their uniforms. The uniforms were green shirts with long, slightly tight sleeves and a split shirttail that hung to the knees.

"You also have a leathered wooden sword. In the space provided, mark your name. These will be your practice swords. You are to bring these every day," Price said with a strict tone. Cadfan looked over the sword in front of him. It was three feet long with a curve in the blade.

Price continued. "This is a very rigorous training course. We strive for perfection in swordplay, and if you don't obtain it, you will not succeed. Today we will start by learning where a good strike is, so open your *Human Anatomy* books."

* * *

Dysan was barely able to contain his excitement as he joined a group of other apprentices. After thirty seconds, he could calm himself no longer. "Are you all as excited as I am to begin Dynami apprenticeship?"

One of the other apprentices, a blond man who was roughly six feet tall like Dysan, responded, "We're all excited. But calm yourself a little, eh, axe-brother?"

Dysan noticed that only a few were fidgeting as much as he was. "Right," Dysan agreed, forcing himself to settle down.

The blond extended his hand, saying, "I'm Jackson."

Dysan shook Jackson's hand. "Dysan. Pleased to meet you, axe-brother Jackson."

At this moment, Dysan noticed three men in the class who could be described as small in build.

Another apprentice with short orange-blond hair introduced himself. "Hello, everyone. My name is Will." After taking a breath, he then directed a question toward one of the smaller apprentices. "No offense, but are you sure you want to take this apprenticeship?"

Two of the men did not look offended, but the other one turned bright red and stepped toward Will. "What makes any of you better than us? Simply because you're bigger, you think we wouldn't be able to handle it and that you are more prone to success?" The third man just stared at Will with ice in his eyes.

"I'm sorry. I meant no offense," Will said. He sounded sincere enough, but the shorter man didn't seem to cool off as he hurled more aggressive remarks toward Will.

As the shouting escalated, a man walked into the room with a snarl on his face. "What the *hell* is going on here?" he boomed.

Dysan was the one to answer. "Sir, axe-brother Will asked if they"—he gestured toward the three shorter men, whom he had gathered were called Seth, Dean, and Adar—"would rather do a different apprenticeship."

The man gave Will a look of both anger and disbelief and asked, "Why the hell would you ask that? We don't pick people just for size; we pick those who want to do it. Just because any of you are bigger does not mean you will succeed. Most apprentices who think that are usually the first to fail and drop the apprenticeship." A thin smile of triumph crossed Adar's face.

The cold stare remained in the man's eyes as he caught Adar's smile and immediately berated Adar and the other young men. "And that doesn't mean the three of you can start arguments. Understood?" Dean, Adar, and Seth nodded. "I want to hear everyone say it!" he yelled.

"Yes sir!" everyone yelled back.

"Find your seats," he said, the anger slowly slipping from his voice. "I am Spyros Girth, your instructor. We start at eight every day. Don't be late. You have a bronze set of armor on your desk consisting of a chest piece, a pair of gauntlets, and a pair of shin-guard boots and a second bronze plate to strap over your armor. Put them on now." Dysan slipped his armor over his chest. It was a tight fit. The bronze armor shone and had a green cloth tasset draped around the shoulders. Dysan looked toward the front of the class and took a notice of Spyros's appearance. He was tall, with medium-length brown hair. He had a beard and, most noticeably, a scar on the left of his chin next to the beard.

"You will have a practice axe that you must bring every day or you will lose points. From eight to ten, we start our drills. You will get five-minute breaks at eight thirty, nine fifteen, and nine fifty. From ten to twelve, we do our combat training. From twelve to one, you get your lunch break. Be back in this room at one or you will be late and lose points. Then from one to three, we will be doing more drills, which is what we will start today. Also, tomorrow I expect you to not make a commotion like today. Your training will be slightly easier if you don't put me in a bad mood."

* * *

Tesni was one of the first few people in the training building. She immediately greeted the other apprentices with warmth and enthusiasm as more people began to trickle in. "Hi, everyone. I'm Tesni. I'm pleased to meet you all."

Two of them were twin women with long blonde braids. "I'm Christina, and this is my sister, Catherine," said the slightly taller woman. Tesni also noticed that she had a small jagged square birthmark under her right eye.

A tall woman with flowing brown hair greeted everyone in the room. "My name's Erika." Four more students, all males, walked into the room and grouped themselves away from everyone else gathered in the center of the room.

One of the men snickered as he stared at the group Tesni was in. "I'll just let you know right now I'm the best this class will ever see. I'm Daniel Nevin. Obviously the most successful person here."

"What makes you so important?" Erika asked, not hiding the irritation in her voice.

"Oh, the real question is what makes you special?" he asked with a smirk.

She poised to slap him but was interrupted.

"What's going on here?" said an eerily calm voice. Tesni noticed a thin man with short blond hair, a clean-shaven angular jaw, and a piercing gaze standing at the doorway. "First of all, knock this shit off. Secondly, I am Peter Gresbin, your teacher. I am your law, as are the other teachers. Walk down the hallway without starting a fight to the third door on the right."

As the Oracle students entered their new classroom and took their marked seats, Peter continued. "Congratulations on being accepted as Oracles. That being said, you earned your spot in this class. Participate proudly. I'm here to train you, and I'm not going to waste time on those who consider this unimportant. If you want to leave, do so now.

"As we learn to wear, fight in, and maneuver in various armors, you are to wear your armor every day or lose a point and waste my time training you." Tesni looked at the Oracle armor on her desk. It was bronze with a bluish-white tint. The armor had a vertical bronze line unpainted in the center. The chest plate, greaves, pauldrons, and gauntlets were all adorned with green cloth. "Your shield and lance are equally important. Bring them or lose points. We train in this class to be agile even in armor, adept at using a lance, equipped in light magic in offensive and healing use, and skilled in the art of blessings to be weapon fighters and medics.

"From eight to ten," Peter continued, "we will focus on combat practice. Ten to eleven, we focus on magic. You get a break for five minutes at eleven. From eleven to twelve, we study magic. From twelve to one, you get your lunch. Be back here at the exact time. From one to three, we will either study blessings or continue in combat training. You are also to bring your books every day or lose points; however, you will not need them at the moment because we are going across the hall to begin learning the forms of combat."

* * *

In the middle of the main room of the Ascalon training building, a group of women stood talking among each other, and a group of men stood over toward the wall. One of the women, with two very long braids that were blue in color, saw Delyth enter and approached her. The blue-haired woman smiled and reached her hand out in greeting.

"Hi. I'm Lisa. Lisa Moren." She and Delyth shook hands. Delyth was astonished at the coloring of her hair. The woman before her had vibrant sky-blue hair, an impossibility among the primarily brown, blonde, red, and black hair that most people in Jylinae had.

"Delyth Vaughn," she returned. Lisa and Delyth walked over to the group of girls in the middle of the room.

"Everyone, this is Delyth," said Lisa. Lisa gestured to the three other women. "That's Nina, Josephine, and Emilyn."

"Hi," Delyth said to the three women. "So would you mind if I asked—"

Lisa answered before she could finish. "Why my hair is blue? No, I don't mind, and people are always curious. When I was younger, I developed an interest in flowers. I crushed some irises and made a dye once and applied it to my hair. I liked it so much that I began to do it regularly every few days. That's usually how long it lasts."

"When we were in school, people always asked about her hair," Josephine stated.

"You should share that with the city. You could possibly start a business or new beauty trend," Delyth suggested. Lisa lightly shrugged.

A group of five apprentices arrived just as a woman entered the other side of the room.

"Well, I suppose everyone is here now. Follow me, students," the woman said kindly. The apprentices followed her through the door she had come through and down a hall to the fourth door on the right.

"Please take your seats. I am Valeria, and I will be your primary instructor. You have chosen to become Ascalons, and we will start your training to evolve you into strong and ready fighters. We start at seven sharp. So get plenty of sleep every night. We begin our training in armor as of today, so put on your armor." Everyone began to put their armor on. It was attached to green cloth, but the armor itself was painted white with an unpainted bronze middle section.

"From seven to nine, we practice our movement training in armor. You will get three ten-minute breaks. From nine to twelve, we train with lances—in combat either against each other or against someone from another guild who uses different weapons than us, or we will be practicing throwing spears at targets." Valeria paused and gazed from one student to another. Long brown hair framed her soft, rounded chin and narrow cheekbones. "During the last hours of the day, we will most likely take a break from the physical parts of training and study either human anatomy or tactics. Or we may go back to training with lances. That mostly depends on how well you all do. Well, are you all ready? Get your practice lances, and follow me," Valeria told her class with a warm, sly smile. "Also, congratulations, and good luck to you all," she added.

Chapter 3

The apprenticeships started right away. Alexander sat in his seat, flipping through his *Sword Mechanics and Human Anatomy* textbook. He was focused on writing the various sword techniques—the report would be due any minute now. This was arguably the most important part of his training due to the potential impact it could have on his life or others'.

"Okay, time's up. Turn in your reports," Regnor said. "Very nice." He gathered all the papyrus scrolls from his students. "Most of you look like you're getting it down. If you can remember this training, it will make a great difference. You don't want to be dealing with bandits and not remember how to fight."

He opened the closet and grabbed a boxful of colored glassy stones the size of a fist, which Alexander recognized as Lapideases. Regnor passed out a Lapideas to every student. He proceeded to pass out some bronze short swords, then demonstrated some strikes with the sword while holding a Lapideas in his other hand. A small burst of fire shot toward the stone wall and quickly burned out. "This handy stone is known as a Lapideas. These stones are imbued with Essence, the very same Essence that imbues all of us in here and others that possess affinities. These affinities are what enable us to do various forms of magic. Lapideases function as sources of Essence. They act as reservoirs and react to the affinity of the user. This means I could give this to a Vivicantern who could then imbue the white affinity into it and use it for light magic. This very reason makes them just as important as any sword, axe, lance, armor, or shield."

Regnor stared down and twirled the stone in his hand. He dropped the Lapideas, and it clattered against the ground but did not break. "Magic is divided into different categories. First, any person with a white, green, gray, hazel, or black affinity can use their Essence to shape and generate shields of Essence," he said as he generated a green rectangular shield the same size as him. "These shields can be changed in size or length depending on the amount of Essence put into them. They can be placed in front of something or even in the air," he said as he generated another shield above his head. The shield floated in the air above him and emitted a sheen. "These shields can be struck or degenerated." As he said this, he held out his hand, and the shields turned into small particles.

"Essentially, any form of magic you release contains Essence. By using your body against the shield, you attach to the Essence and remove the Essence. These shields can also be stopped with dust. This dust seems to lack affinity. For this reason, it can destroy these shields or bind to someone and prevent the use of their Essence. This is why we call it *blocking dust*. Our green affinity allows us to create fire as well as lightning, wind, and water," he said, generating a small contained fire in his left hand. It then changed to electricity and sparked angrily. The lightning then transformed into a whirling of wind and then into a large drop of water that seemed to be suspended above his hand.

"We divide these four elements into the names they had in Niellequaon. *Faer*, or fire; *Fulmenooo*, or lightning; *Vintae*, or wind; and *Vandua*, or water. There is also *Linwae*, or light, and *Skotadae*, or dark. These are also divided into shape classifications. You just saw the base forms, but they can also take on *Xaen*, or ball form." Regnor held up his hand again. Within two seconds, a fireball generated in his hand. Alexander estimated it was close to two feet in height. "The amount of Essence put into this can increase its size," Regnor said while letting the fire die down.

"The next form is *Xel*, or beam. This causes the spell to take on a beam form, which is exactly why I will not demonstrate that here. The third is *Xon*, or disperse. This form causes the spell to disperse over a small area. You would use your Essence and make your spell burst in any direction. The next form would be *Vael*, or shape." He placed his sword on his desk, then held out his left hand and formed a *Faer* spell in it. Gracefully, he moved his right hand toward the fire in his left. He then rapidly moved his right hand backward. The fire extended backward, guided by his right hand's movement, into the shape of a makeshift lance. He returned the fire to his hand, and it burned out to embers.

"The next form is *Vath*, or wave. This allows the user to shape the spell in a small wave, which I will also not demonstrate in this building. The last form is one of the strongest forms to be utilized. That form is *Ruunae*, or rain. This enables us to form the spells into a rain of sorts. *Faer Ruunae* rains down multiple small balls of fire over medium-length ranges, usually fifty to one hundred feet based on the amount of Essence put into them. For this reason, these particular spells require much Essence but are essential to battle tactics. Advanced training can increase this range up to five hundred feet. *Fulmenooo Ruunae* rains multiple lightning bolts over an area."

Regnor set down the Lapideas he had been using and leaned against his desk. "The cause of magic is often not understood. Of course, only those with an affinity can use it. These affinities are thought to be residual energy from the creation of the world and heavens that permeates into the world. This theory is believed to be how we can use magic and how it is absorbed into Lapideases. These Lapideases are mined in mines around Jylinae, other parts of Eltheneae, and all throughout the continent of Thaemell." Regnor paused, took in a breath, and then seemed to snap back into the lesson.

"Now, what is the importance of using a Lapideas?" Regnor asked his students.

"A Lapideas is as much a tool as a sword is. Using it helps with the situation at hand," Alexander answered.

Regnor nodded, and a small smile appeared. "That is precisely why we use them. But you also need to know *where* to use them. Sometimes it is necessary to not use lethal force. It helps if you understand the body to do that." He pulled out a wooden mannequin from his closet and brought it before his class. He then passed his sword along the torso of the mannequin. "What all is in this general region?"

The students tossed around many answers. Some said ribs. Others said the aorta. Some said the spine. "Yes, all of those answers are correct. And one sword swing or fire strike to the area can cause significant damage, intentionally or not. This is why we study anatomy—so that we know where we are striking our enemies should the need arise. Magic can also be used to complement standard fighting. We are fortunate to have affinities to enhance our capabilities. This is also why we put such diligence into our magic training as well as physical training.

"We learn magic for multiple reasons. We are not just scholars of magic who learn the many potentials that magic brings to life; we also must learn to use our magic not only to enrich life but to protect those who cannot protect themselves. You may be assigned to garrisons or maybe even as advisors. Learning to utilize Lapideases is important in order to advise and train others. Does anybody know why we harness Lapideases, though?"

A woman in the first seat of the first row raised her hand.

"Yes," Regnor said, pointing to her.

She lowered her hand as she answered. "We use Lapideases to avoid drawing from our own Essence."

Nodding, Regnor walked back to the front of his desk. "Correct. Lapideas mines and the stones mined from them contain a naturally applied set amount of energy. When we learn to use energy from our own bodies for spells, it can be very taxing, which is why we learn to use Lapideases. A Lapideas, like any tool, must be used properly and trained with to ensure efficiency. Okay, time for your break. Be back in here in ten minutes."

* * *

Jennifer was thirty minutes into her lesson about various parts of the body. She had a wooden target dummy next to her to show examples. "Look at the page about the circulatory system. Scan it for a minute and try to remember everything you see." Jennifer went silent, letting her students follow her instructions. Camilla could see various veins and arteries that lined the body and felt a surge of fascination within her. She found the internal workings and intricacies of the body to be wondrous.

Camilla read the names *aorta, renal vein, jugular vein, vena cava,* and *femoral artery* as her eyes scanned over the anatomy on the page.

"One minute. Time's up," stated Jennifer. "Can somebody come show me where the femoral artery is? Lucas"—she gestured to a young man with short black hair—"show me where the femoral artery is, please."

Lucas rose, walked to the dummy display, and pointed at the leg. "It would be right here in the middle of the leg."

"Excellent," said Jennifer. "Now could somebody show me where the axillary artery is?"

A student named Breeanna walked up to the dummy without prompting. Pointing at the armpit, she said, "It's right here."

"Correct. Camilla, could you show me where the vena cava is?"

Camilla rose and approached the front of the class. "It's the big one right here in the chest. It lies both above and below the heart here and here." She pointed at the middle of the dummy's chest.

"Excellent work, everyone. Knowing where to place a shot can change how you bring down a potential enemy or game—of course, animals have different structures than we do, but this is the precision that we are known for and that we obtain through our training," Jennifer explained, the pride in her guild evident.

* * *

Victor, who was leaning against his desk with his arms crossed, had just finished the time period for teaching anatomy and was starting the next part of his lesson. "Before we head across the hall to begin the fun," said Victor with a slight, almost malicious smile, "somebody explain the importance of stealth."

A woman with dark-red hair raised her hand.

"Yes," Victor said, looking at the name on her desk, "Maria. Explain the importance of stealth."

Maria lowered her hand and then explained earnestly, "Stealth is important because it comprises everything that a Nightcloak does."

Victor gave a look of approval. "Correct. As a Nightcloak, you must be able to come within inches of someone and not alert them of your presence. We must be able to slip into the most fortified castle without a soul seeing us. We must get what we are after and then disappear like dust in a breeze. The reason I tell you this is because we are starting your stealth training today. Now follow me to where that will take place—and quietly too. I don't want to hear any talking in the hall."

The students all rose and followed him out the door. They walked toward the end of the hall and then took a right down another hallway. The walls were black as a starless night, and there was very little lighting. Urien could see only about five feet in front of him. A few moments later, they arrived at a door with a red line around the rim, and Victor stopped abruptly. Some of the apprentices bumped into each other.

Victor spun on his heels to address his students. "Everyone, listen very closely. I'm going into this room. You, however"—he pointed to a bell above the door—"will not come in until this bell rings. Understood?" There were nods and *yes sirs*. Victor then opened the door just wide enough so he could slip through but none of the apprentices could see inside, and an instant later the door closed behind him.

There was silence for a brief period. Urien noticed about ten feet from the door what appeared to be a small bulge under the wall, barely noticeable. The apprentices began to quietly talk among themselves.

Urien watched from the corner of his eye as Michael approached Maria and winked. "Hey. What say you and I have a courting after the day?"

"I'm thinking no," Maria said indifferently. Michael's face contorted.

Urien chuckled to himself. He thought it was funny when Michael's plans failed. When they were kids, Michael and Urien had been put into a team-building exercise at school. Michael had tried to do it his own way but had failed. He and Urien had never gotten along much after that due to Michael's overbearing personality.

The bell above the door rang, and the apprentices made their way into the room where, according to Victor, the fun would begin. Urien, however, had a slight uneasy feeling about what Victor meant by *fun*.

The room was very much the opposite of the hallway they had just come from. The walls were painted white, and a bright light filled the space. On the floor were twenty leather throwing knives, one for each apprentice presumably. Various other items were scattered throughout, including multiple strings attached to bells hanging from the walls and ceiling and across the room, piles of dead leaves, piles of broken glass, and rubble.

Victor was at the far end of the room, about fifty feet away, surrounded by eight tables covered with leather throwing knives. Each table also had a red scarf with a bell attached. "Welcome to the Silence Room," he said flatly. "This is the main room where you will be doing your stealth training. First order of business, behind you there are leather gauntlets and leather chest pieces that you will want to put on." The apprentices donned the leather gauntlets that came up to the elbow and covered all of the hand to the middle knuckle. They slipped on the leather chest pieces, then tightened the straps that pulled the front and back together to cover their backs.

"Next," said Victor, "you'll want to get a leather throwing knife. It may help. Depending on certain conditions, though," he said with slight sarcasm in his smooth, low voice. "Also there are leather face masks behind you. They are mandatory."

An apprentice with black hair combed to the left asked, "Why would we need a face mask? Or any of this stuff?"

Victor raised his eyebrows. "What's your name?"

"Lancet," the student answered.

"Well, Lancet, this is the part in training where most apprentices start to get hurt. The face mask is, well, obviously meant to protect your face from what the training has in store for you. The knife is also used—if you're good enough or lucky enough—to protect you from what will be happening. The leather armor is to protect you in case you fall in the glass." His tone was matter of fact.

"Wait a second. We could fall in the glass?" Michael asked incredulously.

"Yes, you could, if I hear you crunching on it and you get hit and possibly lose your balance and fall in it."

"But that's—" Michael started.

"Dangerous? Why yes, it is. Nightcloaks will often be in dangerous situations, especially in ones where if they are heard or blow their cover, then they could be captured and possibly subjected to torture. If you don't want to get hurt either, don't make any noise for this task, or leave now. You know where the doors are. I and Eltheneae have no need for people who complain about a cut."

Urien was slightly uneasy. He remembered when his father had told him about his own Nightcloak training. He had said there had been plenty of bruises. Urien tried to focus on what was about to come his way.

One woman asked, "What exactly is our objective?"

Victor began, "Well . . ." He stopped.

"Chelsea," she answered the question about to form on his lips.

"Well, Chelsea, your objective is simple. Each of you, in the time provided and in any way you can, is to take one of these scarves from me, provided you can get close enough without me hearing you."

"What do you mean without you hearing us?" Lancet asked.

"If I could see you, it wouldn't do any of you any good. Therefore, I will be blindfolding myself," Victor said as he walked to the table in front of him. He grabbed a black cloth and tied it tightly over his eyes. "You will have thirty minutes. Just a fair warning—I will be throwing these knives at you. And they have a paint pellet in them which will break on contact, meaning I can tell whether you got caught or not. Oh, and one more thing," he added. "Masks on." Urien slipped the mask over his face. It fit tightly and wrapped around his eyes, but he could still see through it well enough. Victor flipped an hourglass. He then almost effortlessly walked back to the spot behind the table where he had originally been standing as his students put their masks over their heads.

Some of the students began to move forward with their best attempts at not making a sound. Michael was the first to falter. He touched a string at his shin, and at the sound of the bell attached to the string, Victor, immediately and effortlessly, picked up a leather throwing knife and threw it at shoulder height. It sailed through the air at amazing speed. Michael attempted to bring his knife up to block but failed miserably, and it hit just above his right eye.

"Owwwww. Dammit, that hurt!" Michael yelled, and as he did, another knife was flung toward him at terrifying speed. Michael tried to block it with his arm but only half succeeded as it hit the bottom part of his arm gauntlet and the top part connected to the front of his mask. He did not say anything this time, seeming to have learned his lesson.

Lancet was in front, carefully trying to move a pile of leaves. He pushed some leaves aside, and Urien spotted a knife whirling at him. Lancet managed to move to his right as the leather knife sailed by, inches from his face—however, as he did, he tripped over a string and fell into two others at his side, setting off their bells. Two knives came flying downward at him and hit his chest.

Urien began easing his way under a string about four feet off the ground. He turned to his right and saw Maria six feet away, slowly working her way over some glass. She stepped with a hard crunch, and a knife came flying at her. It hit her in the shoulder, knocking her off balance and onto one knee and hand in the glass.

A few feet left of Urien's position, one of the other men crunched on some leaves, and Victor quickly grabbed a knife and hurled it in the man's direction. It connected with his face, causing him to double over.

Urien now carefully stepped over a string, which he just barely missed. He made his way under two strings going in opposite directions when he heard glass crunch under his feet. Victor—who, to Urien's unfortunate luck, also heard—flung two knives toward him. Urien tried to move out of the way. As he did, the strings behind him got in his way, and one knife connected to the side of his face and threw off his balance. Even with the mask on, he could feel the impact on his face.

Two more apprentices some feet behind him each took a knife to the face. Michael stepped forward, easing his way over four strings. He got caught in them, setting off a chorus of bells. Victor flung knife after knife in his direction. Two zoomed past him, and the other three connected—two with his face and the third with his chest—as he fell over the strings and hit the ground. "Dammit," Michael said.

Victor, picking up and throwing two more knives at Michael, shouted, "You make too much noise!" Now Victor was throwing knives in every direction, some hitting their marks. Urien stepped forward but pulled a string at his foot, sounding a bell of misfortune. Victor quickly threw a knife at him, which landed a stinging blow on Urien's chin. Despite the mask, Urien could still feel the pain. Michael, after rising to his feet and exhaling, darted forward. As he did, a knife connected with his face and two more with his chest.

As Michael continued darting forward, taking knife after knife, he suddenly was pulled into the air by something unseen. Urien realized it was a trap. "Dammit!" exclaimed Michael, who had been grabbed by a snare around his foot. Victor threw a flurry of knives at him, connecting with his legs and the side of his neck. Michael flung his knife from his right hand in an awkward motion. It sailed through the air at an angle. It skidded across the ground far from Victor. Michael admitted defeat and hung silently in his trap.

"You are all making this really easy," Victor said. Feeling the table in front of him, he added, "Also, it looks like I've finally run out of knives. On one table."

Urien knelt to the ground, watching as the apprentices around him were getting smacked with knives going in every direction. How could he make his way through? He assumed there were traps everywhere. He scanned his surroundings for a possible break in the alarms closer toward Victor. From what he could tell from his position halfway to Victor, the alarms got denser as he and the other apprentices made their way closer to Victor. How could anyone be expected to get through those quietly? It seemed impossible.

As Urien racked his brain, he recalled the bulge in the wall he had seen in the hallway. It had seemed so out of place that he wondered if it held some hidden tool that might help him. He quickly made his way back to the door, being partially careful to not attract attention to himself, but Victor apparently was focused on the sounds that the other apprentices closer to him kept making. Urien very carefully and gently opened the door to avoid making a sound. He managed to open it quietly and wide enough to squeeze through and get back into the dark hallway.

Once in the hall, he walked to the bulge he had noticed before. It was too dark to see clearly, so he ran his hand over it and then slid his hand to the right, feeling for a crack. He found one and gave a quick tug with both hands, pulling back the bulge—which must have been some type of door—and revealing a space just small enough to crawl into. Urien flashed a quick smile and squeezed himself into the space. The stone walls hugged tightly against his shoulders as he shuffled through.

He soon found himself in another small hall, where he was able to stand instead of crawling, with dim light from the Silence Room shining through the vents in the wall. He made his way down the hall, the sounds from the Silence Room filling his ears. A few minutes later, he reached what appeared to be the end of the hall. There was a small carved hole in the wall at about eye level. Urien put his eye to the hole, and he could see the apprentices, barely any farther than they had been when he had left the room, and Victor, approximately thirty feet away from him in the middle of the room.

In the darkness, Urien felt around for a way into the Silence Room and came across another small door like the one he had just crawled through. Being gentle, he pushed it slightly open and squeezed his way through the small opening, not bothering to close it behind him. Back in the Silence Room, Urien, as quickly and quietly as possible, began sneaking toward Victor. He had made it about fifteen feet when he noticed that all the apprentices had stopped in their tracks and were staring at him from across the room.

"You're all being unusually quiet. I'm slightly impressed. Did you manage your way through? That would be a first for any first lesson I've taught. Or are you giving up?" Victor asked with slight disdain. The apprentices closest to Victor began to try moving forward again. A few of them managed to remain silent, until two men in the front stepped on glass. In a flash, Victor began pummeling them with knives, which hit them in the face and knocked one of the men into glass behind him.

Urien inched closer to Victor, and as he did, Lancet's head touched a bell, and Victor launched a knife into his face. Urien was six feet away now, and as he was inching closer, Michael yelled across the room, "Dammit, Urien! How the hell did you get on that side of the room?"

As Michael yelled, Victor picked up a knife in each hand and spun around, then released them in Urien's direction. They flew over Urien's head with a hissing sound. He dashed forward and neared one of the tables. He reached for a scarf. As he got his fingers on it, Victor stepped forward and grabbed blindly down at Urien's arms. Urien and Victor both kicked at each other, which pushed them away from the other. Urien was pushed closer to a table. He reached for a scarf and set off the bell attached. Victor then flung another knife in his direction. An alarm went off as Urien brought his knife up and deflected Victor's, sending it skidding across the floor.

"Impressive," Victor said as he removed his blindfold and looked at his apprentices. "Well, judging from the paint marks all over you, not a single one of you managed to not get hit. But that's to be expected since you are all still brand new to this. How did they do in the other aspects that I couldn't see?" Victor asked.

A form materialized in a puff of purple smoke near Michael and another at the other apparent snare fifteen feet to the right. They were people dressed in black-and-red leather suits with gray robes over them. One pulled Michael closer to the ground and released the snare from around his ankle. He fell to the floor with a thud.

The other spoke. "They did average on performance. No teamwork was used, and as you can tell," he said, gesturing to Urien, "only one had full awareness."

Victor looked at all his apprentices. "This training was to show how to be aware of your surroundings, move in them quietly, and work as a team, because there are times when you will. This is only the beginning of your training as Nightcloaks—or the start of what you could be tasked to do. Now go take your next break."

Urien rolled to his side and rose to his feet. As he removed his mask, he caught Maria removing hers and shooting an astounded look his way. Urien rubbed his now-bruised jaw as he followed the others to the door.

* * *

Eurwen had begun a discussion with her class about medicine. "Why would it be important for us to learn how to make medicine?" she asked. "Why not just stick to magic, right?"

Aeronwen answered her. "We learn medicine in the event that magic is not readily accessible in cases of no energy to perform magic or if our skill is blocked."

"Correct," answered Eurwen casually. "Magic requires drawing Essence from either Lapideases or from ourselves in order to perform. If you are at a point when you cannot use magic to heal someone of any wounds, you would need to use your own knowledge of medicine. We also learn it to stop disease, since the healing we use has no effects on diseases. If I had a wound on my arm, I would need you to use medicine to heal it. We also learn how to use natural medicines in the event of blockage, as you mentioned. Blocking dust is theorized to bind to our bodies, preventing the use of Essence. What would be a good plant to use in this case?"

A male student, while looking in his book, answered her enthusiastically. "Aloe can be used to treat burns, wounds, or rashes."

Eurwen smiled wide. "Correct. Great enthusiasm. I expect you all to learn the information in these books. It will help you in your journey. Now what would be a medicine that we could use to heal skin irritation? Aloe is one. There are more. Can someone tell me?"

Malcolm, who sat in front of Aeronwen, looked through his book for an answer, then spoke. "Arnica could help, but only the roots would help irritation. The rest of the plant could actually cause it or poison if ingested."

"The starvine could also help with that or any ailment," said Aeronwen, reading from her book.

"Good job," Eurwen said. "See, we must know everything about the plants we will use to make our own medicines. We have to know what is used to help people, and we have to know everything that we are giving them. Which is why we must study them. Tomorrow we will be making our first antidote, and in two weeks, we will test over the first two chapters of your *Medicinal Applications* book."

* * *

Cadfan sat twitching his leg and strumming his fingers on his desk. They were almost done with the anatomy part of class, but Cadfan was getting tired of waiting. All he wanted to do was grab his sword and do swordplay. Price, almost as though he sensed Cadfan's readiness, said, "Okay, anatomy is over. Go take your break and then meet back in here in ten. Afterward, we will go across the hall to apply your new knowledge to sword training."

Finally, thought Cadfan as he rose from his seat, grabbed his training sword, and began stretching. He did a few practice swings while waiting for the break to be over. He then realized he should take this chance to empty his bladder. He returned to the room a few minutes later and stood by his seat with his practice sword in hand.

"Okay, looks like everyone is back on time," Price said as he entered the room. "Are you all ready to begin your practice?" His class responded energetically and enthusiastically. "I can tell you are," he said to Cadfan. "All right. Grab your practice swords and follow me." Price made his way to the door with his apprentices, Cadfan first, following him.

They followed him down the hall and into a large spacious room. In the room was a line of twenty wooden training stands spaced about five feet from each other and each with multiple arms attached. There was one set out in front of the others, which is where Price took his spot.

"Everyone take a stand," he said, and his apprentices did so. Cadfan was already at the first one on the left. "The focus of today is to start you with the basics of wielding swords and striking with them. Any sword that we use is designed to be as lightweight as possible and to be used quickly and with precision. We don't use the heavier swords that others use. Now to begin, you will place your feet slightly apart, one foot a few inches forward, and hold your sword with both hands in the middle of your stomach. Don't hold too hard. You want to maintain a steady grip but still slightly loose and relaxed." He took the stance. His apprentices began to mirror the stance he was demonstrating. Price took a step forward and began a few adjustments for some of his apprentices.

"This is the mid front stance. From here you can make various swings, usually downward, on your opponent," he said as he walked back to his stand and took the stance. "You can also raise to the mid high stance or to the lower mid stance." He raised and then lowered his sword to demonstrate both. "I'm going to demonstrate a few strikes from the stances to show what's next." He took the mid front stance. He then drew in a short breath and made a front strike to his practice stand, which made a loud impact. Cadfan smiled excitedly. He thrived on the rush. However, he also strived to be a Royal Guard one day. To do that, his skill would have to be top notch.

Price then took the mid high stance and brought his sword down in an arcing path and hit atop the stand, again making a very loud sound as the woods collided. He swung into the side of the stand. He then lowered his practice sword and turned to face his apprentices. "I want all of you to practice the same strikes I just showed you in the order that I did them," said Price seriously. Cadfan and the other apprentices took the mid front stance. "Begin," Price instructed.

Cadfan, in a blur of speed, performed the first strike, swinging in the same downward arcing path atop the stand, and then dropped the practice sword to his side and swung it into the training stand's side. The other apprentices finished slower than he did.

"Some of you did well," said Price, looking at Cadfan. "Some of you did decent, and some of you did shitty. So you are all going to do it again until I see improvement or until we run out of time. Don't worry, though. If you don't improve today, we will do so again tomorrow. And the next day. And the day after that. Even if you do improve, we will still do it tomorrow until you have that perfect blend of precision and speed. Now again."

* * *

Dysan sat in his chair, wondering how class was going to proceed. So far they had started on a bad note. Spyros reentered the room, seeming less angry than he had been earlier and almost happy in a way that spelled unpleasant news. "Now that you are all aware of what I expect," Spyros said, "we can begin our training. Grab your practice axes and follow me next door to the training room." Dysan and Will rose and were followed by Seth and Adar.

"We'll see who wants to quit first," Adar taunted Dysan and Will. They had all developed a friendly rivalry to motivate each other.

They entered a brightly painted training room. "The first order of business is to start your conditioning. We are known to wear the heaviest of armors and wield the heaviest of weapons. Eventually we will teach you the skill of advanced strength, but until then, it is useless to increase the load without the skill. So to start off, we will be doing axe curls." Spyros held his axe horizontally in his arms to demonstrate. "Like this." Spyros curled the axe up to the top of his shoulder blades and then lowered the bronze axe effortlessly back to the bottom position. "You will be doing this one hundred times."

Some of the apprentices had skeptical looks. Dysan himself had some doubts about what he was about to go through.

"Don't give me that. Dynamis are meant to be physically powerful and are the backbone of garrisons. I expect apprentices to be the same. But you're not doing this alone either. We will be doing this together. So grab your axes as I have mine now," said Spyros, and the apprentices did as he instructed. "Now together. One." He and his apprentices began doing the curls.

They had done thirty curls, and some of the apprentices were beginning to slow down—among them Will. "Come on," Spyros said ardently, "don't slack on me now. We're just getting started."

Adar looked to the side at Will and asked, through heavy breaths, "Ready to give up?"

Will exhaled greatly and answered, "No."

They reached fifty, and some apprentices were struggling even more, continuing only because of Spyros's threats of making anybody who stopped before his say-so do laps in the room while wearing bronze armor.

Dysan exhaled forcibly, feeling the burn through his arms. *Keep going,* he thought. Somehow they managed their way to seventy, and everyone except Spyros had begun to slow down.

"Don't quit," Spyros said with the same ardent seriousness. "If any of you stop, you will be running laps in armor."

They hit ninety now. "Come on—ten more!" encouraged Spyros.

Only ten more. Keep going, Dysan told himself, his arms burning as though fire were blazing through them.

"Ninety-seven, ninety-eight, ninety-nine, one hundred!" Spyros said. "You can all stop now." Everyone let their arms drop with exclamations of relief. "Good job. But it's not over yet. Now we're going to do some practice swings."

* * *

"Why do you believe it is important for us to know the blessings?" Peter asked his class.

"Because historically, blessings have augmented armies and standard military practices," Tesni said.

"Yes, that is correct. So open your books to page twenty. From here to page fifty are various blessings that have been written. Within thirty seconds, I want you to scan over as many blessings as you can and see if you can remember any."

The students cast their gazes downward into their books and scanned and flipped through pages. "Time's up. Close your books," Peter said. "Can anyone remember any blessings they came across?"

A black-haired woman in the second row raised her hand.

"Yes, Fiora," said Peter, looking at his roster. "State a blessing."

"I saw one that said *Spanae Vethin,*" said Fiora.

"Yes. That would be one." Peter looked at his roster again and asked a tall man with short black hair, "Crispin, can you state another blessing?"

Crispin had a thoughtful look across his face. *"Anae . . .* Luma," he eventually responded.

"Excellent." Peter looked around the room for his next target. While he was doing so, Tesni was mentally running through her list of blessings.

"Daniel, tell me another blessing," he demanded.

Daniel twisted his face, but it was to no avail. "How do you expect us to remember this in a split second?" Daniel asked rudely, leaning back with his arms crossed.

Peter stared back with an unpassionate gaze in his blue eyes. "Hold out your arm," said Peter. Daniel hesitated, then extended his arm.

Peter lowered his hand to Daniel's arm. Light-blue runes spread from Daniel's hand to his shoulder. "The runes spread out farther over the body as more of the blessing is applied to something. You will also notice that I had to actually manifest the blessing using Essence and had to apply it like writing. For a reason we do not quite understand, they have to be written, so to speak, and if not done properly, it will not work. So it is common to see them in Onglikae, the spoken and written language in our country, Ciimerii, and Xythuu," Peter explained. Tesni, as well as everyone else, looked bewildered and amazed. "This is why I need you to learn these blessings, though. You're right—thirty seconds isn't always enough," Peter said in a low voice, "but sometimes you may have to go over the list in your head and remember one exact blessing within a second." As Peter finished his explanation, he quickly pulled a dagger strapped to his thigh and brought it down on Daniel's hand. Daniel let out a shriek while the other apprentices gasped. Tesni was astonished, both by Peter stabbing Daniel and at the effect of the blessing, which had stopped the dagger from piercing through Daniel's hand, as the tip of the blade rested atop his hand without drawing blood.

"*Perae Cuutein*, or the stone-skin blessing. It changes the skin composition to rock, making it much more durable. We learn blessings to make objects better. We apply these blessings to anything—armor, weapons, skin, and even the stone walls of the city. We are not better than others. We are the beneficiaries of our brothers," Peter said, gazing at the frightened Daniel, who nodded as Peter resheathed his dagger. Tesni's eyes were still wide with bewilderment. She disagreed with Peter's demonstration on Daniel—it was unnecessarily cruel—but it illustrated to her what she would be learning and would be responsible for.

* * *

Delyth and the other students followed Valeria across the hall to start their training. They entered a room with shining wooden floors, well lit by the sunshine flooding through the elegantly crafted windows. There were multiple wooden circular targets lined up in the room, with a rack holding numerous small metal rods.

"Now," said Valeria, smiling, "during the next two hours, I will teach you the basics of how to hold and thrust a lance. That brings me to these fine devices." She gestured to the wooden rack with the rods. "These are retractable lances designed by the engineers that we will be using quite regularly. They are designed to fold in and out." Valeria grabbed one in each hand, then pressed the buttons so that the lances extended into their full-length forms.

Valeria twirled the lances in her hands effortlessly and elegantly. "So I need each of you to come get a lance, and then we can begin your training." The apprentices approached two at a time, each taking a lance. Lisa, Delyth, Josephine, Emilyn, and Nina proceeded forward, then returned to their spots. The lance was light in Delyth's hand.

"Everyone spread out, and extend your lance," said Valeria. The apprentices followed her instructions and spread four to six feet apart. Delyth pressed the button to extend her lance.

"Here's how we will start." Valeria demonstrated a thrust with her lance. "You will want to place one foot forward and put all the force from your shoulder muscles. Everyone try it." The apprentices all readied themselves for a practice thrust. Delyth placed her right foot forward and thrust her lance, feeling the lance go off balance.

"Not bad. Improvement needed for all of you, but we will train on it. Now here's what I want you to do next. Our armor is designed to be durable and still possess the lightweight capabilities for freedom of movement. However, it still adds extra weight to you. The armor you are currently wearing weighs ten pounds, which adds to you. And that is without vambraces and gauntlets. My point is you can't do anything if you cannot move in whatever armor you are wearing, so I want you all to retract your lances, run three laps around the room, and, after your third lap, run to a target and do a practice thrust into it. Only extend your lances when you get within three feet of a target. I don't want any of you to get hurt. Begin," commanded Valeria warmly but firmly.

The apprentices took off from their positions and began running around the room. Delyth was next to Lisa and Josephine, with Nina and Emilyn behind her. She had made a quarter of a lap when she could feel what Valeria had been talking about. The armor weighed down on her shoulders as she ran.

"This armor feels a lot heavier now," panted Lisa in between breaths. Delyth and Josephine agreed through thick exhales.

They had completed their first lap, and many apprentices were slowing down. "Don't stop. Keep going," Valeria shouted. Delyth and Lisa had pulled ahead of Josephine. Delyth's shoulders felt heavier with each step. They had made it to the halfway point, and Delyth and Lisa were slowing. "Come on, Delyth. We can't let anybody show us up," Lisa said, her words punctuated by gasps for air. "This is a dream that we have achieved!" Delyth knew she was right and sped up with her.

They were now on the last lap, and Delyth could feel the weight in her chest and burning into her legs as well, but she and Lisa kept running, with Nina, Josephine, and Emilyn a few feet behind them. They completed the last lap, everyone breathing heavily in exhaustion.

"Come on—to the targets!" exclaimed Lisa as she followed the other apprentices. Delyth ran to the target next to Lisa's, extended her lance, and thrust it awkwardly into the upper-right side of the target. She removed the lance and began to catch her breath. A few more minutes passed as the last apprentices finished their runs.

Valeria folded her arms and stood firmly. "You all see my point now, right? You could feel the weight of the armor as you continued with each step and each lap. Afterwards, you tried to thrust your lance, which didn't go perfectly because you are not used to running in armor or wielding a lance. But don't get discouraged. This is just day one. There will be more along the way, and with each passing day, you will see improvements. A mountain doesn't grow tall in one day," said Valeria.

"Good job," Lisa said as she, Delyth, Nina, Emilyn, and Josephine shared a smile and a laugh.

* * *

Later that evening, Alexander and his friends, now wearing their normal everyday clothes, gathered at their usual meeting place along the stone wall of the city. "How was everyone's day?" he asked.

"It was amazing," said Cadfan. "I'm already the best apprentice there."

Tesni beamed. "I saw the stone-skin blessing in action. But we also had thirty seconds to remember as many blessings as possible."

"We did that, too, with element magic forms," stated Alexander.

"What happened to your face?" Aeronwen asked, pointing at Urien's bruised jaw. Alexander saw the bruise on Urien's face that she was referencing. *That looks very painful,* he thought to himself.

Urien groaned. "This is what happens when you trip a string with a bell attached to it. And your teacher is trained incredibly well at picking up noises and throwing leather knives while blindfolded."

Cadfan chuckled. "You got hit by a guy who was blindfolded?"

"My day was long," said Dysan. "First we made our teacher mad and then started out with axe curls, then did practice swings, and then more axe curls, followed by push-ups."

Delyth chimed in. "I understand, Dysan. We had to run laps in our armor."

"That sounds rough," Alexander sympathized.

"Yeah, that is exhausting," stated Tesni. "And I can't harness Essence from a Lapideas. Well, none of us could."

Aeronwen nodded. "Neither could anyone from my class."

Alexander laughed. "No one in my class could either."

"Really? And here I thought you were going to be the only one who would be able to. You disappoint me, Alexander," Cadfan said sarcastically. Everyone burst into laughter.

Tesni pushed away from her spot against the wall. "Well, I need to get home."

"We all probably do. Nice warm food, a warm bath, and my soft bed sound good right now," said Dysan. Cadfan, Delyth, Dysan, and Urien began walking toward the middle road through town as Tesni and Aeronwen made their way to the right and Alexander and Camilla turned off to the left road.

"Bye, everybody. See you tomorrow," Tesni called over her shoulder.

Alexander and Camilla arrived at their houses in the next ten minutes.

"Well, today was fun," Alexander remarked, stopping in his doorway since his house was the first along the path.

"No doubt. Good night," Camilla said as she continued walking toward her house a little farther down the road.

Chapter 4

Alexander and his friends underwent a grueling two weeks of training within their apprenticeships. The results of their efforts were showing, but they still had a long way to go. Alexander, Tesni, and Aeronwen were in the process of learning how to use Essence, although they were not yet skilled at using Lapideases. Camilla had made a beautifully crafted bow. Urien was ranked as the number one in stealth in his class, and Cadfan was proving himself to be an adept swordsman—top of his class. Tesni and Delyth were beginning to learn lance wielding and were becoming quite capable of wearing their armor in training exercises. Dysan was regarded as the most dedicated in his class, even though he was currently ranked number five out of the twenty students.

Alexander and his friends, each draped in their apprentice clothing, met at their spot at the wall while the sky was still dark—the sun had not even begun to peek over the horizon. Alexander was leaning over the wall with his elbows folded on top of it as he looked out at the Escali Forest. They began to chat quietly—Dysan and Cadfan particularly, who were always much quieter in the morning when their excitement had not kicked in yet.

Alexander found himself thinking of what would happen after their training. It was very possible they would all be assigned other places. This thought partially troubled him. These were his friends, whom he had known for many years—particularly Camilla, whom he had known the longest. He did not know how to prepare himself for when any of them may not be around.

Cadfan's voice broke through Alexander's thoughts. "Who invented morning?" Cadfan asked sleepily.

Dysan grunted. "Nobody should be up this early."

Urien responded, "Sometimes if you want to achieve something, then you may have to wake before you would like."

Cadfan rolled his eyes. "Your wisdom can be annoying at times."

"You could always quit and go back home to get sleep," said Urien.

"Ugh, dammit. I hate when you're right," Cadfan said.

"Camilla, your bow is amazing!" Tesni said. Camilla grabbed the front of the bow and slung it over her shoulder. It was an ornate carved bow. It was painted blue and was studded with small rocks at the tips. A black leather covering wrapped around the center.

"Thank you, Tesni," Camilla said.

Tesni, running her hand up and down the bow's arch, asked, "Could you carve me a spear?"

Camilla flashed a friendly smile and said, "I might be able to if I have time."

The sky was beginning to mix with pink hues, and they all began to make their way to the middle street behind them. They walked a few minutes, then arrived at one of the many horse carriage stations. A few carriages pulled up, and Alexander and the others climbed into the first one.

They arrived in the center of the city within ten minutes and departed the carriages. "Bye, everybody. Have an amazing day. Let's all meet back here for lunch!" exclaimed Tesni while she and Aeronwen walked west.

The others all walked in the direction of their own guilds' buildings. Alexander soon split off from his friends to slip into his classroom.

Alexander was lost in thought while the other students filled the room with the noise of conversation. Regnor walked into class, looking pleased. "I'm impressed with all of your progress so far. We're going to the training room, and today we will continue learning how to harness Essence from Lapideases. So grab a Lapideas as you walk out," said Regnor, already with a Lapideas in hand and walking out the door. The apprentices piled into a mass and followed through the door two at a time, each grabbing a Lapideas. Alexander grabbed a Lapideas and followed the other students across the hall. Regnor was in the center of the training room, facing toward the apprentices who were walking in.

"Harnessing a Lapideas's energy is not as simple as it seems," warned Regnor. "You must be able to draw the energy from the Lapideas and manifest it into a spell. You must be able to control it. If you don't pull out any energy, no spell can be performed. Or if you pull out the energy haphazardly, it can have malfunctions. So to begin"—Regnor held his Lapideas in front of him and turned to face the other direction, his back now toward the apprentices — "you're going to feel the energy within the Lapideas and pull it slowly, like you would sand in a body of water, letting it slip between your fingers, to the surface. Once you have it there, you must balance the energy as if it were on a scale, but you only do this if you are not yet releasing the energy. Otherwise, one of those malfunctions that I mentioned earlier will happen," Regnor said with a stern chuckle.

"From there," he continued, "you will aim where you want the spell to go and release the energy. This will activate the energy placed into the Lapideas and will launch the spell out. I don't expect that to happen today, but there are always exceptions. Any one of you could be a prodigy. I know many Illustratum more talented than me."

Regnor pointed to two spots on opposite ends of the room. "Ten of you gather at each spot and spread out. Also leave an opening for me to walk between so I can instruct or so I don't get accidentally blasted." Everyone spaced themselves evenly apart as Regnor walked to the center space they had created for him. "Begin," Regnor said.

Alexander was in the group on the right side of the room. He held out his hand with the Lapideas in his palm and tried to withdraw the Essence from the Lapideas. At first, he could not feel anything happening. He tried again, and this time he could detect the energy in the Lapideas, almost like a churning sludge was moving inside of it. It was like he was playing tug-of-war with the stone. Every time he tried to draw his hand back and attempt to pull energy from it, the stone seemed to resist—he felt it in the strain of his arm as he tried to pull back from the Lapideas. He equated the effort of pulling the Essence out of the Lapideas to trying to lift a brick with a string attached to his pinkie. The energy just would not budge from the center of the Lapideas. The other apprentices were having no luck as well.

Alexander closed his eyes, took in a breath, and then released it. *Dad was able to do this. So can I.* He tried pulling the energy once again, imagining lifting a handful of sand from a lake and letting it slip through his fingers as Regnor had suggested. This time, he could feel the Essence budging ever so slightly when he pulled his hand back, but he still did not seem to have the control to bring it all the way out. It was still like trying to move thick sludge. He, along with the two apprentices next to him, dropped their Lapideases from their hands.

"You can feel it in your hands when you try to pull the energy from your Lapideas," said the apprentice directly to his right.

"Yeah. My hands are cramping," Alexander agreed, taking in a deep breath. *I can do this. I will do this.* He leaned over, picked up his Lapideas, and tried once more to loosen the Essence from it. He calmed himself, thought again of sifting sand, and tugged the energy upward. He could feel the Essence budging, a little smoother this time. He pulled it back a little farther. He was able to keep it in place, but it slipped back into the Lapideas the second he faltered.

Alexander gritted his teeth. *Damn stubborn Essence.* He pulled at the energy again but not in the way he had been doing before—this time, it was fueled more aggressively by his frustration. He could feel the energy swirling within his hands, which made him lose his grip on the Lapideas, and it flew from his hand to the floor with a loud clank. He glanced around. Many of the apprentices had frustrated expressions, and Regnor was moving about assisting everybody.

Alexander looked at his hands. The Lapideas had slightly scratched them. Fortunately, his Lapideas was not too jagged. He picked up his Lapideas as Regnor approached him. "It flew from your hand?" he asked.

"Yes."

"That would be because you lost control and were not pulling the Essence calmly. But we will keep practicing this," Regnor said to his class.

Alexander ran his fingers over the hair above his eyebrows and took in a breath to ease himself.

* * *

Camilla and the other Bowmen apprentices had taken their seats for class. Jennifer entered with a cheerful hum. "Good morning," she said as she casually walked to the front of the room. She then sat at the front of her desk.

"Well, I can see some of you have made your bows already. They look good from here. Bring them up here so I can inspect them. Remember, they are due next week," Jennifer said. Camilla, Lucas, Breeanna, and seven other students rose from their seats and proceeded forward to get their bows inspected.

Jennifer looked carefully over the first one. "This is good. Meets all standards," she said. The apprentice, a short boy with orange hair, returned to his seat with a pleased look. Jennifer examined the next two and gave them the approval. Camilla presented her bow respectfully to Jennifer. Jennifer flipped it in her hands and pulled on the string. Camilla was pleased to see her teacher smile and nod as she handed back Camilla's bow. "This is beautiful. Pristinely crafted with your hard work. It's good to use."

Camilla thanked her and returned to her seat as Jennifer examined the other apprentices' bows and stated that they were all clear for use.

As the apprentices returned to their seats, Jennifer continued her morning speech. "All right, everyone, the last two weeks have been decent. Your form has improved enough for me to find you ready for shooting practice." Jennifer walked to a closet near her desk and removed a brown box from it. "So grab your training bows and some leather gloves from this box. In fact, you can keep them until the end of your apprenticeship. Once you graduate, you will have to return them and buy your own. To those of you who have your bows made already, I apologize, but unfortunately you cannot use it yet. I need to see how well you can nock arrows. When we get to the period of training where I will make you use non-notched bows, you can use your bow during shooting."

The students followed their teacher out of the classroom and to a door marked Training Room One. Inside the training room were targets with a thick red outer ring, a slimmer green ring within the red, and a very small blue ring within the green. The targets lined the perimeter of the room. There were lines of targets at distances of twenty-five feet, fifty feet, seventy-five feet, one hundred feet, and continuing in twenty-five-foot increments to six hundred feet at the end of the room. There were also multiple raised targets either under or above various objects. The floor, made of smooth stone, was also marked with numbered black dots about six inches in width. The apprentices marveled at the range and number of targets.

"Impressive, right?" asked Jennifer. "Eventually, in your training, you will be practicing to shoot six hundred feet. However, today we are just starting proper shooting."

Jennifer opened the box she had brought and removed a practice bow and one arrow from a quiver. "To start," she said as she nocked the arrow in her hand between the practice prongs, "you will want to enter the arrow between the prongs like so. Retain a good grip on the arrow, and pull back in the motion that we learned in the last two weeks." She demonstrated the motion and raised the bow close to her face, pulling back to its maximum capacity. "You can close your eye to aim—or not. Whatever works for you." She released the arrow. It hissed through the air and, within seconds, hit the blue center of a target at one hundred feet with a loud thud of metal against wood.

Her apprentices exchanged glances with wide eyes. She turned and said, "Your goal today is to nock an arrow into your bow. And maybe even shoot. Come get a quiver, and take your places on these dots." The apprentices scurried forward to grab their quivers.

Breeanna removed a quiver from the box, and as she made her way to a spot, she turned toward Camilla and said, "Good luck, Camilla."

Camilla grabbed a quiver and took a spot, with three other apprentices in between her and Breeanna. All the apprentices started to nock arrows into their bows. Many did a terrible job. The man to Camilla's left, six feet away, had difficulty holding his bow and trying to nock the arrow in between the training prongs. He was failing numerous times to do so, continuously placing the arrow above or below the prongs.

Jennifer moved about the room to individually help each apprentice. After she did so, they were able to nock their arrows between the prongs. One of the men on the end tried to shoot, but his arm began to waver under the weight of the bow, and when he released his arrow, he shot it downward. It ricocheted across the stone floor. The man next to him brought his bow up to shoot and released his arrow but missed his target by about four feet to its left. A woman to Camilla's right released an arrow but frowned as it fell short of the target and skittered across the floor.

Breeanna nocked her arrow and brought it up to her face fully drawn, then released the arrow. The arrow sailed with a hiss and hit the twenty-five-foot target in front of her in the middle of the green ring. Camilla glanced around—a few of the other apprentices looked on with furrowed brows and lips pressed into thin lines. Camilla could feel the blood pumping through her. She did not want anybody to show her up, especially since she had been practicing for half of her life thus far. She nocked her arrow in between the rungs—not that she needed them, for she could already shoot a bow using her finger to balance the arrow. She brought the bow, fully drawn, up to her face and released the arrow as quickly as she had drawn it. The arrow sailed into the same target in front of Breeanna and thudded into the outer edge of the blue ring.

The other apprentices maintained their stunned looks. Jennifer gave Camilla an approving nod. Breeanna threw Camilla an irritated glare, then removed another arrow from the quiver slung over her left shoulder, nocked it, and released it toward the fifty-foot target. It sailed into the outer edge of the green ring. Camilla nocked another arrow into the prongs of her bow and fired it at her fifty-foot target—it landed with a heavy thud in the middle of the green ring. Camilla looked at Breeanna, whose deep frown indicated that she was not amused. *Looks like I'm going to have a rival,* she thought.

* * *

When Urien entered his classroom, Maria greeted him.

"Good morning, Urien," she said with a wide smile on her face.

"Good morning, Maria. Are you ready for today?"

She let out a laugh and said, "I'm ready for anything" as they made their way to their seats. The students sat for a few minutes, the sound of light chatter filling the room, before Victor walked into the room. The chattering died down as the students turned forward in their seats.

"Good morning," Victor said gruffly, looking out at his class while rubbing his face. After a few long seconds of silence, he spoke again. "So far, your training is progressing well. Not too well but not bad either. Your stealth training isn't near the level it needs to be, but we've still got quite a ways to go. This morning, we're going to have some more fun," he said with a slight smirk. Some of the students sighed lightly. This meant they were probably going to leave their session with bruises or scrapes.

"Let's make our way down the hall, and I'll reveal what I have in store for your morning," Victor said as he stepped out the door. The Nightcloaks tailed him down the dark hallway. Four doors down on the left side, they arrived at their destination. The sign on the side said Training Room Three.

Victor opened the door, and his apprentices followed into a room that was very long, well lit, and dotted with various wooden obstacles—some on the ground, and some about twenty feet off the ground over water—and randomly placed nets that led to the water. On a platform at the end of the room were twenty flags, one for each apprentice. All around the room were other, more advanced Nightcloaks standing in place.

Victor stood before his class almost grinning, much like he had on their first day. "Here's the fun part. As you all know, Nightcloaks are renowned not only for their stealth capabilities, knife skills, and counter techniques, but they are also well known for their abilities to climb and enter spaces that many people would consider impossible or impassible. Today we are going to start that training with this basic course. Your objective is to simply navigate the course, retrieve a flag, and bring it back to me. This is why knowing how to swim is a requirement to be a Nightcloak. These obstacles are suspended twenty feet above a small pool of water, itself about ten feet deep."

Some of the apprentices exchanged worried glances. Urien knew the course in front of him was going to be challenging and exhausting. "Not to worry," Victor said. "Your training will be at times dangerous, but we do have safety precautions in place. Can't have any of you dying on me."

Victor motioned for his students to gather at the starting points. "You will have until the end of this period to bring me the flags. There are three starting points, each marked with a red arrow. You can begin."

Only three? Urien thought. *Surely he wants us to all line up, thus wasting time.* Urien observed the course as the other apprentices began scrambling to the starting points, one on the far left, one in the middle, and one on the far right. Urien saw no other way to the flags except for the marked paths. For the moment, he would try that way.

He, Maria, Lancet, and a few others went toward the left starting point. Maria arrived first. From what he could see, Urien noticed that at the start, they were to run up a five-foot wall. From there, they were to jump across a four-foot gap to a foot-wide plank. At the end of the plank, the paths branched out, but from where he stood, Urien could not make out what they led to.

Maria ran up the wall, then seemingly effortlessly pulled herself up. She kept her balance and then just as easily jumped to the plank and began making her way to the end of it. Lancet proceeded to the wall and ran up it—though not as easily as Maria, who was already crossing another gap by swinging from bar to bar while her feet dangled in the air. Lancet slowly rose to his feet, carefully maintaining his balance. He jumped for the plank but was thrown off balance and landed on the side of the plank. He careened over it, managing to catch the edge with one arm as his feet dangled in the air.

Urien ran up the wall, pulled himself to the top, and leaped across the gap, landing just a few inches shy of Lancet's hand. Urien grabbed Lancet's free hand just as he was beginning to slip. Urien slowly heaved Lancet upward, struggling to find good footing on the narrow plank as Lancet grabbed hold with the hand that had slipped off, pulling himself up next to Urien.

Lancet, heaving heavily, said, "Thank you, Urien."

Urien looked at him and said, "You're welcome. Now let's get going." He made his way quickly and easily to the end of the plank. From there to his right he could see the bars that Maria had crossed—she was now farther into the middle of the course, pulling herself with her arms across a long horizontal bar. In front of Urien was a wall much like the one he had just climbed, except this had flat bulges coming out of the front. It was about six feet high and led to a series of horizontal metal bars, which he imagined he would have to carry himself across. To his left, a rope was extended to another platform, where a twist of metal bars rose up to the second level.

The other apprentices were in the middle and far right of the course, still on the same level he was. *Which way should I go? If I go right, I might catch up to Maria, but I could get stuck behind her the same way Lancet is behind me,* Urien thought as Lancet brushed past him, taking the metal bars to the right. The next apprentice to pass Urien made his way to the rope on the left. *That way leads directly to the next level; however, it seems like more effort to get over there, which would be a great loss of energy.* Urien ran up the wall with bulges, catching each one in his hand to help propel him up. At the top, he walked over the metal bars until he reached the end and stopped.

Lancet had begun to make his way across the long horizontal bar. He proceeded three feet and lost his grip, crashing into the water. Maria sat on a platform in the middle of the course, clearly trying to figure out her next move. Michael, positioned on the left side of the course, locked eyes with Urien and smirked. He then stepped onto a ten-foot-long plank that had handles on it at the three-, six-, and nine-foot markers. As he stepped, the plank tilted to the side and sent Michael plummeting downward into the water. *Ha. Idiot. At least now I know if I use that, I have to catch the handles,* Urien thought. He had finished observing the next parts of the course. He then jumped from the bars he was on and caught the narrow rope that hung in front of him. As his momentum carried him across, he released his hands, sailing downward toward the next platform.

He landed on his feet, which slipped from underneath him, bringing his chest to the platform while his feet dangled in the air. He grunted with the effort of clinging to the platform while trying to pull himself up. He took in a few breaths, exhaled heavily, and managed to pull himself onto the platform, then immediately jumped to his feet. He bolted to the end of the platform and leaped at the end to the left, catching the short horizontal rope that was suspended over a gap. He swung his feet forward and then back, building up momentum. Urien repeated this motion five times and launched himself across the five-foot gap to the next rope.

He caught it, but his left hand's grip slipped, increasing the pressure on his right. His leather gloves took some of the strain. He gritted his teeth, then brought his left arm back up to the rope, managing to reach and grasp it. He then repeated his swaying motion and launched himself to the next rope, catching it. His arms and core were beginning to feel the effort of his endeavors. He still had one more rope in front of him and, after that, the last gap to the next platform. Should he miss either, the rope and gap in front of him would send him plummeting into the water, and the last gap would have him land on a net that would roll him into the water.

Urien took in a few more breaths and held them in his lungs for a few seconds each. He expelled the last deep breath and started swinging his legs once more. He swung seven times, and when he had built the momentum on the seventh swing, he released himself toward the next rope. He caught the rope in his right hand, his pinkie slipping from the rope. Urien could feel the strain of the effort run down his arm and into the muscles of his shoulder and upper back. He managed to get his pinkie wrapped around the rope with the rest of his hand.

Heaving and clenching his jaw with effort, he reached his left hand up to the rope, feeling the strain of doing so in his right hand. After a few seconds, Urien managed to grip his left hand around the rope, feeling the tension in his right arm lessening and equaling that of his left. His lungs rasped with the strenuous effort of stabilizing himself as well as now just hanging by the rope.

He took in one more deep breath, exhaled, and began the same swinging motion. After eight repeats, he launched himself forward. He soared through the air, descending toward the platform below him. He landed on it heavily and rolled forward from the impact. He flashed a victorious smile and rose to his feet, fully feeling the exertion he had put on his body. He quickly made his way to the end of the platform. From there, a large metal post with horizontal metal rungs rose four feet into the air. Urien climbed the metal rungs and scooted around to the other side of the post. Three feet above him was another metal post with rungs on it. He reached above his head for it and grabbed the rungs and pulled himself off the bar he was currently on.

He could feel more tension build in his arms as he pulled himself from one rung to the next until he was able to get his feet on the rungs. Once his feet were in place, he climbed the metal rungs with ease onto the second level of the course. Urien was pleased with himself. While he usually did not make games of things, he felt some competitive satisfaction that he was the only apprentice on the second level of the course. He had even beaten the apprentice who had taken the rope—he had fallen into the water.

Even Maria, who had started the course with ease, was not on the second level. From what he could see, Maria was climbing a set of walls similar to the one he had climbed to get to the metal bars leading him to the ropes. He saw that some of the apprentices were only about halfway through the course, including Michael, who had taken a different route after restarting.

In front of Urien was a square wooden plank with handles on it. He stepped carefully on it, and when he did, the plank swayed slightly to the side he was standing on. Using the handles to help his footing, he quickly crossed the square to the other side.

Maria, at that moment, transitioned from a wall onto the platform of the second level. Rising to her feet, she said, smiling, "Hi. Nice to meet you up here."

Urien smirked. "I thought you would be the first one up here."

Maria laughed, brushing her red bangs back to clear the sweat from her brow. "That was the plan, but clearly that didn't work out. Do you know how much time we have left?"

Urien looked at the clock toward the front of the room. "We have an hour left."

"Well then," said Maria with a light shrug, "let's see who can get on the next level first or get a flag first."

Urien replied confidently, "Well, I'm more than positive it won't be you."

Maria smiled. "I didn't take you for being presumptuous."

* * *

Aeronwen sat waiting for class to begin. Marcus walked over, then placed his hands on her desk and leaned toward her slightly.

"Good morning, Aeronwen. How are you this morning?" he asked.

"I'm fine," she replied. "And yourself?"

Marcus smiled warmly and said, "I am great this morning. Ready and energized. I was wondering . . . ," he began, "would you join me with my friends today at lunch?"

Aeronwen looked at him blankly for a few seconds. At first, she thought he was just asking due to boredom, but now she was surprised about the manner in which he had asked. "Is tomorrow better? That way I can let my friends know I will not be with them. I don't want them to think I am avoiding them."

Marcus grinned and stood up straight, taking his hands off her desk. "That's perfectly fine."

"So yes, I will join you and your friends for lunch tomorrow," Aeronwen said. Aeronwen was not exactly interested in romance with him—if that was what he was after—but was looking forward to making new friends in her training. She was also aware that perhaps she could change her mind.

Eurwen walked into the room, and everyone went to their seats, including Marcus. "Good morning, everyone," Eurwen said, smiling at her class. "That's not what some of you are thinking, though. You're thinking 'Shut up. It's too early for this,'" she said, and her students burst into laughter. "That's better. Bright eyed and able to still embrace laughter. Believe me; I know sometimes mornings just do not work, but that's just how life goes. Anyway, your training is coming along excellently. Your knowledge of medicine has greatly improved. So this morning, we will not be studying medicine. We're going to learn the other aspect of healing. Today we're going to learn to harness energy from Lapideases." Some of her apprentices exchanged eager glances. "Exhilarating, right? I remember doing this for the first time, feeling like I was going to explode with excitement. We're going to start with healing before we move on to offensive light magic. So follow me to the training room." She took a chest from her closet and proceeded out the door.

They walked toward the end of the hall and took a left turn, where the training room awaited them through the second door to the left. They walked into the bright white room. The walls were adorned with flowing white drapes with elegant red-and-blue patterns on them. Wooden mannequins wrapped in fresh pigskin, with meat underneath still attached, were scattered around the room. Eurwen took a few more paces forward, then dropped her box on the ground in front of her. "Come get a Lapideas from this box, and we will begin our training. Find a mannequin to partner with," she said with a chuckle, "and we will begin."

Aeronwen and the others each made their way first to the box to take a Lapideas from it and then to a mannequin. Aeronwen took one on the right side of the room, with Marcus and two of his friends down the line to the right of her.

"Fortunately, we are practicing on mannequins and not real humans or animals. That would be a disaster. But one day you may have to use light magic on someone or something to save them. That's why we are Vivicanterns. Now, harnessing the energy from a Lapideas at first can be quite challenging. The energy inside of one must be pulled out with the perfect balance of force and gentleness. It can be equated to pulling sand from the bottom of a lake or ocean and letting the sand slip slowly through your fingers. The Essence must be pulled as gently as a string. Also, you will need to be close. This generally only works within two feet of the target. So before you can save lives, we must practice and perfect these methods of extraction," Eurwen explained. "Take your Lapideas in both hands—for now it will take both—and try to pull the energy from it."

Eurwen then faced one of the mannequin bodies in front of her. She held her hand up, and a *Linwae* generated in it. She launched the shining white light at the body in front of her. Within a few seconds, wisps of smoke arose from the charring of the pigskin that had covered the mannequin. Eurwen then walked forward and put her hand to it. "This is one reason we learn what we do. Light magic can cause slight burns to the skin that burn out quickly," she said. Her hand then glowed, and she began to move it over the mannequin. To Aeronwen's astonishment, it did not repair the skin. "Burns unfortunately cannot be healed. Healing spells can provide some relief but ultimately do not repair the damage done. You may see these in your journeys. I hope you truly do not and have a peaceful service. But this is one of the reasons we learn to harness this," Eurwen stated seriously.

"Another reason we learn what we do is to counteract dark magic. It works against our own in a push-push manner. One has to pour more Essence in to remove the other. The main version of dark magic functions as masses of cold. When it strikes something, it makes it colder. There are two other forms we counteract: curses and drains. Curses function in two ways. They fill the afflicted with an overwhelming sense of violence and rage but, when cast, can be refined and used to control the rage of the individual. They also function with that push-push manner I mentioned. Curses have to be removed by generating your Essence into the afflicted. If only part of it is removed, the curse can still take effect. It is also possible for the afflicted to completely overcome it by sheer willpower, if they can manage. Then there are drains. These sap out the life energy of someone over the course of minutes, hours, or even days, eventually resulting in death. The more Essence put into it, the faster the action. The caster can even put more Essence in if near the afflicted to massively increase the speed of the decay of the afflicted. Now return to your training," Eurwen instructed.

Aeronwen held her Lapideas in both hands and imagined pulling sand from a lake and letting it slip through her fingers. For a brief moment, she could feel the energy of the Lapideas rising from the center of the cool white stone, shining brightly with white light as it did so. It then proceeded back to the center of the stone as she lost her pull on the energy. Aeronwen glanced around and watched as a few of the other apprentices attempted the same thing but failed too.

Aeronwen focused once more and began to tug the energy from the center of the Lapideas. When she had pulled the energy halfway, she imagined a gentle string gliding slowly through her fingers. This time, the Lapideas shined brighter and stayed that way.

Eurwen looked bewildered. "I've never seen anybody be able to do it this quickly. You have to be able to hold the energy there, which you don't seem to be having trouble doing. Now here's where you apply it. I warn you: this may be graphic," she said. Eurwen knelt down and removed a short knife from a kit next to the mannequin. She then stabbed it into the mannequin's arm, right below the elbow, and slit from the point of contact to the other side of the elbow.

Aeronwen grimaced slightly as blood oozed from the wound.

"To apply the healing to the wound, you have to use the same concept of the string. The motion used to extract this Essence and apply it is a gentle motion. Due to this, the Essence must be extracted and applied delicately. Otherwise it would not work. Now try once more,"

Eurwen instructed. "Your hands or a Lapideas must be near the wound. The Essence then radiates from one to the other and causes the skin to heal. This mannequin is made of pigskin, which will show if your efforts are effective or not."

Aeronwen knelt next to the mannequin and began to apply the healing to the wound in the mannequin, with the concept of a string still in her mind. She watched, amazed, as the wound in the pigskin began to reform.

"Slowly move your hands over the course of the wound," prompted Eurwen. Aeronwen very gently moved her hand over each inch of the wound in the mannequin's arm little by little until no cut was left.

"Excellent," said Eurwen with a smile. "We will keep practicing, because I will show how to use the energy to cover larger areas at once, but good work." Eurwen rose and went to assist her other apprentices. Aeronwen felt confident that she would be able to help others in the future should the need arise. She knew not to get in over her head because there was still more to learn, and it may not be easy, but she would apply herself nonetheless.

* * *

Cadfan was filled with morning tiredness, but it was soon replaced with an aggressive enthusiasm as he made his way through the doors of the Lepides training building. He sauntered down the hall to Training Room Two, where Price had told them to meet at the end of last week. He slipped through the azure doors and saw multiple apprentices warming up.

Cadfan stretched his arms and then his legs and began a few warm-ups of his own. He began by taking his practice sword into a downward swing, followed with a horizontal side swing that led into an upward slash. He chained it into a downward diagonal swing and spun into a shoulder thrust. Cadfan lowered his sword, puffing his chest up in pride.

Price walked into the room, a deep frown on his face. "Everyone line up," Price barked as he walked to the front of his class. His apprentices lined up in front of him. "Your skills are sloppy right now. Most of you are progressing poorly, which is my fault, but I will make you proceed more smoothly." His tone held a touch of disappointment. "So spread out, and this morning, we are going to train hard."

Cadfan and the other apprentices spread out about six feet from each other in line and readied themselves for what Price had in store for them. "Front ready stance," instructed Price, and his apprentices lowered their swords just to the middle of their stomachs. Cadfan could feel the tension build in his arms and run through his body. "To start," Price said, "you will do a downward slash, do a quick step forward with your left foot, proceed to an upward-left diagonal slash, enter mid high stance, and do a quick step to the right while doing a downward-right diagonal slash. Begin."

Cadfan brought his sword downward quickly and with great force, stepped forward with finesse, brought his sword upward in a left diagonal slash, held his sword slightly raised and parallel to his shoulders in the mid high stance, and swiftly stepped to the right while simultaneously bringing his practice sword downward diagonally with a heaviness behind it, until his sword was an inch above the ground.

Price still held his deep frown, but he granted them a nod of approval. "Again." The other apprentices and Cadfan moved back to their starting points and proceeded again with their instructions. Cadfan began his downward swing and connected it to the other moves, ending once more with his sword just above the ground.

"Again," Price demanded, and the apprentices once more repeated their demonstrations. They continued this for an hour until Price instructed them to stop.

"Getting better. Here's how we will test it. First, get two wrist weights from the closet, and strap one to each hand. Then don a set of training gear."

Cadfan hurried to the closet near the door, as did the other apprentices. The apprentices each pushed through to the closet to retrieve wrist weights and padded leather armor sets. Cadfan strapped on the black wrist weights and donned the leather armor over his head while making his way across the room to the red rings painted on the floor. He could feel the inside foam padding of the leather armor against his arms and his thighs as he strapped the pieces to him. He held the helmet in his left hand as he arrived at the cluster of training rings each placed about five feet apart from each other.

Price instructed his students to form a line behind him. They did so, and he stood before them. A grim smile slid across his face. "Let's make this more interesting," he said. "Now we all have access to the hazel affinity; otherwise, you would not be my students. This affinity is harnessed to increase our movement speed. This movement speed can be minor or to extremes. Harnessing the affinity protects our bodies during movement. It also increases our reaction time and awareness while in use. To harness the Essence required of the affinity, think of yourself as a well, and you're pulling a pail of water up. So what I want is for you to attempt to retrieve your own Essence and practice moving and attacking each other in addition to standard practice," he said. He stood motionless for a moment and then darted to the other side of the room in a blur. "That's what I want you to do," he said.

"So two to a ring. First we will do three-minute sparring sessions." Price paced around the training rings. "As you know, the rules are fairly simple. Each successful strike to the legs, chest, arms, or head is worth one point. This is only to show your precision. In a real fight, this is not practical. If you are knocked off your feet, you lose, because in reality if you are taken to the ground, you have already lost control of your stance, even if you manage to rise back to your feet without getting impaled. If your weapon is knocked out of your hand, you lose as well. Now I need two in each ring."

At each set of rings, two apprentices made their way into the centers. Cadfan was waiting at the ring farthest to the left. His leg bounced up and down. He had never liked waiting, and watching people practice made him want to join in. He desired to be known for his skills and talent. There were not enough rings for him to participate this round, so he would have to watch for now. All apprentices took the front ready stance.

Price looked at a small hourglass resting on his palm. "Begin!" he yelled, starting off all the matches. In the ring in front of Cadfan, a shorter apprentice with blond hair hanging under his helmet, Trevor, started with a lower strike to the larger, shaggy-haired Gareth, who blocked with his sword, pushed Trevor back, and brought his sword downward into Trevor's. Trevor blocked the following strike to his side, then parried Gareth's strike, pushing forward, and swung his sword directly into Gareth's stomach; then he backstepped while slashing his sword downward onto Gareth's shoulder.

"Two points," yelled Price as he pointed their way and moved to other rings to referee. "Focus on harnessing your affinity," he shouted to everyone around him.

Hmm. Not bad, I guess, Cadfan thought while twiddling his helmet in his hand.

Gareth stepped forward, heaving his sword downward. Trevor raised his horizontally in front of his face to block Gareth's, pushed Gareth's downward, and brought his sword into Gareth's chest while hooking his leg around Gareth's. Trevor then pulled his leg back along with Gareth's, throwing the larger boy off balance, and then kicked him in the back and sent Gareth crashing into the floor.

"You're finished!" Price yelled from the other side of the room. A minute later, Price called time, and the in-ring apprentices left.

Cadfan tugged on his helmet and tightened it, and his opponent, Arthur, entered the ring. Cadfan held his practice sword in his right hand, twirling it mockingly.

"Begin," said Price in a boom. Arthur quickly stepped forward, bringing his sword down in the arcing motion they had learned. Cadfan tightened the grip on his sword now and sidestepped to the right while propelling the sword, still held in his right hand only, hard into Arthur's chest. There was a loud ring of leather and wood colliding. Cadfan then spun around Arthur and brought his sword into the right side of Arthur's body while sweeping his legs out from under him and simultaneously pushing him with his left arm. Arthur tumbled to the floor and rolled several times.

"Match," Price called from the ring next to them. Cadfan removed his helmet and shot a defiant look at his opponent, feeling the pride of his accomplishment.

* * *

Dysan and the Dynamis gathered in their training room.

"Are you ready for today, Dysan?" Jackson asked.

"We are all born ready!"

"Ready for anything? Including wrestling wolves or carrying Ydaeriin rhinos on your shoulders?" Adar asked from a few feet away.

"If it comes to it. Plus, wrestling a wolf would be fun!" Dysan replied.

Adar rolled his eyes. "Well, even if that happens, we," said Adar, gesturing to himself, Seth, and Dean, "won't let you beat us."

Spyros entered the training room with a mischievous-looking grin on his bearded face. "Are you all ready for today? To start," he said, "strap on a wrist weight, and start with two laps around the room." The apprentices began as instructed, not showing any signs of contempt, knowing that Spyros would make it worse if they did.

Dysan and Jackson, behind Adar, Seth, and Dean, made their way to the supply closet on the right wall. Jackson reached into the closet, grabbed two pairs of weights, and passed one to Dysan. They strapped the weights around their wrists and then sped into a jog around the room. Dysan and Jackson kept a steady pace as they rounded the first corner. *This seems easy,* Dysan thought. They had just finished their first lap and were still running easily. A minute later, they had finished both laps and waited for the rest of the apprentices to finish. When they did, Spyros made another announcement.

"Today you are going to get to wear heavier armor. You'll be wearing a set of pauldrons that drape over your chest plates. The bottoms of these pauldrons will also have grooves in them that can fit another piece of thin armor. You will be wearing a plate on the front and back of the pauldron set," Spyros said. Dysan grinned widely. "In order for you to become a

Dynami, you must become accustomed to wearing many different types of armor, most of which are heavy. So this is what you will do. Get a set of bronze armor pauldrons from the armor closet. You will put it on over your primary armor and then do two laps around the room once more. You may start now."

The apprentices clambered to the armor closet next to the supply closet. Jackson and Dysan were the first to make it there. Jackson grabbed the handle, heaved the door open, and stepped inside. Dysan followed Jackson into the armory closet. Each set of armor was bound together with a leather strap with a looped handle. Dysan wrapped his hand around a handle and hoisted the armor up. The armor was actually heavier than he had imagined. He slipped a thin piece of bronze into notches at the bottom of the armor. He found two small indentations in front of the notches and pushed them through holes at the top of the plate. He then locked them in place. Dysan began to put on the back plate of bronze, which he found more difficult to do. He realized he should have probably put the back plate on first and then slipped on the pauldron. He carried the set of armor out of the closet, passing the other apprentices on his way out.

Next he slipped on the greaves and tightened them with the attached straps. The greaves fit comfortably on his legs, and the linen inside felt smooth beneath his feet. He reached for the helmet and placed it on his head, tightening the strap under his chin. A little uncomfortable, he admitted, but the helmet fit, and the cloth inside felt nice against his scalp. He slipped on his right gauntlet and pulled the leather strap that ran over it to tighten it.

The gauntlet provided protection while still allowing his fingers mobility. He slipped the other one on, tightened it, and stretched his arms. The weight of the armor pressed against his body. His hands felt heavier, and he raised them with difficulty. His feet felt awkward with the weight of the greaves on his legs, even though they fit comfortably. His head felt slightly heavy, but he could still move his head with ease.

By this time, the other apprentices had finished armoring up. "One more thing," Spyros added. "You will be running with your axe in your hand. You may begin."

The apprentices ambled into a slow jog. Adar, Seth, and Dean took the lead, running slowly side by side. The weight of Dysan's armor sank even more into his shoulders, but he passed Adar, Seth, and Dean, who had slowed slightly. Dysan rounded a corner, breathing heavily between his teeth. His entire body burned and ached tremendously, and he could feel the strain of the armor weighing on him with every step he took, but still, he felt proud to be wearing that armor.

* * *

Tesni, alongside Christina and Catherine, was in the training room where Peter had told them to meet when he had entered the classroom earlier. Dotting the room were the multiple person-shaped targets they had used last week.

"What do you think we're doing this morning?" Tesni asked.

Christina, smoothing strands of hair between her fingers, answered, "Looks like we might be doing javelin training. Or maybe we're doing combat training."

Peter walked through the door carrying a box in his arms. "Gather round, everyone," he said as he set the box on the floor. The apprentices congregated near him, all peering around each other to try to peek at what was in the box. "The last two weeks, we started by getting you to maneuver in your armor, which is getting better. We also learned some lance play. Today we will be adding a degree of challenge to it." Peter removed the two-inch-thick lid of the medium-sized wooden box. Tesni looked into the box and saw a dazzling glow of white stones roughly the size of a fist—some smooth and others slightly jagged. They were Lapideases.

"Since you now know how to harness Essence, you will put it to use. That in itself should be challenging to begin with. However, you're all going to take it one step further. You will be doing that while also doing maneuvering and thrusting training with your lances."

Christina, nudging Tesni in the arm, said, "I told you."

Peter gestured to the targets placed throughout the room. "You will each grab a Lapideas. Your goal is to try to pull the Essence to the surface of the Lapideas. You will start at the first targets. Run toward them while zigzagging, do a spinning horizontal slash to it, proceed to your next target while still zigzagging, and perform a thrust just past the side of the neck. Zigzag toward the last target, and perform a chest thrust, and if any of you manage to pull the Lapideas's Essence to the surface, you will finish by doing a backstep removal of your lance and launch the spell at the target."

At this point, the apprentices snatched up Lapideases and returned to their spots.

"Ready!" Peter exclaimed, and the apprentices stood completely straight with their lances parallel to the shoulders of their dominant arms. They clutched Lapideases in the hands of their other arms, which they had their small bronze shields strapped to, holding the arms at a forty-five-degree angle across their chests.

"Begin," he ordered.

After they heard *begin,* Tesni and the other apprentices lifted their lances a foot above the ground and tilted them forward slightly while moving their shield arms to the sides of their bodies. Tesni, with her lance in her right hand, sped forward. Her armor had some weight to it but was still light and flexible to allow her freedom of movement. She had also been wearing this same armor for two weeks now, with the exception of removing it after getting home from her day of training and on the weekends, when she did not have class. Because of that, she could easily run in the armor over short distances without needing to stop.

She increased her speed as she closed in on the first target. She found it incredibly difficult to imagine the instructions Peter had given while running toward her target. *That's the point of this training, then,* she thought. She spun to the left, scraping her lance across the torso of the human-shaped wooden training dummy, and darted forward, barely moving the energy from the Lapideas's center as she began to zigzag from one spot to another. She kept going like this for about thirty feet to the next target. Tesni brought the edge of her lance through the neck of the wooden dummy, and a shower of splinters shattered off of it. She burst forward, zigzagging as she did. The energy in the Lapideas in her left hand pulled up from the center and receded back to it in a tug-of-war effort.

She was now close to the last target. She had managed to pull the energy halfway out of the Lapideas but could not bring it any farther from there. It was more difficult for her to concentrate on the Essence while also doing everything else. Closing in on her last target, she raised her lance higher, pulled it back in her right hand, and, with the force generated from her shoulder, thrust it forward into the wooden dummy, creating a loud impact as it went halfway through the stomach of the wooden dummy. She quickly backstepped and removed the lance with slight resistance, pulling small scraps of wood with it.

The other apprentices were finishing up as well, none of them able to produce the magic from the stones in their hands. Peter called loudly across the room, "Now repeat it. Keep repeating it until your break." Tesni let loose a loud exhale. *This is going to take some time,* she thought. *I guess I'll just have to keep redoing it until I succeed.*

* * *

Delyth, Lisa, Josephine, Emilyn, and Nina gathered in the training room, where multiple circle targets were scattered at ten-, fifteen-, and twenty-foot markers, each spaced about two feet to the left or right of one another. All the apprentices had already followed Valeria's earlier instructions to take ten extendable lances from the training closet. They stood with the lances strapped to various spots on their armor, waiting for Valeria to arrive. She entered the training room a few moments later.

"Good morning, my young and eager apprentices," she greeted joyously.

She motioned for them to gather around. As they did so, she continued with her instructions. "Great effort that you have all applied in the last two weeks. You're starting off well, and you are incredibly driven, which I admire. For today's session, we are going to do target practice. Within the last two weeks, I taught you the mechanics of thrusting, slashing, and throwing techniques. Today, you will be using the same throwing mechanics. Your targets are placed at various lengths, as you can see. The goal is to get six hits before you run out of lances. We will be doing this for the first part of our morning, so by the time of your break, I would like you to at least have hit fifty targets. That's how we will grade today. Any questions?" No hands were raised. "Spectacular. Let's get started. Take your places in front of the targets. The first three will be thrown at the ten-foot marker, the next three will be thrown at the fifteen, and the last four at the twenty. You can begin now."

Delyth, her friends, and the other apprentices took their spots in front of the targets. Delyth drew one of the lances strapped around her arm and extended it. She gripped the lance in her right hand, holding it horizontally toward the target. She then pulled it back, feeling the contraction in her shoulder, and launched it at the ten-foot target in front of her. It landed with a loud smack slightly outside the center. She then took another lance and extended it. Delyth arched her arm and shoulder back and hurled it at the target. The lance sailed through the air with a hiss and hit above the previous one.

Lisa looked at Delyth with a grin. "You're doing really well."

"So far," Delyth said.

"Let's see who can score more hits and who's more accurate."

"I'll accept that challenge," Delyth responded without hesitation as she threw her third lance, which landed just a few inches next to the previous one. She watched Lisa throw her third lance near the center of her target. So far, they were tied. They both had hit the first target three times near the middle or center of the target.

Lisa and Delyth each extended another lance. Delyth raised her right arm up, lance in hand, and stepped forward, then threw at the fifteen-foot target. The lance thudded into the upper-right section of the target. Delyth glanced to her left and saw Lisa launching hers—it sailed into the lower-right part of the target.

Delyth's next lance hit about six inches below the previous one.

"Looks like we're back to square one," Lisa said. She extended a lance and propelled it toward her target. It hissed through the air until it smacked into the lower-left part.

Delyth extended another lance and paused. She looked at her target fifteen feet in front of her. If she could throw her lance evenly, she might be able to hit the center, but so far that had proven to be a challenge. *Okay, Lisa. I can't let you win, so this one is going to the center,* she thought, willing it to happen. Delyth raised her lance in a throwing position, closed her eyes, and imagined the lance going into the center of the target. She then opened her eyes, took in a quick breath, and sent her lance through the air. It hissed directly into the center of the target with a loud thud.

Lisa looked fairly surprised. "Not bad. Let's see if you can hit the last target the same way," she challenged, waggling her eyebrows at Delyth.

Lisa then threw a lance at the last target, and it nicked the edge, cascading to the floor with splinters of wood.

"What was that about hitting the last target?" Delyth teased. She grabbed a lance strapped around her leg, extended it, and threw it at the twenty-foot target. The lance hissed toward the target, lowering and barely hitting the edge before it skidded across the ground.

"Nice one," Lisa said sarcastically.

Delyth threw another lance, which managed to land on the target a few inches from the edge. Lisa's next lance landed in the same spot on her target as Delyth's had.

They were each down to their last two lances. Delyth could hear Valeria instructing people as she focused her thoughts on her target—she tried to tune everything else out. Delyth grabbed her last two lances and extended them, one in each hand. She looked at her target, once more imaging the lances hitting it. She drew in a breath and threw both lances toward her target. Both lances hissed through the air and smashed the bottom edge of the target; they and chunks of wood clattered onto the floor.

Lisa's mouth dropped open before she looked Delyth's way and laughed.

Valeria walked over to Delyth, also with a stunned look on her face. "Nice job. You still need practice, but that was incredible."

"Thank you," Delyth said humbly.

Lisa extended her hand to Delyth. "Good job. It seems we both have much still to learn, but this was fun. After this, let's see who can make it to first." Lisa grinned.

Delyth shook her hand fervently. "I accept this challenge!"

* * *

Alexander and his friends sat on the wall at their usual spot. The sun was a fading orange color, which looked beautiful as it mixed with the dark-green hues of the Escali Forest. He and his friends were dressed not in their apprentice clothes but in the normal clothes they wore on a regular basis.

"How was everybody's day?" Tesni asked cheerily.

"Well, I wasn't able to draw out a Lapideas's energy. I was only able to pull it halfway from the center," Alexander answered, fiddling with a stone on the wall beside him.

"Me too!" Tesni exclaimed. "I also had to try to pull it out while charging targets with my lance, which makes it even more challenging. Aeronwen, were you able to pull out a Lapideas's energy?"

"Yes," Aeronwen answered simply.

"What? No fair!" Tesni feigned offense, but Alexander knew her well enough to see that it was all in good humor. "How was it?"

Aeronwen shrugged—seemingly casual—yet her eyes lit up as she spoke. "It was incredible. Just like everything I imagined as a kid. The stone glowed, and the wound on the practice dummy closed up."

"Tesni, have you started throwing practice yet?" Delyth asked, jumping into the conversation.

"We have. We did some this afternoon. Camilla, what did you do today?" Tesni turned in Camilla's direction.

"I made a rival today. We kept showing each other up shooting arrows at our targets," Camilla said.

"I did that today too," said Delyth. "One of my friends challenged me to see who could hit more targets."

"That's amazing," Dysan said.

"What did you do today, Dysan?" Delyth asked him. Alexander listened while his friend explained.

"This morning we did our standard warm-up laps with wrist and ankle weights attached and then we got to wear our pauldron armor sets and do more laps. Then in the afternoon, we did brief combat practice," Dysan answered.

"We did that today too," Cadfan said. "My opponent was beaten within seconds of the match beginning. Urien, what skills mentioned in legends and whispers did you learn today?" Cadfan's sarcastic tone was clearly meant to tease Urien.

Urien answered, "You know how Nightcloaks are famous for those *legendary* skills you just mentioned? We did some of those today. This morning we climbed through an obstacle course that was raised in the air over nets and water."

Cadfan smirked. "Did you fall in? We can't be friends anymore if you did."

"No, I didn't. Michael did," Urien said. Cadfan burst into laughter and slapped the back of Urien's shoulder roughly. His laughter died down after a few seconds. A few minutes of silence passed before anyone said anything.

"Well, time to go home and get some grub and then some shut eye. You know greatness needs rest to be great the next day," Cadfan said. They all laughed as they made their way to their houses. Alexander and Camilla walked together toward their houses as usual, and along the way, he wondered where he and his friends would be in five or ten years. He felt that they would still be friends, because Tesni had made them promise that they would be, and they never broke their promises to Tesni. He imagined what they would all be doing.

Since his first day, he had often pictured himself as a member of the Royal Magic Court, whose role was to provide magical knowledge and protection to the royal family and other royal families that comprised the court. He had imagined that Cadfan and Urien would be part of the Royal Guard, the personal bodyguards of the king or other royal family members. He knew that Dysan was quite capable of succeeding and imagined that he might be a general of Eltheneae one day. He believed that Tesni and Aeronwen would be regarded as the greatest healers in the city. He imagined that Delyth would be an Ascalon teaching at the guild. He also imagined that Camilla would be known as a great Bowman and would teach future students. Alexander walked through the door of his house, wondering what the future would bring for him and his friends.

Chapter 5

Alexander and his friends had undergone a long four months of training. Alexander, Tesni, and Aeronwen were now capable of drawing energy from Lapideases and producing shield walls and were trained in magical combat. They had learned how to counter blocking dust, a naturally occurring substance that prevented the use of Essence within someone. Camilla was able to shoot an arrow accurately at a two-hundred-foot range. She and Urien had become novice trackers. Dysan now wore thick bronze armor permanently during training days.

Alexander felt the biggest change was the feeling of the trust placed in him. At this point, just one month before they graduated from their apprenticeships, each apprentice who had trained to use weapons was allowed to carry a real weapon as a sign of trust. He and Aeronwen carried short swords and leather satchels filled with multiple Lapideases. Tesni carried the same satchel in addition to a medium-weight combat lance. Delyth had the same lance and a satchel filled with numerous extendable lances. Urien wore six belts, each containing ten throwing knives, strapped to his waist and legs as well as four longer, heavier knives and a short sword. Camilla carried her bow and a quiver of eighty arrows on her back as well as a short sword. Dysan and Cadfan each had their weapons—a long slender sword for Cadfan and a bronze axe for Dysan—strapped to their sides.

They were at the wall discussing what they wanted to do for their Friday night as a celebration for making it as far as they had. All of them had seen several fellow apprentices drop out of their apprenticeships.

Looking out at the short field that spread before the walls of Jylinae, Alexander instinctively brushed aside the hair that hung above his eyes. He closed his eyes as he listened to his friends. Aeronwen, Tesni, and Delyth were discussing one of the restaurants along one of the canals in the middle section. He could hear Dysan and Cadfan playing a game of slaps while occasionally adding their opinions to the girls' conversation. All of them were dressed for the occasion. The ladies all wore shin-length robes in blue, white, purple, and pink, one for each of them. The men each wore brown pants and black, red, or brown robes with them. Alexander had also draped his father's cloak around his shoulders.

He opened his eyes now and looked at the edge of the Escali Forest, where something caught his eye. It was a glint, like light reflecting off of metal. He stared for a few brief seconds, wondering what it could be. It was far too noticeable from this far away to be a knife or spoon or other small object. A second glint appeared five or so feet away from it, as far as he could tell. More now appeared, in equal distance from each other, until a total of twenty glints could be seen.

The soldiers stationed along the wall were now speaking about the glints, with audible concern in their voices. The girls' discussion trailed off as they caught wind of the conversation happening near them. Dysan and Cadfan scrambled up so they could peer out over the wall with Alexander.

Then Alexander heard the sound of whirling metal. He made eye contact with Cadfan, who shook his head, clearly uncertain of where the noise was coming from. Moments later, he saw what appeared to be giant drills breaking through the surface of the ground. Within seconds the machines had emerged in full. They appeared to be vehicles of some sort but were nothing like what he had seen before. They had metal wheels with leather wrapped over them and what appeared to be smaller versions of the Lapideas-powered artillery that Eltheneae and other countries had used for centuries.

Alexander was frozen in place as he watched. The vehicles charged forward as the soldiers on the wall yelled that they were under attack. The horns were blown down the length of the wall and at the corner towers. The approaching vehicles shot an incredibly fast barrage of fire blasts from their cannons up and down the city's wall, not quite able to reach the top, where Alexander and his friends stood. Alexander watched two of the vehicles dip into premade sinkholes. The buzzing sound of fire being blasted filled Alexander's ears as the soldiers manning artillery near him were shooting at the vehicles to no avail, most just missing the fast targets. Some projectiles collided with the bronze plates that framed the outside of the mechanisms.

A burst of unidentifiable objects were launched from the edge of the forest, hitting along the top of the wall. Some flew over his head as he and his friends ducked and cried out in panic. Tesni and Camilla grasped each other's hands, huddling down behind the wall. Alexander scanned his friends quickly to make sure they each appeared unharmed. He heard the sound of shattering as a glass object impacted the rock behind him, just inches from his arm, releasing the pink color of blocking dust. Panicked, he yanked his cloak up to cover his mouth and nose. He did not know if he had already inhaled any.

When things had been quiet for a moment, he turned and peeked over the top of the wall. Eight more drills were breaking through the ground, revealing even larger vehicles, each painted at the front with a black rectangle with a thin horizontal red line through the middle, which he knew to be the flag of Xythuu. The sides of the vehicles then opened upward, and at least two dozen soldiers poured out of each one. At this moment he could also hear the heavy whirl of large arrows being launched from the ballistae, which smacked against the white walls of the kingdom as another wave of fire ascended from the forest.

"Alexander! We have to get out of here!" he heard Camilla scream. She and Tesni stood and bolted for the stairs, followed by their other friends. A projectile smashed through the top part of the wall a few feet to his left while another landed in the wall just a few feet below him. His breath caught in his throat as he realized how close they had come to hitting him.

As the approaching enemies were reloading, he scanned the forest once again and saw yet another unfamiliar sight. Three blue lights dotted the forest—on the far left, far right, and middle—and were increasing in size. He was about to sprint toward the stairs his friends had just descended when he saw the blue lights being fired from the forest's edge. He turned away immediately.

The wall he had been crouching behind burst into a shower of rocks a few feet away from him, which knocked him onto his chest. His body slammed hard into the ground, knocking the wind out of him and sending an ache through his joints. He was facedown, and he could hear the muffled frightened yells around him. He slowly lifted his head, feeling it ache as he did. His ears rang as he heard the muffled sound of soldiers telling someone to evacuate—his friends?—and insisting that apprentices were not ready for this sort of thing. Around him, he could see shattered white rocks of Jylinae's wall. Smoke filled the air.

His friends rushed toward him, and Urien tucked his arm under Alexander's shoulder and lifted him up. Alexander tried to shake off the dizziness and focus on what Urien was saying. "Alexander, they've ordered an evacuation."

Alexander was well aware that during events like these, apprentices were also evacuated along with civilians.

"Are you okay?" Aeronwen asked, brushing off some gravel and bits of stone that had dug into Alexander's arms.

"Yeah, I think so," he said, touching his fingers to a bit of blood on the left side of his face, next to his eye.

"You have to get to an evacuation point," ordered one of the soldiers near them. At that moment, another blue light smashed through the wall, showering pieces from it. Alexander lifted his hand and created a small green shield to block some of the debris coming in their direction, surprised and relieved that he had not breathed in any blocking powder. The chunks of rock ricocheted to the ground.

"We have to go," said Urien, beginning to jog and pulling Alexander along with him as his other friends followed. They took the stairs down to the first level and then ran fifty feet down the road and over the bridge of a canal of the Grand Courtyard.

Soldiers were directing people to the evacuation points, so Alexander and his friends made their way to a staircase by the bridge.

Alexander and Urien, with the rest of their friends tailing behind them, descended the stairs to their right and into the main plaza. Alexander, Aeronwen, Camilla, Tesni, Delyth, and Dysan all stopped.

"What are you doing?" Urien asked incredulously. "We need to keep moving."

Alexander looked back in the direction they had traveled. "We should go back. They need our help," he said.

"I understand you want to help, but we aren't skilled enough to provide assistance. We still haven't finished our training. And you know the protocol for those that haven't graduated from their apprenticeships is to evacuate with the citizens to provide their protection," Urien insisted.

Cadfan stepped forward. "I think we should fight. I'm eager to cut up some of these bastards."

"Cadfan, you can't be serious?" Urien asked.

"I *am*. This is our home."

"Plus, this is what we were training to do. One day this is to be our role," added Dysan.

"Urien, I know you want us to get out of here, and I agree that we aren't finished training, but we have to help," Tesni pleaded, laying a hand on his shoulder.

Urien sighed. "You're right. We need to help."

Explosions sounded from the way they had come. More explosions were heard toward the western part of the courtyard. They could see a wall of defensive Eltheneaen troops fighting off Xythuu forces. The Xythuu forces then pressed farther into the Eltheneaen troops, and the drills came crashing through the walls. More Xythuu troops pushed out of the vehicles. Alexander burst into a run, back the way he had come, and made his way to the entrance of the courtyard.

Camilla chased after him. The others followed suit, yelling for Alexander to stop. As Alexander got closer to the fight, the sounds of weapons colliding, and the smell of smoke overwhelmed his senses. He took a spot toward the back left of the formation that had now assembled and raised a Lapideas in his left hand. He then withdrew the Essence within and launched three rapid *Faer* spells. The small balls of fire sailed toward the enemy and were deflected into the ground. The troops next to him ordered him to evacuate. A group of Xythuu soldiers then stepped off to the side of the formation and hurled lances at them.

Alexander, Tesni, and Aeronwen darted forward, each making a shield that spanned five feet in front of them. The lances ricocheted off of them and collided into the ground; the shields then timed out as the Essence used for them ran out. Alexander launched three more balls of fire toward the approaching group. The Xythuu soldiers scattered in an attempt to dodge the incoming fireballs, which they did successfully. To his right, Tesni generated another shield. The Xythuu spearmen extended lances and aimed while Camilla launched an arrow into the arm of one. The other two threw their lances against the shields, which caused them to dissipate into small particles. They rushed forward, covering the distance quickly.

Two more lances were thrown at Tesni and Aeronwen, who brought up more shields while two other soldiers rushed toward Alexander. He shot a fireball at their legs. It knocked one of them off of his feet. Next to him, Tesni threw a blast of light from the Lapideas in her left hand, knocking over two Xythuu soldiers. The one whom Camilla had shot earlier threw a lance with his uninjured arm. It sailed toward Tesni, who was pulled out of the way by Urien. The lance landed next to their legs.

Four axe-wielding Xythuu charged forward, breaking through the side of the formation and heaving their axes down, one aimed at Cadfan, one at Delyth, and two going for Dysan. Dysan managed to evade one and barely blocked the other.

Cadfan sidestepped the blow aimed at him and brought his sword horizontally across the soldier's arm, but he barely scraped it. Delyth blocked the axe blow, kicking her assailant backward. Two spearmen drove their lances forward at Tesni and Aeronwen. Tesni blocked both and repelled them to the side. The men attacked once more, and Aeronwen brought up a shield on her right side to block an incoming lance. It impacted against the shield, which then dissipated into particles. Tesni attempted to dodge a lance but was cut on her leg. Aeronwen shot a blast of light, knocking Tesni's attacker to the ground while another attacker slashed his lance horizontally, cutting across Aeronwen's shoulder.

Urien ran forward, slid under the soldier's feet, and threw him off balance. He caught the soldier's foot in his hand and pulled him closer, then drove a heavy knife into the soldier's thigh, just below his groin, causing him to scream in pain.

Alexander was doing his best to dodge the blows of the two attacking him. His shields were being destroyed after each hit the two landed. A lance scraped the left side of his abdomen, sending pain coursing through him as it cut him. He pulled a soldier forward by his lance and brought the Lapideas in his right hand up to the soldier's face and blasted fire into it. The soldier fell backward, screaming in agony. Camilla launched an arrow behind Alexander directly under the eye of the other soldier near him.

Cadfan was dodging each attack his opponent threw at him. He had managed only minor damage to his assailant. The soldier raised his axe and brought it down with amazing force. Cadfan raised his sword to block. As the two weapons collided, the force knocked him to the ground.

"Cadfan!" Dysan shouted some feet away while he blocked an attack to his right, kicked his opponent back, and brought his axe twice across the face of the other. He ran toward the soldier standing over Cadfan, but Alexander did not think he would have enough time to make it over there. Delyth blocked her opponent's attack, swept his feet out from under him, and drove her lance through his neck. She grabbed the lance he held and turned, then threw it at the soldier standing over Cadfan. It landed in his arm, which stopped him. Cadfan swiftly rose and thrust his sword into his opponent's neck, piercing his armor. He removed his sword and backstepped while Dysan crashed his axe into the Xythuu soldier's face.

"Thanks," Cadfan grunted.

More Jylinae soldiers flooded into the area.

"Get out of here," one of them ordered.

Alexander and his friends ran from the incoming Xythuu soldiers, with some of the Jylinae soldiers escorting them. Alexander could hear the sounds of fighting and explosions in the middle section of the city. They made their way down a road leading away from the Grand Courtyard. He looked back over his shoulder and saw numerous soldiers at the courtyard entrance get knocked back as it was blasted into pieces by Xythuu soldiers. He and his friends hurried down the road and turned right through a narrow alley. A few moments later, they had arrived at one of the underground entrances that were used as evacuation points. Jylinae soldiers were directing people through it while arrows, lances, and various forms of magic were launched into the area, colliding into the shields that the Illustratum had put up.

Tesni and Aeronwen stopped at this moment to heal the wounds Delyth and Alexander had received. Blood had dripped down Delyth's leg and soaked her purple dress, and Alexander's own wound had drenched his shirt with blood. Aeronwen had healed her wound quickly enough to not lose much blood.

"Thank you," Delyth said, once her cut was healed. They all ducked at that moment as a large fireball spell crashed into one of the shields, exploding it into particles. Another was launched seconds after and smashed into the tunnel entrance. Shattered rocks tumbled over the entrance, sealing it off. The spell dispersed from the impact point and rained a shower of small balls of fire and rocks. Alexander, Tesni, and Aeronwen brought green shields over their group, protecting themselves from the shower of rocks that collided into the shields.

As they rose, they could hear the sound of fast-paced feet moving on stone behind them. A group of Xythuu soldiers—ten with lances, two with curved swords drawn, and two wielding Lapideases—advanced through the same alley that Alexander and the others had gone through earlier. Alexander grabbed a Lapideas from his bag in his left hand and shot *a Faer Xaen* from it and a *Vintae* from the other. The ball of fire instantly got bigger and fanned over the area. It was blocked by a Xythuu soldier before it could hit anyone Alexander had aimed for.

A Xythuu wielding a Lapideas then drew the fire upward and shot it back in two beams of condensed fire. Alexander and some of his friends dropped instantly to the ground, and some jumped to either side of the narrow walkway. He heard the hissing sound of fire over his head and the cries of anguish from those who had been hit by it. The Jylinae Illustratum behind him had put up several horizontal and vertical shields, some over Alexander, in an attempt to protect those in the area.

Alexander shot multiple small blasts of water at the feet of soldiers, hitting six of them. He heard them muttering something. He quickly raised up his other hand and shot a blast of lightning out of his Lapideas. The parts of the ground that were wet instantly conducted, causing the drenched soldiers to scream with agony. Alexander shot another blast at the stone ground. A javelin flew through the air and hit the top of his hand, smearing blood across the top of his hand and knocking the Lapideas away from him.

Cadfan rose and charged forward, gripping his sword in both hands. Two Xythuu spearmen tried to impale him with their lances. He slid under them and rose once more. He had now made it to the wounded Lapideas bearers. He rapidly slashed through the neck of one and brought his sword across and through the chest of the other. Before he fell to the ground, the second man shot a condensed beam of electricity from his hand. Cadfan sidestepped but not fast enough. The spell grazed a few inches of his side and forced him backward, rolling him onto the ground. A small wisp of smoke appeared on his clothes, and he quickly beat it out.

Alexander, his friends, and some of the Jylinae soldiers charged forward as Aeronwen rushed to Cadfan. He grunted as she arrived and rolled him onto his back.

"Be still," she said as she pulled a Lapideas from her satchel and placed it against his side. She withdrew the energy from it and began to heal the wound.

Alexander was launching multiple fire blasts from a new Lapideas, either missing or not hitting where he wanted. Camilla released arrows at Xythuu soldiers as they were fighting Jylinae soldiers; some of them were blocked with shields, but some hit their marks. Tesni and Delyth were both vigorously fighting one spearman while other Jylinae soldiers collided their spears or swords with the others'. A lance cut across Urien's arm; he pulled the soldier's lance closer to him and jabbed one of his big knives through the bronze armor and into the neck of the spearman wielding it. He then spun and threw a knife into the neck of another who had just dug his lance into a downed Jylinae soldier. After a fierce barrage of attacks and counterattacks, one of the Xythuu swordsmen met his end as a lance impaled him, splashing the ground with blood.

Dysan had his hands full with another swordsman who had already landed two cuts to his arms. They had been using guerrilla tactics, which Dysan was having trouble countering. The soldier now stood ten feet away from Dysan. He dashed forward in a blur and released two attacks, one of which cut horizontally across Dysan's clavicle. The swordsman swung his weapon downward. Dysan took a small step back and to his side. He rushed forward and caught his opponent's hand. He struggled momentarily to stay in control but managed to wrench his opponent's hands downward. With full force, he swung around so that his opponent was behind him, removing his opponent's grip on his sword and sending him rolling. Before his opponent could escape, Dysan darted forward and brought his axe down on his opponent's head.

All around the sounds of chaos were escalating. Fierce fighting, explosions, and the clatter of rubble could still be heard from the Grand Courtyard, including near the apprentice buildings. Jylinae soldiers were trying to escort civilians across the raised stone wall while a multitude of spells, arrows, and lances were being blasted at it. Jylinae Illustratum did their best to keep shields up.

Most of the Xythuu soldiers they had fought from the alley had been defeated, so the Jylinae soldiers ordered the apprentices to continue down the road to the nearest escape tunnel. A group of Illustratum followed them. Dysan lifted one of his shoulders under Cadfan to support him, and Alexander stayed by their side to create a shield at any incoming objects. As they dashed toward their escape, a barrage of blocking-dust-filled glass jars was launched across the road. The Illustratum were hit directly, and their shields soon dissipated into small green particles. As this was happening, a helmetless Xythuu soldier ran forward with a combat lance in his right hand. He extended a lance in his left and hurled it forward, barely missing Alexander and Camilla.

The soldier continued forward, passing two Jylinae Lepides and grazing one's side with his lance. He thrust his lance forward, aiming at Cadfan, who still had his back turned while being supported by Dysan. Delyth jumped forward and knocked his lance to the side, with it barely missing her leg. They exchanged a flurry of attacks, blocks, and dodges. The soldier thrust his lance forward. Delyth sidestepped, slashing downward—but not quickly enough. They simultaneously struck each other—Delyth getting the left side of the soldier's face and the soldier striking her hip. Each cried out in pain. Delyth shoved her lance up toward his throat, which he swiftly blocked.

Urien launched two knives at the soldier, both of which missed. The soldier, with blood pouring down his face, charged forward again. He extended another lance and threw it, which cut across Camilla's leg as her arrow hit his shoulder between his armor. He then dropped his other lance, and Tesni leaped forward and thrust her own lance. It impaled the man's thigh. She quickly removed it and kicked her foot into her opponent's. He tripped, and she thrust her lance into his neck. Blood spurted on the ground and on Tesni's clothes as the man fell. She removed her lance while a barrage of arrows and spells were launched from behind them.

Alexander and Tesni each threw up a set of three shields, one after another, in front of them, and the barrage of arrows and spells collided into them. The first of their shields broke into particles. Alexander launched multiple blasts of fire backed by gusts of wind, increasing the size of the fire. Alexander and his friends dashed once more down the road. Alexander, Tesni, and Aeronwen put up shields to block incoming spells and arrows as they ran.

They had only twenty more feet to go when an unrelenting barrage of fire, lightning, water, ice, and light spells were shot in front of them, forcing them to stop and spin to the side to put up more shields. Alexander threw up one shield after another as each was destroyed by spells. He breathed heavily, wondering how much more he and his friends could take. Their training had increased their stamina and stores of Essence, but he, Aeronwen, and Tesni were nearing their limit in energy due to shield magic use. Delyth, Cadfan, Urien, Dysan, and Camilla were also beginning to show signs of exertion from their efforts.

The shield in front of him broke into particles, and a blast of fire flew toward him. He dropped the Lapideases he was holding and caught the blast of fire in his hand, sliding back a few inches. He heaved with the effort but managed to split the blast in two and return the blasts near to where they had come from. Another medium-sized ball of fire flew in his direction. He managed to catch it in front of him in the same manner but was pushed back about two feet. If he went back ten more feet, he would crash into a building behind him.

He exhaled heavily with the intense effort of holding the ball of fire while standing his ground. His control over magic was still a long way from perfect. He managed to take a few slow steps forward, heaving labored breaths. He took a few more steps. Another medium-sized ball of fire was blasted toward him, which collided into the current one held in front of him and pushed him back quickly. Urien yanked Alexander from the line of fire, and both fireballs crashed into the wall behind the two. The fire exploded in a three-foot radius. The resulting force from the blast pushed Alexander, his friends, the remaining Jylinae soldiers near it, and chunks of rock flying all around.

Alexander hit the ground with a hard thud, ending up on his stomach. He could feel a painful scrape on his chin, and blood slowly oozed from it. His vision was blurry again, and his ears rang. Through his blurred vision, he could see the enemy troops being engaged by Jylinae soldiers. Many of the teachers from the various apprenticeships were engaging enemies. Valeria commanded a square-shaped formation, her lance and others' drawn forward. He could also see Victor engaging one on one and Regnor shooting blasts of fireballs and purple electricity at other troops who got too close to Victor. He also spotted Urien's father, Logan, and Cadfan's father, Broderick, fighting Xythuu soldiers.

His hearing and vision gradually returned to normal as the sounds of fighting filled his ears once more. Most of his friends had risen to their hands and knees and were coughing. The heavy smell of smoke wafted into his nose.

"That was horrible," Cadfan said. Alexander rose to his knees, coughing while doing so. Urien moved to him and helped him to his feet.

"We have to go," Urien insisted. They were still fifteen feet from the underground escape tunnel. Numerous Jylinae guards stood in front of the five-foot-wide stone entrance, directing citizens into it.

Alexander and his friends, with Urien leading them forward, ran as fast as they could to the entrance. They were a few feet from it when a ball of fire hit the ground near them and the guards, knocking over everyone near the impact. Alexander coughed once more as he rolled to his side, the smoke filling his lungs. As he did so, he saw another medium ball of fire colliding into the tunnel entrance, shattering the stone above it and covering the entrance in rubble. He stood as quickly as he could.

The guards began directing everyone toward another entrance on the other side of the plaza, about fifty feet away. Alexander and his friends ran through a sea of chaos. All around them lay soldiers who were wounded or already dead. Blood drenched the ground underneath, and the excruciating screams of pain rang in the air. Citizens were being grabbed and forced to the ground by Xythuu soldiers. Many were covered in either dirt, soot, or blood.

A blast of fire went over their heads, and another struck the ground, making them trip and roll. A Xythuu soldier charged forward, lunging with his lance while Camilla unsuccessfully shot an arrow at the enemy who had shot the blast of fire at them. Cadfan caught the soldier's arm and pulled him forward while thrusting his sword through the thin armor wrapped around the soldier's neck. He removed his sword, and the soldier was then sent crashing to the ground by a blow to the head from Dysan's axe.

The Xythuu soldier who had launched the fire met his demise to a Jylinae Ascalon, giving Alexander's group the opportunity to reach the escape tunnel. As they neared the entrance, they collided with a group of people who were also running to the tunnel entrance. Alexander noticed that one of them was a Nightcloak apprentice, still wearing his apprentice cloak over blue silk clothing.

"Urien?" The apprentice noticed Alexander's friend. "Oh, thank the gods and saints. I was wondering if anybody had made it."

Urien helped his fellow apprentice to his feet while responding nearly in a yell, "Lancet! I wondered the same thing. Have you seen Maria?"

Lancet dusted himself off and replied, "No, I haven't. I haven't seen anyone from class besides you."

They all continued to the entrance, now twenty feet away.

"Urien, I think we should help fight," Lancet said.

Alexander glanced at Urien to see how he would react. He and his friends had already tried to convince Urien earlier.

"Believe me, I want to help too, but they ordered evacuation, including for apprentices. And currently, I'm not sure we would be much help. I'm sure they're ordered to attack anyone. We've already intervened and met a handful of resistance," Urien said.

As he finished his sentence, a flurry of arrows was launched in their direction. Some whizzed over their heads, but a few hit some citizens who had been running with them. Alexander and the others ducked in an effort to avoid the arrows. He attempted to generate a fire but felt a tingle in his hand as he tried to withdraw his Essence. It was now low, and he could no longer generate his own magic.

Camilla released two arrows in quick succession at the Xythuu soldiers against one of the apprentice buildings. One arrow missed, and the other slammed into the neck of a Xythuu soldier. Camilla released two more arrows, each of them hitting their targets.

They kept moving forward as arrows hissed into the ground around them. Another arrow launched toward Urien and Lancet. Lancet dived forward, pulling a citizen to the side as the arrow grazed his shoulder. Camilla and a Xythuu archer raised their bows and released their arrows at the same time. Her arrow sped into the archer's neck while the enemy's arrow flew in Urien's direction. Lancet leaped forward, pushing Urien to the side so that the arrow slammed into his own forehead. His now-lifeless body fell backward to the ground. Urien stood still briefly, looking stunned. Alexander then heard Urien yell out in anger.

Three Xythuu soldiers rushed forward, lances pointed out, only to be swept off their feet by a moving blur. The blur of a person thrust his sword through one soldier's neck. The other two rose but were each stabbed in the neck in succession by an invisible man, who then materialized. It was Logan. Broderick quickly appeared next to Logan—he had been the quick-moving blur.

"Dad!" Cadfan shouted.

"Cadfan, get out of here. This is no place for an apprentice," Broderick said. "Take the tunnels, and meet up with the rest of the evacuees and Jylinae guards, and go where they instruct you."

Cadfan took a small step forward. "But, Dad, we want to help. That's what we've been training for!"

Broderick turned slightly to look at his son. "I said go. If you stay, I don't know what will happen to you, and that thought doesn't please me at all," he said very seriously.

"What about Mom? Is she safe?" Cadfan asked.

"When the alarm was sounded, I rushed from here to the house. She had left earlier to do errands, but no one said she had returned. Shortly after arriving there, the area was flooded with enemy soldiers from those damn drills. It weighs on my heart, but I do not know if your mother is safe. That's why you must go now." Broderick laid a hand on his son's shoulder.

Explosions could be heard at the far end of the plaza, and more Xythuu troops pushed their way through the defenses on that side. Soldiers poured into the plaza. Broderick and Logan began to cross the plaza. Alexander and his friends hurried to the entrance of the underground tunnel but paused as Cadfan stopped.

"Cadfan, I'm worried too, but our fathers are more than capable of handling themselves and surviving. They've done so many times before," said Urien. As he spoke, two more large drills bored through the stone-paved ground, just twenty feet in front of Broderick, Logan, and some Jylinae Ascalons.

More Xythuu soldiers poured out of the vehicles. One in particular caught Alexander's eye. He had thick blond hair mixed with tones of brown and gray with a thin beard of the same colors. Over the black Xythuu robes, he wore bronze armor with many blessings inscribed into it. Four red-and-yellow tassels were draped over his shoulders, and a red cloak was attached to his armor. He carried a strange lance in one hand with swirling blue energy wrapped around the lance and up the spear-head. He held his helmet in the other hand. Alexander was sure the man was a figure of command.

Worry washed through Alexander, making him nauseated and causing his legs to feel heavy. Most of what had happened already did not make much sense. How could Xythuu have gotten so far into Eltheneae without reports of an attack coming in? Even though he was an apprentice and did not have access to information, they should have known at least something. He believed Xythuu's underground drills might have had something to do with the lack of detection, but that also raised the question of where they had gotten them or how they had made them. He thought of the cannon that had blasted the wall apart and the lance carried by this newcomer. They did not have the properties that the artillery did. There was something different about them. Something he could not explain.

The Jylinae guard and Xythuu forces engaged in a devastating clash. Cadfan's father moved in a blur from one target to another, striking them or sweeping them off their feet, while Logan went invisible and threw knives at the ones whom Broderick did not kill. One of the Jylinae troops made his way quickly and nimbly to the man with the strange lance.

From what Alexander could tell, the man had a smirk spread across his face as he put his helmet on. The Jylinae soldier raised his sword in one hand and his shield in the other, then slashed his sword downward. The Xythuu man stepped to the side, and the sword clanged against the ground. The stranger held back his lance, which now had more blue energy swirling around it, and thrust it at the Jylinae soldier's leg. It melted through his armor and made him cry out in pain as it pierced through his leg. The soldier fell to one knee and swung his sword horizontally at his assailant. The Xythuu man ducked, and as the sword went over his head, he sliced through it, sending a chunk of the blade to the ground. The Xythuu man then slashed his lance across his opponent, once more melting through the armor, and then thrust his lance into the chest of the Jylinae soldier. He removed his lance, and his opponent collapsed with a heavy thud.

Broderick darted toward him, moving in zigzagging blurs at his opponent, and attempted to slash through him. Broderick's sword grazed the man's armor as he barely dodged a counterstrike. Flaming knives shot at the Xythuu man's back—Alexander assumed those were from an invisible Logan. Two of them grazed the man's armor while one went over his head, and another cut across his tassels and cloak. The Xythuu man spun and cut off his flaming cloak.

Cadfan was watching intently.

"Cadfan, we need to go. We might not get another chance to leave," Alexander said as he tried to pull him to no avail. Dysan grabbed Cadfan and lifted him off of the ground.

"Hey, what the hell are you doing? Put me down!" Cadfan yelled as he squirmed and hit his head against Dysan's. He managed to wriggle free.

Broderick dashed forward once more in a barely seen zigzagging blur, with dust kicking up as he did. The Xythuu man dragged his lance along the ground and melted a small trench into the stone, then melted two more behind it. Broderick now closed in, tripping over one of the holes but quickly righting himself. His opponent brought his lance sideways, dodging Broderick's attack and scraping his lance across the front of

Broderick's armor. Broderick went rolling to the ground, clutching the side of his chest. Logan once more threw flaming knives at his opponent. The knives grazed his shoulder pauldrons. The Xythuu man held out his lance and shot a blue blast of energy from it, which hit the ground and burst the stone into a shower of rubble.

Broderick staggered to his feet and attempted to strike the Xythuu man, who managed to dodge it. Broderick bolted forward with his sword aimed toward the soldier. The Xythuu man barely dodged, and Broderick's sword caught just a bit of his armor. Before Broderick fully passed his opponent, though, the Xythuu man slashed his lance over the top of Broderick's right forearm, sending it and his sword crashing to the ground beside him.

Logan materialized, no longer invisible—Alexander guessed he did so to draw the soldier's attention away from Broderick—and threw his last bronze, oil-soaked flaming knife. The Xythuu man ducked under it and drove his lance through Broderick's neck, separating his head from his body.

Cadfan instantly let out a cry of anguish. *"No! Father!"* Dysan held him back. Logan lit a fuse on a glass oil-filled knife and threw it at the Xythuu man, who brought his lance up and fired another blast of energy from it. The blast of energy hit behind Logan, sending him flying forward to land near Broderick.

Urien shouted and attempted to run forward, but Alexander grasped Urien's shoulder. He could not imagine the agony they were feeling. His own father had died but had not been killed in front of him. The glass knife hit the Xythuu man's armor. It caught fire and exploded, pushing him to the ground. A slow wave of water pulsed out of one the blessings on his armor and dispersed the flames. The Xythuu man rose, noticeably slower but hardly seeming hindered. His armor sizzled and showed a barely noticeable scorch mark, but physically he was unscathed.

Dysan, Urien, and Alexander were trying to pull Cadfan into the entrance of the tunnel while he screamed, "Let me go! He has to pay!"

The Xythuu man raised his lance upward and pointed it at Logan, who had his head slightly lifted off the ground as he gazed at his fallen friend. Alexander and the others had managed to get Cadfan into the tunnel entrance. Urien was the last to go in. He looked back to where his father, Logan, was lying as the Xythuu man fired a blast of energy at his father's head. Urien turned away, hurrying into the tunnel entrance and down the stairs with tears streaming down his face as a Jylinae guard closed and locked the door behind him.

Alexander felt a mix of emotions tangle his insides. He was grateful they had made their way into the tunnels but had no idea what pain his friends were feeling.

"I am terribly sorry," Alexander said sadly.

The tunnel was wide enough to have two caravans of horses pass through and was dimly lit by torches on the wall. Guards were in the tunnel directing them forward.

"We should go back!" Cadfan screamed hoarsely. Alexander looked at his friend with sympathy and gently placed his hand on Cadfan's shoulder, staring at him with what he hoped was a sympathetic and reassuring gaze.

"Cadfan," Alexander said softly, "Camilla and I both know what it's like to lose a parent. We know the pain, the anger, the bitterness, and emptiness that follows it. But at the moment, the best option we have is to go to Ilgeth with the remaining forces and finish our apprenticeship training. We're no good to anyone dead."

Cadfan lowered his brow. "Your father and Camilla's may have been killed," he said in a low voice, "but they weren't killed in front of you! You can't imagine the anguish and anger I feel right now! That's why we must go back!"

"Cadfan," said Urien bluntly, "he is right. We need to go to Ilgeth and finish training. Believe me; I feel the same rage you do, but now it would only get us killed. I saw my father get killed, so you're not the only one in this. But I've known your father since we were children. He would not have taken kindly to you just charging in and doing something stupid like that."

Cadfan was heaving breaths in and out quickly, backed up against the wall by all his friends. After staring at Urien for a moment, he lowered his head and softened his expression. He closed his eyes with a short intake of breath. "You are right, Urien. He would not want me to just throw away this opportunity he gave me. Or any. I'm sorry, everyone. Especially to you and Camilla," he said to Alexander. He paused and, after a few seconds of silence, raised his head and added, "Let's go. We have a long way to the end of this tunnel to reach the halfway mark. And afterward, when we resurface, we have another bit of travel to get to Ilgeth."

Aeronwen nodded and added, "But first, let me and Tesni take the time to heal the wounds we all received. I lost some of my Lapideases when the wall was hit, but I have a few left. They should be able to last us until we get to Ilgeth."

After a few minutes of Aeronwen and Tesni healing the wounds they had all received, they continued forward fifty feet until they reached a triple split in the tunnel. The path to the left was blocked by large chunks of rock and rubble that had fallen in front of it. The middle and right paths were unblocked. Jylinae guards in their armor and white robes were directing them to the right path, which would take them halfway to Ilgeth, at which point they would resurface.

"Over here. We're directing everyone to Ilgeth. This way," one of the guards said. Alexander and the others began stepping toward her and the other guards and stopped as small pieces of rock dropped from the ceiling. "It's okay. That's been happening since the start when they were able to get to the middle section. It hasn't done much damage."

Dysan eyed the ceiling warily. "Let's hurry up and get this over with," he said as he bolted forward. As soon as he did, the ceiling in front of him caved in with a barrage of falling rubble.

"Dysan!" screamed Alexander and Delyth. The rocks had dropped just in front of Dysan, the force of the impact knocking him down. The dust was clearing. Dysan was on the ground, his head and shoulders raised while he lay there and coughed vigorously. He had some cuts and scrapes on his elbows, legs, and arms. Delyth and Tesni slid beside him. Tesni held out her arm with a Lapideas in hand.

"No, don't," Dysan said hoarsely. "Just a few scrapes. We need to keep going."

Tesni looked at him decisively. "Dysan, that's admirable, but these need to get healed. They could get infected, and I won't allow that. Also, you could have broken bones," she said as she brought her Lapideas to his chest. A swirl of white light circled around the Lapideas as she moved it slowly over every inch of his body. She held her Lapideas over his arms and began to heal the cuts on them. Aeronwen now joined her to help and speed up his healing. The wounds on Dysan's arms gradually closed, and the small amount of blood that had come out remained on his arms. They repeated the process on his legs and healed them within a few minutes. Cadfan extended his hand to Dysan, who pushed his legs into the ground as Cadfan pulled him up.

Aeronwen looked at the rubble that had blocked their way along the right path. The guards with them began to make way into the middle chamber. "Looks like we will have to take the middle route now," a guard said.

"We will. And that one only goes just outside the capital," Camilla said.

"Even so, we have to take it. We will just have to make our way aboveground to Ilgeth," Alexander said as they hurried down the middle tunnel.

Along the walls of the middle path were numerous straw bundles that were packed with emergency items. There were markings on the outside describing the size of garments contained within. They each rummaged through them until they found a bundle that would suit them.

Urien pulled out a map of the country. "Okay, we have that. That's good. We will need one just in case," he said.

"Is everyone ready?" Alexander asked. They all nodded. With that, they made their way farther down the tunnel.

* * *

Just over an hour had passed, and they were nearing the exit of the tunnel.

Urien gestured for them to stop. "I don't wish to say unsettling news, but we need to form a backup plan just in case we cannot make way to Ilgeth," he said. They all stood there. Alexander believed that the remaining forces in the city and survivors would be evacuated to the coast cities.

"If we are unable to make our way to Ilgeth," Aeronwen said, "then we should go to Fort Ydaeriin. If Jylinae should fall, they will see the beacon and realize they need to develop a plan. And also, it's a long shot, but if we have to go there, we could ask Ciimerii for aid." They all agreed with her plan.

Convincing Ciimerii to aid us is going to be almost impossible, Alexander thought to himself. He believed it was possibly an option, if the commanders of the forces agreed to it. Then a shudder ran through him. This would work only if the other cities were still standing and not captured. He had no way of knowing if Xythuu forces had moved into other parts of the country. For all he knew, they could have, given that Jylinae had not foreseen an attack.

Alexander made his way up the stone stairs. Once at the door, he paused and took in a breath.

"Be careful," Urien said. "There could be Xythuu soldiers around."

Alexander nodded and slowly pushed open the door just enough to see through the one-inch opening. He could see the trees around the entrance that kept it hidden. "I don't see anyone," Alexander whispered. He poked his head farther out of the exit and, upon seeing no one around, pushed the door completely open and walked out, with his friends, the surviving Jylinae guards, and others behind him.

They were surrounded by the trees that concealed the entrance. They made their way to the edge of the trees and saw no one around. Thirty feet in front of them was the road outside of Jylinae that led to Ilgeth. To their left, numerous bushes and trees dotted the side of the road.

"Stay in the bushes and off the road," Urien said as they began trekking alongside the road.

Alexander stopped and turned. He looked at the once tall, proud white walls and towers of the place where he had spent his boyhood.

Now some of them were shattered, and smoke and flames rose over most of the city.

He felt some relief to have escaped, but his heart still filled with so much dread looking upon Jylinae in this state—as well as anguish of not knowing whether people he knew, such as his teachers, his neighbors, or even his own mother, were alive. He turned and continued forward with his friends, leaving the despair of his hometown of Jylinae behind him.

Chapter 6

They were trudging alongside the road to Ilgeth and had covered only a tenth of a mile so far, with no encounters with Xythuu forces. Urien, who had taken the lead, signaled for them to all drop. Alexander and Urien crawled slowly to the edge of the bushes, just barely able to peek through them but with enough cover to not be seen. Numerous Jylinae soldiers lay on the ground, surrounded by dozens of Xythuu soldiers, some holding lances, swords, or Lapideases at the Jylinae soldiers.

"Dammit. They must have been doing patrols on the outskirts of the city when the invasion happened," Urien whispered.

"I can't believe they have already advanced this far out of the city," Alexander whispered. Anxiety filled the pit of his stomach.

"We have to get out of here. There are far too many of them to fight."

They could see the Xythuu soldiers spread out across the road and heard one say, "Move out. And if you find anyone, capture them. If they resist, kill them."

Alexander and Urien crawled backward and returned to the group. They relayed the information to the guards they were with.

"What's happening?" Aeronwen asked in a whisper.

"The road is crawling with Xythuu soldiers. There are too many of them. We have to find a way around them," Alexander responded.

"We may have to backtrack. There is so much open terrain," Delyth said.

Urien glanced around, then motioned forward. "Follow me. Stay as low as you can, and be quiet," he said as he rose to his hands and knees and moved through the tall grass. Alexander and the others followed suit.

They slowly crawled under and between the bushes as Xythuu soldiers moved forward alongside them. A group of Xythuu soldiers dragged the Jylinae prisoners upward by the ropes, binding their hands. Three Xythuu spearmen made their way very close to the hedges in which Alexander and his friends were hiding, and Alexander froze as they drew near. He heard some commotion on the other side of the road.

"We found some more," a Xythuu soldier called loudly. Alexander peered through a bush and saw the Xythuu soldiers ordering some Eltheneaen soldiers to drop their arms and surrender. He wanted to rescue them, but if he got captured too, he would be of no help. There were far too many to fight.

He glanced back at his friends behind him. Dysan, Tesni, and Delyth wore the same frustrated looks on their faces as they inched forward. He motioned for them to stop moving, knowing they were so close that the soldiers might hear them. His friends stopped. He felt as though he should fight, but he recalled stories from his father. His father had told him once about a time when he and a handful of other soldiers had hidden from enemy forces that had far outnumbered them. He had said that sometimes you had to do something necessary to ensure you carried on and that sometimes it was wiser to not fight.

Looking up ahead, Alexander saw Cadfan's face twist into a grimace. He knew that Cadfan had a different idea. Cadfan probably felt like a coward for not fighting, but they seemed to have talked some sense into him after his earlier outburst.

The noise from the Xythuu soldiers moved farther down the road. Tesni shifted and, in the process, snapped a twig on the ground. She cringed.

"What was that?" Alexander heard one of the soldiers ask.

"It was probably just a fox or something," he heard the other say. Nervous sweat dripped into Alexander's eye. The soldiers were closer now, prodding into the bushes with lances.

"See, I told you it was nothing," said the younger-looking one after a few quiet moments had passed. But they continued to prod the bushes with their lances. Alexander's mind was racing. *What do we do? We need to move, but if we do, they will see us.*

The Xythuu soldiers now physically pushed through the bushes.

"See, nothing," the younger one said again.

At that moment, they bumped into Urien.

"What—" one of them began to say, but Urien quickly pulled the soldier into his lance. He then shoved two knives into the man's neck as his arms crisscrossed each other. Urien pushed upward and then slammed the soldier down onto his back. Blood poured down the soldier's throat, and he gasped for air as Urien dragged his knives across the Xythuu soldier's neck. He lay on his back, not moving, as Urien removed his knives.

The younger Xythuu soldier attempted to spear someone with his lance while yelling "Hel-" but was cut short as Dysan pulled him down and pushed his axe edge through the young man's neck. Unfortunately, he did not remove his axe fast enough or do so in the same quiet manner as Urien.

Alexander could hear a Xythuu soldier farther up the road yell, "We're under attack!" Next he heard the whiz of lances flying into the bushes, one going just over his head, one scraping the side of Urien's bundle, and one sailing next to Dysan, cutting his cheek.

Alexander rolled out from the bush that had been hiding him. "Stay in two rows. Aeronwen, Tesni, and I will move in the back to provide cover," he said. Some of the guards with them gathered to the sides, each with lances extended and bronze shields on their arms. The other guards were around some of the citizens who had escaped with them.

His friends had all risen from their hiding places, and they began a full sprint along the side of the road as lances were thrown in their direction. Some arrows flew from behind, whizzing overhead. They dropped to their knees to duck under the arrows, then leaped back up. A group of Xythuu soldiers were right behind them and threw more lances, which barely missed them. Another group of Xythuu soldiers swept to the side of the road and attempted to attack over the hedges with axes, lances, and swords, forcing Alexander and his friends to make a left turn. They continued in that direction as the two groups of Xythuu soldiers gave pursuit.

Camilla turned and released two arrows in rapid succession, one of which hit the neck of a Xythuu soldier. Alexander shot a blast of fire from a Lapideas he had managed to pull from one of his pockets while running. It impacted on the ground, bursting the grass into flames, stopping the group of soldiers in front while the other group circled around and continued pursuing them.

Alexander gritted his teeth as they ran. They had now been thrown off of their initial course and were being pushed away from the road and closer to the Ydaeriin Plains. There was less cover in the plains, and being sent into the plains unprepared could prove hazardous. There were fewer and fewer bushes to cover them as the ground became slightly more jagged and rocky. More lances whizzed past him, with one tearing across his shoulder, causing him to scream out in pain. Arrows were also launched at them, hitting the shoulders of some Jylinae guards.

He kept running as fast as he could with blood dripping down his shoulder. He and Camilla both turned to attack. She launched an arrow, which hit inadequately into the armor of one the soldiers, and Alexander shot another blast of fire, but a lance whizzed under his arm, the back end of the lance hitting his wrist. This caused the Lapideas to drop out of his hand. Tesni launched a *Linwae* spell, and Aeronwen did the same; the lights collided into two targets. A quick burn surged over the Xythuu soldiers who had been hit.

Alexander removed another Lapideas from his bag and shot lightning at the ground, causing the grass in front of his opponents to once more burst into flames. There were some cavalry now riding in toward them, but the sudden flames startled some of the horses, and they threw their riders to the ground. Alexander launched a flurry of *Faer* spells toward the back of the group of horses. This startled them again, and the horses began to run straight toward Alexander. He caught the bridle of one and slid along the ground as the horse kept going. He struggled but managed to pull himself onto the saddle of the horse. Urien and Camilla managed to quickly grab a horse and pull themselves up.

The horses in front of them neighed violently as the others attempted to grab hold. More lances hurled toward them as they lifted themselves atop the horses. Camilla pulled her stolen horse forward, then turned back and launched an arrow. The arrow landed directly in the chest of an enemy spearman.

Alexander launched a few *Faer* spells, keeping the ground ahead of the enemies burning with flames to prevent them from following. He then launched lightning from his Lapideas toward them. It connected with some, searing them. As the fire and smoke slowed the troops' advances, his friends managed to take hold of the spooked horses that had made their way to them. Some of them shared horses, but they all had a ride now. They pushed their horses forward as more lances sailed toward them, most hitting the ground as the horses outran the aim of the soldiers. One, however, crashed into Urien's bundle, shattering it to pieces and strewing its contents along the ground. Their horses picked up more speed as they approached the Ydaeriin Plains. Alexander felt shame welling in him. They had not planned on leaving the guards behind, but the nature of the battle had forced them away.

Alexander and his friends crossed into the plains and kept going for about four hundred yards. They slowed the horses to a trot and stopped to look behind them. They could not see any Xythuu forces pursuing them. Alexander leaned forward on his horse and breathed heavily, trying to compose himself. Running for his life had taken its toll on him. *I need to get better at running,* he thought. The others, especially Tesni and Aeronwen, showed signs of exhaustion too.

"Can we stop running away for one minute?" Cadfan asked between heavy breaths.

Alexander gritted his teeth. "What exactly do you want us to do? Charge sword first into Jylinae with no plan?" he asked, anger seeping out in his voice.

"We need to think of our next plan. We are not enemies," Urien said.

Alexander let out a sigh. "I'm sorry, Cadfan."

"I'm sorry too," Cadfan said. "You're right—if we went back any of those times, we would have been killed either because of being outnumbered or vastly outclassed. I think we did well against some of the ones that we did fight, but it might have been luck too. I just don't like running away. My father always taught me to stand my ground. I don't like having to run away from something and not being in control. So now what?" He dropped to the ground and crossed his hands over his knees.

Alexander looked at the sun slowly slinking below the horizon. The battle at Jylinae had gone on for some time, and it had taken them an hour and a half to get out of the city. He estimated they had only about thirty minutes of daylight left. "First of all," he said "we need to find some shelter and count everything in our emergency kits."

Urien nodded. "Agreed. That should be a good place for the night," he said as he pointed to a tree about fifty feet away.

Alexander and the others nodded. They walked their newly acquired horses over, tied them to the tree, and then removed their saddles. They each then sprawled around the wide tree, which had enough cover to block any severe sunlight or weather. Each of them, except Urien, placed their bundle on the ground and removed the lid to inspect what was inside. They each removed four sets of clothing, a sleeping fur, a wooden jug with water, a fire-starter kit, dried meats, a cup, a bowl, eating utensils, coffee, salt, sugar, a map, a compass, and some medicine in wooden bottles.

"Yes, food. We won't have to go without," Cadfan said happily as he grabbed a piece of dried chicken and began eating it.

"You should wash your hands off first," Aeronwen said as she poured water over her hands and washed dirt off of them. The others did the same. Tesni and Delyth filled some cups with water and passed them around. Alexander and Camilla grabbed a jug of water each. They moved a few feet away and placed some bowls on the ground. They then poured water in them, and the horses drank gratefully. Dysan gave some dried meats to Urien, who took them and sat back against the tree to eat.

Alexander sat next to Camilla and looked at his friends. Each of them, including himself, had various tears in the clothes they were wearing, and each was covered in dirt and soot. Some had dried blood on their clothes. He bit off a chunk of dried beef and swallowed.

"Camilla, are you okay?" Alexander asked gently. She turned to look him in the eye. He thought, oddly, that despite the dirt and soot stains on her face, the glow of the setting sun made her green eyes stand out.

"As fine as I can be in this situation," she said. He welcomed the comforting warmth that her presence brought.

Silence fell over the whole group. None of them knew for sure if their family members were alive. None of them knew if their classmates and teachers were alive either. Alexander was fortunate to know that Camilla and his friends had survived, but he knew nothing of his mother's situation. He assumed his friends thought the same.

He contemplated the fate of those who had stayed behind in Jylinae, of the last soldiers who had defended the city. What had happened to all of them?

Urien broke the silence. "Should we still try to head to Ilgeth?"

Delyth put her cup down. "If they were looking for Jylinae troops on the outskirts of town on the Ilgeth side, then I believe Ilgeth might be their target. And with those machines, they could get there quickly. More quickly than we could."

Urien nodded. "Plus, strategically speaking," he said, "if they controlled Ilgeth, they could make their way to Port Ivory and even Hyybeth if that is their goal. And control shipping into the area."

"I believe we must make our way to Fort Ydaeriin and inform them of the situation. If no one from Jylinae has sent out messenger eagles yet, then they may not know that an attack has occurred," Aeronwen said. "And like we discussed in the tunnel, we could request aid, if necessary, from Ciimerii."

Cadfan scoffed. "Those bastards are not going to do anything that compromises their damn neutrality. They will not aid in battle or send supplies. At most, they will probably just let us or anybody else stay there for refuge," he said bitterly.

"Port Ivory would be our best chance," Camilla said. "From there, we could send out word to the rest of the cities and have the armies mobilize. Do we have an agreement?"

They all nodded or shrugged in agreement. The sun had set now, and the sky had turned a light shade of black. On the horizon, an orange flash of light burst into the sky behind them, which meant Jylinae had activated its beacon as a sign to the neighboring area that it had fallen. They all grew solemn. Alexander felt as if a heavy weight had been dropped on his chest. He felt breathless, and the weight sank into his stomach, and it tightened.

He stood, looking at where the flash was. In that distance was Jylinae, his home. His childhood. His memories. The capital of the kingdom of which he was a citizen. He gazed at the smoke rising above and thought of his mother. He suddenly felt shame run through him, as if he had let down his father. A single tear then rolled down his cheek as he realized Jylinae was gone.

After a few minutes of silence, Urien spoke. "We should all go to sleep. We have a long journey ahead of us," he said.

"Will our supplies last that long?" Delyth asked worriedly.

"We will have to worry about that tomorrow. We all need as much sleep as possible. We should probably also take watches just in case Xythuu troops are pursuing us. Two hours each. I'll go first."

"So I take it that also means no fire too, right?" Cadfan asked.

"Correct," Urien answered. "We can't chance it until we know we are not being pursued."

Cadfan scowled. "Fine. I know it would lead them to us and we may not have the skill to fight them off. I guess we are fortunate this did not occur later in the year. The night weather should be mild. I am not too keen on being in the dark and not seeing what is around us, though."

"That is why you have a fur blanket. I do not want to be in pitch blackness either, but I believe the risk is too high," Urien said.

Dysan moved from the tree and stretched. "Urien, I'll be on watch with you," he said.

"Delyth and I will go after the two of you," Tesni stated.

"We'll do so after the two of you," Camilla said, gesturing to Alexander.

"So me and Aeronwen will do it after that if the sun hasn't risen by then," Cadfan said.

"Thank you, my friends. Now go to sleep. You will need it," Urien said as he and Dysan moved to the other side of the tree. Alexander laid his sleeping fur next to Camilla's and stretched out on the ground next to her, wondering how the future was going to unfold now. He also thought, as he closed his eyes, that no matter how strong his enemies or how brutal the trials he would have to undergo, he would fight, to his last breath if necessary, to free Jylinae and Eltheneae from the people who had invaded it. A new thought occurred to him. The childhood friends he had been hesitant to leave behind after his training were now the only parts of his life not taken from him. He thought about what the future was going to be like and how drastically different it was going to be now, and then he drifted off into sleep.

Chapter 7

Alexander felt the rays of the sun shining upon his face, which woke him from his sleep. He and Camilla had woken earlier in the night to do their watch. He still felt the exhaustion from the day before and the poor sleep, but he knew the rest of them would be tired too. Cadfan stretched and rose to a sitting position. He yawned heavily and drank some water from one of the bottles that was in his kit. The others had risen already.

"Those Xythuu asses are going to pay for taking me away from my bed," Cadfan grumbled irritably.

"Sometimes, even comfort must be given up, especially in our line of work," Aeronwen said.

"Yeah, I am aware. You never realize how much we take beds for granted, though," he replied.

Urien shrugged. "That is not important right now. We have enough food to last at least the time frame for us to get there. We need to get moving—"

"I understand our direness," Dysan interrupted, "but could we at least go through our morning routine, at least to relieve ourselves?"

Urien nodded his head in apology.

There was a set of bushes about twenty feet to the side of them, where the girls headed first. They returned after a few minutes. Aeronwen walked toward Cadfan with an unpleasant look on her face.

"Cadfan, I agree with you. That was unpleasant," she said grimly.

"You don't have to tell me about the unpleasantness and uncomfortableness of war," he said as he sauntered with the other three guys toward the bushes.

They returned a minute or two later. Urien rummaged through Dysan's kit and pulled out the map and compass.

"Urien, I know we are refugees from our home," Cadfan said bluntly, "but can we have some coffee first?"

Urien was looking intently at his map. "Yes. Go ahead." Cadfan and Dysan eagerly grabbed some pots and coffee and started a brew.

"How bad is our journey ahead?" Alexander asked as he sat, eating some dried chicken and offering some to Urien. Urien took it but did not eat it right away.

"We have miles to go to either get to Port Ivory or Fort Ydaeriin and through some of the rugged parts of the plains," Urien said, then took a bite of the chicken in his hand. "Also, we do not know if we will encounter more Xythuu troops. I'm sure that the beacon was seen by the other cities, but I doubt they have any information on how it happened and how quickly it happened." He sighed deeply.

"I guess we'll just have to go through the plains and inform them ourselves if they haven't gotten any information. We also have horses now, so that makes this a little bit better," Alexander said confidently. He was trying to be optimistic, but he knew—and the others did as well—that they now had to ration their water with the horses.

They finished their breakfast of coffee and dried meats. Urien made his way to the horses and filled bowls of water for them. Aeronwen, Tesni, and Delyth removed the Xythuu tarps that were draped over their horses. They then proceeded to cut the tarps into strips with small daggers. This way they could use them as ties if needed. Then they gently placed the saddles on the horses' backs. Once they finished, the group began making their way toward Port Ivory.

* * *

Alexander and his friends were moving fast. It had been three hours since they had departed.

"Urien, how far have we gone? Can we stop? We must have covered at least ten miles by now," Cadfan said with slightly heavy breaths.

"Yeah, we can stop to take a break for fifteen minutes," Urien said, also breathing heavily. Tesni and Delyth slowed, and the others came to a halt behind them. They hopped off the horses and began to drink and let the horses do the same. Dysan dismounted and led his horse to where the bowls had been placed. His mouth was turned down in a scowl.

"What's wrong, Dysan?" Delyth asked after finishing drinking her water.

"I miss my armor. It was something that became an integral part of my life. By the time we got to keep it, it felt like it was a part of who I am. Now I feel exposed and like I am missing some part of me," Dysan said.

"I think you may be exaggerating just a bit there," Cadfan said with a smirk.

"Maybe, but we earned that armor, which is why I wish I had it, but you don't always get what you want, I guess."

"I do understand, though," Cadfan said, clutching his sword. "This sword was a gift from my father. Now it is the only tangible memory of him."

Alexander and Urien, after downing some water, bent over the map to study it. "We should be somewhere right here," Urien said, pointing at the map. "I am not sure we should continue on, though." He looked up at the sky. The clouds were thick, gray, and heavy.

"Agreed. It looks like a storm is coming," Alexander said.

"The storms here are supposed to be bad too," Camilla added.

"Let's hope that part of grade class was wrong." Urien looked around. "I think we should stop." The clouds were growing thicker by the second, and the sound of thunder popped.

"That's . . . not good," Cadfan said. The horses spooked slightly at the thunder. Urien, Alexander, and Camilla searched for a suitable place to ride out the storm. The ground was mostly covered in rocks and grass with only a few trees and some bushes around but too far to get to fast enough.

"Over there," Alexander said, pointing to a trench in the ground about ten feet away. They rushed to it, pulling their horses behind them, as heavy rain started to pour. The trench stretched about twenty feet long with small slopes rising from the end of it.

There was enough space between the slopes for the horses to enter and slightly less toward the side they were closer to. The horses went into the far side of the trench. Alexander and the others squeezed into the space between the slopes, which went down about five feet, with the slopes curling over their heads. It was a tight squeeze for the eight of them, as there was barely any room between them. The rain was now pouring down fiercely. They had cloaks inside their kits, which they quickly removed and donned. Alexander draped himself in his father's cloak. He then removed a cloak from his kit and handed it to Urien, who draped it around himself.

"I hope these things work," Alexander said, hugging his father's cloak closer to himself while he and his friends huddled into the tiny space under the ridge.

Thunder cracked while lightning flashed across the sky, the wind blowing turbulently, throwing rain into the area under the ridge. The frightened neighs of the horses filled the area along with the sounds of thunder cracking above. Alexander and his friends spent four hours in the storm, with their cloak hoods over their heads. They had kept them mostly dry, including Alexander's father's cloak.

"Is it over?" Cadfan asked incredulously. The rain had mostly stopped. Delyth and Tesni inspected their kits for any damage or missing supplies and found that none of it was gone, damaged, or wet, except for the clothes they had been wearing when the storm had begun. Only the outside of the kits were wet. Cadfan and Urien checked the horses for any injuries and to calm them.

"So should we keep going?" Dysan asked.

It had been a little after noon when they had stopped to rest and had had to ride out the storm. "We have at least another three hours of sunlight left, which I think we should utilize to the max potential," Urien stated. They all agreed and rose from their spots. They climbed the ridge and continued once more on their way to Port Ivory.

It was close to sunset when the group decided they should rest for the night. They stopped and set up under another tree near a cluster of bushes and other greenery. Swirling fields dotted the rest of the landscape. The horses had been unsaddled and were grazing at the bushes.

Cadfan dropped his kit on the ground and plopped down next to it. "Finally," he said wearily. Urien and Alexander had set up a spot to make a fire and were getting it started. Flames were soon crackling and spreading warmth around them while everyone was laying out their sleeping furs. They then all sat around the fire, eating and drinking.

"Are you sure we can risk a fire?" Dysan asked.

"I believe that we can. I have not noticed any signs of us being followed," Urien said. They continued resting in comfort for about ten minutes.

"What's wrong, Urien?" Tesni asked.

"I feel uncomfortable. Something is not right," he said uneasily.

"I feel it too," Alexander said. His training had taught him to always be aware of his surroundings and to trust in his senses. Right now, he listened intently and could feel every part of his body tense up.

"So do I," Camilla said, eyeing the foliage near them. Some rustling was heard in the bushes, and all of them grew silent. The horses whinnied. At that moment, a pack of wolves, about fifteen of them, rushed out of the shadows, snarling and howling.

Camilla leaped up, snatched the bow she had left by her pack, and launched two arrows, both of which landed in the skulls of her targets.

Alexander scrambled to reach into his pack, then shot blasts of wind from a Lapideas while Tesni and Delyth each launched a spear at the wolves, with one landing in its target and the other missing. Urien flung a knife into one's throat as it got closer.

The wolves darted to the sides in two groups, flanking Alexander and his friends and forcing them into a tighter circle. The horses kicked at some of the wolves and managed to break apart part of the wolf formation. One lunged at Urien and pinned him to the ground, its teeth snarling just above him. He quickly removed a knife from a belt strapped to his right shoulder, then sliced it across the wolf's neck and stabbed its head. Alexander's heart raced as he helped his friend to his feet so he would not be in a vulnerable position. Urien then replaced his knife and removed his sword.

Dysan had also been taken to the ground by a wolf latching onto his arm. He punched the wolf with his left hand while Camilla shot arrows at some of the others that were circling around him, Tesni, and Delyth. Dysan managed to wrap his arms around the wolf's throat. It released his arm and tried to squirm free, but Dysan snapped its neck. Two more went for his shoulders but were stopped as Delyth and Tesni impaled the wolves with their lances.

Some of the wolves circled around Cadfan and Aeronwen but darted away whenever Aeronwen fired blasts of light from a Lapideas. One of the wolves lunged at Camilla, knocking her down. Alexander hit it with a blast of wind and sprang a few feet forward. He managed to reach his satchel and pulled out another Lapideas. He shot a blast of lightning at the wolf attacking Camilla, which hit its shoulder and sent it scurrying away, whimpering in agony.

Another wolf near Alexander lunged at him. Its snarling teeth whizzed past his head, and it knocked him to the ground. The wolf lunged again, and Alexander felt terror tear through him. His heart pounded vigorously in his chest as the wolf just barely missed his face. He managed to raise the Lapideas in his left hand and blast the wolf's face with electricity, which sent it flying five feet away from him.

The rest of the wolves fled back into the bushes while Camilla slid next to Alexander. She assisted him to his feet. He had minor scrapes on his shoulder with a bit of blood oozing out. His shoulder ached. The rest of them gathered around, with Dysan and Urien clutching their arms. Each had minor scrapes on their arms with some blood. Delyth ripped off part of her robe and wrapped it around Dysan's arm gently to stop the bleeding. Urien cut off part of his shirt and did the same with his arm. Cadfan quickly fetched a kit of medicine from one of their packs. Camilla took it from him and applied a salve to Alexander's shoulder. He flinched as her fingers touched the wound, but he knew it was for his own good.

Only Aeronwen and Tesni could heal their friends with magic. Traditional medicines such as the salve would still help, since they still ran the risk of infection through the open wounds. Aeronwen stepped toward Urien with pursed lips, then peeled back the bloody cloth to inspect the wound.

"Worry about him first," Urien said, gesturing toward Alexander. "His wounds are much worse."

"I agree. Heal Urien too. We won't make it very far without either of them," Dysan said.

"Way to underestimate yourself," Cadfan muttered. Tesni grabbed a Lapideas and placed it on Urien's arm while Aeronwen did the same with Alexander. A white light glowed from the Lapideases and penetrated the darkness around them while the wounds slowly closed. They then did the same with Camilla and Dysan. Afterward, salves were placed on all their wounds to further prevent any unwanted conditions and to soothe the wounds.

Camilla knelt down next to Alexander. Cadfan, Delyth, and Aeronwen briefly patrolled the area to ensure they were in the clear.

"Are you okay?" Camilla asked, breathing heavily.

"I think I will be okay," he said, with breaths just as heavy.

"Just do not scare us again," Camilla said.

"I honestly cannot guarantee nothing else will happen," he said, feeling a wave of gratitude wash through him.

"Well, we could fry up one of these wolves and make some jerked wolf meat," Cadfan suggested.

"And get more water if it rains again," Dysan added.

"Now, in the meantime, we should change. We've worn the same clothes since Jylinae," Aeronwen said as she pulled a change of clothes out of her kit and made her way behind a tree. The other ladies followed suit.

"Don't look either," Aeronwen said as the others turned around.

A few moments later, the women rejoined the group in new clothing. They wore nearly identical long white robes with the same footwear they had previously been wearing.

Alexander and the other guys took their clothes now while the ladies turned away from the tree. Alexander changed very carefully, as his shoulder still ached when he pulled his shirt over his head. The air around him filled with a cool breeze. He now wore the same shoes with a pair of gray pants under his shirt. He reached for his father's cloak and draped himself in it once more, then tied the front of it. The other three guys wore similar clothes.

Urien, Dysan, and Alexander slumped against the tree while Cadfan fetched the wolf that Alexander had blasted in the face earlier. Dysan grabbed the other dead wolves. Cadfan began to skin one while Camilla quickly added more tinder to the fire, then sat next to Alexander and leaned against his nondamaged shoulder. Cadfan spent a few minutes skinning the wolf and was now attempting to make jerky of it by laying pieces on a stick suspended over the fire. While waiting for the food to be cooked, Tesni and Aeronwen inspected the horses for wounds and began to heal the small injuries that they did find.

The clouds darkened against the sky, and thunder rumbled loudly.

"Now what?" Alexander asked. Irritation filled him, as he felt they had had horrible luck. Lightning flashed across the sky, and rain started to fiercely pour, blowing sideways because of the wind, so there was no good shelter from it. It quickly extinguished their fire.

Alexander pulled the hood of his father's cloak over his head while the others got soaked as they removed theirs from their kits and donned them. Urien instructed Cadfan to retrieve wooden cups from his bag. They grabbed a total of eighteen wooden cups and took off the lids. Once the cups had filled with rainwater, they tightened the lids and returned them to their various bags.

More lightning flashed across the sky in violent purple dances. Alexander and his friends huddled together once more as they had during the previous storm, this time under the sparse shelter of the tree. The rain poured fiercely downward on them.

More lightning cascaded across the sky, and one strike darted into the tree, bursting it into flames. Some of the branches fell off of the tree and onto some of the kits that were placed around them. Alexander and his friends hastily gathered what they could and rushed forward as the flames spread and at the same time sizzled from the water hitting them. The flames licked at the rope that was tied to the horses, then severed it entirely. They neighed with fright.

Cadfan, Aeronwen, Delyth, Tesni, and Dysan tried to recover the frightened horses but to no avail. The horses slipped through their fingers and darted into the darkness of the night. Cadfan and the others then followed Alexander, Camilla, and Urien to a tree with a wide trunk and a slight trench around it. They dropped against it and wrapped around the trunk. Ice-cold raindrops fell onto the earth. Alexander's jaw started to shiver. He wrapped his father's cloak tighter around him and lowered his head. This helped block the rain from hitting his face, but a cold draft still blew into it. He then placed his head in his lap and began to warm his face while the rain poured down around him. A loud crack of thunder exploded in the sky.

"What rotten luck," Cadfan said, groaning and cursing angrily.

"Will this ever end?" Camilla asked. Alexander's shoulder was nudged as she buried her face next to it. He could not find an answer as he listened to the rain crashing down.

Chapter 8

Alexander tossed in his sleep as his dreaming mind showed him horrific events. He watched Jylinae troops being killed by various means. He heard the screams as people ran from Xythuu soldiers who were attempting to capture citizens of Jylinae. He could feel himself being thrown from the wall again and hear the shower of rocks and ringing in his ears. He saw himself and his friends fighting Xythuu forces as one of the Xythuu soldiers was thrown off the raised wall and crashed into the ground.

He awoke with a fierce, sudden jolt. The rain was still slowly drizzling, and the natural trench that he and his friends were in was slick with mud. His face was still wet, and parts of his cloak were covered in mud. His shoulder still throbbed from the wolf attack but was not feeling as bad as it had. A soreness ran through his whole back, making it feel tight and painful. He rubbed his back with his arm in an attempt to massage away his stiffness.

Camilla awoke next to him. He noticed red lines running across her face from her sleep. "Are you okay?" she asked with mixed gentleness and tiredness.

"I dreamed of the invasion," he said wearily.

Camilla looked at him, and he felt like she could see right into his thoughts. "I know the same feeling. It was much like being an animal. Kill or be killed. It is terrible, but the fact that you feel fear after trauma shows the humanity in you. I did not expect to be thrust into war so quickly," Camilla said.

"I do not think anyone does," Alexander said. He saw her eyes flick away and lower to the ground. Her expression showed subtle signs of pain. *The very same we all feel,* he thought. The others rose from their slumber.

Cadfan groaned and then asked, "Five more minutes, please?" He slowly sat forward, clutching his back. "Trees don't make good beds." The others grumbled, too, as they sat forward.

"What's the plan today?" Cadfan asked as he ruffled his shoulder-length red hair.

Urien pulled out the map from his pocket under his rain cloak. His black hair hung down as he viewed the map. He brushed his hair to the side of his face and then placed a finger on the map. "The horses are gone, so this will take a bit longer, but we were lucky to get them anyway. We still have a lot of ground to cover. We are going to have to conserve as much water as possible. At this rate, if we keep moving, it will take us about fourteen days to make it to the Escali River," he said, pointing down at the map. "Then we go west to Port Ivory."

"Let's get going," Urien said gruffly as he climbed out of the trench and assisted Tesni up the slippery slope. The others climbed up and began nibbling on some jerked beef they had from their packs. "Good thing we were able to get that wolf meat," Dysan added.

"We should also take an inventory of our supplies. We are down three kits now, which means we have less food, which will slow us down," Urien said.

They briefly rummaged through the emergency kits that they had left. Urien did a count of all their food and supplies. "We might have enough to get there. That wolf meat needs to be salted now so we can preserve it." Urien did not hide his frustration. It was scrawled across his face. "We also only have eighteen cups of water between the eight of us. That will not last long. On horseback, it would have taken maybe a week to get to Port Ivory if the horses were being pushed to their absolute limit. Since they are no longer with us, it will take us longer to get there. With a dwindling water supply," he said calmly.

"We have a solution to that," Cadfan stated, uncrossing his arms. "Alexander can just give us water."

"No, I cannot," Alexander said, shaking his head. "Someone asked Regnor this once in class. *Vandua* spells are made out of Essence and are therefore not drinkable. If you were to drink one, it would damage the inside of the body. We will just have to conserve carefully." He remained calm, but internally he felt a stab of fear. The thought of dying of thirst greatly terrified him. *There are quicker ways to die,* he thought. He did not want to watch his friends experience that. He pushed the thought out of his mind and began to mentally prepare himself.

Each of them pulled out wolf meat. Alexander began pouring copious amounts of salt on the wolf meat, and Urien joined him. They mixed it in with the meat for a few seconds. Once they had finished, Urien grabbed the meat and placed it in Alexander's pack.

Everyone gathered around as Alexander generated a weak *Vandua* in his hand. He dispensed small drops of the water onto the hands of his friends. Each rubbed the water vigorously between their hands. They then made their way from the tree and farther into the plains. A few hours passed with the group moving swiftly.

Urien stopped first at the front of the group. "Take a break," Urien said as they stopped under a short tree with a small stream nearby. "We can break here and refill on water." Each of them either downed some water or ate small bites of jerky. The trip had become more arduous since the loss of their horses, but they had still managed to cover several miles. Much of their training had prepared them all for this level of exertion.

"I am going to get some water," Cadfan said. He walked slowly toward the stream. Alexander heard a low grunting call somewhere in the vicinity of the area, and he quickly scanned the horizon.

"What was that?" Cadfan asked wearily.

"That cannot be good," Urien said.

"That is because it is not," Camilla said. "It sounds like a male Ydaeriin rhino. My dad and I would come here to camp all the time, and we could hear them. This is not good. If there are others nearby and he gets startled, the rest of the herd will attack." Alexander met her gaze; her brow was knit with worry.

As she finished her sentence, the rhino made its appearance near the edge of the stream. It was a younger rhino but was still large enough to trample them. It stood from foot to shoulder about six feet from the ground and had sandy-yellow skin. A large bony frill jutted out from the back of its head, and it had a short, curved horn on each side of its face as well as one on top. It also sported a bony horn on its nose as well as many pointed, triangular armor plates on the front of its chest and halfway down its legs. The armor continued on most of the body but transitioned into flat plates as it went from the front to the sides and back.

"Nobody make any sudden movements or loud noises, or you'll scare him, and he'll charge," Camilla warned in a whisper. They slowly grabbed their things and began to edge away from the tree. The rhino raised its head and looked in their direction, eyeing them cautiously. Alexander and his friends froze.

"Keep moving slowly. If you stop too long, he will believe you challenged him. Also, do not look him in the eyes," Camilla instructed quietly. They continued to back away from the tree, now about four feet away from it. Delyth, not looking behind her, stepped on a stone, twisted her foot, and toppled to the ground. Alexander flinched at the noise of snapping twigs. The rhino looked at her and made a bellowing sound while scraping the ground with its front foot. Dysan attempted to help Delyth to her feet as the rhino bellowed once more and charged. Dysan braced himself with his axe held in front him.

The rhino quickly closed the gap between them, its horns pointed forward. It barely brushed by Delyth and crashed into Dysan's axe, knocking him backward. It began its charge at Dysan again. Dysan jumped toward the rhino and wrapped his arm around its neck, driving its head toward the ground. The rhino's horn grazed his shoulder, cutting him slightly.

Dysan lost his grip on the rhino's neck. The rhino bellowed loudly again, stomped his feet angrily, and charged for Tesni, who was the closest to the tree, with Urien not far from her.

As the rhino charged closer to Tesni, she hastily threw up a shield, and the rhino collided into it, instantly destroying it. While the shield dissipated into particles, Urien darted toward the rhino with a knife in hand and leaped onto its back. He grabbed one of its horns and attempted to pull the rhino's head back and thrust his knife into the rhino's face. The rhino threw Urien loose, knocking the knife from his hand and sending him to the ground. It stomped once more, with more force. It lowered its head and thrust its horns toward Urien.

Tesni threw up another shield in front of Urien, into which the rhino crashed. She raised her left hand with her Lapideas in it and prepared to fire a blast of *Linwae* magic.

"Tesni, don't!" Alexander exclaimed. "If you hit the rhino and kill it, it could collapse on Urien!" The rhino tried to gouge Urien unsuccessfully. The rhino trampled over Urien, rolling him, its feet just missing his head. Urien managed to jam a large knife into the side of its stomach. He pulled the knife downward along the rhino's stomach, drenching himself in its blood as the rhino kept moving forward. Urien rolled from under the rhino's feet as it weakly moved a few feet farther.

Tesni rushed toward Urien and slid next to him. Dysan and Cadfan ran toward the now-unsteady rhino. Dysan swung his axe, which crashed into the side of the rhino's head, sending it to the ground. Cadfan, exactly as the rhino hit the ground, thrust his sword into its heart. The rhino bellowed once and then made no more sound. Dysan lowered his axe and head and sighed heavily.

"I would have rather not done that," he said with remorse.

"We didn't have much of a choice. It's not like you can negotiate with an animal that is trying to kill you," Cadfan said.

"I'm sorry," Delyth said as Dysan made his way closer to her.

"It's not your fault, Delyth. Nature happens. The important thing is that none of us got incredibly hurt in the process," he said.

"That's an understatement. Pulling you to the ground hurt a whole lot," Cadfan said with a grin.

"But you're hurt. Your arm is cut open. Urien might be hurt," Delyth said almost sorrowfully.

"Calm down, Delyth," Aeronwen said as she made her way to Dysan. She held up her Lapideas and started healing the cut on his arm. Tesni approached too, with Urien behind her.

"Delyth, none of this is your fault," Tesni said warmly. "And Urien is fine. I should be the one upset. I could have accidently killed him." Aeronwen had finished healing Dysan's wound and motioned for Alexander to join them. He and Camilla trotted over to where everyone else was standing.

Aeronwen used her Lapideas to scan Dysan's and Alexander's arms while Tesni did the same for Urien. "Your bones have healed slightly but still not all the way," Aeronwen said. "I'm actually surprised you were able to move your arms."

Dysan smiled. "When the need arises," he said with a wince as Aeronwen handled his arm.

Alexander felt guilty. "Well, I probably could have taken a shot while it was charging," he said.

"Do not worry," Cadfan said casually. "You may have not even been able to hit it. And when it was closer, you could have hit any of us. Also, Urien is covered in rhino blood, so I won't forget this anytime soon." He laughed.

Dysan walked over to the now-dead rhino and stared at it. "Well, I suppose there is no point in leaving this rhino here to rot. We might as well use it for food. Or maybe find some other uses for what we cannot eat."

Urien walked up to the rhino and crouched next to it. "Lay in peace, rhino, and we shall use every bit of you to continue life." After a few seconds of silence and bowing his head, he took a knife in his left hand and began stabbing the point into some of the rhino's armor plates. He did this for a few minutes, grunting, and managed to pull a triangular plate from the rhino's body. He then did so to another plate. Once he had two out, he placed them together, one on top of the other. Urien smiled slightly. "We can use these."

It took them an hour to fully cut off the plates and carve out the meatier parts of the rhino. They had removed the inside of the rhino's stomach and were in the process of cooking some of it. Cadfan and Urien vigorously cut into the rhino and removed the tendons and put them on the fire in an attempt to turn them into cords. After they had removed the meat, plates, skin, and tendons from the rhino, they gathered its bones and respectfully buried them in a small pit they had dug. They salted the skin and gathered everything into their kits, and once more they were on the move.

They stopped in the middle of an open field once nightfall arrived. They sprawled their sleeping skins over the ground, spread around a fire they had made. They sat in silence as the fire crackled and illuminated the blackness around them.

Alexander looked at the starry sky above him. A few meteors streaked fast across the sky and then quickly vanished. He returned his gaze to the fire. Tesni gazed at the fire quietly, with an empty, emotionless stare on her face.

"Tesni, are you okay?" he asked.

She continued to stare at the fire. "No," she said, her voice cracking some. "I keep thinking about my sister. She could be hurt. She could be dead. She could be slowly dying." She began to tear up. "She could need help right now, and I am stuck out here, not able to get to her. She could need me, and I am running away." The tears then flowed freely down her face.

Aeronwen was next to her and embraced her. She placed her chin atop Tesni's auburn hair, drowning her friend in her own long white hair. She then placed one hand behind Tesni's head and the other on the back of her shoulder.

"You are not running away," Aeronwen said gently.

"Tesni, I can assure you Xythuu will pay for their actions," Cadfan said, gripping his sword tightly.

Alexander wanted to agree with him. He personally wanted every Xythuu soldier to be cut down. He knew, though, that first they would need reinforcements and a plan. He felt some confliction. He knew rage was not something to give in to; however, he despised Xythuu. *What would my father feel in this moment?*

* * *

Urien woke his friends early at the start of the day.

"This better be important," Cadfan grumbled. "The sun has barely risen."

Urien rolled his eyes. "Fine, you can go back to sleep while the rest of us move forward."

Dysan rose up with a groggy look on his face. "Are we at least closer by now?"

Urien shook his head. "We've still got a long way to go. That's why we have to get going soon. We need all the day we can get."

Dysan packed his stuff quickly in his kit, then vigorously shook Cadfan, who had not moved. "Come on; get up."

"Can we at least make some coffee first?" Cadfan asked.

"Well, obviously."

A few minutes later, everyone was up and had their stuff packed into the kits. The leftovers from the now-missing kits and other things gathered on the way were tied to Dysan's back. They made some coffee and downed it very rapidly, then went on the move once more. They were moving faster than they had the day before and climbed over short hills, made their way through a scatter of trees and bushes, and eventually crossed wetlands from the many streams that spread across the plains. Toward the end of the day, they stopped by a stream and washed their dirty clothes and refilled their water supply.

They spent the next ten days gaining more and more ground. They saw no signs of Xythuu forces, and for all they knew, the other cities may have already been attacked. As they made their way closer to the

Escali River, they crossed streams more frequently, which helped them keep their thirst quenched. This part of their journey had involved fewer encounters with other creatures.

They were now moving through the wet grass of a flooded plain, and the sounds of bugs and running water could be heard. Their hair stuck to their faces with the sweat of exertion and the humidity of the area. Some forty feet away, they could see the end of the Escali River. The fiery sun shone down on it, mixing sparkling blue hues with the green of lush vegetation around it.

"We made it!" Dysan shouted, and he and Cadfan bolted toward the river at full speed.

"Wait! You do not know what is over there," Alexander cautioned, but his friends did not slow. "Do they ever think?"

Urien shrugged. "I believe they do; they just let their excitement take over their cautiousness," he said. Dysan and Cadfan had now made it to the river and splashed into it, sprawling out in the mud at the river's edge and drinking the clear water voraciously. The others joined in on drinking the water and relaxing in its coolness with casual cheers and smiles spread across their faces.

Chapter 9

Alexander and his friends camped at the edge of the river for four days, gathering as much water as they could. Urien made a makeshift net by cutting the skin of the rhino into pieces and stitching them closed with its tendons. They had caught and cooked many fish and believed they now had enough to get to Port Ivory. They had also used some of the dried rhino skin as bags, which they were going to use to carry what they had gathered.

Cadfan and Dysan strapped the rhino-skin bags to their backs, and the others held the remaining kits. Urien and Alexander were not completely comfortable leaving their only possible water and food source behind but knew that they must get to Port Ivory or Fort Ydaeriin. Alexander did not believe that either of them had heard news of the fall of Jylinae. At most, they might have seen the beacon activate but received no messages from anyone from Jylinae.

He and his friends departed early on their fifth morning at the Escali River and spent three rough days crossing the plains toward the west. Unlike the first part of their journey, it did not rain, and the temperature on the west side of the plains was not mildly warm; it was gruelingly hot and very humid. They were making their way into the drier part of the plains. They had to stop multiple times each day and were consuming more water than they had anticipated. They now held less than half of the total they had collected before leaving.

Urien, after downing half a bottle of water, pulled the map from his pocket and sat on the ground.

Cadfan had also taken a spot on the ground and consumed some water voraciously. "How much further do we have?" he asked.

Urien sighed. "We should be just about halfway. We could still cover a lot of ground every day, but the climate in this area is slowing us down." He studied the map a bit more.

"At least it is not winter," Cadfan said.

After a short silence, Dysan spoke. "I could give my water away," he said. Cadfan shot him a sharp look.

"Do not be foolish, Dysan," Alexander said. "There would be no point in making you weaker and more prone to dehydration by relinquishing your water." They all sat in silence. Alexander knew there had to be a solution—he just had not thought about it yet.

"We could travel by night," Tesni suggested.

"That could work," Urien said. "However, there is the problem of having nothing to keep the sun off of us during the day. We have not seen a tree, bush, or slope for days."

A realization dawned on Alexander. "Put your cloaks on," he said.

Cadfan shot a critical look at Alexander. "Has the sun fried your brain?"

Urien looked rather embarrassed. "Wow, it took me this long to figure it out. You are not hot under that thing, are you?"

Alexander grinned. "No, I feel relatively cool. But since I never remove my father's cloak unless I have to, it has kept me cooler." Urien took his out and inspected it. "Ah, I see. The outside feels like cotton, and the inside is silk with a cotton layer. The back has a removable wool layer to keep warmth or take it away." Urien then threw his cloak over his back.

The others now donned their cloaks with the hoods over their heads and let out sighs of relief.

"Wow, it actually works," Cadfan said incredulously. They all sat in the cooling effects of their coats for a few minutes.

"This should help us stay more hydrated," Urien said, breaking the silence, "but we could still run out of water before we get there."

"We will just have to ration better now. Only small amounts here and there," Alexander said. That was going to be difficult and painful, he knew. They rested for an hour and then rose to continue on their journey. They started in a trot.

Dysan began to sing an Eltheneaen battle hymn. "With running blood," Dysan started off softly, "like fire through our veins; with adamant hearts, like the sun shining bright."

He sang with increasing volume, and he and his friends increased their speed. "We will crash through the walls that hold us back. We will run, like a wave over land. The thunder will sound, but we will stand tall. The lightning will crash, but we will not cower. The roar will engulf the sky, filling everywhere with its chaos. And we will know we are afraid. We are afraid, but we will run strong. We will run boldly. We will run as lions toward our prey."

He sang now even louder while he and his friends darted with agility over the plains. "We will bleed, but we will bleed proud. We will hurt, but we will hurt proud. The sound of the horn's thunder will ring in our ears, but we will scream. With pride. With honor. For one another! As the fire burns around. As the smoke fills the sky. As the axes are dropped behind. We will run. We will run. We will run forward! You will then know. Just who we are. We are the warriors. That you could not keep down. We are the warriors. That you could not keep down. We are the warriors. That you could not keep down!"

Cadfan burst into energetic laughter. "Dysan, you really know how to motivate someone!" He and Dysan laughed together. They kept running for half an hour until they came across a sight that they had not seen for days: a tree. They ran up to the tree in a slower trot and slid into the grass in the shade the tree provided. There was laughter as they all rolled or just lay in the grass.

Alexander looked at the evening sun as it hung low over the horizon. It was a brilliant crimson and was painted beautifully across the sky. He had never ventured this far into the plains before. Most people did not and usually stuck to normal routes outside of it. His mind then went to Jylinae, and a haze came over his vision. It was as if he was seeing it all in front of him again. He shook his head, and his eyes came back to the sun on the horizon. "We should probably make camp here for tonight," he said.

"Agreed," said Cadfan lazily as he rested on the grass with his hands under his head.

They set up a fire and ate their dinner of rhino jerky while night descended upon them. They told some short stories afterward and prepared to sleep with the night. Cadfan and Dysan volunteered to do the first watch.

* * *

Tesni and Camilla were on watch when Urien awoke from his slumber and made his way some fifteen feet away from the tree, where he sat, gazing at the star-filled sky above him.

"We should go see what's wrong," Camilla whispered to Tesni as they sat by the tree. "Tesni, go talk to him. You have an empathy that cannot be rivaled or copied."

Tesni liked the compliment that Camilla had given her, but even that could not bring a smile to her face right now. It pained Tesni to see Urien, whom she thought was always so regal and resilient, showing obvious discomfort or anguish. She slowly rose and ambled over to him.

He was still sitting, gazing up into the sky, when she approached. She was about to speak but was cut off.

"You can join me if you want, if that's why you came over here," Urien said in a passive tone, not even turning toward her. Tesni was shocked.

His skills of perception were astounding. He would indeed make a great Nightcloak once they were able to officially finish their apprenticeships. She sat next to him on the grass, in total silence for a few minutes.

She finally spoke. "Urien, what's wrong?" She turned her head toward him, only a few inches away. He looked down from the sky now and into her eyes.

"Tesni," he said softly, "you already know what is wrong. We have all been feeling it, even if we try to hide it." He was right.

"I know. I constantly wonder about my family. I wonder if my parents and my sister are alive. It's a torment that knows no bounds, but also I wonder if something worse than death happened to them," Tesni said drearily.

"My mother could very well be dead," he said in a low voice. "It haunts me. The same for Maria." They sat in silence once more for a few minutes. She gently placed her hand on his shoulder.

"Urien, I understand most of your agony. We all do. And Cadfan understands the other part of your agony." She then pulled him close to her and wrapped her arms around him in a gentle hug. "We're here if you need us," she said, releasing him now. "Try to get some sleep, please."

Urien looked at her kindly. "Thank you, Tesni," he said, and she rose and made her way back to the tree.

"Is he okay?" Camilla asked.

"In some ways he is," Tesni said, "but in others he is not. He, like all of us, is experiencing the tragedy of war, one that has claimed our home and possibly our families. It will be a while before he overcomes that painful burden."

Urien rose and made his way back to his sleeping fur.

* * *

Alexander tossed and turned in his sleeping fur. In his mind he saw Jylinae once more with smoke filling the skies and blood on the ground. He saw himself flying off the rock wall that he and his friends had sat at for so long. He saw people running toward the underground tunnels to evacuate.

Then his mind took him to a ship at sea. On the horizon, he could see land and a blue flag with three gold buck deer in a circle, the flag of Hyybeth, flying over the shore.

Then he turned and saw his father on the boat. His father stood tall, with white-and-blue-painted Oracle armor over brown clothes, his brown cloak draped around his shoulders, and his sword hanging at his side. The flag of Eltheneae, a green field with three white vertical stripes, was on the front and sides of his armor and sewn to the neck of his robe. He looked the same as when Alexander had last seen him. Tall and broad shouldered, with long brown hair that was tied back, with two strands of hair hanging over his right eye. Camilla's father, Geoffrey, slightly shorter and with neat long blond hair that hung freely, stood next to him. He wore the same white armor and brown clothes underneath with a short red scarf around his shoulders and a bow and quiver filled with arrows on his back.

"Dad! Dad!" Alexander called out, but his father did not seem to hear him. Two more ships arrived next to the one he was on, and an alarm horn sounded. The ships moved closer and launched hooks onto Patrick's ship. Patrick swiftly created blessings on himself and Geoffrey as pirates boarded the ship and flooded it, attacking anybody they could get their swords or axes into.

Geoffrey began to launch arrows at targets while Patrick launched large balls of light magic at the opponents rushing toward him. Patrick pulled out his sword and fought off pirates to his side while more of them boarded the ship. A sudden glass object flew at Patrick and broke as it hit his side and dispersed blocking dust, stopping Patrick from using magic. He fought off seven pirates at once, some of them wounding him, while Geoffrey battled pirates next to him with his bow or by jamming arrows into some of them. Two more glass objects flew at Patrick and Geoffrey, releasing something that instantly made them cough heavily.

Patrick killed a pirate but also got impaled through his lower abdomen under the edge of his armor. Geoffrey jabbed an arrow into one's throat but also got hit on the side of the head. Blood began pouring over his face.

"Dad! *Dad!*" Alexander screamed as he watched. He could see Geoffrey say something to his father but could not hear what he said. Patrick scoffed and said something back. Alexander thought he heard his father say that Geoffrey was going to see his wife and daughter again and told him not to go just yet. He and Geoffrey coughed more while pirates surrounded them.

They fought off as much as they could. Patrick coughed again and stabbed two pirates before he was impaled through the throat. Blood poured down his neck as the sword was removed, and he fell to the ground. Geoffrey jabbed an arrow into a pirate's eye and then was knocked down. A rapier point went through the chest of his armor. Blood spilled from his mouth, and he collapsed backward. Other members of the crew fought back the pirates as Alexander watched in horror.

Alexander jerked upward, his eyes wide and sweat pouring down his forehead. He heaved quick breaths as he looked around. The sun was just beginning to rise, with pink hues bursting over the horizon. He saw Camilla lying just a foot away from him, and the rest of his friends were scattered around. Delyth and Aeronwen were awake, sitting at the tree.

"Alexander, are you okay?" Aeronwen asked.

He tried to slow his breathing as he answered. "I'm fine. Just a bad dream." He rose and made his way about ten feet away from where he had been sleeping under the tree. He stood there for a few minutes with his hands on his hips. Camilla approached him.

"What's wrong?" she asked kindly, with sleepiness still in her voice.

"Another dream. I saw Jylinae again, but this time I also saw our fathers the day they were killed," he said despondently. Camilla was silent. After a few moments, she wrapped her arms around him, and they stood motionless for some time.

"I don't know if that helps," she said, "but I feel it's the only thing I can do for now."

They returned to the tree to begin packing their things.

Cadfan was rummaging through his kit frantically. "Come on. Where is it?" he muttered hysterically. He looked at Dysan. "Dysan, do you have any coffee?"

"No. Unfortunately, I am all out," Dysan answered.

Cadfan threw his hands up. He made his way over to Aeronwen and began to rummage through her kit before she snatched it away from him.

"Come on. There has to be some in here," he said.

Aeronwen glared at him. "Hey, you don't just rummage through a lady's stuff!" she said, slapping his reaching hand away. "I don't have any coffee left."

He looked around at all of his friends. They each shook their heads.

"Clearly you don't need it," Urien said. "You're already wide awake and energized looking for it."

Cadfan turned toward Urien, who stood some five feet away from him. "Shut up, Urien. Not having coffee is an emergency like a natural disaster."

Urien sighed. "Look, all of us are out of coffee. I don't know what to tell you. Just get over it."

Cadfan twisted his face. "Fine," he grumbled. "But when we get to Port Ivory or Fort Ydaeriin, I'm getting some coffee."

Urien shrugged. "Tell you what. If you down some jerky and water so we can get moving, I will personally buy you some coffee when we get there. Or you can stay here and complain about needing coffee while we leave you behind."

Cadfan grabbed his kit and dug through it for some food. "You wouldn't leave me behind," he said to Urien.

"Maybe. Maybe not. Maybe we would have to drag you," Urien said as they continued on their journey.

They traveled hard and fast and covered much ground over the next four days. During the tail end of that trip, they ran into some luck, as it rained continuously, and they replenished their drinking-water supplies.

They did halt briefly, at a small stand of trees, on the eighth of the month of Portokali. They stopped to celebrate Urien's nineteenth birthday.

"Well, everyone, thank you for this birthday. It's not the most ideal, but there are worse ways to spend it," Urien said. It was true. They had had some terrible days recently—their trek had been dry and hot, and they had run low on water. The last few days of rain had saved them.

"Do you feel old yet?" Cadfan asked as he ate a small piece of jerky. Alexander noticed as Cadfan's gaze was drawn to something a few hundred feet away. The others turned to look at what had caught his eye. Alexander narrowed his eyes. In the distance, he could see what looked like a caravan of five carriages with people around them. Attached to the side of one carriage was a flag.

"That looks like people," Alexander said, his heart racing as hope and uncertainty pounded through him.

"Should we check it out?" Dysan asked. "They could help."

"It could also be a trap," Aeronwen stated.

"Yeah, but people have stuff. We do not have much of anything," Cadfan said. "Even if it happens to be bandits, maybe we could take those carriages and use them to get to Port Ivory. It is worth a shot and better than trying to walk the rest of the way with our dwindling supplies."

"We could take a vote," Delyth suggested.

They all murmured some agreement. Delyth asked who wanted to make contact with the caravan. Dysan, Alexander, Tesni, Camilla, and Cadfan raised their hands. Delyth hesitantly raised hers as well. Aeronwen and Urien were the odd ones out, and the question was not even asked.

They rose and slowly approached the caravan, which had stopped a few hundred feet away. Once they had covered more ground, they could see a flag of three vertical white lines against a field of green. The Eltheneaen flag waved gallantly next to the carriages. Hope filled Alexander at the sight of the flag, and he and his friends began to dart toward the caravan. As they got closer, the members of the caravan noticed them.

"Hold!" one of them shouted out as he raised a bow upward. A few others did the same. They had not yet drawn the strings of the bows, but they had arrows in their hands ready to fly.

"What business do you have?" asked the man who had called out before.

"We are Eltheneaen travelers," Alexander said as he raised his hands above his head. "We seek passage to Port Ivory. We have urgent news to deliver."

"How do we know that this is not a bandit ploy to get us to drop our guards?" the archer in the middle of the caravan asked.

"In all honesty, if we were bandits, we would have ambushed you and not have shown ourselves. We are residents of Jylinae."

"You might be," the archer answered. "Let us do a test. Who is the crown prince of Eltheneae?"

"Prince Ethan," Urien answered. The archer darted his eyes back and forth between the two.

"Name the three uniters of Eltheneae," the archer demanded sternly.

"Pogeaeran the Wise," Dysan answered, seeming to catch on to the tactic Urien and Alexander were using.

"Mistia the Brave," said Delyth.

"Teshan the Influential," Cadfan answered.

The man eyed them and then signaled the archers to lower their bows. "I suppose if you wanted to, you *would* have attacked by now," the man said. Now that they were closer, Alexander saw the man was wearing some wool robes and leather armor. He sported curly graying hair and a thick beard. "What are a bunch of kids doing in the middle of the damn Ydaeriin Plains?" he asked incredulously.

"Well, sir, we came from Jylinae and have struggled to survive to this point. We seek refuge in Port Ivory and have some grim news to deliver if they are not aware," Alexander said in response as he lowered his hands.

The man first looked at him sternly, but his expression softened slightly. "We're heading to Port Ivory. We can take you there. 'Tis much better than walking and dying out there in the plains," he said. He motioned for them to climb aboard.

Alexander and the others proceeded to the back of the same carriage the man was sitting in. There were two other people inside who helped them up. As Alexander and the others were situating themselves among some back supply seats, a few jugs of water were passed out between them. They drank it eagerly and thanked their unlikely rescuers as the carriages then pulled forward.

There was a silence among the cart's occupants. Only the sound of the wheels turning vigorously and horses moving and heaving could be heard. The back of the cart was packed with some trade goods—mostly wooden jars filled with food and some bundles of cloth. It was a tight fit with Alexander and his friends nestled near the back with the supplies. The flap over the cart kept it cool. There was enough space for a breeze to come through the opening of the flap. Through the gap, Alexander could see the coachman and one of the guards next to him. The other guards were scattered between the other carriages. Each carried a small sword and a bow and wore leather chest plates. He assumed they were mercenaries.

"So there is something on my mind, probably on everyone else's too," said the coachman. "Why are you in the plains? You mentioned that you had survived since Jylinae. Survived what?" The coachman briefly turned his head to look at them.

After a small pause, Alexander answered. "Jylinae was attacked," he said flatly. A look of confusion, then sadness, scrawled across the coachman's face.

"What do you mean, lad? This isn't a joke, is it?" he asked as he turned his head forward again.

"It is no joke," Delyth said softly.

"What do you mean it was attacked?" the front guard asked.

"Xythuu led an invasion into Jylinae," Urien answered.

"But how?" the guard asked, his volume rising. "How could they get an army across the borders without us knowing?"

"They have some form of transportation vehicle," Alexander said. "Possibly capable of traveling hundreds of miles. These vehicles are also capable of boring through the ground, which took Jylinae by surprise. The size of their force was also quite large. They most likely have a larger standing army than we do."

There was silence; then the coachman spoke, his voice cracking. "So we are at war?"

"Yes," Alexander answered. "As far as we know, we are the only survivors of the attack. They ordered an evacuation so that all people could regroup. We got thrown off course during the attack. We do not know how much of the army at Jylinae remains. That is why we were in the plains. Our plan was to go to Ilgeth, but we were diverted. We then believed that we must make our way to Port Ivory to relay the warning." There was now silence that lasted for most of the day's trip.

Later in the evening, they stopped to make camp. The horses were unsaddled and tethered. A fire crackled, and the caravan members gathered around it. Alexander sat at the edge of the wagon they had ridden in, a few feet away from the fire, and stared into the flames. The smell of salted chicken and spiced rice filled the air as the caravan guards and the others ate.

The coachman slowly walked over to Alexander with two bowls of food. "You should eat, young man," he said as he sat down and held a bowl in Alexander's direction. Alexander, for a brief moment, still gazed into the fire. He then registered that the man was offering him food and took the bowl that was held out to him.

"Thank you," he said kindly. "Truly for all the hospitality." He took a small bite of the food and stared back into the fire.

"Well, lad, I've seen some things in my day. Back in my younger days, I was a foot soldier in the army. I have fought bandits and learned that not all people can be trusted. But you and your friends—I can tell that you are honest kids who have experienced a great deal of torment. If I had left you, what type of man would I be? I would be the type that contributes to that pain. If I can, I will help whenever possible."

Alexander let the words run through his mind while he ate his food. Later that evening, he lay in his sleeping fur, wondering what had happened to his hometown. What was the purpose of the invasion? How would the outcome affect his own future? He remained lost in thought for some time before he drifted into sleep.

In the morning, they awoke and ate breakfast in a rush. They then boarded the wagons for the rest of the journey to Port Ivory. Halfway through the day, the coachman explained they were about three days away from Port Ivory. The plains with their rugged crags and sparse trees passed by in view. They stopped only for relieving themselves and for food. The day passed just as quickly as it had begun, as did the next two days. They were now on their fourth night. As the camp was being set up, the caravanners talked about how they would reach Port Ivory by the next evening. Alexander and his friends sat around the fire, eating and discussing their expectations.

"Do you think it will still be there?" Cadfan asked.

Urien wiped his face with a cloth and responded, "Considering what Xythuu has, it is possible they could cover a lot of ground shortly. They could be just as close as we are right now. However, we also do not know the full extent of the ranges."

"Let us hope they are not." Aeronwen sighed heavily. "Port Ivory is a major logistical site for most of the country."

"They could be going for control of the entire east coast," Camilla said. "That would hamper our ability to get trade and sea resources."

Alexander had just listened as his friends spoke, but now he presented the questions that had been running through his mind every day. "We have to ask ourselves, though—what is their goal? What is the point of their war? Why waste the time and effort? They do not need land, and as far as we know, they should have plenty of resources, so why go through with it?"

"Who knows?" Cadfan answered, casually shrugging. "Power. Stroking the king's ego. We have had issues with them through some of our history."

"Those were centuries ago," Tesni argued. "Why do it now?"

Cadfan shrugged once more after swallowing some food. "Do the relationships between tribes, clans, countries, or any other organization of people ever change? What if this is just a repeat on the wheel of history? It should be reasonable that they will not change. The only option is to be stronger than them and get them out of our lands and make it a lasting memory for them," he said. His words echoed through Alexander's mind as the night drifted onward.

* * *

Alexander awoke to the sound of bustling activity as well as Urien telling him to wake up. When he rose, he could see the camp around him being packed. Urien gave Alexander some hot oats and told him to eat it quickly so that the utensils could be cleaned and packed. He began to eat the food he had been given. It had a sugary taste and was mixed quite well. Camilla emerged from behind the carriages.

"Are you okay?" he asked. He thought he saw a look of annoyance on her face.

"Fine. Just ready to get to a city with working plumbing." He knew the feeling, although he knew his struggles with that were easier.

He proceeded behind the carriage to relieve himself. After a minute or so, he made his way to the sleeping area. The coachman asked if everyone had eaten and relieved themselves. No one objected to moving forward, so everything was loaded up. The horses were saddled and brought over to the carriages. Alexander picked up a basket and followed the others to the inside of a carriage. A guard took his basket and loaded it and others into the underside of the carriage and then put some in the sitting area with the trade supplies. Two of the guards then proceeded toward the front near the coachman while Alexander and his friends piled behind them. They started their journey.

"Seems a bit unreal that we should make our way to Port Ivory today," Camilla said. The others agreed with her. They then began to converse about their priorities and goals for when they arrived in the city.

"I can't wait to get some nice food from a local vendor," Dysan said.

"Our main priority is reporting our findings to the city governor, though. We should have time for fun later," Urien stated.

"Learn to relax, Urien," Cadfan responded. "I understand our priority, but we have all had a difficult time. I think we deserve some fun."

Urien did nod in agreement but also made his view clear again.

"Do you think Port Ivory is how it was described in our school?" Dysan asked.

"We'll soon see," Aeronwen stated.

In the distance as the evening sun hung over the horizon, they saw it. Port Ivory some few hundred yards away. The white docks sheened as the sun's light cascaded onto them while the grand, eloquently designed buildings with stone bridges crisscrossing over one another towered over the water. The flag of Eltheneae still flew over the many buildings and at the gate—it had not been taken yet. A smile slid across Alexander's face as the caravan pulled closer. A sense of indescribable joy filled him and spread across the faces of his friends as they made their way to the shining jewel before them.

Chapter 10

Alexander and his friends arrived at the giant wooden gate of Port Ivory in the middle of the stone wall that wrapped around the city. Soldiers at the top of the wall armed with bows or lances stopped them. Four soldiers at the door crossed their lances to prevent them from entering as the carriages drew closer. One walked forward. The coachman in the front carriage gave him a list of the items the caravan was carrying and how many people were expected to be in the carriages. The letter had a red wax seal at the top. The soldier walked behind and peered into the carriage. He immediately motioned for everyone to step out. Alexander, his friends, and the carriage guards stepped out as instructed while the coachman sat at the reins.

"Who are these people?" the man asked. "Your paper only listed thirty people. This is suspicious. Either you enslaved them or they are possible refugees from bandit encampments." He motioned the other troops over, and they roughly pulled the coachman down from his seat at the front of the carriage.

Alexander darted forward. "These men did not enslave or capture us nor are we from bandit camps," he insisted. The troops seemed almost challenged by his words as they moved swiftly toward Alexander, their intentions unclear.

Cadfan, Urien, and Dysan stepped up next to Alexander with their weapons drawn. The archers placed at the top of the gate yelled and then, after being signaled by the man on the ground, fired warning shots that landed near the feet of Alexander, Dysan, and Cadfan. The soldiers drew closer, and Alexander immediately generated a massive shield in front of them and then held his left arm up in front of him and his right arm above his head. A fire generated in his hand. He then launched a small brief stream of *Faer Xel* over his head.

He yelled out at the top of his lungs, "We are not enemies!" The *Faer Xel* burned for a bit, and then he let it extinguish above him. "We are from Jylinae, and if you have not heard reports of its beacon being activated, I can tell you that it is true!"

The soldiers stopped inching forward toward the shield and peered at him. Another tactic crossed Alexander's mind. At least three of the soldiers were young, roughly nineteen to twenty-one in age, if he had to guess.

"I am Alexander Kai. My father was Patrick Kai. He was an Oracle who was slain in a pirate raid."

Two of the soldiers exchanged quick glances.

"You are Patrick's son?" one man asked.

"Yes," Alexander answered proudly.

The soldiers lowered their weapons.

"Patrick was a hero. We learn to honor his sacrifice in our training," one of them said.

Tesni then stepped forward until she was next to Alexander. "This is a true statement. I am Tesni Glenice, an Oracle apprentice. I have learned of Patrick Kai of Jylinae, and I can verify that this is his son, Alexander, and that he and the rest of us are from Jylinae and bear no ill intent," she said boldly.

The man stood motionless and studied Alexander briefly. Alexander held his chin high, trying to prove himself worthy of the association with his father and his city.

"Let them in," the man called to the guards at the gate. The gate swung open with a loud sound of heavy chains turning and the creak of wood. The troops moved to each side of the gate as Alexander and his friends made their way through the opening, followed by the caravan. Once inside, they turned to see the man they had spoken to coming through the gate. He wore bronze armor with the Eltheneaen flag sewn on his shoulder. He was draped in white and blue robes underneath his armor. On his left shoulder was the insignia of his military rank. He had short blond hair with sky-blue eyes surrounded by a slightly tanned complexion on a taught face and appeared to be in his early thirties.

"My name is Captain Riley Spearus," he said and then made a short bow. Alexander and his friends returned the bow. "What news do you have of Jylinae? We were aware of the beacon but have not come across refugees."

"For starters, Xythuu managed to move massive forces across the border with little detection," Alexander explained. "They have some sort of vehicle capable of boring through the ground. It may be possible that the border was even destroyed or passed in some other manner." A shudder ran through Alexander at his own words.

"Follow me. The governor will want to know this information immediately," Captain Spearus said.

"One moment, sir," Alexander said and approached the carriage in which they had ridden.

"I suppose this is where we part ways," the coachman said.

"Sir, what you have done for me and my friends is a debt that I do not know how to repay," Alexander said.

"Just knowing you got here alive is fine for me, lad," the coachman said. He reached into his pocket and held out a black coin purse. "It's eight hundred Endariins."

Alexander shook his head. He should have been offering the coachman money, not the other way around. "I cannot possibly take this," he said.

"Please, lad. You and your friends need it more than I, and I have still have fifteen hundred with me. Each guard will get two hundred, and then I will collect one thousand after dropping off these supplies."

Alexander wanted to refuse, but he knew they would need the money to buy food and shelter. It would be foolish to turn down such generosity when they were desperate. Alexander accepted the money in his left hand and held up his right wrist at an angle. The coachman brought up his left wrist at the same angle and nudged it against Alexander's own.

"Thank you, sir. I hope one day we will meet again," he said.

The coachman then dropped his arm and went on his way.

Alexander returned to his group and began to follow Captain Spearus through the bustling city of Port Ivory. The smell of the sea entered his nose as they passed many vendors selling wondrous goods ranging from fine linens to beautifully crafted swords and various food items. Cadfan nudged Urien as they passed a stand selling bags of coffee. They still had a small bag of Endariins that they had brought with them when they had left Jylinae. Cadfan picked three to his liking, and Urien handed the vendor Endariins. Dysan bought four of his own as well.

After twenty minutes of moving from street to street, they arrived at the governor's building, which towered over them and housed not only the governor and governor's family but the attendants as well as the garrison leader of the city and some other people who were stationed there. It would also serve as a hotel for important people such as ambassadors, military units, and the royal family or other royals. The two soldiers at the door snapped their feet together when Captain Spearus approached, and they opened the door for him.

Inside, the walls were a dark blue and adorned with many paintings, and lamps illuminated the walls with a white-orange glow. Captain Spearus walked toward the counter at the end of the room. There was a woman on the other side who appeared to be in her late twenties.

Captain Spearus approached her, and she smiled. "Anna, can you give our guests a room?" he asked. Alexander felt uneasy—what if the coachman's money did not cover the cost to stay in such a nice place? He had imagined they would just stay in smaller inns in the city, possibly even sharing rooms to save money.

"Yes, we can do that," she said warmly.

"I'll take care of the expenses," Captain Spearus said. Alexander's shoulders relaxed.

Captain Spearus turned to face the group. "Anna will make sure you are well taken care of. You all relax, eat, and freshen yourselves. I know that the road can be weary sometimes. I will go to the governor and give him the information at once. We will send for you later." He spun back around, bent over the counter, and kissed Anna's cheek. "I have to go see the governor. I'll see you later tonight," he said gently. He then hurried up one of the spiraling staircases.

Anna looked at the young people before her. "Well, let's get you all a room. You must be exhausted," she said as she led them to a different staircase. "I hope my husband didn't alarm you too much at the gate."

They made their way up the stairs and down a red hall. Drapes lined the walls, giving the space a luxurious atmosphere. Anna stopped at two doors next to each other. She pulled a key out of her pocket and opened one and then the other. "This room is the gentlemen's room," she said, pointing at the door in front of her. "The ladies' is on the left. We'll have clean clothing brought for you. If you need more, feel free to ask. We can also wash your other clothes for you if you want." She entered the guys' room and turned to the right and opened a compartment, which had a small bell inside attached to a tight string that ran down the narrow shaft. "If you need anything, ring this bell, and someone will assist you. I will now let you relax." She handed a key to each of them and returned down the hall. Alexander and the other boys went into their room while the girls did the same.

* * *

A few hours had passed, and Alexander and the others had still not heard word for them to speak with the governor. During that time, they had each bathed and changed into a fresh set of robes of various colors.

Cadfan looked at himself in the mirror and moved so that the robe swished around him. "Damn, I look good in blue." Alexander sat on one of the beds and counted his Lapideases while Dysan relaxed into an elegant chair and Urien started strapping his knives to his chest, waist, and legs. Someone knocked on the door.

"You may enter," Alexander called out, and another young woman with curled blonde hair entered.

"My lords, the governor wishes to speak to you now. Could you please follow me?" she said. They walked into the hall, where the girls, each dressed in flowing violet robes, joined them. They descended the stairs they had come up previously and were led up the stairs that Captain Spearus had used earlier. The new floor had many doors to new rooms, and they walked a few feet down the hall before entering a wide circular room with a long table in the middle. Captain Spearus was seated at one end next to a young man who held the position at the head of the table. The man had pale skin, was dressed in a purple robe, and had shoulder-length brown hair.

"My name is Maximillian Burke, and I am the appointed governor of Port Ivory," he said as he looked at Alexander and the others. "Please have a seat." He gestured to the empty seats next to him and the captain. Alexander stepped forward to take the seat next to Maximillian.

"I understand you have information about Jylinae?" Maximillian asked.

"Yes. We were at Jylinae when Xythuu forces attacked us," Alexander said, taking the lead for his group.

"How did they manage to take Jylinae? Not only that, but how did they even get that far into Eltheneae?"

"That is why we came here, sir," Alexander said. "This is what I know based on what I saw. They seemed to have some sort of advanced weapons. They were like giant drills that emerged from the ground. They can move more quickly than their appearance might suggest, and each is fitted with multiple small cannons. They are made of wood and iron. They seem to have two types of these vehicles. One seems to be just a smaller operated unit. It seems it is used to cover distance as quickly as possible. They deployed them in formations of five or six and used effective tactics with them, which might suggest that they have been training with these for some time. The other seems to function as a troop transport. The transports are apparently big enough to carry large amounts of troops, at least two dozen. The pitfall traps did seem to damage them or stop them from working."

He paused briefly, took a breath, and continued. "They also have another weapon, but I do not know what it is. It's like . . . a cannon, but it does not fire magic or traditional artillery like rocks. It seems to fire some unknown form of energy which is capable of shattering rock, blessed or not, into pieces. We were at the top of the wall when a blast shattered through it with ease," Alexander said. "They had three of those and had at least one dozen of the drill vehicles—maybe even more. Also, in regards to the strange energy fired from the cannons, there was a Xythuu man who had a lance that was wrapped in the same energy, covering the spear tip."

To his right, Cadfan clenched his fist at the mention of the man who had killed his father.

Alexander continued. "His lance was wrapped in the same energy, it seemed, as the cannons were firing. It was able to cut through a sword and pierce through someone's armor with no resistance at all. He was also capable of firing the energy from his lance at short distances. Lapideases are put in cannons, and I know that is how we use them. This just did not seem like a Lapideas."

Maximillian maintained his composure, but the wrinkles in his brow betrayed his worry. "Captain, send immediate word to other cities of our information. I also want all fortifications to be double manned and given more powerful blessings. I also want Illustratum teams to go make more pitfalls, each armed with oil canisters," Maximillian commanded.

Captain Spearus rose from his seat and quickly left the room.

"We also thought we might seek aid from Ciimerii," Alexander said.

"I doubt they would be willing to help," Maximillian said, "but I could send word to them stating everything I have learned here. Also, you are apprentices, correct?"

"Yes," Alexander answered. "We were one week away from taking our final tests."

Maximillian paused briefly, pondering something. "I think it would be best, then, if you finish your apprenticeships while you stay here. You will do so tomorrow."

Dysan fidgeted in his seat.

"Do you have objections?" Maximillian asked, looking directly at Dysan.

"No sir," Dysan answered. "I just do not know how I will do that without my armor."

Maximillian cracked a bewildered smile. "Do you really think that I would make you complete your training without the necessary gear? The supplies will be delivered to your rooms. That includes armor, weapons, satchels, and apprentice clothing as well as traveling kits and any other clothes you may need. Do you have any questions?"

Alexander shook his head. "No. Thank you for your hospitality." He and his friends rose and left the room.

Now it was dark. The sun had set an hour previously. They sat in a dining area and ate a dinner of crab-and-lobster stew and then returned to their rooms. When Alexander opened their door, they saw a surprise. Dysan gasped in excitement, and his eyes lit up the same way a child's would at the sight of presents. He dropped to the ground next to the shining iron armor. It had a piece of paper with his name on it.

"It's so beautiful," he said as he placed his head near it.

Alexander saw a bag with his name on it and picked it up. Inside was an apprentice cloak. He draped it over the robe he was wearing. There were also numerous Lapideases and another satchel, which he began filling up. Urien donned a green-and-brown cloak and two more throwing-knife belts, each of them also holding various vials. Cadfan pulled on a green shirt with long sleeves and with short tails in the back and front.

"It feels good to be in green again, even though I am ready to upgrade," Cadfan said.

The light of torches shone through the window, filling the room with a pristine glow. Dysan and Cadfan began to arm wrestle. Alexander found a game of chess under a table and began a game with Urien. Cadfan and Dysan got progressively louder as their wrestling matches went on. They did this for half an hour until they heard a knock at the door. When Alexander and Urien answered the door, they saw Camilla, Tesni, Aeronwen, and Delyth standing before them. They all wore their apprentice clothing, although Tesni and Delyth were not wearing armor over the clothes.

"Hi," Alexander said with a cheesy grin on his face.

"It's a little late for roughhousing, don't you think?" Camilla asked him with her eyebrows raised in an authoritarian manner.

"Cadfan and Dysan are roughhousing. Urien and I are just minding our business," he said casually. Cadfan took this opportunity to slam Dysan's arm down while he was focused on the scene at the door.

"That is not fair," Dysan complained.

"No one said it had to be," Cadfan responded while leaning back in his chair. Alexander slowly began to close the door, but Camilla stopped him and proceeded into the room with the other girls following her.

"Really, I'm just saying it's late to be doing this," Camilla said loudly.

"Oh, come on," Cadfan said, seemingly unconcerned. "We've been traveling for months and have had one hassle after another. We deserve a little relaxation."

Aeronwen sighed heavily. "Actually, we were enjoying our relaxation too. We're not saying you can't. We just wondered if you could do it quietly." Suddenly they all heard a heavy crashing sound, like the breaking of rocks.

"That did not sound good," Aeronwen said. Dysan and Cadfan stopped what they had been doing while Camilla and Alexander walked over to the window. When he peered outside, he saw troops rushing out from their barracks.

Multiple horns sounded off as audible shouts began to increase in volume in the streets below.

The door opened, and a frantic maid entered. "We're under attack. Please follow me," she said. Dysan rose quickly, donned his armor, and took his axe in his right hand. Camilla and the other girls ran to their room and soon returned with weapons. Camilla had her bow ready in her hand with two quivers of arrows on her back and a sword on her waist. Tesni and Delyth each had a lance in their hand as well as a bag of extendables draped around them. Aeronwen had two satchels around her lower back.

They followed the maid to the main room on their floor. Captain Spearus and other soldiers were directing people through open doors.

"We want to help!" Alexander said as they approached Captain Spearus.

"Good! You're all with me! Armor up!" he shouted as the apprentices made way to an armor closet. Alexander grabbed armor plates, greaves, and vambraces. He slid into all three, as did the others, with the exception of Dysan. He slid on a bronze chest piece and then slid on pauldrons over it. Alexander then slid a helmet over his head and strapped a sword in a leather sheath around him, followed by a satchel of Lapideases around his chest. The others donned armor and various weapons. They all returned to Captain Spearus.

"Captain, everyone from the floor has been evacuated," said one of the soldiers.

"Good. Everyone in," Captain Spearus said, pointing to a bronze, gleaming oval-shaped pod. The captain, the apprentices, and twenty soldiers dropped into a pod. Captain Spearus pulled the lid down while the others strapped into seats that circled the pod. He strapped in and turned a stone key in a carved keyhole next to him. A heavy clunk sounded underneath them. They plummeted downward to the first floor and stopped with a sudden halt. Within a few seconds, they all unstrapped and poured out of the top of the pod.

The soldiers and apprentices followed the captain toward some stairs.

"Riley!" Anna said from behind them. Captain Spearus spun and embraced his wife. "Please be safe," she said.

"I will come back for you, Anna. I promise," he said and then kissed her. The governor and his tall blonde wife approached Anna. His wife escorted Anna to a door on the side, which they disappeared through. The governor himself stayed and was wearing bronze armor over his red tailed shirt, with a gold-hilted sword strapped to his side.

"Sir, are you sure about this?" Captain Spearus asked.

"This is my city, Captain. I was placed in charge of it to lead it and protect it and its citizens," Maximillian insisted.

"Very well," Captain Spearus said. He turned and led the group up a short flight of stairs to the outside.

Alexander looked up at the tower that rose above him. All around were magic shields that covered up to three-fourths of the height of the building that towered at the center of the city. He was in awe. Those shields must have taken a massive amount of Essence to put up. He could feel his heart beginning to pound vigorously in his chest. His breathing became labored as he thought of Jylinae.

Fireballs from a *Faer Ruunae* spell rained down but collided into one of the shields. The group entered a pod that carried them rapidly to the front of the city. From there, Captain Spearus bolted up some stairs to the top of the three levels of the wall. The apprentices, soldiers, and governor followed him. The sound of artillery and explosions filled the air. The captain took the spot where he had been stationed when Alexander and his friends had first arrived earlier in the morning.

"Apprentices, this does not sound like a quick, easy fight," Captain Spearus said. "Gather around me." He gestured to Alexander's group and the governor. Captain Spearus held up his hand. Blue glowing runic script moved from his hand and down the various body parts of Alexander and the others. Multiple blessings wrapped down their arms, over their chests, down their legs, and over their eyes, with lines sprawling out from the blessings. "I have given you the stone-skin blessing, making your skin act as a second armor; the vitality blessing, increasing your stamina;

the sight blessing, increasing your night vision; and the speed blessing, increasing your movement speed," Captain Spearus said.

"Sir, are you sure you can spare the Essence use for these?" Alexander asked.

"Well, it does drain my Essence, but I have trained for years to increase the amount of Essence I can use. This is only a small amount." Alexander was astounded. It reminded him of stories his father had used to tell him. Stories of how he had trained and become capable of using more and more within a certain time frame. Alexander wondered what that was like. Nonetheless, he felt some anxiety. He did not want to have Captain Spearus use all his Essence. He was also not fully sure what was about to happen.

Alexander looked out to the plains stretching out from the city. His gaze fell on a large formation of troops, two flanks of cavalry on the sides and a center formation of soldiers on foot. They held up battle banners that were a black field with a thin red line, representing Xythuu Army forces. The sides of the cavalry were also flanked with more drills. Siege weapons stood behind parts of the formation. The cavalry and drills then charged forward.

Alexander looked over the battlefield with keen clarity. The blessing had greatly improved his vision. Four of the drills had met their demise to the pitfall traps and were ablaze and pouring thick black smoke off of them while the others had gathered at the horizon, likely preparing for an assault. The functioning vehicles proceeded forward in three formations. They charged Port Ivory's stone wall from the front, the right, and the left while Port Ivory's cavalry charged forward. There were magic users at the front being carried as the cavaliers' passengers who put numerous shields in front of their respective cavaliers. The enemy infantry charged forward in slow-moving formations. Following that was a barrage of arrows from some of the Xythuu soldiers. The siege weapons hurled various items from their positions.

Alexander, Aeronwen, and Tesni joined with Lapideases held up in their hands while Port Ivory's own soldiers launched massive amounts of arrows, artillery blasts, and fire, water, lightning, and light magic at the Xythuu forces.

Alexander heard a barrage of arrows colliding into their shields and watched several shields dissipate into particles. He heard some explosions, too, as various forms of magic collided into parts of the wall below him or whizzed over his head. Captain Spearus instructed the Illustratum to unleash a barrage of *Xel* spells onto the advancing force.

Alexander leaned over the wall and blasted a beam of fire from his Lapideas while many others did the same with beams of lightning or fire, which collided with the charging mass of cavalry, either into the shields they had generated or into the units themselves. The middle mass of the charging units toppled over, some on fire, while the ones on the sides kept charging. Captain Spearus ordered a launch of arrows on the mass of soldiers. Camilla nocked two arrows and then, with the other Bowmen, launched them into the air with an arc.

The volley of arrows landed with a heavy impact while dozens of artillery blasts were shot from the wall, lighting the dark night sky with blasting gleams of fire. Alexander saw a formation of four vehicles, some forty feet away, speeding toward the wall. One barely crashed into a sinkhole as one tire fell over the edge, but the rest of the formation sped forward.

Alexander raised his Lapideas and blasted another beam of fire at the metal-and-wooden vehicles. The fire clashed with the front vehicle briefly, and it burst into flames. A large artillery blast hit the wall in front of him, knocking his Lapideas from his hand to the ground below and causing him to stumble backward. All of a sudden, his vision narrowed, and his hearing dulled.

He turned and saw Aeronwen leaning over him as Camilla and Urien stood by, looking down at him from above. Aeronwen was asking him something, but he could not hear what it was. He saw some Port Ivory soldiers who were manning artillery take arrows to the chest and collapse. Urien, Cadfan, and Dysan took up the soldiers' stations and started shooting blasts of magic artillery fire.

"Are you okay?" he heard Aeronwen ask loudly. The chaos of the fighting returned to his ears. The air smelled heavily of sweat, metal, soot, dust, and burning flesh, which wafted into his nose, nearly making him gag. He rose to his feet with Aeronwen's help. They quickly ducked behind the rock wall as a barrage of blessed ballistae bolts crashed through the top of the stone wall and tore through numerous soldiers.

A reverberating thud caught Alexander's attention. The drill vehicles had now collided into the wall and the gate. Tesni and numerous other magic users hurried to the top of the remaining wall and let loose a barrage of magical attacks.

Arrows whizzed over their heads. Captain Spearus yelled a command that involved the drills, since many had now made their way close to the walls. Alexander looked out to the ground below him. The drills were advancing, with the cavalry charges some distance behind. Some of the cavalry had fallen victim to pitfalls, strewing the field before him with twisted, mangled horse and human bodies tossed about.

Oil canisters were being dropped on the vehicles as more burst through the ground and hordes of soldiers popped out of them. Fires burst from the dropped canisters, and screams of burning people could be heard from the top of the wall. The Xythuu forces quickly extended ladders to the top of the wall and began climbing as arrows, lances, and magic were exchanged from both sides. A blast of fire destroyed the artillery that Cadfan, Dysan, and Urien were manning and knocked them backward to the ground. The Xythuu forces climbed over the stone walls. Captain Spearus and the other soldiers at the top clashed with them. Alexander watched Captain Spearus thrust a spear through someone and Maximillian slash through a Xythuu soldier's neck.

Urien jabbed a knife into someone's neck while Cadfan slashed through the chest of one and then threw another over the top of the wall. Camilla launched arrows at soldiers farther down the wall. Alexander launched a *Faer Xel* downward at the mass of Xythuu soldiers below the stone walls. A javelin sailed next to him, catching him off guard. Two Xythuu soldiers charged toward him, lances fully extended. One crashed into Camilla and knocked her down and her bow slightly out of reach.

"Camilla!" Alexander yelled as he charged to the right a few feet from where she was. The other Xythuu soldier used his lance to slap the Lapideas out of Alexander's hand and then slammed the blunt end into his face, knocking him to the ground. Captain Spearus charged forward and thrust his lance into the stomach of the soldier and spun him around and into the ground. He then jabbed his lance through the Xythuu soldier's neck, causing blood to spray all over the stones. The other soldier over Camilla was hit in the back by two blasts of light magic from Tesni and Aeronwen. The soldier was knocked off balance, and Camilla quickly rose and grabbed an arrow and thrust it into the soldier's neck. Delyth charged forward and thrust her lance into the back of the soldier. Captain Spearus held out his hand to Alexander and helped him up.

"It's good to keep your feet on the ground, Alexander," Captain Spearus said. He pulled a bandage from his pocket and applied it to Alexander's now-bloody face. The sound of the drills breaking through the walls and the wooden gate roared.

"All forces except artillery head to the ground floor!" Captain Spearus bellowed. He and the others began to run toward the first level. Alexander looked at the lower levels of the battlefield, just outside the city wall. He could still see hordes of Xythuu forces on all three sides, some pinned in place with their shields, defending against artillery attacks. The cavalry were still regrouping.

He bounded down two flights of stairs and out the door of the fort tower. The black moonless night sky looked so strange. The light from the torches on the wall illuminated the immediate area, but the night was also lit up from the many spells and projectiles being volleyed and from the fires that danced in lamps and on the ground all around.

At that moment, Alexander saw a blue glow on the horizon, where the Xythuu artillery was positioned. Three thick beams of blue energy were launched at the walls of Port Ivory. They tore through the walls for a few brief moments. A thunderous sound of rocks being torn filled the area, and chunks of them landed all around. A few crashed near Alexander and his friends. The force of their impact sent out a wave and knocked him and the others into the dirt.

Alexander coughed as he slowly pushed himself from the ground. Blue particles filled the air from the destroyed blessings of those around him, which meant that the blessings had either expired or taken damage and been destroyed. He had some cuts on his arms, and his chest felt incredibly sore. He was amazed that he was still alive.

"Camilla, are you okay?" he asked as he helped her up. She had a cut on her eyebrow and some scrapes on her arms.

"I do not think I am mortally wounded, but I have been better," Camilla said with a wince.

"Your mystery weapon?" Captain Spearus asked gruffly.

Alexander nodded. Cadfan pushed himself up from the ground with help from Urien while Dysan helped Delyth to her feet.

"Let's hope that doesn't happen again," Cadfan said with a groan. They were just bruised and battered.

"Take this. It should help with pain," Tesni told her friends as she gave them a green mixture in a vial. She then assisted the soldiers who had fallen with them. Some had broken bones and scrapes along their arms. Tesni placed a Lapideas on one of them and began healing scrapes while Aeronwen did the same for another. Captain Spearus immediately stopped them.

"I appreciate that, but these are my soldiers, and I can heal them. Save your Lapideases," he said as held up his left hand. White light filled the area and surrounded those who were injured. He did this for thirty or so seconds, and the wounds on the soldiers began to close.

"That should help but will not fully heal them. Broken bones will not be fixed, but any other wound should be," Captain Spearus said. The governor, a few feet away, rose, clenching his teeth and breathing heavily. Alexander could see a white nub covered in blood protruding from his left arm, and he bore a sharp piece of rock in his right leg.

"Governor," Captain Spearus said as he walked closer.

"What are we waiting for?" Maximillian asked with heavy gasps of agony. "They are closing in."

Captain Spearus raised his hand and said, "With all due respect, sir, you are not going anywhere." He had to yell over the sounds of fighting.

"But I have to fight them off!" Maximillian insisted.

"You are in no condition to do so. Use your head. You are wise enough to know that you need treatment," Captain Spearus said calmly. "My magic should assist in the healing and pain but will not be able to close a wound that big." He motioned for some Oracles farther down the road to come to him. They attended to Maximillian while newly arrived Vivicanterns got busy healing the others who had also been knocked down by the force of falling rocks. Captain Spearus turned and motioned for Alexander and his friends to follow him. They took a few steps and were stopped.

"Captain!" Maximillian said. Captain Spearus turned his head halfway to look at him. "Give them hell," he said, and Captain Spearus nodded and then bolted toward the city gate.

Alexander had lost his blessings and was also beginning to feel the physical effects of the battle. His legs buckled slightly underneath him, and exhaustion shot through every part of his body. He saw the same look across his friends' faces as they were running. They were getting just as tired. He began to be concerned about Captain Spearus's remaining Essence. He felt like his own was starting to dwindle. They took positions at ground-level windows along the gate wall, with other soldiers around. The sound of the fighting intensified, and the smell of burning and smoke filled the air.

Alexander was concerned. He could see no sign of the vehicles that had burrowed through the gate and parts of the wall. He pulled a Lapideas from his satchel and aimed at the mass of Xythuu soldiers in front of the gate. He launched a medium-sized ball of fire while Tesni and Aeronwen each held a Lapideas and launched a *Linwae Xel*. The magic crashed into the Xythuu forces and scattered them over the ground.

More ferocious barrages of magic, arrows, and javelins were exchanged, each side receiving casualties. A flurry of lightning magic was shot at the wall where Alexander and the others were. Captain Spearus generated a vast shield in front of them, which the lightning thudded into. Some of the magic then dispersed into smaller balls of lightning over the area. Alexander could hear it crackling along the shield and the ground. He launched another *Faer Xaen* from his Lapideas.

Camilla landed an arrow directly in the throat of a Xythuu swordsman. She shot another into the shoulder of an archer. Xythuu magic users released a flurry of fire and lightning magic toward them. Alexander told Camilla to lay out five arrows for him. She did so, then turned away to continue firing at the enemies. While multiple exchanges of magic, arrows, and lances came to and from their wall, Alexander lit the tips of the five arrows on fire and told Camilla to shoot them. Delyth and Tesni threw lances at the proceeding Xythuu forces fifty feet away. The Port Ivory soldiers who were behind small walls and wagons up front were beginning to be slowly pushed back by Xythuu forces.

Camilla quickly launched one of the flaming arrows. It collided into the shoulder of a Xythuu soldier. His clothes caught on fire, and he fell into others and set them aflame. Agonizing screams filled the air around them. Camilla launched three more of the flaming arrows, each hitting and setting someone aflame. As she aimed her last flaming arrow, Captain Spearus sent a medium ball of light magic from his hand, which separated into many smaller balls of light that exploded into bursts of light magic as they hit the Xythuu forces, further breaking them into a chaotic mass. Camilla released her last flaming arrow, which collided with the head of a Xythuu soldier, who collapsed and set others ablaze. Several jars filled with blocking dust were launched at them. Captain Spearus created another shield a few feet in front of the current one. The incoming jars hit it and dissipated it into green particles. The enemy prepared to launch more, but Aeronwen blasted a beam of light at the wooden launcher, bursting it into pieces.

Multiple drills then broke through the surface in front of the gate wall. One busted through the ground at the front, near the gate, flinging many Port Ivory soldiers into the air. The drills aimed their cannons upward and let loose a barrage of energy blasts. Each drill strafed back and forth. Alexander heard the sounds of magic energy hitting the stone walls, the thick thud as it hit the shield in front of him, and the cries of the people who were hit by the energy. Some blasts struck about fifteen feet above him and the others. Multiple jars of oil were hurled at one drill and exploded into flames on contact. The drill, still burning on its lower sides, kept doing strafes of artillery fire.

Alexander and many others shot blasts of *Faer Xaen* at the drill. They collided into it and exploded into an enormous fire, which blasted chunks of rock and metal in all directions. More drills, some of the transports as well as smaller ones, broke through the ground. Dozens of soldiers poured out of the transports while groups of four exited from the smaller drills and charged over every corner of the area and clashed with the Port Ivory forces. From a distance, Alexander saw another familiar sight stepping out of a transport. The man who had commanded the forces at Jylinae just one month prior.

Captain Spearus caught Alexander's gaze. "Is that the man?" he asked loudly.

"Yes," Alexander answered with a yell.

Captain Spearus jumped over a five-foot wall and into the plaza below. "Stay here," he said. "He looks dangerous, and I don't want any of you getting hurt by him. If things take a turn for the worse, I want you kids to leave. I have escorts at the end of the town that are carrying refugees. If we begin to get overrun, head there, and go to Fort Ydaeriin," he said somberly.

Dysan shook his head in evident disbelief. "But we can't just leave you here," he insisted.

"You must if I believe that you should. Don't think of it as an order. Think of it as a promise. Promise to leave if we begin to get overrun," he said, looking back at them.

Dysan lowered his head for a moment, then raised it. "We promise," he said. Captain Spearus nodded and then ran to the growing chaos on the other side of the gate wall.

They could see Captain Spearus twist and turn, avoiding thrusts of lances and slashes of swords while he countered his opponents, leaving them wounded or dead. At that moment, a *Faer Xaen* crashed into the few steps they were standing on, sending Alexander and some of his friends stumbling to the ground. Alexander landed with force, his vambraces colliding with the ground first. His blessings and those of his friends now turned into particles, destroyed. He lifted his head to see about ten Xythuu soldiers charging in their direction. He rose quickly and blasted one of them with a *Faer Xaen* while the other soldiers dove to the ground. They rose and continued their charge. Camilla shot two arrows in rapid succession, both piercing the armor of her targets.

Dysan stood at the front of the group. A Xythuu soldier swung his sword at Dysan, who managed to block and attempted a counterattack but failed. The soldier moved a few feet to the right in a blur. He moved again in the same manner and cut Dysan's arm armor. Simultaneously, the soldier got his ribs bashed by Dysan's axe.

Dysan punched the soldier to the ground. He went for an attack but was stopped as a Xythuu soldier lunged a lance past his shoulder. Urien flung a knife toward the face of the soldier, but it was blocked by the armor on the Xythuu soldier's arm.

Cadfan stepped forward and moved in a short blur and jabbed his sword into the armpit of the soldier followed by Dysan bashing the man's head with his axe. The other Xythuu soldier held his lance forward, slowly moving and eyeing those around. The soldier lunged with his lance, and Dysan jumped toward it. His axe caught the lance, and they each struggled to gain control. Cadfan quickly made his way forward. He slid behind the Xythuu soldier and slashed his leg. The soldier fell to the ground but then wrestled his lance free from Dysan and pulled Dysan to his knee. The soldier jabbed the back end of his lance into Cadfan's leg and knocked him to the ground. Dysan rose and moved forward but was kept back by the sharp end of the lance. Cadfan rose and slashed under the armpit of the soldier. He lowered his lance, and Dysan then struck the soldier down. A formation of Port Ivory troops formed in front of the gate walls as another Xythuu formation neared.

Alexander, Aeronwen, and Tesni put up shields toward the front of the formation. Parts of the wall exploded, letting in Xythuu forces. They charged near them, yells filling the area. Camilla launched an arrow into the shoulder of a foot soldier followed by Delyth sweeping him off of his feet with her lance. Dysan and Cadfan were busy fighting another Xythuu soldier, evading lance thrusts while Tesni dodged axe blows. She thrust her lance into the Xythuu soldier's leg. She quickly removed it, backstepped, and shot a *Linwae* from her Lapideas at the soldier. The soldier proceeded closer to her despite being hit by another blast of *Linwae* from Aeronwen. Urien charged the soldier and jumped on his shoulders. The soldier flailed about, attempting to throw Urien off. Urien managed to remove the soldier's helmet but was thrown to the ground, his knife falling from his hand. Tesni stepped forward and slashed through the soldier's neck as he stepped toward Urien.

While Alexander and Camilla were busy shooting distant enemies, Cadfan and Dysan had their hands full fighting the same Xythuu soldier. Cadfan had been knocked to the ground while Dysan slashed at the soldier's arm. The man dodged Dysan's slash effortlessly and hit Dysan in the chin with the back end of his lance, knocking Dysan's head back. The soldier then jammed the same end into Dysan's face, knocking him backward to the ground while blood ran from Dysan's nose. Tesni slid next to him and jabbed her lance into a new approaching enemy's neck. While her assailant dropped to the ground, she reached for a Lapideas from her satchel and placed it to Dysan's nose to heal him.

Cadfan sprang to his feet and moved in a blur once again toward his opponent. He reappeared next to the soldier and slashed quickly but was blocked. He and his opponent exchanged a flurry of blows, each dodging and being pushed about. The Xythuu soldier kicked Cadfan back, then charged forward and thrust his lance at Cadfan. Cadfan managed to move to the side but not quickly enough. The tip of the lance pierced the side of Cadfan's hip, just under his armor. Cadfan held his hand to his now-blood-covered hip and slowly sank to the ground. Alexander pivoted to where they were and launched a *Faer*. It hit the soldier's leg, which began to catch fire. Frightened screams came from the soldier as part of his robes burned against his skin and he attempted to stamp it out.

Two other soldiers moved forward. To Alexander's right, Aeronwen launched a *Linwae*, and it dispersed into small pieces. They hit the soldiers in multiple spots, searing through their robes. To his left, Alexander saw Camilla raise her bow and launch an arrow. It sailed into the head of the left soldier, and he fell backward. She launched another that pierced the neck of the other. Blood poured onto his hands as he grabbed his throat. The other had put out the fire and was seated with his lance in hand and raised above his head. He prepared to throw, but Camilla released another arrow that landed in his eye. He slumped back, his helmet falling off as he hit the ground.

Alexander, Camilla, and Aeronwen slid next to Cadfan. Alexander grimaced. The smell of burning flesh filled his nose and made him want to vomit. The Xythuu soldiers they had defeated lay on the ground, their blood staining the stones beneath them. Aeronwen placed her Lapideas next to Cadfan's hip.

"Are you all right?" she asked loudly.

"Perfectly fine," Cadfan said in return.

A barrage of arrows and spells hit the shields behind them. Alexander and Tesni generated another shield in front of them and began blasting spells at the incoming Xythuu forces. Delyth threw lances at opponents who proceeded too close to the shields, one landing in the chest of a Xythuu soldier. Camilla launched an arrow at one, and it landed in his eye. Delyth landed a lance in the thigh of a spearman. Urien darted forward and grabbed the lance of one the soldiers. He pulled the man closer and brought the knife in his right hand through the soldier's neck. He grabbed his arm and spun him to the ground, then lunged at another soldier. Urien jammed his knives into the man's eyes, and he screamed in agony. Urien kicked him backward and spun around. He crisscrossed his arms and brought both of his knives into the necks of the downed soldiers.

Alexander moved to Cadfan and grabbed his arm, pulling him backward to the corner of the wall behind them. They would have to heal Cadfan and get out of the corner quickly. Three blasts of fire hammered the shield at various spots, and several Xythuu soldiers ran forward.

Urien flung a knife hard into the neck of one of them, piercing the armor. Tesni, Urien, and Delyth were busy holding off other Xythuu soldiers. Delyth kicked her opponent back, who then took an arrow to the side of his helmetless head. Dysan dodged attacks from the Xythuu soldier he was fighting, who then slammed the shaft of his spear into

Dysan's chest. Dysan's armor absorbed most of the blow, but it still seemed to take the breath out of him. The soldier backstepped and thrust his lance toward Dysan's neck. Dysan caught the end of the lance with his free hand, the tip inches away from his throat. He dropped his axe and brought his other hand up to resist the lance. The leather padding on his palms tore open, and his hands began to bleed as he struggled to move the lance away from himself. He managed to move it to his shoulder, and the lance began to slowly dent his armor, digging into the flesh underneath.

Delyth stabbed an extendable lance through the lower back of the Xythuu soldier attacking Dysan. She then slashed her heavier lance through the side of his neck. Shards of bronze armor fell to the ground, and blood spurted from his neck as Delyth removed her lance and hit the soldier's head with it. She then turned and looked at Dysan with a softer look on her face.

In the distance, Alexander saw Captain Spearus fighting a few soldiers, with the Xythuu commander a few feet behind them seeming to size up his competition as he watched them fight. At that moment, Captain Spearus shouted something to nearby Port Ivory soldiers, and then seven horns were sounded off in rapid succession. He was calling for retreat. Alexander's shoulders sagged. Many of the Port Ivory soldiers started to fall back into the deeper parts of the city.

Aeronwen finished healing Cadfan's wound, and he and the others rose. They made their way to a flow of retreating soldiers. Alexander turned and generated a shield to block any incoming magic. He launched a *Faer Xaen* spell from his Lapideas, which crashed into his foes, sending some into the ground and others bursting aflame. Camilla launched three arrows in rapid succession, all of which hit their targets in the chests fifty feet away. They then spun around and continued toward the back gate of the city.

From the corner of his eye, Alexander could see Captain Spearus and the Xythuu commander now exchanging a flurry of blows, each dodging, blocking, sidestepping, and spinning their lances. Captain Spearus took a cut to his shoulder from the strange energy lance his opponent carried. Alexander skidded to a halt to watch. His friends stopped in place.

Captain Spearus prepared to use a spell but was interrupted by a Xythuu soldier throwing a glass jar that impacted him in the chest. Alexander looked on in disbelief as the blocking dust within it burst out. Captain Spearus coughed and appeared unable to generate his spell.

Alexander tensed and tried to move forward, only to be stopped by Dysan gripping his shoulder.

"We promised we would go to Fort Ydaeriin," he said.

Alexander looked back at him, saying, "We can't solve our problems by running away!"

Cadfan looked at the Xythuu commander with a burning rage in his eyes. He gripped his sword and stepped forward. Urien grabbed his shoulder as Tesni and Delyth stepped forward to stop both Cadfan and Alexander from moving.

"There is no way we are strong enough to take them. Our parents wouldn't want us dead," Urien said.

"We should not just leave," Alexander insisted. His mind drifted toward Anna. Some blasts of fire flew over their heads, just barely missing them. Urien and Dysan pulled Alexander and Cadfan back with them and urged them to run.

"We can discuss it later," Urien said.

Though he was sure of Captain Spearus's strength, Alexander did not want to leave him alone against the Xythuu commander, but he knew Urien was right.

Alexander turned his head back. Captain Spearus had already defeated the foot soldiers around him and now exchanged more blows with the Xythuu commander. He saw Captain Spearus take a searing cut down his right arm through his armor; his skin burned, and the blessing on his arm began to heal his skin. Alexander, still letting his friends lead him away from the battle, watched Captain Spearus go for a lunge attack but miss. The Xythuu commander then cut through Captain Spearus's lance. Captain Spearus began to fight with the two pieces of his lance. The Xythuu commander blocked all attacks and cut down Captain Spearus's right shoulder and quickly hit his right eye. Alexander still watched as uneasiness crept in. Captain Spearus fell backward, his hair coming loose over his forehead. The Xythuu commander then slashed his lance across Captain Spearus's chest and thrust it through his heart. The Xythuu commander removed his lance, and Captain Spearus fell to the ground, lifeless.

Alexander and his friends stopped, and he let loose a scream of agony. Alexander looked on at the fallen body of the captain, disbelief washing over him. Dysan grabbed his shoulder, and they continued on to the west exit.

Seven minutes later, they arrived at the west door, with the roar of Xythuu soldiers still flooding their ears. They met their escorts, consisting of numerous cavaliers. There were many carriages in the area with some soldiers in them. Civilians piled into the carriages and began to rush out of the city. The cavaliers extended their arms to Alexander and his friends, then pulled them onto the backs of their horses. Alexander and the others donned harnesses and strapped themselves to the saddles of the horses. The cavaliers then motioned for their horses to move, and they bolted forward into a rapid gallop.

Within moments, Alexander and his friends were outside the walls of Port Ivory.

Chapter 11

The group was riding fast on the dirt roads. The trees on both sides passed by in a green blur. Alexander turned his head at the sound of more horses galloping closer toward them. About fifteen feet behind them, he could see roughly eleven Xythuu cavaliers, each carrying an archer. The Port Ivory cavaliers shouted to each other and spread out on the road. As they did so, Alexander heard arrows whizzing next to him. An arrow hit one of the Port Ivory riders, and he fell to the ground.

As the Xythuu archers began to ready more arrows, Alexander, Tesni, and Aeronwen generated small shields. The arrows collided into them as the Xythuu cavaliers maneuvered to avoid crashing into the shields. Alexander could feel his magical energy dwindling. Would he even be capable of making more shields?

The Xythuu archers prepared to fire more arrows. Alexander aimed a Lapideas at the Xythuu horses and shot a *Faer Xaen* at their hooves. It collided with the ground, throwing shards of rock and dirt around while knocking two of the Xythuu cavaliers to the ground. Alexander looked to the left at Camilla, making sure she was safe. The Xythuu archers launched more arrows, which whizzed all around them, one hitting another Port Ivory cavalier.

The Port Ivory cavaliers then split apart, half going to the right side of the tree line and the other half going to the left. Alexander and Camilla locked eyes as they were taken to opposite sides. Alexander's horse weaved through the thick copse of trees.

"What are you doing?" Alexander asked the cavalier guiding his horse.

"We need the trees to cover us," he responded.

More arrows whizzed past them, hitting trees all around. Some of the Port Ivory cavaliers let go of their reins and turned halfway in their saddles with bows in hand and managed to hit two of the Xythuu cavaliers. Alexander looked around, quickly finding Dysan, Cadfan, and Tesni in the spread of horses. He launched a blast of wind from his Lapideas while Tesni launched a blast of light from hers, each hitting a target and knocking back horses. The Port Ivory cavaliers weaved left and right, dodging the arrows being shot at them, and some fired arrows backward at the Xythuu cavaliers. Alexander launched another blast of wind from his Lapideas, knocking over several of the horses.

The two remaining Xythuu cavaliers fired off more arrows. One arrow barely avoided Alexander's head. His horse stumbled as it jumped over a rock, which knocked Alexander loose. His harness held his legs as his upper body fell off to the right side, dangling just inches above the ground. Arrows whizzed past him, hitting the surrounding shrubbery. He caught the left hand of the cavalier above him. The cavalier struggled to hold Alexander up.

Tesni pulled out a Lapideas from one of her satchels and launched a *Linwae* from it. Two more arrows whizzed past Alexander while Tesni's light magic hit her targets and dispersed into a giant spinning whirl of light energy that shot smaller blasts from it, knocking the Xythuu horses and their riders to the ground.

The cavalier held Alexander's arm and heaved him back onto his horse. They rode forward through the trees and shrubs for a few more minutes and then began to gradually make their way back to the road.

The cavaliers pulled out from the trees and onto the road, still galloping at a lightning pace. Alexander looked to the left and saw, to his relief,

Urien, Aeronwen, Delyth, Camilla, and their cavaliers coming forth from the tree line on the other side of the road. They all merged into one group and continued their course. For the next few hours, everything seemed to pass in a blur. Many riders with them held up *Faer* spells for light.

Alexander spent most of the trip looking into the whirling orange glow as it pierced its dark surroundings. He wondered how much farther they had to go. His lower back and bottom were getting to be in a state of mild pain after this rough ride. Alexander's rider signaled to the other riders, and they all slowed to a trot and eventually stopped at the side of the road. The riders began to set up tents while one of them placed a bundle of wood down and started a fire.

"You can get off now," the rider said to Alexander.

Alexander unfastened his harness and slid off of the horse's saddle and onto the ground. The moment his feet hit the ground searing pain shot through his whole body. His back ached tremendously as he tried to stand up straight.

Cadfan groaned with agony as he walked up to Alexander with the rest of their friends. "Damn, I've never felt so sore in my life," he said. He stopped and rubbed his legs.

Even Dysan had a grimace on his face.

The cavaliers had finished setting up the tents and were now removing the saddles and gear from their horses. A few minutes later, the cavalier with whom Alexander had ridden turned and removed his helmet. A young man with brown hair brushed to the side stood before them.

"Hello. My name is Lieutenant Morgan Lydennan. We are about five hundred and fifty miles away from Fort Ydaeriin. We could probably push further today, but I believe that you and our horses need a rest. We have food provided for you as well as sleeping materials. Eat and rest, because we will be riding the first hours after sunrise, which is about six hours from now, and we will not be making any stops unless absolutely necessary. I apologize for the soreness from the ride. No matter how much of an experienced rider you are, you never get used to it. We will have two shifts of watch. Four of us will be out here at any one time and will be doing three-hour shifts. I myself will be taking the first shift with three others. Since we are your escorts, I do not expect you to participate in the watch," he said.

Alexander and the others gathered around the now-roaring fire and slowly ate chunks of ham and bread as well as rich crackers. While chewing his food, Alexander looked into the fire, his thoughts whirling through his exhausted mind. He gazed at the fire for some time, ignoring the small chatter around him until Camilla broke his concentration.

"Alexander, what's wrong?" Camilla asked him.

"Nothing," Alexander answered hollowly.

"Do not lie to me," she said, staring at him intently. "If something is wrong, I want to help."

Alexander took in a breath and exhaled it slowly. "Xythuu has caused so much destruction—for what purpose? I hate them. Every last single one of them." Alexander's volume rose steadily as he spoke.

Camilla's gaze was soft and appeared sympathetic. "I wish I knew the answer to that. We cannot, however, lose ourselves to anger and hatred. If we do, we become no better." Her voice was quiet and gentle.

Aeronwen nodded in agreement. "If we allow hatred and anger to fester within us, we will be infected, much like a sore. I do agree, though, that we must rectify this injustice for all—but not with hate in our hearts."

Alexander stood up now, feeling that he could not sit still during this conversation.

"Xythuu is the cause of all of this! The only justice they deserve is none whatsoever!" Alexander exclaimed as all the rage that had built up and been compressed over the last month began to rise to the surface.

"They killed my father and destroyed our home, and you expect me to just forgive them?" Cadfan asked, jumping up and standing beside Alexander. "The very notion is absolutely absurd."

Aeronwen looked at him in dismay. "This is what I am talking about. I want to seek justice for our country and all the wrong that Xythuu has caused too, but I don't want to be hateful when doing so. Please just try to let go of the hatred. It will consume you and warp you into a face you no longer recognize. You are a good person, and I do not want that to happen to you."

"How would you know if hatred consumed you? Have you ever been through it?" Cadfan asked.

"I am in the same position you are, Cadfan. While I did not see my father get killed in front of me, I do not know if he is alive. If he is, I do not know how he is being treated," Aeronwen shot back, her previously gentle voice now sharp and loud.

Urien stood up now. "Enough," he said calmly. "While I agree that anger is pointless and will solve nothing, I also know that arguing among ourselves is equally as pointless and will not solve anything."

They all grew quiet and listened to the cackle of the fire. Some mutters of annoyance and concurrence were uttered by the cavaliers with them.

Cadfan sighed. "I hate to admit it, but he is right."

Alexander took a moment to calm his racing breath; then he sat quietly beside Camilla. "Camilla, I am sorry."

"We are all entitled to our own opinions. Some of us have more barriers when adjusting. Try to get some sleep." She flashed a gentle smile and then pivoted away toward her tent. Alexander and the other males slowly walked to their tent. Alexander picked the nearest sleeping fur and dropped onto it. It was quite crowded with himself, his friends, and some Port Ivory citizens. He buried his head in the furry pillow that came along with it and drifted to sleep.

Alexander tossed and turned in his sleep. He could hear the sounds of artillery being fired and of rocks crashing and breaking apart. He then stood in the middle of the field around Port Ivory. Dead Port Ivory soldiers lay all around him, and the smells of dust and soot wafted into his nose. He walked past a body, which immediately reached its rotten hand around his ankle. He kicked and squirmed but could not shake the corpse's hand free. It then spoke to him.

"Even though you had the help of hundreds of thousands, you could still not protect Eltheneae," the corpse said in a grotesque gargle. "You are not strong enough to do so. You are not strong enough to protect your friends or family. You are not strong enough for anything! Everyone you love will die!" the corpse screamed.

Alexander removed a Lapideas from his satchel and blasted the corpse's head into pieces with fire. More corpses rose from the ground and began to reach for him, each one saying different taunts.

"Failure," one corpse said.

"Weak," another said.

Alexander ran forward into a thick fog.

He kept running until he heard no more noise from the corpses now behind him. He tripped over a tree root and rolled forward several times. When he rose, he saw the magnificence of Jylinae before him. Feelings of nostalgia whirled through him. His home looked so pristine with the lamplight and the orange setting sun illuminating it. He heard somebody stumble to his left. He turned his head, immediately raising his Lapideas. A silhouette took a few shuffled steps toward him. Seconds later, the silhouette changed into visible form. His mother stood before him.

"Mom? Is that really you? Mom, I've been worried so sick about you. I thought you were dead," Alexander said as he ran toward his mother, tears rolling down his face. He stood in front of her now, but something was not right. Her eyes appeared dull and listless. She fell forward into Alexander's shoulder, and he caught her. Alexander felt something warm cover his arms and chest. He looked down to see a massive spot of blood oozing from her chest and shoulders. He screamed as she fell to the ground.

He heard an armored footstep to his right. He turned his head to see Cadfan getting speared with a Xythuu soldier's lance.

"You could have saved me," Cadfan said.

He turned to see his other friends lying on the ground with arrows or swords piercing their bodies. He screamed once more as he took a step back.

"You're nothing. Nothing at all," a familiar gentle voice said. Camilla stood before him. "I thought I might be safe with you. I thought that being near you would slowly lift the burdens of this calamity. But clearly I was wrong. You're too weak for anything," Camilla said with a flat voice and eyes that showed no emotion whatsoever.

Alexander stammered. "Ca—" He choked down the sore lump in his throat while tears streamed from his eyes. "Camilla, please . . . please don't say things like that. You can't possibly mean it."

"I do. You're weak. Worthless. And a complete waste of time," Camilla said flatly. Alexander looked down at her feet to hide his anguish and noticed that her feet had turned to ash. The ash slowly rose up her body.

"See," Camilla said dryly, "you couldn't even keep me from fading away." The rest of her body turned to ash and drifted away with the wind.

"*No!* Camilla!" Alexander screamed.

Alexander woke up with a jerk. He looked around to find himself still in his tent. Sweat dripped down his forehead. He ran his hands through his sweat-drenched hair and made his way out of his tent. Outside, he could see the second shift of cavaliers doing their watch. He walked past them until he was about fifteen feet away from the tent and sat in the damp grass and cool night air.

Alexander did not return to a restful sleep and so was already awake as the cavaliers began to rise from their slumber. Alexander sat outside the tent in the middle of the camp, where the ashes from the fire of the previous night were.

Cadfan walked out of the tent sleepily and yawned. "What's for breakfast?" he asked.

"No time unless you shove a handful of jerky in your mouth," said Lieutenant Lydennan as he dragged his foot in the dirt to cover the ashes. The rest of the cavaliers had gotten their horses saddled and almost ready for the trip.

"Can we at least have coffee?" Cadfan asked.

"Also no time for that. We have to get to Fort Ydaeriin quickly. While I don't believe it will be attacked and defeated so easily," said Lieutenant Lydennan, "we will want to be on the other sides of the walls when our enemies come. They might have more right behind us, and with their drill vehicles, they could probably cover this distance for their whole army within a few days. We need to be ready."

Cadfan cursed under his breath. The others were now outside and were helping break down the tents.

"You expect that they will attack Fort Ydaeriin?" Delyth asked.

"I am almost positive that they will," the lieutenant said.

"Another battle?" Tesni asked.

Lieutenant Lydennan nodded. "Sadly, yes, more than likely. You are apprentices. You all chose to be apprentices in fields of battle, right?" he asked. Tesni nodded. "It is the unfortunate nature of the beast," he said. The tents had been finished and were strapped to the backs of the horses, so their riders as well as Alexander and his friends mounted the horses and sped off in a dash.

For the first thirty minutes of the ride, Alexander could see nothing but the blur of the countryside around him—flashes of the green rolling hills and flashes of some of the brown, rougher, rocky terrain. They rode fast and hard for another three hours. The horses then slowed to a stop in a small clearing of trees.

"Am I missing something? We are in the middle of nowhere. Why did we stop?" Cadfan asked.

Alexander looked toward Lydennan with a doubtful expression. "Sir, should we keep moving like you said?"

"Yes," Lydennan said as he slid off his horse and made his way to a stump. He knelt down next to it and messed with something Alexander could not see on the stump. A heavy stone nearby began to make grinding noises as it slowly moved. "We are exactly where we need to be," Lydennan stated.

Lydennan led the way, with his horse's reins in hand, down some stairs within the hole that the stone had revealed. He held his hand to the wall, up against what appeared to be a lamp. Alexander could not see it directly in the dark. Lydennan then struck a flint on it, and the lamp lit ablaze. The light cascaded down a series of lamps into the distance.

Alexander was astounded. His friends gasped in awe too, accompanied by muffled astonishment from the many people with them. Not at the lamps and the instant flash of light but at what was before them. Before them stood a beautifully crafted tunnel.

"This tunnel was made to connect the two cities for this very purpose. We have extra supplies stored at certain intervals if we need them. The lamp system goes on for about half a mile and then disconnects. There is a new system at each interval. We should be able to move through over the course of the next six or so days. Not to worry—there is an extensive air-supply system that was carved to allow the flow of air into the tunnels," Lydennan said.

They stopped where they were and started setting up camp. Alexander felt the soreness in his legs and began to rub them while setting up a tent. Soon the smell of stew wafted through the area, and dinner chatter sounded all around. Afterward, pots were cleaned, and the sounds began to die down as everyone settled to sleep. Alexander, Urien, Cadfan, Dysan, and two other people entered their tent. Alexander shuffled over to a cot within the spacious tent. He collapsed onto it. He saw the others doing the same. Soon, he drifted to sleep. He tossed and turned and woke once within the night. He looked around. The dim darkness in front of him shortened his range of vision to about two feet. He drifted back to sleep.

The sound of chatter and moving feet woke him, and he rose with everyone and assisted with teardown. Within an hour, they were on their way, riding for long periods of time. The next five days, they repeated the same routine. On the sixth day, they had made their way toward the end of the tunnel. Alexander saw a light shining through at the end. Lydennan rode forward and dismounted his horse. He nudged the door and pushed it open. Brilliant sunlight then flooded in from the open door.

Lydennan led his horse out, with the others following. The smell of grass greeted Alexander. People around him raised their hands up to cheer. Lydennan then closed the door behind them once everyone had made their way outside.

Alexander and the others looked upward. Before them, some three hundred feet away, they saw the massive layers and layers of white rock walls that made up Fort Ydaeriin. They could also see four concentric moat rings encircling it. At each moat was a small fort with up to four small wooden towers around it. It took Alexander's breath away.

The cavaliers proceeded forward at a gallop. When they were close to the first moat ring, one of the lone cavaliers removed a flag from his back and began to wave it through the air. The first of the small stone forts lowered a wooden drawbridge over the moat and directed the riders to cross.

Once they were closer to the drawbridge, they were directed to stop. The soldiers there made a salute of two fingers to their throats directed to Lieutenant Lydennan. He returned the salute and was motioned through. They did this two more times. Once they were stopped at the last gate, Alexander looked at the walls of Fort Ydaeriin. They shone brilliantly as the sun reflected off them. The group of travelers was motioned through and proceeded to the middle of the city. An enormous white stone building stood in the center.

Lieutenant Lydennan slid off of his horse and instructed Alexander to do the same. Once Alexander and his friends had touched their feet to the ground, the cavaliers removed the gear from their horses and handed the horses as well as their saddles to the workers of the stables some ten feet from the white stone building.

The spearmen guards opened the doors, and Lieutenant Lydennan and the others walked through. They entered a brightly lit red hall, where a lone soldier sat at a desk fifteen feet away. The lieutenant walked over to the desk, with Alexander, his friends, and the other cavaliers following shortly behind. The soldier stood up and snapped his arms to his sides.

"At ease," Lydennan instructed. "I need to speak with the governor regarding an urgent matter. Governor Burke should have sent a sealed envelope explaining the matter," Lieutenant Lydennan said.

"Yes sir," said the soldier. "He received it earlier today. He has been expecting a sortie from Port Ivory." Another soldier entered from the left side of the hall. "He will escort you to the governor's meeting room on the fifth floor." The first soldier pointed to the other.

The other soldier, who wore a sword at his side, motioned for them to follow him. They followed him through the door that he had entered from and up some stairs.

Once on the fifth floor, the soldier led them through two large wooden doors into a room with a large circular table draped with a red velvet cloth. Around the table sat many wooden chairs and one particularly large chair draped with red and blue velvet and silk.

"The governor should be in shortly," the soldier informed them. After a few minutes, the wooden doors heaved open. A stout man with short black hair, a thick black beard, and tan skin wearing white robes with a red cloak draped over his right shoulder proceeded through the doorway, followed by a tall armored man with brown curly hair and a brown beard. The soldier, Lieutenant Lydennan, and Alexander and his friends all snapped their heels together when the two walked in the room.

"Please take your seats," said the man with the red cloak draped over his shoulder as he made his way to the large seat. "My name is Amatus Vanerin, appointed governor of Fort Ydaeriin. This is my commander, Marshal Lynus Holstead. I have read the information that Governor Burke sent. Do you know of his condition?" the governor asked.

Lieutenant Lydennan had a flat look on his face.

"We were with him during the attack on Port Ivory," said Alexander, "but we know not of his condition."

Urien added an extra bit of information. "He was with us until we went to the ground to assist. He had lost one of his hands. We had to force him to stay there and get treatment while we all left to help defend the gate. We do not know if he survived, and if he did, we do not know if he evaded capture."

The governor nodded solemnly, the news evidently weighing on him. "That is sad news to hear. He's such a headstrong young man who greatly carries the weight of being a governor. From his report, he said that Xythuu has a form of advanced weaponry that is capable of obliterating stone walls. He also said that apprentices gave him this information. Would that happen to be the eight of you?" he asked.

"Yes sir," answered Camilla. "We saw it firsthand at Jylinae."

He looked at her for a moment and sighed deeply. "That is a very painful burden to bear. Deeply troubling news too. I do not know why we were thrown into this attack, but we must fight back any way we can. Later you will receive information on your placement in the field. For now, all of you should go rest. Apprentices, you will be given rooms and new clothing to replace your torn robes. You and all the others from Port Ivory will be given rooms at no expense. You shall escort them to their rooms," he said to the soldier as he slowly rose. The others snapped their feet together as Governor Vanerin and Marshal Holstead moved closer to the door. As they walked out, Lieutenant Lydennan turned to the soldier.

"When they get a room set up, please let me know," said Lieutenant Lydennan.

"Yes sir," the soldier said as he motioned for the others to follow him.

A few minutes later, Alexander and his friends had followed the soldier down the hall to their rooms. Alexander thanked him, and he went about his way. Some few hours later, Alexander and the other boys were bathed and wore brown, red, or black robes that draped over their bodies down to their knees. Cadfan was looking out the window while Alexander lay on one of the beds. Urien and Dysan were sitting in the leather-lined wooden chairs at the table in the corner of the room.

"So what do you guys think?" Alexander asked.

"Personally," Cadfan said without turning around, "I think we should get as close as possible on the field. I'm tired of being at the top of walls while others do the fighting first."

Dysan shifted in his seat. "I agree," he said. "I know the closer we are, the more danger it will present, but if I die, I would rather die right there, holding off an enemy advancement."

Urien drummed his fingers with a puzzled look on his face.

"You disagree, don't you?" Dysan asked.

"Actually, I do not," Urien said.

Cadfan turned around, clearly surprised.

"I want to be there too. Plus, somebody has to be there to look out for you."

"Well, that is good. We got Urien's approval. What do you say, Alexander?" Cadfan asked with his head turned to Alexander.

"I agree," Alexander said. "I will be right there beside you all, but it is not my approval you need. We would need to ask Camilla, Delyth, Tesni, and Aeronwen. I am also assuming that since we never formally finished our training and were given assignments, Lieutenant Lydennan assumes command over us, so he would need to give permission for that." There was silence for a few seconds.

Cadfan walked toward the door. "Well then, let us go ask them," he said, halfway across the room. A knock sounded at the door.

"Come in," Alexander said. The door opened, and the women walked through. They wore brown and black robes that hung down to their knees.

"Well, we were just on our way over to talk to you," Cadfan said, now standing in the middle of the room. Tesni and Delyth took seats at the table while Aeronwen and Camilla sat on the same bed as Alexander.

"We were discussing something, and we wanted to know what your thoughts on it were," Camilla said.

"What would you like to discuss?" Alexander asked.

"When we have to go to battle again, we would like to be as close as possible to battle. We were thinking maybe we could be in one of the forts at one of the moats," Camilla said.

"What a coincidence. We were thinking the same thing," Cadfan said, "and we agree."

Alexander nodded. "We may have to discuss it with the lieutenant."

Another knock sounded from the other side of the door.

"Come in," Alexander said.

Lieutenant Lydennan walked through the doorway. The others moved to stand up. "Sit down," he said as he stopped in the middle of the room with a few big bags in hand, which he dropped to the floor. He was wearing a blue tailed robe with white pants and brown leather boots.

"We were just wondering if we could ask you something, sir," Alexander said.

"Whatever we need to discuss, we will after I give you some things." The lieutenant picked up one of the leather bags he had set on the floor. He pulled out a curved single-edged sword. "Cadfan, this is for you." Lieutenant Lydennan handed the blade hilt first to him. Cadfan removed the sword from the sheath and looked at the blade. It was lined with a white edge. He spun it in his hand.

"It is remarkably light," Cadfan said. "What is the white on the edge?"

"It's a bone mixture painted on the blade," said Lieutenant Lydennan. "This is also for you." He pulled out a leather shirt with small bronze plates attached over the chest and shoulder areas. Cadfan tried the shirt on.

"Wow, this is very light. It should come in handy. I accept these gratefully, sir," Cadfan said humbly.

Lieutenant Lydennan pulled two black lacquered knives and a small bronze sword from his bag and motioned for Urien to grab them. Urien took them and unsheathed them. The blades were black and lined with the same white edge as Cadfan's sword. "They are also lined with the bone mixture. I also have a task for you if you are up to it, but we will discuss that later," Lieutenant Lydennan said. "This is also for you." He handed Urien a leather armor chest piece with bronze plates woven at the shoulders. "It is light enough to not hinder your movement. Tesni, Delyth, I got these for you." He gave each of them a thin ornate black lance with a white edge at the tip. "They are also mixed with bone," Lieutenant Lydennan said as they took the lances. He then pulled out a thick, doubled-layered armor set consisting of a chest piece, vambraces, pauldrons, and boots. "Dysan, these are for you. Try them on."

Dysan took the chest piece and slipped it over his head. It seemed to fit him well. Dysan had a grin that spread from ear to ear.

"Alexander and Aeronwen, I got these for you," the lieutenant said as he placed a set of leather armor vambraces and two bronze swords in front of them. The vambraces also came with a leather chest piece that had a small plating of bronze on the front. "Try the gloves on. They have the same property," said Lieutenant Lydennan.

"These are amazing," Alexander said.

"Camilla, I did not forget about you," Lieutenant Lydennan said as he gave her a set of leather armor with bronze plates. There were small openings within them, suitable for a few arrows to be stored in each. "I also got you one hundred arrows and a sword." He placed a quiverful of gray-tipped arrows on the ground. Camilla looked at the leather armor thoughtfully.

"This is lovely," she said. "Did you buy all of these yourself?"

"I did. I just wanted to get them for you all. You have been through a lot," the lieutenant said softly. "Now on to briefings. There should be one tomorrow at noon and another the next day after a set of Nightcloaks come back with information. Which is what I want to speak with you about, Urien," he said as he locked eyes with Urien.

"What did you want to discuss, sir?"

The lieutenant cast a thoughtful look at Urien. "As I said, a group of Nightcloaks are to gather intelligence on the placement of the enemy. They wish to know if you would join them."

Urien gasped for a brief second and glanced at his friends. "But, sir, I am still an apprentice."

Lieutenant Lydennan's look changed from thoughtful to quizzical as he crossed his arms. "But, Urien, that's what this is about. They have requested to help you with your final training."

Urien just looked stunned, and Alexander felt surprised as well. Urien was quiet for a moment. "Sir, I agree. I am ready and willing to begin my final Nightcloak training."

Lieutenant Lydennan smiled. "Very well. Follow me, then. They are ready for you now," he said as he turned and headed to the door with Urien behind him.

* * *

Lieutenant Lydennan and Urien descended two sets of stairs and came to a blue door. Lieutenant Lydennan knocked twice. The door opened, and the two proceeded in. Urien found himself in a Nightcloak training room, much like the one he had trained in back in Jylinae.

A Nightcloak with chin-length blond hair and a beard walked forward from the center of the room where twelve other Nightcloaks were gathered. They all wore loose-fitting sleep clothes. The approaching Nightcloak stopped in front of them with a victorious grin on his face.

"So he decided to join in," the man said.

"Yes, he did," answered Lieutenant Lydennan with obvious pride. "Urien, this is Lieutenant Garrett Baethalin. We attended officer training together. There is no finer leader to follow. He kept me out of many troubling situations," he said with a grin.

Lieutenant Baethalin scoffed. "Oh, please. I did not do anything great," he said. "Anyway, Urien, are you ready to become a Nightcloak?"

"Yes sir," Urien answered loudly.

"Very well. We will go over all of the training you have accomplished. You will demonstrate your stealth training, your obstacle training, your ranged training, and your hand-to-hand combat training. We should finish within an hour or two. And then tomorrow you will go into the field with us as your final test. We must begin now. We will start with the stealth training first," Lieutenant Baethalin said as he, Lieutenant Lydennan, and the other Nightcloaks moved to the sides of the training room.

The lights extinguished, and Urien could hear something mechanical rising up from the floor. The lights flickered on dimly, which helped Urien vaguely make out an obstacle course in front of him. He could see the silhouettes of walls surrounding the course. "Your objective is to make it to the other side without being seen, heard, or caught. If you are seen or heard, you do not fail but must evade capture," said Baethalin from somewhere above at the end of the course.

Urien assessed his options carefully. He saw two openings, one on each side of the course. In front of him, there was a wall about six feet tall. Urien, as quietly and quickly as possible, ran to the wall. His foot connected with it, and his momentum carried him upward to the edge, where he then pulled himself on top of the wall. He crouched in place and scanned his surroundings. In front of him was a walkway that extended toward the end of the room. To his side were many smaller walkways. He dropped quietly to the floor and proceeded to the left narrow path. Once there, he snuck up next to a wall and peered just a few centimeters over the edge of the wall. He could see nothing and heard no presence. He cautiously stepped out in a low crouch.

After a few more feet, walkways emerged from both sides. Urien decided to take the right path and crept to the next intersecting path. He could make out the form of a figure fifteen feet to his right.

The person looked in his direction for a long minute and dropped to a low crouch. For a moment, Urien thought that he had already been caught. The other person moved quickly along the path, out of Urien's sight. Urien stepped toward where he had seen the person and came to yet another split path. To his left he saw a corner, and he saw nothing to his right. He moved slowly toward the end of the left path and peeked around the corner. Seeing no signs of the other Nightcloaks, he paused.

This seems almost too easy, he thought. He moved forward, carefully placing his feet. Once he was at the end of the path, he scanned his surroundings. There were four different paths, each going the same direction but spaced out about ten feet apart.

This must be a trap, he thought. Suddenly, one of the Nightcloaks grabbed hold of him from the left. Urien shifted his feet to counter being pulled by his assailant. He slid his foot down beside the inside of the Nightcloak's foot. Urien then brought his other leg forward and kicked it into the side of the Nightcloak. He pulled the Nightcloak's arm and swept his right foot out from his body and kicked him back into the wall with a heavy thud. Urien spun and darted away, passing the first two passages and turning into the third. He continued to run until he reached the end and slid under a low barricade. Once through, he quickly crouched and looked to his left and right.

To the right, the path went on and on for about fifty feet before coming to a turn. To his left, the path went for about ten feet and turned right. He slowly, quietly, and cautiously proceeded to the right in a low crouch. Urien stuck close to the wall and stopped about four feet away from the turn before continuing. He knew that more Nightcloaks might be hiding around the corner as the previous one had been. So far, he could see nobody hiding. He proceeded to the corner and turned carefully.

To his right, as he turned the corner, he barely saw a hand reach for him. He quickly turned and slapped the hand, then caught it by the wrist. He pulled the assailant toward him. His assailant attempted to lift a knee into Urien's chest. Urien blocked it with his raised right leg and wrenched his opponent's arm, bringing him closer. Urien kicked the Nightcloak's foot out from under him, pulled on the Nightcloak's arm, and rolled him onto the ground.

Urien darted forward once more. He ran a few feet and jumped over a barricade. Ahead of him was the vague shadow of a horizontal bar, about the height of his shoulders. He grabbed the bar and used the momentum to pull himself under in a rapid slide. Once under, he rose to his feet.

He could see nothing but shadows all around him. The sound of clapping broke the silence as new torches were lit and windows opened, illuminating the area. Lieutenant Baethalin stood nearby with a wide grin on his face as he clapped loudly.

"That was incredible," Lieutenant Baethalin said. "You certainly have some talent for this. Well, you pass the stealth portion as well as the maneuverability portion. You did well. You still have two more tests. The range weaponry and the hand-to-hand combat portion. Let us start with the weaponry."

The mazes and pillars began to retract into the floor and were replaced with many small walls and pillars with targets on them. Another Nightcloak brought a bag of weapons to Lieutenant Baethalin and placed them at his feet.

"Let's get this show started, then," Lieutenant Baethalin said with evident excitement.

Lieutenant Baethalin opened the bag at his feet. He removed two throwing-knife belts, a pack of throwing needles, a small black pouch with unknown contents, and a fist-sized black item with a prong on each side of it.

"You should be familiar with these," said Lieutenant Baethalin as he tossed the knife belts and needle pack at Urien, who caught the belts in one hand and the pack in the other. Urien strapped the knife belts across his chest and the needle pack to his leg. "I am going to introduce you to two new weapons," Lieutenant Baethalin said as he opened the pouch and pulled out a knife no more than five inches long. "This is what is known as a False Blade. It is so called for this reason. You can plainly see the knife blade as well as the two buttons on the side," Lieutenant Baethalin said as he gestured to the side buttons, one near the top of the blade and one close to the hilt. "The top button serves as a retraction for the actions of the bottom button. Now the bottom button is different." Lieutenant Baethalin placed his thumb on the bottom button and held it in place. He then quickly threw the knife into one of the wooden posts in front of him. It hit the post with a thud. "If you would follow me," Lieutenant Baethalin said as he and Urien stepped forward. At the post, Lieutenant Baethalin removed the knife and showed it to Urien.

Urien could see another smaller blade that had opened from the hilt of the knife.

"You can see the blade coming out of the hilt. This doubles your chances for either blade to land in the target," Lieutenant Baethalin explained. "Also, if an assailant were to grab hold of your arm or hand, you could use the lower knife to loosen their grip because the force of the spring load will pierce directly into their skin. Now this weapon should also be used sparingly. For obvious reasons, if you hold the knife wrong in your hand, the blade could pierce your hand. So it is best used only for throwing. I will let you hold on to this." Baethalin handed the knife to Urien, who strapped it to the belt around his waist. "The next weapon might be difficult for you."

The lieutenant picked up the fist-sized object. Baethalin turned a small knob on the front of the object and pulled it downward. The object folded out into a bow. Urien remembered seeing this late in his training.

"The point of this is to be able to carry a bow without it being seen," Lieutenant Baethalin said as he turned the front knob back to its first position and pushed the bow into its retracted form. He handed the bow to Urien. Urien clasped the bow over the cloth on his bottom knife belt.

"Now," Lieutenant Baethalin said, "you have thirty arrows"—he tossed a quiver of arrows to Urien—"two sets of twenty throwing knives, twenty throwing needles, and ten False Blades, giving you one hundred weapons total. Your goal is to hit your targets at least seventy times. You will also be moving from one point to another throughout this course and must watch for the targets to spring up. This course will test your quickness, accuracy, and awareness. You will have fifteen minutes to proceed through the course. If time runs out and you have not finished, your session will end, and any targets you have hit will be counted. You finish if you cross the finish line marked at the end of the course. You will start at the starting line." Baethalin gestured to a thin white line at the front of the course. He pulled out a goat horn from the bag at his feet. "Are you ready?" he asked seriously.

"I am," Urien said calmly, feeling confident in his abilities to ace this course.

The targets popped out, and Urien darted over the starting line. He threw three knives in rapid succession, each flying seven feet and landing in the center of the circular targets. Two more targets popped up. Urien flung one knife at the left target, which landed in it with a thunk. He turned and threw one at the other target, but it missed as the target swung back to its original position.

"Move forward," Lieutenant Baethalin called. Urien took a few rapid steps forward as eight targets popped up over a horizontal log. Four knives were flung into the targets, followed by two more that slammed into the targets. Urien then threw two more; one landed in the wood just below the target, and the other missed as the targets went back down. To his right, a target popped up, and Urien hurled a knife rapidly into it. Another two popped up to his left, and he landed two more knives.

At this point he was instructed to move forward. He passed through an opening, and multiple targets popped up around him. Urien, as quickly as possible, moved and turned while throwing a knife into each target. He moved forward, and two more targets popped up on his left, which he hit with two needles from his leg pouch. In quick succession, Urien nailed every target that popped up in this section.

Urien was instructed to move forward again. He came to a thin bridge, barely wide enough for him to step on, that hung over a pool of water beneath him. He had to cross, so he carefully placed his foot on the bridge. He stepped on. As he did so, two targets popped up on his left. Urien slowly reached for his needles and, while carefully trying to keep his balance, managed to throw one into the target. He repeated this process and hit the second target in its center.

Urien neared the end of the bridge, where there was a five-foot gap to the other platform. While he teetered on the edge, a target popped up on the other side of the platform.

Urien jumped off of the bridge, over the gap. His hands caught the edge of the platform as his feet hung just two feet over the water below him. A target popped up from the wall to his left. Urien pulled himself farther up. He hung there momentarily, his left arm straining to hold up his full weight. He reached for a needle with his right hand and then grabbed the ledge with his right, moving the needle into his left hand. He now held on to the ledge with his right arm and flung the needle at the target. It hit the target, just barely landing on the edge of it. Urien pulled himself up over the ledge and then flung a needle into the target two feet in front of him. Two targets popped up to his left and one to his right. He rapidly flung a needle into the right target, hitting the center. He turned and threw two needles at the left targets. One hit in the upper right of the target, and the other hit the edge and ricocheted to the ground as the target went back down.

Urien ran forward as three more targets popped up. He quickly flung his needles to the right and spun and threw one at the left target. A fifteen-foot rope leading to the upper level hung before him. He grabbed the rope with both hands, wrapped his legs around, and heaved himself up, the weight of his body pulling him down. Urien was five feet up when a target popped out to his right side.

He braced himself with his left hand and reached for the needles on his right side. His left hand began to slip and burn as he clutched the rope. He grabbed hold of a needle and threw it horizontally at the target. It landed on the target's edge. Urien grasped the rope and continued his climb.

He was now five feet away from the top platform when another target popped up to his left. He gripped the rope in his right hand until his knuckles turned white. He carefully reached across his body and managed to pull a needle from his pouch. He raised his left arm up and hurled the needle toward the target. It collided into the target's edge.

Urien raised his left hand back onto the rope and pulled himself up. He reached the platform at the top and lifted himself onto it. He looked forward at the rest of the course. The whole upper level hung over the water and had many teetering bridges. He took a step forward, and as he did, two targets popped up on the right side in a curved line and quickly began moving toward the left side of the course. Urien flung a needle into each one as they passed the middle of the course.

He arrived at the first of the teetering bridges. He saw four targets, two on each side. He carefully placed his foot on the bridge and felt it sway to the right.

"Seven minutes left," Lieutenant Baethalin shouted from the floor.

Urien proceeded into a slow crouch across the bridge. It wobbled under him. The first target was now about five feet to his right. He very cautiously reached for a False Blade and threw it at the target. As the blade hit the target, he slightly lost his balance and felt the bridge shift to the right. Urien leaped to his feet and ran across the bridge. As he did so, he flung another False Blade into a target on his left and jumped from the first bridge to the second. It began to tilt and wobble as he tried to walk across. The bridge balanced out as Urien made his way to the center. He flung a False Blade to a target on his right.

He moved five more feet very quickly. As he did, the bridge shifted to his left. He moved to the right and managed to balance the bridge. He flung a blade at a target on the left. It landed in the center of the target as the bridge now swayed to the right. Urien's feet slipped slightly as he moved to the left side. He jumped to the next bridge and stayed low as it swayed heavily.

Six targets, three on each side, popped up. He threw two knives to the right, each of them hitting the targets as he moved to the left to balance the bridge. He threw two more to the left, hitting the targets, and then slid to the floor of the bridge as it began to pull to the left. He inched closer to the edge. He slowly rolled to his right as the bridge came into balance.

He rose to his feet, extracting his bow and releasing an arrow at the last target to his right. It landed near the center. He shot another at the left target, and it missed as the target moved downward.

"Four minutes left," shouted Lieutenant Baethalin. Urien now bolted across the bridge.

He leaped over a three-foot gap and rolled over a wide plank. He rose to his feet with his bow fully drawn, then began firing off arrows at any targets that appeared.

Urien, in a crouch, moved slowly across another swaying bridge, balancing carefully and shooting at all the targets. He hit most of them but missed one as he swayed.

"Thirty seconds left," called Lieutenant Baethalin. Urien ran across another plank and onto another tilting bridge. This one was much more unstable than the last, but he managed to release multiple arrows in rapid succession. The first two hit the outer edges of the targets, and the last missed the bottom of the target by a few inches. A timer horn sounded.

"That's time," said Lieutenant Baethalin. "Well now," he continued as he rubbed his hand on his chin, "not bad. Not bad at all. Excellent, actually. You missed seven targets and had three unused arrows—so a ten-point deduction, making your score a ninety."

Urien retracted his bow into storage form and made his way to a ladder on the side and slid down. He and Lieutenant Baethalin moved twenty feet away from the course as it repositioned back into the ground.

The other Nightcloaks were clad in padded leather training gear. Lieutenant Baethalin removed some from a bag and gave it to Urien. He then proceeded to put some on himself.

"Now the last stage," Lieutenant Baethalin said as he slid a leather mask over his face, muffling his voice, "will be the hand-to-hand combat. You will be tested on how effectively you can fight multiple opponents at once, how effectively you can escape from holds and attacks, and how effectively you fight. You might want to put your mask on. This part usually hurts." The other Nightcloaks gathered around them.

Urien slid his mask over his face. "I am ready," he said in a muffled voice.

Lieutenant Baethalin instructed the others to begin. Three of the Nightcloaks in front of Urien charged toward him. He blocked a punch from the first and managed to grab his wrist, pull him to the side, and kick him down to the floor. The other two Nightcloaks began to strike at his sides. Urien blocked and dodged multiple strikes. He punched one of the Nightcloaks in the face and then did a front kick to his stomach, sending the Nightcloak to the ground while the other landed a punch to Urien's cheek, knocking him back a step. Urien felt the sting on his face.

The Nightcloak closed the gap between them and threw a flurry of punches. Urien blocked and backstepped and caught the Nightcloak's arm and jerked it downward diagonally; then he kicked the Nightcloak's knee and threw him to the ground, away from him. The Nightcloak rose, as did the other two, and sprang for Urien. One threw a punch and kicked Urien in his side. The force of the kick sent Urien to the side, where one of the other Nightcloaks locked him in a bear hug from behind.

Urien threw his head backward into his assailant's and slid his foot down into the man's shin. Urien then broke free of the bear hug and grabbed the man's wrist. He pulled on his arm and kicked his chest, then hurled him into one of the other Nightcloaks, sending them both crashing to the ground.

The remaining Nightcloak moved to the right and connected his fist with Urien's face. Urien was thrown back, and the Nightcloak launched a roundhouse kick, which hit full force into Urien's side. He went for more strikes, but Urien blocked the blows. The Nightcloak connected a punch with Urien's chest, which sent him tumbling. As he fell, he grabbed hold of the Nightcloak's arm and pulled him to the ground with him.

They locked on to each other. He kicked the back of the Nightcloak's head and slammed him into the ground. Lieutenant Baethalin sent in three more Nightcloaks. Urien was still on the ground when one darted up to him and swung his foot toward his chest. Urien rolled to the side, then onto his feet. The Nightcloak in front of him launched an aggressive onslaught of kicks, which Urien did his best to avoid.

Another Nightcloak darted at him and punched toward his head. Urien blocked and deflected the punch but was then hit in the stomach by the first Nightcloak's kick. The Nightcloak joined his hands together, raised them over his head, and dropped them with incredible force. Urien managed to step back and dodge the attack and brought his knee into the Nightcloak's chest but was then hit in the face by the other Nightcloak. The third Nightcloak caught Urien's arm and began to move it down in an arm bar. Urien felt the strain in his arm as it was pushed farther. He moved with the force and spun around his opponent, wrenching free of the arm bar. Urien kicked his opponent's back and pushed him forward.

Another Nightcloak hit him in the face, kneed him in the stomach, and then brought his hand down toward Urien's head. Urien caught the Nightcloak's hand and kicked into the instep of his foot, dropping the Nightcloak to one knee, and then, rotating with full force, punched the Nightcloak in the face, knocking him backward. Another Nightcloak punched Urien in the side of the head, causing him to take a step back, while another kicked him hard in the leg, dropping him to his knee.

One Nightcloak brought his fist to Urien's face, but Urien managed to block it with his hands. He tossed the Nightcloak to the side and rose to his feet, only to be kicked by another Nightcloak. They exchanged blows until Urien managed to hit the Nightcloak's face and sweep him off of his feet.

"Everyone stand down," said Lieutenant Baethalin. All the Nightcloaks stepped to the side. Lieutenant Baethalin stepped forward and took up a fighting stance. "Now come at me, Urien," he demanded with ferocity. A twinge of anxiety coursed through Urien's body as he panted heavily. *Suppose I have encountered worse,* he thought.

Urien took a few small steps forward, carefully assessing Lieutenant Baethalin's stance. He then took a huge step and threw a punch at Lieutenant Baethalin. The lieutenant blocked it and pulled Urien into a hard punch to the face, which caused him to roll to the ground. Lieutenant Baethalin darted forward, then brought his foot down toward Urien. Urien rolled to the side and punched his opponent's knee. He rose and hit Lieutenant Baethalin with an uppercut.

Lieutenant Baethalin grabbed Urien's arm, pulled him forward, and tossed him to the side. He ran at Urien and launched a sidekick at him. Urien barely dodged, then grabbed hold of Lieutenant Baethalin's foot. Urien swept Lieutenant Baethalin's other leg out from under him.

Urien began a downward punch, but Lieutenant Baethalin kicked Urien back. Lieutenant Baethalin sprang to his feet and tackled Urien. Urien blocked an incoming punch and headbutted Lieutenant Baethalin.

Urien pushed him upward and rolled him over, then punched his face hard. Lieutenant Baethalin pushed Urien off of him and jumped to his feet. They exchanged blows briefly. Lieutenant Baethalin caught Urien's arm and pulled him toward a punch, but Urien deflected the punch and kicked Lieutenant Baethalin in the knee and then punched him in the face. Lieutenant Baethalin shoved his hands into Urien's face and then, using his foot, pushed him up and backward. He grabbed Urien in a headlock, but Urien broke free and then threw a punch that was blocked. Urien kicked him and went for another punch. Lieutenant Baethalin caught Urien's arm and threw him over his shoulder, then attempted to place Urien in a choke hold. Urien broke free of the grip, shoved Lieutenant Baethalin back, and spun onto his feet.

Urien prepared for Lieutenant Baethalin to charge and raised his hands in a fighting position, but Lieutenant Baethalin held up his hand, gesturing for him to stop.

"That is the end," Lieutenant Baethalin said. He motioned to one of the other Nightcloaks, who went to the bag that Baethalin had taken his gear from, removed a rolled piece of paper, and brought it over. Lieutenant Baethalin took it and removed his mask.

"Remove your mask, Urien," Lieutenant Baethalin said. Urien did as instructed. Lieutenant Baethalin unrolled the paper and began to read what was written on it. "Attention, attention, attention," he read as he, Urien, and the other Nightcloaks snapped their heels together, "to whom it pertains, this states that Urien Maldwyn, who was seen before me, Lieutenant Garrett Baethalin, is deemed fully worthy of obtaining the title of Nightcloak of Eltheneae." He removed a capped seal from his pocket, took off the cap, and stamped the paper. He also removed a small blue hexagonal badge from his pocket.

He handed the paper to Urien. Lieutenant Baethalin then pinned the blue badge on Urien's shirt. Urien made the two-finger throat salute, and Lieutenant Baethalin returned the salute. One of the Nightcloaks brought a mottled-black Nightcloak cloak and handed it to Lieutenant Baethalin, and he draped it over Urien's shoulders and shook his hand.

Urien looked down at the badge on his chest. It had a picture in black ink of a hood with a knife behind it with the words *Eltheneae* above it and *Nightcloak* below it. Urien felt overwhelmed by the pride and honor filling him.

"Now," said Lieutenant Baethalin, "get plenty of sleep. Tomorrow we will meet here at seven p.m. and then make our way to the front gate to meet with a group of cavaliers. From there, I will give the brief, and we will begin our mission. Be sure to be in your cloak and any armor you wish to bring. You are now free to go. Do not lose the paper either. We keep copies. The process is just very tedious to replace it."

Urien rolled up the paper and placed it in his pocket. He was escorted out of the training room and led back through the halls to his room. He stopped at the door before entering. A tear escaped each eye, running down his face. He was proud to now be a Nightcloak but wished he could tell his parents of his accomplishment. It was all he had ever worked toward, and they had only ever supported him. He still felt so much dread knowing his father was dead and not knowing if his mother was even alive. He wiped his eyes on his shirt and then opened the door.

All his friends were sprawled out across the floor or beds. Alexander and Cadfan were playing a game of chess while Aeronwen, Tesni, Dysan, Delyth, and Camilla played a card game with detailed drawings.

Cadfan looked up, and a grin slid across his face. "No way," he said. "Look at Urien. Did you fail?" he asked. Urien removed his paper and showed it to them. Cadfan whistled in surprise. They all rose with excited grins on their faces and congratulated and hugged him.

"I cannot believe that you are a Nightcloak now!" Dysan stated with excitement. Urien made his way to his bed and draped his cloak over the post. He removed his badge and placed it on his cloak and then collapsed onto his bed with excitement in his heart and drifted off to sleep.

Chapter 12

Alexander awoke to find his friends dressed in their apprentice clothes—with the exception of Urien, who wore his Nightcloak robe over his dark-brown clothes.

"About time you woke up," Cadfan said as Alexander sat up groggily. "If I am awake before you, that must be an issue."

Alexander had fuzzy thoughts. *Cadfan is really more awake than I am,* he thought. He rose from his bed and ran a comb through his hair in the bathroom. A minute later, he walked out of the bathroom and slipped into some white cloth pants and a brown long-sleeved shirt. He then draped his apprentice robe over his head and his father's cloak after that. He slipped on his long brown boots over his pant legs and followed his friends out the door.

The girls were outside of their door waiting for them.

"Good morning, sunshine," Camilla said, smiling warmly. They proceeded down the hall and took the first set of stairs on the right side. They walked down until they reached the first floor, then went out the front door. The fresh morning air wafted into Alexander's nose, and he heard the chirping of the birds as they flew about.

"Lieutenant Lydennan said he would meet us at the Dawn Kitchen," Urien told Alexander.

"He also said he would have news for us," Tesni added.

They made their way down the road and took a right. On the left side was the Dawn Kitchen. Lieutenant Lydennan, wearing a flowing blue robe that ended at his knees with black pants and brown boots, stood outside the entrance with another person, a tall man with short blond hair who wore a brown leather suit with black boots.

"Ah, good morning," Lydennan said as they moved closer. "First of all, your request to be right at the front of any possible battle was denied due to your inexperience." Alexander was taken aback at the bluntness right off the start. He sighed slightly. Part of him felt relieved. He had experienced much in a short amount of time. Another part of him, though, felt eager. He did not want to just sit back in their ongoing struggle. "Urien, I see that you became a Nightcloak. Congratulations." The lieutenant made a short bow.

"Thank you, sir," Urien said.

"Now, as I said, you will not be at the front fort. They did, however, agree to place you at the second one, so I wanted to introduce you to the man who will command you," Lydennan said as the other young man took a step forward.

"My name is Captain Hayden Thaenin, and I will be your commander in the field. Tomorrow we will meet here at noon to discuss any information," he said.

"Also, there will be a briefing in the Hall of News today at noon. You will attend because you are not needed elsewhere, and it will discuss information pertaining to what is known so far of the ongoing Xythuu advancement. That is all I have for you," said Lieutenant Lydennan. Alexander and the others entered the Dawn Kitchen.

Alexander sat with his friends at a table and stared at his food, just pushing it around with his fork. He kept thinking back to the battle at Port Ivory. His mind drifted to the lance cutting his face. He rubbed the newly formed scar on the bridge of his nose.

"What is wrong?" Camilla asked him, a look of worry on her face.

"I never thought we would be sitting at a table, still relatively young, having survived two major battles and preparing for a possible third or more," Alexander muttered with a slight twinge of cynicism in his voice. "I never would have imagined that I would have caused serious harm to another person at such a young age." He continued to just stare at his food. The others paused eating and looked at him. He glanced up at their faces, each twisted to various degrees.

"I suppose that is part of the nature of joining what we did. It is good that you feel this," Urien said. "Shame is part of being human, and you would not be fully human if you did these things without feeling."

Dysan looked blankly at him. "I believe I can guess the other thing you are feeling. Your mind keeps taking you back to the battles. At least I think it does. I know mine does too. I can assume that the others' do too."

Alexander darted glances at each of his friends. They nodded in agreement to what Dysan had said.

"But how do we balance the feelings of being warriors fighting for our own cause while not succumbing to our own feelings of shame? How do we know we are not monsters deep inside who try to fight off the shame of harming and killing other people while at the same time feeling so much anger towards the very same people who we delivered the harm and death to? How do we live with that?" Alexander asked.

The others went silent and stared at each other blankly.

Cadfan snorted. "Who cares about living with shame about killing some worthless Xythuu pieces of trash," he said snidely. His friends, except Alexander, had looks of shock spread across their faces.

"Cadfan, surely you do not mean that?" Aeronwen asked.

"I do. Xythuu deserves to be destroyed."

"How can you say that? Every country and being has a right to exist," Aeronwen said.

"Even if they have committed horrible acts?" Cadfan asked. "We may have not been alive during them, but Xythuu has started two wars with our country in the past, and you honestly think they will change?"

"Yes, I do. Peace and compassion are things that can be learned," Aeronwen insisted.

"Even if they might have killed your parents or could be torturing them or using them as slaves?" Cadfan shot back.

Aeronwen's face turned bright red, and she stormed from her chair and toward the door. The other girls walked after—Alexander supposed they went to comfort her. He was slightly shocked. He had never seen Aeronwen angry before in his life, but he felt that Cadfan was right. Or maybe Alexander had let hatred take over him.

* * *

Later in the day, Alexander and his friends met up at the orator building in the center of the city. Aeronwen still looked upset, but she kept her cool and put on a good front, Alexander thought.

She looked directly at Cadfan. "I thought about what you said," she said. "I do realize it is hard to forgive people who have wronged you. I do not know if my parents are alive, but I realize that we have also committed harm on other beings. So in some ways, we are exactly the same. Please do not allow these acts to change who you are, my friends," she stated softly.

Nobody had anything to say in response, so they slipped quietly into the orator building. The main room was already packed. Alexander and his friends managed to find some seats at the back of the building and squeezed into them. A few minutes later, the roar of the crowd died down as Governor Vanerin and Marshal Holstead took the stage. There was a podium with a sound amplifier placed at the front of the stage to which Governor Vanerin proceeded.

"Good afternoon," he said into a horn with many tubes connecting to the walls, thus filling the whole building with the sound of his voice. "I thank you all for gathering here today, for this is an urgent matter which must be addressed. We have been given the news of the attack on Jylinae and Port Ivory by the Kingdom of Xythuu. Both of their beacons have been activated and observed from trade caravans, meaning that both cities have fallen," he said, his tone low and serious.

He paused briefly and then continued. "That is why I have gathered you all here today. We have reason to believe that they will make their way here to Fort Ydaeriin next. This is an act of war, and it will not be tolerated. We will defend our city and our country. We believe they are just about one hundred and fifty miles away from the city and expect them to arrive within three or four days. Do not be alarmed, though. All military members will be in place, ready to fight them off, and all civilians will be moved to the underground forts. We will not surrender to Xythuu's will, and we will not lose this city easily. We have received word from Ilgeth that Xythuu has pushed closer to their city. Currently, the city still stands under our control. We have received no word from any of the eastern cities, meaning that they have either fallen or have not sent any messages of attack because the Xythuu Army has not advanced that far yet. I am uncertain. Anyone who wishes to volunteer to fight should report to Marshal Holstead before sundown today. We will receive more intel on the advancing Xythuu Army at a later date. We will defend this city," Governor Vanerin said, with passion flaring in his voice now.

Everyone let out a cheer.

"Looks like we will be in another battle here soon," Delyth said somberly.

* * *

Later in the evening in the boys' room, Alexander and the other three were relaxing and playing chess on the floor.

"Are you guys ready for another fight?" Dysan asked, moving his pawn to another space on the board.

"You know it," Cadfan answered with obvious pride. "Ready for justice."

Alexander looked blankly at the chessboard. Would his father have approved of his new attitude and feelings toward Xythuu?

There was a knock on the door. Dysan rose and made his way to the door and opened it. A group of Nightcloaks stood outside their room.

Urien jumped up. "Lieutenant Baethalin," he greeted. Alexander peered at the door to get a look at the man who had put Urien to the test previously.

"Good evening. May we come in?" Lieutenant Baethalin asked.

"Yes sir," said Dysan as he moved to the side.

* * *

Lieutenant Baethalin and some of the others walked into the room. One of them dropped a bag at Urien's feet.

"Get your cloak, and suit up in your armor," the lieutenant said.

Urien rummaged through the bag and strapped every piece of the leather armor to his body.

"Arm up too," Lieutenant Baethalin said. Urien strapped on all the weapons—three belts of throwing knives, two holsters of throwing needles, one holster of arrows, two small packs filled with needles, False Blades, a sword strapped to his leg, and vials. There were also two tridents, which Urien strapped to his legs. He also strapped another weapon he had never used to his side: a small curved knife intended to pierce and cut armor.

"May I ask what all of this is needed for?" Urien asked.

Lieutenant Baethalin looked at him apologetically. "It is confidential information," he said. There was a silence between them. Camilla and the others stood in the doorway, likely having heard the commotion from next door. Lieutenant Baethalin sighed. "I guess you and your friends have a right to know. We are making our way to the Xythuu Army's campsite. A scout tower sent information after spotting them." His expression was stern.

Urien's friends looked at him in apparent alarm. This would be the first actual mission any of them had been on.

"Very well. I will go," Urien said.

Lieutenant Baethalin smirked a little. "You did not really have a choice, and I requested that we were not going to leave without you. You need to get experience. Now I need you to sign these," he said as he pulled out two papers from his pocket.

Urien read over the papers. One was a will, and the other was a paper that stated who should be contacted and who would get his Endariins in the event of his death. It also stated that he would now be getting paid the amount of one thousand Endariins monthly plus five hundred extra for his mission. He signed that his friends should be contacted if anything were to happen to him and that they would receive all his money and possessions. Urien returned the paper to Lieutenant Baethalin. He placed them in an envelope and wrapped it in a red cord.

"Say your goodbyes. We are leaving right now," he said.

His friends gathered around him. Dysan and Cadfan each shook his hand and pulled him in for a quick hug. Alexander gave him a tight hug.

"Keep your head up. You have always been good at it," Alexander said.

The girls now gave their hugs. Tesni hugged Urien last, and when she did, she held on tighter and longer than everyone else.

"Be safe, and come back," she said warmly. Urien felt a mix of emotions. He felt some fear, but it was overshadowed by determination. She let go of him now and turned toward Lieutenant Baethalin. "Can I give him a blessing?"

"Only if you can do so quickly," he said with slight impatience.

Tesni instructed Urien to hold out his arm. She held her hand over his until the stone-skin and heal blessings were etched over his arm in Onglikae runic script. "They should last for a few hours," she said as she looked him in the eyes.

"I will see you soon, my friends," Urien said as he grabbed his knives and strapped them to his hip and followed Lieutenant Baethalin and the other Nightcloaks out the door and down the stairs. They made their way outside. The night air was cold, and the stars shone down from the sky with brilliance. They arrived at the gate to the city and stopped. Lieutenant Baethalin had a brief and unheard conversation with the guards. The gate then opened, and they were instructed to follow him. They wove through the vastness of the city until they reached the next gate and passed through it.

Urien looked around. There were not many people around with the exception of guards on night shift and a few other people just out in the night. From there, they sauntered down the side of a wall. A guard opened a hatch in the wall that revealed a hidden passageway, and the Nightcloaks slipped inside.

Lieutenant Baethalin took large steps and moved quickly, with Urien and the others tailing him. They turned a few times and then proceeded down a long corridor. After about twenty minutes of traversing down the corridor, they reached a set of stairs that went up five feet to a door. Lieutenant Baethalin opened the door and pushed his way outside. Urien followed through and could smell the night air again. They were now outside of the outermost moat that wrapped around the city.

Lieutenant Lydennan greeted them. Urien spotted a group of horses and their cavaliers nearby.

"Finally. We have been waiting," said Lydennan sarcastically.

"Yeah, yeah," Baethalin responded. He instructed everyone to gather around. The cavaliers stood a few feet away now. "We have been tasked with a mission tonight, which is why we are gathered here now. Our job is to get intel on how much more ground the Xythuu Army has to cover as well as the strength of their army and their equipment. Also, if at all possible, we are to sabotage them in an effort to delay them. As I said earlier, this is a classified mission, meaning besides us, only the governor and the marshal know exactly where we are going," he said, turning his head to Urien. "Urien, like I said, I requested that you come along due to the fact that you need the experience and that you are incredibly skilled for someone just starting. Now, this mission is also incredibly dangerous." He distributed small slips of paper to the Nightcloaks.

"These basically state that the governor has authorized the use of poison," Baethalin said. He folded a map out before them.

"We will be taking you to this location," Lydennan said as he pointed to a spot on the map. "We'll be going about forty miles out. The intel we have so far suggests that the army was estimated to be one hundred and fifty miles away, but we now believe they could be much closer. At thirty-eight miles, we will slow down, and once we hit the forty mark, we will stop and set up a hidden campsite. From there, you will not be able to have our support and will have to make the rest of the way on foot. We will be waiting for you at the campsite. We have been instructed to return you and the intel before nine a.m. tomorrow morning. Right now it is about ten p.m."—he glanced at a pocket watch— "and we can be there in approximately two hours, which gives you seven hours to get the intel, do any sabotage as need be, and return in time to travel back to here. Any questions?"

No one asked anything.

"Okay then. Let's get saddled up. We have some ground to cover," Lydennan said. Urien and the others jumped on the backs of the cavaliers' horses and moved away in a trot that exploded into a gallop as the walls of Fort Ydaeriin shrank behind them.

They rode for close to two hours as the countryside passed by in a blur. Urien was beginning to feel the soreness from the ride in his thighs and lower back. His rider told him that it would still be about ten to twenty minutes before they would arrive at their destination. He groaned with impatience. He remembered the stories his father had told him when he was a child of how he would have to ride horses sometimes and how he had always dreaded it.

It pained his heart to think of his father now. He had so many good memories of his father. His father had taught him how to throw knives when he was nine and had begun to teach him how to fight as well. He greatly missed his father, and there were some nights when he would wake from his sleep because of nightmares of his father's death in Jylinae. He cleared his mind for now and realized that they had slowed to a trot. They kept this pace for a few minutes and then stopped on a ridge in a clearing with some surrounding trees. Urien realized that he was back in the Ydaeriin Plains.

"We have arrived," Lieutenant Lydennan said as he dismounted his horse. Urien slid off as well and felt the soreness run through his lower body. Moments later, the Nightcloaks gathered around the trees while the cavaliers removed the saddles and gear from their horses and poured water from a pot into a container for them to drink out of. "We will pitch our tents in and around this area," said Lydennan. "We will post guards and rotate every two hours. Even if we see you returning, we will ask you a pass question. The question will be 'What is moonlight?' The response will be 'The reflection.' Please remember it. If you answer incorrectly, we will consider that you may be acting under duress and assume that enemies are present. That is all I have. Good luck," he said as he went to help the cavaliers set up camp.

Lieutenant Baethalin had the Nightcloaks gather around him. He unfolded a topographical map in front of him. "We are currently at this location," he said, pointing to the map. "We will move from here to the suspected location of the Xythuu Army. Prior intel suggested that they should be in this spot." He pointed to another area on the map. "Their location is surrounded by a group of trees on two sides. They will obviously expect us to use the trees as cover, but we are still going to use them," Baethalin said.

Urien looked at the other Nightcloaks. Some glanced at each other in confusion.

"We will only send in two teams of two to each group of trees. Urien and I will be one team on the right side of the camp. We will have four other teams moving to the camp from this location." He dragged his finger along the map. "The lack of moonlight tonight should help conceal our movement, but they will most likely be doing patrols. Move low and move slow. Attacking is authorized if you must. The outside teams will wait once they get one hundred feet away from the camp. We are primarily here to assess their numbers and equipment, but I wouldn't mind trying to sabotage. When you hear an explosion inside the camp, the outside teams will move in closer to attempt more sabotages on that side. If after thirty minutes of waiting at your locations, you do not hear any explosions or other signs of our presence, proceed back to your starting positions. Once done, we will all reconvene at this point." He tapped the map. "Any questions?" None of them asked anything. "Okay. Let's get a move on." They all rose.

Urien and his team moved over low ridges and shrubs for ten minutes before they arrived at their destination. There was shrubbery all around them, with some holes and dips in the ground that would conceal them. They came to a group of bushes with a small hole that dipped into the rock and grass around it.

"This will be our recon spot. From here, we will split into our groups. We will still use the same security question that Lydennan gave us," Lieutenant Baethalin said. He began to assign the other Nightcloaks their positions. Urien, Lieutenant Baethalin, and two other Nightcloaks moved eastward while the other teams moved to their locations. It was dark, and Urien was glad there was no moonlight. They moved low and slow, using their cloaks to keep them covered. The other two Nightcloaks branched away fifteen feet from them to take up their positions for executing the plan.

They moved over the grassy plains and low ridges for ten minutes and then stopped. Urien could see the lights of torches and silhouettes of tents about two hundred feet away. The enemy had small fences scattered at certain points around the camp. Baethalin made a birdcall to signal the other team to stop. Baethalin removed a scope from his side and extended it.

"Well, there certainly are many of them standing watch," he said in a gruff whisper. "However, I cannot see anything past the first tents." He seemed to ponder for a moment. "We should get closer. We need to see the size of their army."

Urien hesitated briefly and then spoke what was on his mind. "Sir, with all due respect," he said in a whisper, "I believe we should turn back now. We know how far away they are, and judging from the number of torches, we have a rough estimate of the size of their army."

Baethalin turned his head toward him. "You are very astute, but we need to get closer and see what they have. The forest appears unguarded, but be wary," he said almost disdainfully. He made a different bird-call that signaled the other team to keep moving. Urien trailed after Baethalin, feeling slight anger bubble inside him. He felt this was a foolish ordeal, but he also knew this was a Nightcloak's job—to sneak into enemy strongholds and camps. He just hoped he could trust Baethalin's judgment.

They crept closer to the tree line, now about fifty feet away from the fence of the camp. There was just a small gap between the end of the tree line and the outside of the fence. About twenty feet to their left was a Xythuu guard pacing slowly beside the fence as he watched the area around him.

Urien and Baethalin crept along farther. The soldier patrolling the fence stopped and looked in their direction. Urien and Baethalin lay flat on the ground. The soldier held his gaze over the area for some time, which to Urien felt like an eternity. Urien could feel the man's stare, and sweat began to run down his spine. The soldier, after some time, turned to the left and made his way back to the other end of the fence. Urien and Baethalin remained on the ground, then began to crawl carefully. They made some more progress and paused briefly, waiting to see if anyone had noticed their movement.

They were still approximately thirty feet from the fence. On the ground, Urien felt that it might be a mile away. He and Baethalin moved in a slow crawl once more, covering eight more feet. The Xythuu soldier turned once again but this time took a step toward the trees, lighting the darkness with the torch in his hand. Baethalin and Urien lay still in the grass, looking at the man who gazed in their general direction. He took another step toward the trees and then proceeded back to the fence and paced a bit.

Urien and Baethalin moved forward, now close to fifteen feet away. They moved slightly to the right so they could stay out of the light cast by the torch he carried.

Urien could see out of the edge of the trees and also felt the effort of the crawling in his sore body. The man walked alongside the fence and moved in their direction. His torch went out as he stopped just over ten feet away from them. Urien held his breath as his heart pounded wildly within his chest. The soldier fumbled with getting more fluid from his satchel.

Baethalin slowly crawled closer to the soldier. Sweat dripped down Urien's arm. He was trained to remain calm in these situations, but he could still feel the anxiety welling within him. This was his first mission, after all. He could be killed. He found it ironic. In Jylinae and Port Ivory, he had not felt like this. Maybe he felt different due to trying to stay hidden.

Lieutenant Baethalin now leaped up and tackled the soldier, then thrust the knife into his leather-covered neck before he had a chance to yell out. Blood spurted from his wound over Baethalin's face, and the man made a gurgle and stopped moving.

They moved into a low crouch and returned to the tree line. Urien could smell the trees and grass around him. The light was dimmer in the trees, concealing their movements better, though they would still have to move with caution. Baethalin took a step forward, carefully placing his feet. Urien followed, moving through the trees parallel with the fence, which were close together, creating narrow passageways. They moved a few feet and stopped.

Approximately fifteen feet in front of them, outside of the enemy's fence, stood an enemy archer carrying a long bow. Baethalin looked up and around, and Urien followed his gaze, seeing nothing at first. He then spotted another archer to the left, about four feet away from the first. Baethalin equipped a knife in each hand and hooked them into the trunk of a tree, then used them to slowly climb upward. Urien followed suit using his knives and pulled himself up. From here, he could see most of the surrounding area below.

The glow of torches could be seen some distance away, closer to the heart of the enemy's camp, but he could not make out any other details. Urien followed Baethalin, who had begun moving from the branches of one tree to another. Urien grabbed hold of the branches and swung himself over to the next tree. He caught up to Baethalin and stopped. A bird landed in front of Urien, rustling some leaves to the ground.

One of the Xythuu archers readied an arrow.

"Relax," Urien heard the other one say. "It was most likely a bird."

Urien moved no part of his body and took in shallow breaths. The bird jumped nimbly from branch to branch, pecking at the tree. The bird proceeded to do this for a few more seconds and then flew away. Baethalin waited for a couple of moments and then inched forward. Urien followed shortly, but Baethalin instructed him to stop and pointed ahead. Urien looked to what he was pointing at and noticed the camouflaged outline of a person's hunched body in the treetops. It worked well to make the person blend in with the tree, but Baethalin's experience had helped him see through the tactic.

Urien hoped Baethalin was coming up with some strategy to avoid the area. Urien then heard an arrow whiz past him, just over his head, toward where he had been earlier. The archers on the ground responded to the sound and snatched arrows from their quivers.

"Are there bugs on the ground?" one of them asked. Urien guessed that was a code phrase, but he figured the hidden enemy would not want to reveal their location unless need be.

Another arrow whizzed over Urien's head. Baethalin removed his bow from his side and extended it. He nocked an arrow and released it at the enemy in the treetops. It hit his hand, and his bow dropped to the ground. The bow landed with a loud thud, crunching sticks under it. The archers launched arrows at their location. One whizzed just a few inches past Urien's shoulder, and the other landed in the tree.

Baethalin whispered, "Take care of them; leave the other one to me." He jumped to the branches of the next tree. Two more arrows were launched into the tree Baethalin had just jumped into. Urien heard the impact of a knife being thrown into wood. The archers moved to the side, launching their arrows in the direction that Baethalin had just gone. It was a good thing that the enemy archers were too proud to call the alarm.

Urien slowly slipped down the tree and landed on the ground. He moved toward the archers, who now had their backs turned to him. They wore black Xythuu robes with leather-and-metal armor pieces over them.

The flag of Xythuu was stamped on the shoulders. He knew he might have to get closer.

Urien crept forward and was just a few feet behind his targets. He silently unsheathed one of his knives. He jumped and thrust his knife into the side of one of the archers' necks. The archer fell to the ground with blood spurting from his neck. Urien removed his knife and lunged to the surprised other archer.

"We're under att—" he tried to yell, but Urien had already landed his knife in the man's throat, so the volume of his yell was hardly audible. Blood poured from his throat, down his body, and onto Urien's hand. Urien hastily removed the knife and jammed it in his chest and slammed him into the ground, soaking the ground around him. He resheathed his knife and then leaped to the area where Baethalin had gone, hoping he was still alive.

Moments later, he spotted Baethalin twenty feet away as he got thrown to the ground. The enemy from the treetops moved in closer. Urien extracted his bow and released an arrow at his target. It missed just over his shoulder, and the enemy threw a knife at him and charged. The knife passed by just three inches from Urien's face.

Urien launched another arrow, hitting his target in the chest, but the man just threw another knife and kept charging. The second knife grazed Urien's leather armor on his shoulder.

The enemy closed the distance and crashed into Urien, knocking him and his bow to the ground. The man began to thrust a knife downward. Urien caught the hilt of the blade in his hands and could feel the strength and downward force that his enemy was using. His hand ached intensely with the effort. Urien managed to roll his attacker off of him and kick his head. He lunged with his own knife in hand, but his attacker rolled to the side.

They both rose to their feet, and the enemy threw a knife at Urien, which cut across his cheek. The man charged at him again with a knife in hand and unleashed a flurry of stabs, punches, and kicks. Urien blocked the punches and kicks and dodged thrust after thrust of the knife. Their knives crossed blades as they dodged and blocked each other's attacks.

Urien kicked his opponent's knee, throwing him off balance, and then lunged for his neck. The enemy rapidly regained his balance and caught Urien's arm and threw him to the ground while wrenching Urien's right arm. The attacker brought his knee rapidly and forcefully to Urien's elbow, which shot pain through his arm and caused him to drop his knife into the dirt and leaves around him.

The enemy tried to bring his knife into Urien's neck. Urien caught his opponent's hand as the tip of the knife just touched the flesh of his neck through the leather armor that wrapped around his throat. He felt a trickle of blood on his neck as the knife was close to going in. The pressure on his arm and the force of his opponent's grip were almost too much. At that moment, a knife landed in the cheek of the attacker. Urien saw Baethalin charging forward.

Urien broke free of the enemy's grasp and threw him toward Baethalin, who lunged onto the man, jamming another knife into his neck and slamming his skull forcefully into the ground. Blood gushed out of his neck and onto Baethalin. Baethalin removed the knife and looked at Urien.

"Don't you go dying on me. You just started," he said gruffly with heavy breaths.

"Thank you, sir," Urien said, panting heavily.

Baethalin gestured that they should keep moving. They crept low in the grass-and-leaf-covered ground. Looking around, Urien could see no sign of more enemy resistance. Their fight had not attracted any attention. They were not far from the fence now, but they stayed hidden in the shrubbery. Urien, judging from the size of the camp, guessed that it contained at least one hundred thousand soldiers. He felt a sense of accomplishment having gotten this close to an army this size almost unnoticed.

"We need to get inside and set off a fire," Baethalin whispered to Urien.

"Sir, should we not head back?" Urien asked.

"The governor wanted us, if possible, to do anything to delay them," Baethalin said quietly. "I believe we can do the daunting task in front of us. Urien, I have led people before, and I would not risk their lives on a whim. Do not undermine my authority. This army could arrive at Fort Ydaeriin in a day or two. If we manage to do this, we can delay them. Even though Fort Ydaeriin is well fortified, we need to add extra defenses against an army of this size. Not all of our extra defenses are ready." Baethalin's tone was serious and authoritative.

"I apologize for my attitude," Urien said.

Baethalin smirked, lightening up a bit. "You remind me of myself when I was just starting out." Baethalin turned to scan the camp in front of them. "We do not need to get inside. If we can just light the fence, it may just spread over the camp," he whispered half to himself.

"But would they just put the fire out with water magic?" Urien asked.

"Even *Vandua* spells cannot put out an oil fire," Baethalin said, still smirking. Urien nodded now, understanding the logic in this choice. "This is going to be painstaking, but we have managed so far," Baethalin said. "We will need to crawl until we are about fifteen feet from the fence. The grass is tall enough to cover our movement. Then"—he jerked his chin toward two foot soldiers patrolling the area — "we will need to take them out without drawing attention. We're going to use one of the poisons we brought with us to ensure no errors occur. After that, we will need to pour oil on the fence." He pointed to four spots along the fence.

"The plan is to soak at least a few spots. Once we have the oil on the fence, we make our way back over here and launch some flaming arrows at it. After that, we will regroup with the others. We're going to wait until the flames of their oil lamps are halfway depleted. I want them to be tired so we increase our chances of not being caught during this. Then we will crawl toward them. Once the oil goes out and they change it, that's when we will launch the poisoned arrows. Get an arrow ready now. Get comfy too. We could be here a while," Baethalin said.

Urien lay under the shrubbery, watching the two soldiers outside the fence. When they had been lying in place for an hour, the oil in the soldiers' lamps had depleted to almost empty. Urien was feeling tired from just watching the two soldiers, who moved only a few feet every five minutes. He was doing his best to maintain his patience. Baethalin smirked. Urien's whole body ached.

"Not the most exciting part about being a Nightcloak," Baethalin whispered to him. Urien nodded in agreement.

"What do I do if I have to go?" Urien asked.

Baethalin snorted. "Piss your pants. Or if you don't want to do that, find a tree back there, but be careful. Make it quick too. These lamps probably have a few more minutes. If you have to shit, try to not fall in it."

Urien wondered if Baethalin had experienced that once. He slowly crawled backward until he was behind the shrubs and trees. He lifted himself off the ground, and aches ran through him. He found a tree and began to urinate on the tree. The chill of the night air got to him now that he was up and moving. His mind went to his friends back in Fort Ydaeriin and his parents. Had his mother survived the attack? Thinking of his parents brought a severe pain to his heart, so he tried to brush away the thoughts.

He finished and removed a vial of a green material from a pack he carried and rubbed it onto his hands and between his fingers.

He thought of Lancet. Urien vividly remembered how Lancet had moved him aside to save him from an arrow, dying in the process. Maybe that was why he was here now just outside a Xythuu camp. *They must face justice for the actions they committed,* he thought.

Urien crawled back to the spot where they had begun their hour-long endeavor.

"Good thing you're back," Baethalin said. "It's almost time." He motioned Urien forward, and they began to crawl into the grass in front of them. From Urien's viewpoint on the ground, the grass might as well have been a mountain. It rose high above his head and scratched his face and his hood as he and Baethalin slowly crawled through it. They covered about six feet and then slowed.

Urien and Baethalin watched the dimming shadow created from the fire of the soldiers' lamps. It waned some more, and Urien and Baethalin continued to inch through the thick grass. They were close now and stopped to avoid detection from the light cast by the lamps. The light was now close to disappearing. Urien could hear the men move for their oil. Baethalin signaled to him. They both rose rapidly into a crouch, with their bows and poisoned arrows in hand. Instantly, they let their arrows fly at their assailants, hitting each one in the neck.

The action took the men by surprise. They tried to yell for help, but their mouths started to froth. They clutched their necks, gasping for air and trying to speak but to no avail. They slumped to the ground. Urien and Baethalin walked forward in a crouch. Once they arrived at the bodies, they each took the remaining oil vials from the soldiers and proceeded to the points at the fence that they were targeting.

As Urien snuck closer to his target, he heard commotion inside the camp. He quickly and as quietly as possible poured oil along the fence. As he did so, a horn sounded from inside the camp, and he heard everyone inside hustling about. He realized this was a horn of alarm.

Suddenly, from his peripheral vision, he saw a slight movement as two arrows were launched in his direction. He evaded to the left, and the arrows hit the wooden fence just inches to the right of his face. He could not see who had shot the arrows. Two more were launched at him, both missing by just inches. The shooters were not visible, but when the arrows were launched, the arrows became visible, indicating that his adversaries were using their affinity to conceal themselves.

Urien dropped to the ground and began to pour the other vial of oil onto the same spot as the previous one. He heard a tent flap somewhere far to his right and a shout of "Intruder!" He crawled quickly through the grass. The arrows had been launched from his left. He threw a knife up in the air and rose to a crouch as more arrows whizzed past the knife. He launched another knife in the general direction of the enemies, managing to hit one of the attackers in the neck, making him visible as he hit the ground.

Urien darted back to the ground as another arrow flew from the second attacker. Urien held his bow horizontally and removed a match from his pouch. He thought for a few seconds of the catastrophe that would be caused by his actions. It was his only hope of getting away from the camp, so he proceeded to light his arrow. He swiftly nocked the arrow and tilted his bow up at a thirty-degree angle, then launched the flaming arrow into a tree. The tree started to burn, and he crawled forward some more. He lit another arrow and rose. He felt an arrow pierce his cloak, missing his body, and he released his flaming arrow. The arrow hit the attacker directly in his lower chest, and Urien heard him frantically scream as he started to burn.

Urien darted toward the tree line. He launched another arrow at the enemy, which hit his head, killing him. Urien lit another arrow, turned, and launched it at the spot where he had poured the oil. In an instant, the oil ignited and exploded into a flurry of flames. He ran through the dense foliage as the flames burned the fence. A small tinder flew off of it, igniting more. Another explosion sounded in the distance behind him. He crouched behind a tree, away from the flames, and waited for Baethalin to show up. Urien heard two more explosions on the other side of the camp and concluded that the other team had done their part. Within a minute, he heard footsteps moving rapidly toward him.

He quickly called out, "What is moonlight?"

"The reflection," he heard Baethalin state. Urien moved out from the tree and joined Baethalin, and they continued forward.

As they wove through the trees, he heard the thundering of feet hitting the ground behind them in the distance. They took cover behind a tree, and Baethalin began to light an arrow.

"What are you doing?" Urien asked incredulously.

"Holding them off," Baethalin said as he shot a flaming arrow at a tree. "Get out of here!" he commanded as the tree began to burn, and he moved to take shelter behind another tree. Arrows and javelins whizzed past them. Urien lit an arrow and poked his head out from behind the tree. He saw a large force of about thirty soldiers.

He launched the arrow back the way he had come. It hit a soldier, who started to burn. His anguished screams pierced the night. Smoke and flames were filling the area. Baethalin launched another flaming arrow at the ground, igniting the leaves settled in the dirt. More arrows and javelins whizzed past both of them. A blast of light magic flew by Urien, destroying a chunk of the tree he was hiding behind. He launched another flaming arrow at the ground near an archer.

A flaming arrow landed somewhere between the trees Urien and Baethalin were using for cover. Fire started to blaze dangerously close to them.

"Get out of here! Now! That's an order!" Baethalin yelled as an arrow and a blast of light magic barely missed him. He turned and launched an arrow into an archer and took two arrows to the left shoulder.

Urien bolted from the tree and heard arrows whizzing behind him. He kept running for two minutes and made his way out of the trees. He could see the other Nightcloaks heading toward him, hands on their weapons.

"The reflection," Urien stated loudly before they could even ask the question. They lowered their hands as he caught up to them.

"Where is the lieutenant?" one of them asked.

"He stayed behind to hold off the enemies and ordered me to continue onward," Urien said somberly. They made their way back to their camp and slowed to a trot. The guards and the sleeping cavaliers were alerted to the noise.

"The reflection," one of the Nightcloaks stated as they proceeded closer. Lieutenant Lydennan emerged from his tent in his leather suit, half-asleep.

"Nightcloaks never make this much noise," he mused. "Where is Baethalin?"

"He stayed behind," Urien said solemnly.

Lydennan let out a heavy sigh. "All right, I want this camp ready to go in five minutes!" he ordered. He walked over to Urien. "He wouldn't have wanted you to get killed or captured on your first mission."

Urien just stared at the lieutenant, his chest tight. He felt shame, guilt, and anger tearing through his mind. Lydennan put his hand on Urien's shoulder.

"This is how war goes, Urien. War doesn't care who dies and lives or who gets captured and imprisoned." He swiftly turned back to his tent. Within five minutes, as Lydennan had ordered, the tents were packed, and everyone was in gear and ready to go. Urien climbed on his horse behind a cavalier, the events of the night whirling through his mind as they galloped toward Fort Ydaeriin.

Chapter 13

After two hours of hard riding, Urien, the other eight Nightcloaks, nine cavaliers, and Lydennan arrived back at Fort Ydaeriin and were proceeding through the smaller forts along the entranceway to the city. Once past the last entrance, after their horses had been delivered to the stables, Urien followed Lieutenant Lydennan, who took every step forward with a fierce determination. An early-morning sunrise filled the sky as they hurried up and down crisscrossing streets until they reached the governor's manor in the central part of the city. At the front gate, an Ascalon and a Bowman stood watch.

"We are here to see the governor on information relating to a classified mission that we have returned from," Lydennan said to the guards. They opened the gate, and Urien followed Lydennan through. Due to the mission, neither Baethalin nor Lydennan had worn the armor attachments that marked them as officers of the Eltheneaen military. Urien felt odd passing through an entrance and not seeing Lydennan get saluted.

Just inside the gate were many ornate gardens and statues. Urien thought they were very decorative but also somewhat unexpectedly flamboyant of the governor. They arrived at a secondary gate, which stood fifteen feet from the door of the tall, elegant manor.

"We need to speak with the governor about critical information," Lydennan informed a guard.

The gate opened, and they proceeded to the main door, where more Ascalons and Bowmen stood guard. "I need to speak with the governor. Would you be able to wake him?" Lydennan asked. One of the Ascalons fidgeted and passed an uneasy look to the others. The Ascalon on the right gave her an approving nod.

"Wait here, sir," she said as she turned toward the door. Urien stood there observing the intricacies. Flowers adorned the edge of the fence, which Urien gazed at for a while. They made him think of his mother. She had always liked to sort flowers. He could feel his throat start to swell and his eyes water. He thought of something else to keep his mind away from painful thoughts.

He thought instead of surviving the hostility. He thought about one day falling in love and having children and being a family, with his friends as part of that family. That made him think of Maria. His heart pained to think about her. There was an affection that had developed between them during their apprentice days. He dismissed the thought of her from his mind and instead thought of all the mornings, evenings, and nights he had spent with his friends on the walls of Jylinae or within its many fine dining halls. He decided those memories would give him the strength to carry on.

The Ascalon returned and told them to follow her inside. They passed through the doorway and stood in a large room with halls to the sides and a tall winding staircase draped with crimson liners.

"The governor will be right with you," the Ascalon said. Lydennan thanked her, and she resumed her post outside.

The inside of the manor was even more elaborate than the outside. Urien figured that it must have changed through the years from governor to governor. Governor Vanerin then appeared at the top of the stairs in brown silk nightclothes. He was rubbing the sleep out of his eyes.

"Lieutenant, I trust you have the information we need?" he asked groggily, taking slow steps down the stairs. He stopped rubbing his eyes and looked around with a disturbed expression. "Where is Lieutenant Baethalin?" he asked somberly.

Urien took a step forward and raised his eyes to meet the governor's. "Sir, Lieutenant Baethalin did not come back with us. He and I were proceeding to a fence of the enemy camp, where we started our mission. We killed a few enemies. The rest of the camp was then alerted to our presence. We then began an escape away from the enemy camp but became pinned down by magic, arrows, and javelins. There was also fire spreading on the enemy's side of the trees as well as where Lieutenant Baethalin and I were pinned down. He ordered me to escape," Urien said gravely.

"Well, that is grim news indeed," Governor Vanerin said. "I do not blame you, Urien. You did your duty to your commander, and he did his duties. I pray he is well," he said.

"We did, however, get the information we need," Urien stated. "They are approximately fifty miles away. They could be here within the next two days—three or four if they take the time to repair the damage from tonight."

The governor looked at each of the men, nodding. "I thank each of you for your dedication and effort. It does not go unnoticed, and neither will Lieutenant Baethalin's valiant efforts. We will prepare more defenses tomorrow. Now, go get much-needed sleep," he said. He made his way upstairs, and Urien and the others exited the building. They proceeded through the gates and back to the central building where their rooms were located. Urien could still feel the weight in his heart, sitting there as if it were lead.

* * *

The next morning Alexander was awoken by a knock on the door. Dysan rose to answer it. Alexander could just barely see Lydennan standing there in brown robes.

"Your fort commander would like to speak with all of you in an hour. How are you all?" Lydennan asked.

Dysan shrugged. "We are fine, sir."

"Be at the second fort in an hour," Lydennan instructed. After that, he went about his way, and Dysan closed the door. Alexander had risen out of his bed and proceeded to dress in a purple robe. He then threw on his father's cloak. After getting his pants and boots on, he made his way to the counter at the end of the room and grabbed a bagel and began eating. Dysan had walked over to his closet and dressed in a leather suit and draped himself in a fur cloak.

"Cadfan, wake up," Dysan said.

Cadfan rolled over groggily. "I need some coffee," he groaned. Alexander started the coffeepot, and as the scent of freshly brewed coffee wafted through the room, Cadfan rose from his bed, made his way to the counter, and made himself a cup of coffee with milk and sugar. He raised the cup to his mouth and downed the still-hot contents. He gave a satisfied smile and walked over to the closet. After a few minutes of rummaging through his clothes, he dressed in a black robe and leather cloak.

"What about Urien? He is back now, right?" Dysan asked. Alexander had heard Urien slip into the room early this morning, but Dysan must not have even noticed that Urien's bed was filled.

Urien slowly rolled to a sitting position. "Yes, I'm back," he said groggily.

"How was the mission?" Cadfan asked.

"That's classified," Urien stated dryly.

"We have to be at the second moat fort in less than an hour," Alexander informed him, in case he had not overheard the exchange at the door. Urien dressed quickly in brown robes and draped himself with his Nightcloak robe.

"Welcome back," Dysan said, slapping Urien on the shoulder. They exited the room and met the girls in the hallway outside. Each of them was wearing pants, a cotton robe, and a leather cloak with fur sewn on the outside.

"Welcome back, Urien," they all said excitedly. Tesni in particular looked ecstatic, Alexander thought.

"How was your first Nightcloak experience?" Delyth asked.

"I can't talk about it," he said apologetically.

"That doesn't matter," Aeronwen said. "The important thing is that you have come back safely."

"Let's go get this over with." Cadfan darted down the hall, his friends following.

They scurried down the stairs and then out the wooden door on the first floor of their building. A gust of cold wind blew through the air. There was even a light snow falling. Alexander looked around. Everyone was busy preparing for the advancement of the Xythuu Army.

He and his friends hurried down the first street, where they could see many buildings having blessings applied to them. People were moving their goods into storage containers by their houses and locking them inside. Horses leading a carriage galloped past them.

"It looks like everybody is preparing for this," Aeronwen observed.

"They're not going to get into this city," Dysan said fiercely. "You can count on that."

The hustle of the city brought Jylinae to Alexander's mind. He could remember Jylinae with the same exciting crowd. But his childhood home was gone now, either destroyed or occupied by the Xythuu Army. He would not let them take this city too, even if it meant he would die.

They arrived at the gate to the city and made their way out. Tents had been constructed around every moat fort and on the strips of land between the moats. There were also trenches dug around the forts and between the moats, each being fortified with wood or stone walls and cannons. The fortifications and tents surrounded every inch of the moats and land around Fort Ydaeriin.

Alexander and his friends passed through two moat forts and continued on to the next, which was where they would be fighting. There were numerous others behind them, making their way to the same location. At the fort, a group of people was already gathered in front of them. Captain Thaenin stood at the top of the fort, waiting for them.

"Gather around, everyone," he yelled. "Can everyone hear me?" The group responded collectively with loud yells. Alexander looked up at the man who would be in charge of the whole area over the next few days. "As we all know, the Xythuu Army is on its way for this very city," Captain Thaenin said as he moved slowly across the platform. "We know this thanks to the intel provided by a brave group of soldiers."

Cadfan nudged Urien in the arm with a proud look on his face.

"This means that each of you has been assigned to me and this area. To start, we will go over the plans. Starting tonight, every one of you will be sleeping in these tents. Until the army has been driven back, this is where you will sleep. My assistants"—he pointed at a small group of people below—"will be giving out paper slips. This slip of paper will tell you where you will be placed during the battle. It also states your tent grouping and your manning time. We will have at least half of you here on watch at any given time over the next few days. My assistants will explain that more in depth. Lastly, I would like to thank all of you for that which you are about to endure. It may get gruesome, but we will defend this city from Xythuu. We will not bow down to them or their king. I thank you all for making the commitment to do that. That is all I have," he said, and the crowd surged to the four assistants on the ground.

Alexander and his friends moved forward with the crowd as they drew closer to the assistants. There were at least fifty people in front of them as the assistants began to explain that everyone would be doing watch duty. They also explained that the tents would be labeled for males or females. They then separated the groups into four lines by last name in alphabetical order. Each assistant held a piece of parchment with the letters marked on them. Alexander's group split off into the appropriate lines, and Alexander quickly arrived at the front of his line. The assistant held a book and parchment in her hand and asked for Alexander's name. She gave him a piece of parchment. Alexander joined a few of his friends who had already finished as well.

Alexander looked at his piece of parchment. "Well, I'm on the morning watch from six a.m. to noon and assigned to tent one hundred," he said.

"Isn't that fortunate," Cadfan said. "Same thing."

"I've got the same ones too," Urien stated.

Aeronwen and Tesni now joined them.

"What did you guys get?" Tesni asked.

"We all got the morning guard shift," Cadfan stated.

"So did we," Tesni said.

A few minutes later, Dysan, Camilla, and Delyth joined them.

"What shifts and tents did you get?" Aeronwen asked.

"Tent two hundred and the morning shift from six a.m. to noon," Delyth stated.

"I got that too," Camilla said.

"That's where we're staying too," Tesni stated excitedly while gesturing to Aeronwen.

"Dysan, where are you at?" Cadfan asked. "You better not ruin it!"

"Tent one hundred and morning guard shift," Dysan answered proudly.

If Alexander had to guess, Captain Thaenin had kept them together on purpose. He was not sure of the motivation behind that decision, but he was grateful to have his friends by his side. They had always had each other's backs.

The assistants told everyone to gather around. They each gave brief speeches on who they were and what to expect. They were told to have a change of clothes in their tents ready by the end of the day. The first night shift was to take place that night. They were also told to find their spots for the battle, which were located on their parchment.

Alexander and his friends then went to find their tents. They walked through the maze of white leather tents draped with fur and eventually found theirs.

Alexander and the other boys walked into their shared tent. It was warm inside, warmer than Alexander had expected. Inside were rows and rows of cots, possibly enough for fifty people. There was fire in the middle of the tent with small holes in the top cut for the smoke to pass through.

"Well, this is cozy," Cadfan said. The others agreed and stepped back outside. More snow was beginning to fall, and the smell of food, metal, and snow filled the air as the girls joined them. They all returned to their rooms in the city to collect their things.

* * *

Later that evening, Alexander and his friends had gathered their belongings and were settled within the tents. They were now in the food tent, gathered at a table and enjoying some deer stew.

"Well, this will be the story of the ages," Cadfan said. He then changed his voice to mimic one of an elderly man. "Kids, I was at Fort Ydaeriin fifty years ago holding back the Xythuu Army. They were some tough old bastards, but your grandpappy was a tougher one. I fought off every one of them, and then they left crying."

The group burst into hysterical laughter.

After the laughter had stopped, Aeronwen spoke. "Your humor makes all of this more bearable."

They all fell silent. With the exception of Urien, they were all still apprentices and had already experienced the harshness of battle. It was almost unheard of in Eltheneae for apprentices to have experienced that. Many did not even experience full battles right after graduation, yet this would be their third one in less than a year's time. Alexander realized they all could die within the next few days, and he tried to suppress the painful sadness that came with that thought.

They sat there for a few moments, hands bound together in silence. Alexander thought if he were to die in battle within the next few days, he was glad to spend this time with his friends.

* * *

The next morning, Alexander and his friends had completed a long first watch in the cold morning air. After they were done, they all met at their battle location. Alexander looked around. Four towers stood above each fort: two in the middle that rose high and two on the sides that were shorter. They had been assigned to the top of the right lower tower and were part of an artillery support team with sixty other people, and each of them was going to learn how to properly use artillery.

Their instructor told them to take hold of the cannon stem. Alexander and Urien were on these. He then told them to lean into the stem and embrace the impact. He had all the cannons aimed at a wooden target fifty feet away and instructed them to fire. Alexander pressed the buttons on the side of the cannon's handle and watched as a flaming projectile fired at the box. His shots came within a foot of the target and burned the ground around it. They were trained until six that evening, and by the end of it, each of them had a basic understanding of how to use the cannons. They were taught how to accurately aim, fire, and reload as well as about the types of ammunition and the kind they would be using in the battle.

* * *

The next two nights passed by more quickly than any of them could have imagined. It was shortly after sunrise on their third morning shift, and Alexander and Urien were overlooking the plains.

"How hard was your Nightcloak training?" Alexander asked as they patrolled the walls.

Urien was about to respond when a horn sounded, and voices shouted that enemies had been spotted. Multiple horns blasted now, and everyone rushed to their predetermined stations. Alexander and Urien sprinted to the top of the lower tower and were met by their friends. They were each already in their armor that Lydennan had given to them as gifts, for they had been wearing them during their watches. Each also had a white robe with an Eltheneaen flag on it, which had been given to them during their first night watch.

Alexander, his friends, and many other soldiers gathered to the right side of the wall, looking out over the right side of the battlefield. Urien, Dysan, Delyth, and Cadfan proceeded to the four cannons while Alexander, Camilla, Tesni, and Aeronwen moved next to them. Other cannons and ballistae in the area were also occupied with soldiers and magic users and Bowmen.

Alexander peered out past the moats and saw line after line of soldiers, siege weapons, cavalry, and the infamous Xythuu drills lined up in formation. Alexander gasped at the sheer mass of their army.

"There must be thousands of them," Dysan stated flatly.

"There are thousands of us too," Alexander said.

The Xythuu Army had sent out a group on horseback, who attached a message to a hawk and sent it toward the Fort Ydaeriin formations. Someone intercepted the hawk in the middle of the first fort and gave it to Marshal Holstead, whom Alexander could see at the top of the first fort. He read the message briefly and then returned the message to the hawk and sent it on its way. The hawk landed on the arm of one of the Xythuu men. He read the reply and then turned his horse around, not appearing particularly pleased.

"They wanted us to surrender," Urien stated. Alexander had assumed that as well.

"Like hell we will," Cadfan said fiercely. "Over my cold, dead body."

Alexander turned to the left and looked at the middle tower of their fort. Captain Thaenin stood there, seemingly undaunted by the army in front of him. Someone shouted "Ready!" and every Illustratum at every fort, trench, and wall threw up dozens of shields. Alexander, Tesni, and Aeronwen joined in, and multiple rectangular magic shields were now in place.

Alexander watched the center of the field as the Xythuu Army generated their own shields over their units and drills. The drills then charged forward at full speed, as Alexander had seen before, and Illustratum inside the drills generated shields as they moved. The drills began to fire from the small cannons attached to them while both armies launched a flurry of ballistae bolts, artillery blasts, long-range magic, and jars filled with blocking powder.

Balls of fire and lightning bolts rained down upon Fort Ydaeriin's shields. The thundering noise of the bombardment filled Alexander's ears. Alexander watched as the drills avoided attack after attack.

The shields above him began to dissipate as more magic rained down. He and the others could hardly generate shields fast enough to defend against the steady bombardment. He turned to the right side of the battlefield, where he could see the Xythuu drills charging forward and attacking the other forts in the same manner.

Some of the shields over the trenches were entirely destroyed, and the entrenched Eltheneaen Army was hit by various long-ranged attacks. Chunks of stone, people, and fortifications flew in multiple directions. He then saw a wave of Fort Ydaeriin cavalry rush forward, with Illustratum on the cavaliers' horses generating shields around them. Bowmen on other horses then launched a volley of arrows into the enemy lines. The Illustratum at the second fort rained down fireballs, lightning bolts, and giant blasts of water on the enemy while the surviving teams in the trenches near the first moat began to launch artillery and magic attacks.

Soon, all Alexander could see in the distance was the battlefield being lit up with magic and blasts of artillery fire. The Xythuu forces were now in range of artillery from the second moat ring. Urien, Cadfan, Dysan, and Delyth turned their cannons and began to fire at the forces now close to the fortifications on the first ring. Chaos ensued as troops from both sides were hit by the other's attacks. Bodies were flying as the artillery fire that Alexander's friends and others unleashed hit their targets.

Some of the enemy's smaller drills collapsed into sinkholes. To finish the job, fire magic was launched at them, bursting them into pieces. Enemy troop transport drills then broke through the ground, with shields quickly being generated around them as Xythuu troops poured out. They gathered into formations rapidly, then charged multiple Fort Ydaeriin fortifications.

An order to cease fire was given so as to not hit Eltheneaens with friendly fire, so Alexander's friends stopped their attacks. A group of Fort Ydaeriin cavaliers dashed from an area behind the first moat ring toward the advancing Xythuu forces.

Alexander and his friends now watched intently because they knew Lieutenant Lydennan was among the cavaliers. The group crashed into the Xythuu forces, leaving bodies behind them as they surged through the whole group, turned around, and charged again. Some of the cavalry members dropped to the ground as fighting broke out. The rest of the group was hit by blasts of purplish-black magic.

"No, they can't be doing that!" Aeronwen screamed out as some of the cavalry members began to grab their heads and scream in agony. Alexander's stomach sank as the group began to fight among each other.

"They're using dark magic to take control of them!" Aeronwen stated loudly.

"Unfortunately there was never any treaty not allowing it. I hate curses too," Alexander said.

He and his friends watched as Vivicanterns and Oracles began to try to remove the curses from the soldiers from a distance. They had to remove the magic one person at a time; some of them succeeded quickly while others either struggled to remove it fast enough or failed entirely. Eltheneaens clashed with and killed each other. *Faer Ruunae* spells rained down on the front of the Eltheneaen Army, destroying most of the soldiers in the area.

The Eltheneaens formed up once more and moved, continuing to generate three-layer magic shields in front of and on top of themselves. Urien, Dysan, Cadfan, and Delyth began firing artillery blasts at the advancing Xythuu soldiers. Other cannons opened fire as the swarm of Xythuu soldiers moved closer to the first moat ring. From the corner of his eye, Alexander saw boulders being hurled through the air from both sides, and another group of enemies charged for the fort.

A boulder crashed nearby below them, hitting a window and shattering it. It pierced the surrounding area with a loud thunderous sound.

The Xythuu forces formed more shields, returned to their formation, and pushed to the edge of the first moat, one hundred feet away. The teams near the moat now began to unleash a savage assault on the advancing forces. A barrage of jars were launched on the Eltheneaen troops, some reaching even as far as the second moat fort. Two shattered on the tower just a few feet below Alexander and Tesni. They held their breath as the pink dust dispersed.

Alexander launched a *Faer* spell from his hand successfully. Urien, Dysan, Cadfan, and Delyth launched more artillery blasts from their cannons at the Xythuu forces. Alexander launched a *Fulmenooo Xel* from a Lapideas. It collided with a shield.

A *Faer Xaen* hurled toward them, but Aeronwen blocked it with a shield. An exchange of spells was launched back and forth.

A glowing assault of spells was also fired from the main tower of the second fort, the left tower, and the many trenches on the ground. Alexander, Tesni, and Aeronwen generated a total of six shields around them. Spells bombarded the shields. Camilla, and other Bowmen, readied an arrow with a small oil container on it and fired it at the ground near the Xythuu forces. The arrows burst into flames in front of their shields.

While the enemy troops were trying to douse the flames, remove water from the moats, and protect their army, Alexander launched another *Fulmenooo Xel* at the enemy units. It collided with a shield and broke through it. A barrage of jars crashed violently into the unprotected group.

Alexander blasted lightning through a unit, knocking several off their feet. Camilla and others launched a deadly barrage of arrows, which hit many Xythuu soldiers in the enormous formation. A *Faer Xaen* was launched at Alexander's tower. Alexander, his friends, and the other soldiers on the tower took cover. It destroyed a chunk of the tower, and pieces of rock flew overhead.

Alexander looked at his Lapideas, which had now turned gray. The Essence within it had been depleted, and he tossed it to the ground. He reached into his satchel and grabbed another Lapideas. He launched a medium-sized ball of fire at the Xythuu forces. It collided into the front troops and burst everything in the surrounding area into flames. Two arrows whizzed over his head as he ducked back below the stone of the tower.

A boulder crashed into the tower, spraying the area with a splash of debris that hit many of the soldiers on the tower. A small chunk of debris cut across Dysan's arm. He kept firing while blood poured down his arm. Aeronwen, who stood five feet to the left of Dysan, moved closer, held a Lapideas to his arm, and began to heal the wound while more spells and arrows collided into the shields of both armies.

The Xythuu forces had now breached farther along the bridge of the first moat. Moments later, two *Faer Xaen* crashed into the area near Alexander, destroying one of the cannons and knocking Cadfan, Alexander, and Urien to the stone of the tower under their feet. Alexander's head hurt, and he coughed as he slowly rolled to his knees. Dysan and Delyth stayed on their cannons and returned fire at the Xythuu Army. Camilla looked at Alexander, her brow knit with worry. She turned, drew an arrow, and launched it, hitting a distracted Xythuu magic user in the head.

Tesni slid next to Urien and generated a shield on each side of them as well as three above her, Cadfan, and Urien. Aeronwen moved next to Alexander. She yelled for another healer and then held her Lapideas to Alexander. Another healer came running and began to check if Cadfan was injured. *Faer Ruunae* and *Vintae Ruunae* spells rained down, heavily barraging the shields with falling fire and vertical, forceful gusts of wind. Alexander generated more shields under Aeronwen's, relieved he could still use magic.

Urien pushed himself up from the ground, against Tesni's pleas for him to stay down because she was not finished healing him and took hold of one of the cannons that remained and began to fire at the Xythuu forces. The fire from his, Dysan's, and Delyth's cannons fiercely collided into the army, destroying some of the advancing forces. Aeronwen then instructed Alexander to get up. Cadfan had already gotten up. Alexander pushed himself up to his feet and stumbled over to the cannons—the pain was less severe after Aeronwen's healing, but she had not eliminated it entirely.

Once at the wall of the tower, he saw multiple troop transport drills push over the bridge of the first moat ring, and hundreds of Xythuu soldiers poured out, with magic shields deployed in front of their armies.

Eltheneaen troops on the middle tower of the second fort grabbed their heads and faces as a purplish-black material was shot upward from the ground and rained down on the area. *More dark magic,* Alexander thought with dread. In an instant, he saw two Eltheneaen soldiers on the other side of their fort tower attack and kill other Eltheneaen soldiers. A flurry of soldiers began to attack each other all over the fort tower and in trenches below.

Three infected Ascalons charged toward Alexander's group, killing the Vivicantern who had healed Cadfan. They then thrust their lances at Dysan, whom Cadfan managed to shove out of the way. Aeronwen moved behind one of the Ascalons and held out her hand and attempted to remove the dark magic from him. He stopped momentarily and held his hand to his head. Aeronwen held him in place, her hand glowing a pale white, but the Ascalon resisted and turned and slashed at her. His spear cut across her arm, and she cried out in agony. She evaded the next slashes.

Cadfan and Dysan were evading blows, clearly hesitant to attack the other two Ascalons. Tesni came up behind one and began the process of removing the curse from him while the other continued to attack Dysan and Cadfan.

Alexander tackled the Ascalon near Aeronwen and pinned him to the ground while Aeronwen continued to try to remove the curse. The soldier thrashed against him angrily and managed to throw Alexander off. The Ascalon then thrust his lance, and Alexander rolled to the side. The lance tore part of his white Eltheneaen robe and his father's cloak. He rolled to the side again and again, avoiding the lance as it stabbed into the stone beneath him. Aeronwen moved closer and continued to pull at the dark magic. The Ascalon stopped in place. Then he stepped forward and thrust his lance toward her, which cut across her shoulder and knocked her to the ground.

Urien charged the Ascalon from behind and tripped him. Meanwhile, Dysan and Cadfan were trying to not attack their opponent, and Tesni had the third Ascalon on the ground, slowly getting an advantage over the dark magic. Tesni then managed to pull the dark magic out of him, which came out as a dark-purple smoke and then disappeared as the light magic cut through it.

Urien had the other Ascalon pinned to the ground while he thrashed against him, trying to violently attack him in any way. The Ascalon even attempted to bite Urien, who barely prevented the man's teeth from clenching his neck. Tesni held up her hand and began to remove the curse from him. The purple smoke came out of him piece by piece. Tesni removed the final bits of the curse from him, and he stopped thrashing about.

Cadfan and Dysan were still caught up evading strikes from their cursed attacker. Cadfan dodged his lance and then kicked the Ascalon hard in his right knee with enough force to break it. The Ascalon pushed through the pain and still tried to attack him. At that moment, Alexander, Aeronwen, and Tesni generated more three-layer shields over their heads as *Faer Ruunae* spells rained down.

The cursed Ascalon thrust his lance toward Cadfan. Cadfan parried the heavy lance to the side, but his attacker lunged forward and put his hands around Cadfan's throat as they fell to the ground. Cadfan started to gasp for breath as the Ascalon choked him. Dysan ran to them. He dropped his axe and punched the Ascalon vehemently several times until the Ascalon had lost his grip and was thrown off of Cadfan.

Tesni and Aeronwen slid next to the Ascalon and each held out a pale, glowing hand. They quickly removed the curse. The purple smoke was pulled out of him and vanished into the air.

They were all beginning to show signs of exhaustion, particularly Alexander, Aeronwen, and Tesni. Delyth was still firing artillery blasts while Camilla launched arrows at the advancing Xythuu forces. Blasts of artillery from the Xythuu Army hit all around the fort. Alexander could hear nothing but the overpowering noise of artillery blasts as they shot past them or hit close to the ground around him, his friends, and the few remaining forces at the western part of the fort tower. One of them hit the cannon that Delyth was on. It shattered it into pieces and knocked her, Camilla, and chunks of rocks to the ground. Aeronwen tended to her. She was relatively unscathed except for some scrapes on her hands, which Aeronwen held a Lapideas to and began to heal.

Alexander rushed to Camilla. She insisted that she was fine as Alexander pulled her to her feet. The edge of the western part of the fort tower had now mostly been destroyed. The Xythuu forces were still storming the first fort. The trench forces had suffered many losses but were still fighting off the advancement of the Xythuu Army.

The Fort Ydaeriin forces had been greatly diminished. Alexander, his friends, and a small handful of soldiers were the only ones who had survived the attack so far on the western part of the tower. The eastern part had suffered some losses but not as many. Alexander looked up and to his left. Much of Captain Thaenin's force had survived. Many of the soldiers at the left fort tower were still alive. The first fort had taken many casualties, but he saw that Marshal Holstead was still alive and fighting.

The ones who had not survived, however, filled his heart with great anguish. He could see the dead around him and the blood that had been spread all over the fort tower, mixed with dirt and fresh ash. His own white robe was covered in dirt. Aeronwen and Dysan had blood on their robes.

Alexander was getting exhausted. The battle had gone on now for almost two hours. His face was starting to sting from the cold air around him. He thought of his father and mother, hoping such thoughts would give him strength to continue.

At that moment, the enemy forces around the first fort launched a barrage of magic against the second fort and the surrounding trenches. Some surviving Eltheneaen Illustratum generated shields but not enough as spells of fire, lightning, and wind impacted the fort and the ground forces. More purplish-black spells were launched into the air, hitting a handful of people. One just barely missed Alexander while another hit Urien and some others on the tower. Urien and the others began to grab their heads. Alexander's heart sank.

Black lines with purple hues ran to Urien's eyes and covered the sclera. More fighting broke out as the cursed soldiers began to attack their own. Two had charged Dysan and Delyth, forcing them to evade as best as possible. Delyth took a sword slash to her arm and stabbed her lance just barely into the other woman's leg while Dysan was avoiding being hit by a lance. Urien rose to his feet with his knives clenched tightly in both hands.

"Urien, don't!" Cadfan screamed as he charged toward Urien and tackled him to the ground. "You have to fight this!" he yelled as he tried to hold Urien down.

Tesni held up her hand, trying to remove the curse from him. Urien bashed his head against Cadfan's and threw him off. Urien rose to his feet and shoved his knife toward Cadfan with great force. Cadfan rolled to the side and sprang to his feet.

Aeronwen bolted toward Urien, but a cursed Oracle charged and swung a mace at her, which she barely dodged. He kept swinging at her, barely missing or being blocked by the small shields she generated. A cursed Ascalon had charged them and now thrust his lance at Tesni, just missing her and tearing her robe, which forced her to take a step backward.

Delyth, Dysan, and Cadfan were busy evading and not countering as their cursed allies kept up their attacks. Camilla and Alexander rushed the Oracle and Ascalon, attempting to pin them down.

The curse had taken most of Urien's skill with a knife away, but Urien managed to graze the top of Cadfan's hand, knocking his sword to the ground. He dodged two more strikes. Urien then lunged forward and brought his right hand down over Cadfan's face, next to his left eye. Cadfan fell to the ground with his hand over his bloody face.

Alexander had been knocked to the ground by the Ascalon. Alexander, feeling guilt well up inside but willing himself to live with it to save Cadfan and Urien, lifted his hand. With great effort, he launched a *Faer Xaen* at the Ascalon. It crashed into him, bursting him into flames and sending him violently into the right side of the tower wall.

Cadfan lay on the ground, gasping for air. Urien held the knife in his right hand and swung down at Cadfan. Camilla, lying on the ground, snatched up her bow and shot an arrow. It collided with the knife and knocked it out of Urien's hand.

Dysan had knocked the Oracle attacking Aeronwen to the ground. Delyth stabbed another soldier, who had multiple shallow wounds, but Delyth could hold off no longer.

Tesni darted for Urien as he began to bring another knife down. She dropped her lance and jumped toward him. She winced as she caught his hand. They both fell to the ground as she began to remove the curse.

Tears streamed down Tesni's face. She removed bits of purple smoke from him.

"I won't let this happen to you," she said, crying as she removed the last tuft of smoke from him. Urien collapsed, unconscious, into Tesni's arms. Alexander, still on the ground, looked around. Urien had survived the curse, but the others who had charged them had not. Alexander saw many dead bodies on the other side of the tower. He clenched his hand until his knuckles turned white. He was livid, both toward the Xythuu forces and toward dark magic.

More snow began to fall—only it was gray in color. Alexander then realized it was not snow but ash from the fires across the battlefield. The smell of death filled the air and made him nauseous.

Aeronwen stumbled over to Cadfan. She picked up his sword and gave it to him. She held a Lapideas to his face and began to heal his wound.

Cadfan, wincing in pain, spoke. "Promise me none of you will tell Urien what happened," he said loudly. "This will most likely leave a scar. If he asks, just say he was knocked out and an enemy hit my face with a lance. If he knew the truth, he would never forgive himself, so promise me right now that none of you will say how this happened."

They all nodded in agreement.

"We promise," Aeronwen said. She removed a rag from her satchel and wiped the blood from his face. She helped him to his feet, and Dysan lifted Urien onto his shoulder and moved him to the corner where the others were.

They watched as fierce fighting continued between the armies at the first fort. A Xythuu detachment force branched off from the side and launched another onslaught of magic, arrows, and jars at the second fort and the trenches below. Alexander and the others ducked as a spell collided with the shattered walls of the fort. Alexander heard several fire spells whiz over his head. The remaining Fort Ydaeriin cannons launched a flurry of artillery blasts at the detachment, with many colliding into the shields the enemy forces had generated, although some destroyed part of the army.

A *Faer Xaen* spell collided into the wall, sending a spray of rubble over the area. A small chunk slashed through Alexander's left arm. He cried out in pain as blood began to pour from his arm. Tesni grabbed hold of him. They ducked in a low crouch and moved quickly to the tower wall, where Urien, still unconscious, and Dysan were. Alexander collapsed into the corner of the tower, and Tesni held a Lapideas to begin closing up the wound in his arm. As she did so, more spells and arrows collided into the wall, some of them less than fifteen feet away. Seconds later, heavy ballistae bolts smashed into the fort and the trenches below. Several bodies were hit, and he grimaced as they came crashing down all around.

One of the people hit was Captain Thaenin. His chest armor was torn open and covered in blood, as was his face. Alexander looked at him with agony as a Vivicantern held up a glowing hand to heal him.

A barrage of blocking dust jars, *Faer Ruunae* spells, and *Fulmenooo Ruunae* spells bombarded the area. The Vivicantern tried to create a shield over his head, but it was too late. A jar broke over his shoulder, spreading the dust into his lungs.

Alexander and Tesni managed to create a shield in front of themselves while their friends were crouched down with their hands over their heads. Dysan threw his body over Urien's to protect him from debris. A ball of fire then crashed down into the Vivicantern, knocking his flaming body back and launching his arm toward Alexander and Tesni. It landed near them and filled his nose with the stench.

Tesni finished healing his arm and then turned her body to the side and hurled. Hopeful that the Vivicantern had finished healing Captain Thaenin before his unfortunate death, Alexander peered into the debris.

Captain Thaenin lay still, lifeless. Alexander's face stung from the cold, and the slow tears rolling from his eyes froze on his face.

At that moment, Urien woke with a startled and confused look on his face.

Dysan pulled him up. Alexander rose over the edge of the wall and saw the detachment advancing closer. They had crossed the first drained moat and were halfway to the second one. The remaining Eltheneaen cannons opened a barrage of fire, still colliding mostly into shields. The sound of drills breaking through the ground caught his attention.

Tesni and Aeronwen were healing wounded near the wall of the tower when the drills broke through the ground thirty feet below. The next instant, bronze ladders with hooks were being attached to the top left of their tower wall. The Eltheneaen cannons were still firing at the advancing detachment when spells of *Faer Xaen* and *Fulmenooo Xaen* crashed into them, destroying two of them and sending pieces flying. Soldiers on the wall began to throw oil down some of the ladders. Shields generated over the tops of the ladders. Dysan darted to one of the ladders with a can of oil in his left hand and threw oil in front of the ladder and kept moving farther down the wall.

Camilla removed an arrow and wrapped it in cloth. She struck a match to the cloth and launched it into the wall that Dysan had covered in oil. It exploded into pieces, sending flames onto the Xythuu soldiers. There were still too many protected ladders, though, and soldiers poured over the walls. An exchange of spells took place.

A *Faer* spell shot by just two feet away from Alexander's head. Another came at him, and he deflected it with his hand and launched a *Faer Xaen* from his Lapideas, which collided into a group of Xythuu soldiers. One of the aflame soldiers ran to the tower wall, but Urien flung a knife into his head before he got any closer.

Dysan began to exchange blows with an enemy swordsman. Delyth darted in his direction, cutting across a soldier's stomach. Camilla launched arrow after arrow, and they landed in the heads and chests of soldiers coming off of the ladders. Cadfan, whose face was partially swollen, dodged a strike from an enemy soldier who had a heated tip on his blade. Their swords grated across each other as they evaded and attacked. Cadfan blocked a slash that scratched across his sword. The enemy soldier moved forward in a blur and then swung down. Cadfan managed to step to the side, just barely evading the edge of the blade. He caught the man's arm and attempted to thrust his sword into the man's chest, but it landed in his thigh. They caught hold of each other's wrist and tried, with great effort, to push each other away. The Xythuu man managed to shove Cadfan backward, which removed his sword from the man's leg. He lunged forward, but Cadfan caught his sword arm. He shoved his elbow into the man's shoulder and thrust his sword into the man's neck. The man fell to the ground as Cadfan removed his sword.

A Xythuu soldier with a heavy sword was attacking soldiers on the wall. Spells were launched at him, but a group of enemy magic users had generated shields around him. Camilla fired off arrows at the magic users, but they generated more shields to their sides, which blocked her arrows.

Meanwhile, Dysan was fighting a spearman. He evaded a few strikes. One cut across his armor. He then managed to slam his axe into the man's side, which buckled him to his knees. Dysan punched the man's face with his left hand and then brought his axe down onto the man's neck. Another spearman charged him. His lance slightly cut above Dysan's eye. Small drops of blood fell over his eye as the spearman thrust his lance forward. Delyth drew near and thrust her lance into the back of the unsuspecting spearman. She then removed her lance, grabbed the man's arm, and spun the man into the ground. She turned quickly on her heels and thrust her lance into the man's chest.

Urien barely evaded the lance end of an enemy soldier. He hurled a small glass container at the soldier, which hit his helmet and burst into a reddish-orange powder. The man began to cry out in agony as his eyes reddened and teared up. He fumbled with a bottle at his side and struggled to pour water into his eyes. Urien stepped around him. He jumped on the man's back and rammed a knife toward his throat. He caught Urien's hand as the knife barely pierced his neck armor and touched the tip of his throat. He threw Urien to the ground. The soldier readied his sword and prepared to swing, but Aeronwen shot a *Linwae Xon* at him.

The ball of light magic broke into smaller pieces and pierced his body. Tesni launched another from the side, staggering him.

Urien pulled himself to his feet. He charged the soldier, and then, using the Xythuu soldier's knee as a stepping stool, Urien caught hold of the soldier's shoulder and thrust a knife through a helmet eyehole. Urien then spun off the soldier and threw the knife horizontally at an advancing soldier. It bounced off his armor. Urien darted forward and shoved his short sword into his opponent's neck.

Xythuu forces overran the fort. Alexander launched multiple *Faer Xaen*s from his Lapideas, hitting some and causing more chaos as burning soldiers sprawled over the tower walls. Dysan and Delyth managed to run through the vast group of enemies and pushed two of the ladders, with soldiers still on them, to the ground. They fell thirty feet to the ground below. Dysan hit two Xythuu soldiers in the head while Delyth slashed two across the chest with her lance.

Alexander shot more magic from his Lapideas. He and Tesni were crouched against the wall as spells and arrows repeatedly hit near them. Cadfan, still in the middle of the fort, charged at an archer firing arrows at Alexander and Tesni. He slid and thrust his sword into the archer's leg as an arrow flew over his head. He quickly removed his sword, thrust it into his opponent's stomach, and then used the archer's robe to pull him down into the sword.

Cadfan pushed the dead Xythuu body upward and slid behind it as an arrow hit the shoulder of the dead body. He took two big steps forward and then threw the body into a Xythuu archer and magic user, taking them by surprise and making them lose their balance. Cadfan darted forward and slashed diagonally through the archer's bow and neck. He then stepped to the side and turned. He caught hold of the magic user's arm and slashed it off. He pulled the magic user to the side and thrust his sword into his chest.

An order to retreat from the tower was given. Urien and Camilla moved quickly to where Alexander and Tesni were on the tower. Some Illustratum had moved in front of them and generated shields that blocked incoming magic, lances, and arrows. Aeronwen was making her way toward them while simultaneously trying to heal a wounded Eltheneaen soldier stumbling to the stairs. Cadfan, Delyth, and Dysan sprinted down the stairs.

The Fort Ydaeriin Illustratum had thinned the ranks of Xythuu soldiers on the tower, but more still remained as Alexander and the others followed a large group of soldiers down the stairs. Alexander glanced back and saw a shield get destroyed, followed by a *Fulmenooo Xaen*. The ball of lightning crashed into the last cannon. They made their way down spiraling stairs and through ten feet of a narrow hall, which led into a large open room.

Alexander looked around. All the cannons were still there, but some of their team had been killed or were terribly wounded. Aeronwen and Tesni immediately tended to the wounded. Alexander noted that many Illustratum and Vivicanterns in the area were dead. A cannon operator was then killed by a lance that had gone through the three-foot opening in the wall. Urien rushed to the cannon.

Alexander could hear no more sounds of fighting above him. He moved beside Urien's cannon. He did not have the personal energy to generate a shield, but he was still going to help Urien by using his Lapideases. Camilla stood next to him with her back against the wall and her bow aimed at the door. Another Illustratum moved beside Alexander and generated a two-layer shield over the cannon wall opening. Others moved boxes and crates against the door to barricade it, then generated two-layer shields in front of the doorway.

Banging sounds were heard at the door. Alexander turned to look. The banging stopped, and he now heard the sound of flames licking at the door. He immediately reached for a *Vandua* Lapideas and launched a ball of water at the door. It hissed as it hit right as the flames streaked up the door, filling the room with smoke and steam.

An Illustratum launched a *Vintae Xel* spell. The beam of whirling wind tore through the door and spread some of the remaining flames back onto the Xythuu forces within the narrow hall. The smoke in the room was causing everyone to cough. Alexander coughed heavily, and his eyes started to sting. He launched a *Faer Xaen* at the wall opposite the door, which created a small hole. He ran back to where Urien was as the smoke began to funnel out the hole. He could see and hear a fierce and rapid exchange of spells and arrows in the doorway and down the hall. Urien and the others on the cannons were firing heavily at the incoming Xythuu detachment.

Xythuu had shields on their front and sides blocking the artillery fire. Alexander launched a *Vandua Xaen* at the ground in front of the army. Urien destroyed a front shield and then tore many Xythuu soldiers to pieces, taking out two magic users before another two-layer shield was generated. Rapid artillery fire instantly destroyed it. Alexander then launched a *Fulmenooo Xel*, and the beam of lightning sparked and hit the soaked ground below, electrifying any near it.

The Xythuu forces in the hall breached the doorway. They destroyed the shields and one of the Illustratum who had deployed the shields.

Cadfan, Dysan, and Delyth charged forward and clashed with the forces. Camilla shot an arrow into one. Alexander launched another *Fulmenooo Xel* out the window, just in front of a shield.

Cadfan stabbed his sword into someone and barely took a step to the side as a lance moved inches in front of his face. He dodged another slash of the lance and stumbled over a sword on the ground. Dysan quickly brought his axe across the back of the assailant, killing him.

The Eltheneaen forces were dropping fast. Tesni, Aeronwen, and one other Vivicantern struggled to heal all the wounded. Urien was still launching artillery fire at the Xythuu detachment, which had become pinned down in front of the fort.

Artillery fire from Xythuu slammed into the fort, making five-foot-wide holes in the wall and destroying the cannons. Alexander and Camilla both ducked. The blast had caught an ally Illustratum and killed him.

Alexander took cover as best he could as the thick beams of cannon fire continued to assault the fort. He looked out the hole next to him and saw that the Fort Ydaeriin artillery cannons in other places had all focused fire on the bigger Xythuu cannons. A *Faer Ruunae* spell rained down over some of the enemy cannons and troops.

Alexander was appalled that Xythuu forces would fire upon a location knowing that they had their own troops in that location. The Xythuu forces inside the tower with them began to rise. Alexander launched quick blasts of *Vandua Xaen*, which knocked a few soldiers to the ground. A lance was thrown and hit the top of his hand, cutting it and causing his hand to bleed.

Camilla quickly nocked an arrow and launched it at the spearman who had thrown the lance at Alexander. It collided into his chest. She released more, hitting two soldiers. A wounded Eltheneaen Illustratum on the ground opened fire with spells, most of which hit the Xythuu forces. Alexander grabbed his Lapideas and launched a *Fulmenooo Xel* at the wet spot on the stone floor. It electrified a few Xythuu units near it.

Alexander tore a piece of his robe off. He winced in pain as he wrapped his bloody left hand. Afterward, he sat in place with his head against the wall. Most of the front wall was now destroyed, which let the cold in. He huddled in his cloak and robe, looking out the massive holes in the stone wall of the tower. The Xythuu Army had smashed through the trenches and the first fort, destroying most of the units in place. Most of the detachment that had arrived at the second fort had now been defeated.

Alexander was tired. The battle was physically and mentally draining. He had used nearly all his Essence to make shields. It would take him a full day to recover, which he did not have.

The battle had gone on now for a few hours, and it was getting colder. Alexander watched as the Xythuu Army moved closer and closer, feeling the dread flow through his body.

Numerous Eltheneaen forces charged out from the trenches with shields generated in front of and above them. Forces from both sides were hit with vicious attacks. A few minutes of heavy fighting went by, and then the Eltheneaen forces sounded a retreat and began returning to the forts and various entrenchments. As they did so, cannons opened fire at the Xythuu Army. They met a barricade of shields and then destroyed some of them faster than they could be replaced.

Alexander saw Xythuu blasts of artillery hit trenches near the fort they were in. Seconds later, ballistae and oil-soaked flaming rocks crashed through the area, one landing at the base of the fort. Another smashed through the right side of the tower, just ten feet from everyone in the room. Smoke soon engulfed the area, and an order to evacuate was given.

Alexander could feel the smoke enter his lungs, and he started to cough. He, Camilla, and Urien stuck low to the ground and began to crawl across the room. Tesni and Aeronwen had already started to crawl and were halfway to the door. Dysan, Delyth, and Cadfan quickly joined them and helped them to their feet and to the door.

They all hurried down the staircase. In the central room of the tower's first floor, another flaming rock crashed through the ceiling fifteen feet away from them, spraying the area with debris. They joined a group of soldiers escaping out the back door. They followed the escaping soldiers twenty feet behind the tower and slid into a three-feet-deep and twenty-feet-long trench.

Alexander landed in the trench heavily and then moved behind the wooden wall that was in front of most of the trench. He, his friends, and the surviving soldiers sat there for a moment, heaving. Alexander looked at the soldiers who had started the battle in the trench. Only two had been killed, with the ballistae that had done so still pinned through their bodies.

He and the others sat in the trench breathing in the thick cold air, which stung his face. Alexander leaned back into the trench and tried to take deep breaths. The overpowering smell of smoke, dust, and death filled his nose, and he grew queasy. *How much longer will this go on?* he wondered.

Camilla was sitting to his right, with Dysan and Cadfan on the other side of her. On his left side, Urien, Tesni, Aeronwen, and Delyth sat, leaning into the walls of the trench and exhibiting the same exhaustion he felt. It pained him to know that so many people had lost their friends, but he was grateful that his were still alive and breathing next to him. Someone in another trench called out that the Xythuu Army was making camp at the first fort and surrounding area. Alexander sighed heavily and began to mentally prepare himself for the night and the following day ahead.

Other soldiers began to move around and gather supplies. Large wooden boxes were pulled out of surviving storage tents, and the contents were distributed. While others handed out sleeping furs and cooking kits, Alexander climbed out of the trench. Most of the tents had been destroyed, including his own.

Urien, Cadfan, and Dysan climbed out of the trench with him and found a box of supplies. They distributed furs while other soldiers began setting up the logs and pots from the cooking kits.

A soldier with long brown hair and a neat beard spoke to all soldiers in the surrounding area. "The tents are destroyed, which means we will have to set up camp here. We will also need to develop a watch schedule." Some volunteers began to gather around.

Alexander and his friends lay their furs behind the wooden barricades of the trench. A few minutes later, the sun had started to set, and warm fires had been lit all along the trench. The smell of food wafted through the air, which relieved Alexander. A few minutes passed, and the sun had now set completely. The food had finished cooking and was passed out among all present. Alexander sat next to his friends and greatly enjoyed the warm rabbit stew that filled his stomach. Afterward, they sat in silence for some time.

Tesni held her hand out in the middle of their group. Her friends slowly, one by one, put their hands on each of the other's in the middle.

"Promise me," Tesni said solemnly, "promise you will all survive whatever happens tonight or tomorrow or for how long this may go on."

Urien wore a dismal look. "Tesni, that may be something that we cannot promise."

"Please just say it. Even if you cannot guarantee it, just say it for my sake," she said quietly.

"Tesni, then I promise I will not leave you," Urien said.

"As do I," Aeronwen said.

"I promise," Delyth added.

Cadfan nodded. "Me too."

"I promise, Tesni," Dysan said.

"You have my word," Camilla promised.

"Mine as well," Alexander said.

Tesni then smiled and dropped her hand. "Good night, everyone," she said as she made her way to her sleeping fur. Alexander crawled into his. He was warm and cozy, something he was grateful for. He then closed his eyes and drifted immediately to sleep.

Chapter 14

Alexander awoke with a violent twist as he heard shouting in the distance. Camilla had fallen asleep next to him and woke now too. He heard murmurs that an enemy team of spies had been caught and were being fought back. He lowered his head again. He was still exhausted from the battle and had been awoken three times earlier in the night for the same reason.

Camilla spoke softly over to him. "It was just a nightmare. We are all right here," she said. He managed to lay his head back down and drift to sleep.

When Alexander awoke again, the sun had just risen above the horizon, filling the frigid air with small amounts of warmth. Then the sound of stone breaking rang out, and nearby horns blasted. Alexander, his friends, and others in the area quickly rose.

Alexander and his friends gathered their weapons and followed their group to the destroyed fort. They took cover behind the loose rocks and the remains of the fort tower. Eltheneaen troops were positioned along the ruins all the way to the other side of the fort. He looked out over the field and noticed many Xythuu drills, with massive amounts of cavalry following behind. Alexander, Tesni, Aeronwen, and a few others made small shields over the cover of the stone walls.

Alexander watched some of the drills and cavalry fall into pit traps. He also saw flaming ballistae bolts hurled into the Xythuu cavalry, causing them to break formation. But they just kept moving forward.

The drills began to fire rapid blasts of energy from their cannons. Many hit the ground just in front of the stone walls they were using for cover. Alexander heard the thunk of blasts as they collided into the shields in front, weakening them and destroying some altogether.

Some blasts collided into men next to him, knocking them over and showering the area with rocks. He could see the burns on the men's bodies. He had not recovered much of his magical energy and knew he would be able to generate only a few shields.

He shot a *Fulmenooo Xel* while others launched various forms of magic. His beam of lightning collided into one of the drills. He then brought the beam downward at some rapidly advancing drills and destroyed their tracks, flipping them onto their sides. Lightning cackled around his Lapideas, and the yellow turned to gray. He tossed down the Lapideas and then quickly snatched up another. While he did so, magic bombarded the remaining drills, bursting them into flames.

He had only a few seconds to celebrate internally before he heard the ground breaking thirty feet in front of the fort. Numerous transport drills broke through the surface. Many shields were generated around them as magic and arrows bombarded the drills. Xythuu troops with shields strapped on their arms and lances extended overhead broke out in formation. Eltheneaen Bowmen and Illustratum launched an onslaught of arrows and spells.

Alexander fired off a *Fulmenooo Xaen* from his Lapideas. It collided into one of the shields, followed by a barrage of other spells. The shield in front of a group of Xythuu soldiers broke. Camilla launched an arrow at a soldier's neck, which barely pierced the armor. She released another while Tesni shot a spell of light magic, which dispersed and collided into some of the soldiers. Spells of fire and lightning, as well as lances, were unleashed in Alexander's location.

Two lances whizzed past Alexander while spells collided into the stones in front of his friends. A fire spell burst the remaining stones in front of Tesni to pieces, also knocking her to the ground. Aeronwen moved next to Tesni and inspected her. Some rocks had cut across the top of her arm. She placed a Lapideas next to it and began to heal her.

The formation of Xythuu troops kept moving forward, charging the stone formation despite numerous attacks against them. Aeronwen finished healing Tesni's shoulder and moved to assist Urien with a wounded Eltheneaen soldier. The moving formation of Xythuu soldiers began to climb over the crumbled walls, but many were impaled by lances that were extended over the stone. A Xythuu soldier tried to quickly dash toward them, but Camilla launched an arrow in his head.

Xythuu troops began to climb on top of the stones and launch spells downward at the Eltheneaen soldiers. Cadfan knocked one to his knees with his sword and then grabbed the man's arm and pulled him into his sword. The man's blood spilled down onto Cadfan's robe.

More troops poured over the wall, and Cadfan blocked a sword strike with his own sword and began to exchange blows. Dysan pushed a soldier into the stone, and Delyth shoved her lance through a soldier's eye socket.

Urien and Aeronwen, still assisting the wounded Eltheneaen soldier, grabbed hold of him and began to drag him backward. A Xythuu soldier launched a fire spell at them. It barely missed Urien's leg. Urien grabbed a throwing knife from his side and hurled it toward his enemy, who deflected it with a small magic shield. Urien threw another one, and Aeronwen launched a *Linwae Xon* after it. The soldier deflected the knife but could not react fast enough and was hit by the dispersing light magic. Tesni ran at the man and thrust her lance into his side and then slashed across his neck.

A soldier charged at Tesni and collided shoulder to shoulder. The man hit her ankle, tripping her, and then lunged his lance toward her. She caught the body of it, just below the blade. Tesni was holding the lance inches from her face with all her strength. Urien drew in close enough to hurl his knife at the soldier. It bounced off of his helmet, distracting him. Tesni pushed the lance upward and to the side. It clattered on the ground beside her. Urien charged forward and impaled the soldier with his sword.

A horn sounded, and Eltheneaen troops began to fall back, making their way toward the third moat ring.

Alexander and his friends ran at full speed. Camilla tripped over a rock, falling to the ground. Alexander turned to help her and saw numerous enemies either killing or capturing Eltheneaen soldiers. Some were pursuing them. He launched a *Faer Xaen*. It collided into them, burning their bodies. He helped Camilla to her feet, and they continued toward the wall.

More Xythuu soldiers pursued them, assaulting them with arrows and lances. Camilla turned and released two arrows in rapid succession. They met their targets and sent them to the ground. Tesni and Aeronwen launched a set of *Linwae Xon* spells at the Xythuu forces, which dispersed and collided into them. They and hordes of Eltheneaen soldiers kept retreating toward the moat. They had spent a few minutes running. They were now about fifty feet away from the moat. Alexander could see small boats being sent across the moat. They arrived at the moat in time to board a boat. Alexander's lungs were heaving, and the cold air filled them, causing him to cough. When their boat was full, they pushed off across the moat. Their boat was filled with Alexander and his friends, the oarsman of the boat, and two other soldiers.

Xythuu forces now arrived at the bank of the moat and began to fire arrows and throw javelins. The javelins whizzed past Alexander and into the water around him. Eltheneaen Illustratum generated small shields over the edge of the water. The cannons atop the fort and wall behind the moat began to fire at the Xythuu forces.

Camilla stood and launched an arrow, then ducked as arrows sailed over their boat. She rose and shot another as Alexander fired off a *Faer Xaen* and a *Fulmenooo Xaen* from his Lapideases. They smashed into his enemies and exploded over the area. He glanced over his shoulder. They still had twenty feet to go before they would reach the other side of the moat.

Alexander launched multiple *Faer Xaen* spells toward the water around them. The five-foot-wide balls of fire hit the water's surface with a hiss, and steam surrounded them. He then launched more in front of them and to the side. Other Illustratum began to do the same. Soon, a massive wall of thick steam hid them from the enemy.

The Xythuu forces began to blindly launch spells into the moat. The boats pulled in against the shore, and Alexander and the others poured out of them. They ran for a few minutes over a stone bridge that crossed the final moat and then made their way into the final fort. They formed a group along the wall, overlooking the scene on the battlefield. The first fort had been partially destroyed and captured. Parts of that first wall had been obliterated. Bodies lay all over the field, and small fires burned, the smoke filling the sky. The second fort had been demolished completely on one side. Parts of the wall there had been destroyed.

The rest of the Xythuu Army, about half of the original numbers, was spread out across the field. The Xythuu Army began to hurl giant boulders across the moat.

The sound of troops rapidly moving out of drills filled the air. Numerous transport drills had made it to the bridge in front of the final fort. Some of the boulders crashed through the wall. The boulders then stopped flying across the field as Xythuu troops poured out of the transports, and heavy barrages of spells and artillery fire were exchanged.

Alexander heard screams of anguish around him. Small cannons were being carried out of each drill vehicle. Artillery fire was launched at the fort but was blocked by generated shields.

A blue glow emitted from the cannons' openings. A thick blue beam of energy tore through the wall fifty feet left of where Alexander and his friends were located while another hit the base of the wall thirty feet to the right.

Heavy artillery fire barraged the enemy's cannons. Blocking dust jars destroyed the cannons' shields; then the artillery fire destroyed the cannons, causing small explosions. After an onslaught of ordinary spells destroyed the Eltheneaen shields, a rain of dark-purple spells fell on the area. One hit a soldier near Alexander. Purplish-black lines ran toward his eyes. Dread once again filled Alexander.

The man swung his sword at Alexander and just missed the top of his head. He swung again. Alexander launched a *Faer* spell, which knocked the sword out of his hand. The man was still enraged from the curse he was afflicted with and charged at Alexander. Alexander hesitated and was tackled. The soldier gripped Alexander's throat tightly.

Alexander could feel the crushing weight of the man's hands around his throat. He tried to gasp for air, but none made it into his lungs. The soldier's knees pinned his arms to his side. He tried to wrestle free but to no avail. His vision started to blacken. He heard a familiar voice that he had not heard in years whisper in his ear. The voice of his father, telling him to keep fighting back. Telling him to not give in.

Camilla, after knocking a cursed Ascalon in the head with her bow, launched an arrow at the soldier holding Alexander down. It landed in his shoulder under his armor, which loosened his grip. Camilla shot another, which hit his chest. Alexander managed to throw the man's arms off of his throat. He gasped for air, and his throat ached with a strong, burning pain.

Alexander's left arm was pinned to the ground, but he managed to free his right. The soldier still reached for Alexander, clawing at him furiously. Alexander was scratched across the face. The man lunged for his throat again. Camilla readied another arrow but was taken to the ground by a cursed Nightcloak.

Alexander took in a deep breath. He did not want to harm his own but would do so to protect himself and Camilla. He raised his hand and shot a *Faer* spell into the soldier's face. The man fell over to the side, his face burning. Alexander turned over and ran toward Camilla.

The Nightcloak and Camilla were both on the ground. The Nightcloak thrust downward with a knife. Camilla rolled to the side, and the knife landed next to her. She rolled again, and her bow rolled a foot out of her reach. The Nightcloak lunged. She caught his knife between her wrists, and the blade grazed against her leather vambraces. She wrestled the knife out of the Nightcloak's hand. She then freed her hand and punched the Nightcloak in the face. She punched again harder and then punched once more. The force of her punch knocked the Nightcloak back. She rolled for her bow as the Nightcloak rushed her with a knife in hand.

Alexander launched a *Faer Xaen* at the Nightcloak. It lit him on fire, but he still charged toward Camilla. Camilla grabbed her bow and shot an arrow into the head of the Nightcloak. She then rolled two feet to the side as the burning body fell over her. Alexander reached her and dropped to her side.

"Are you all right?" he asked with a rasp in his voice.

"I could ask you the same thing," she said as he helped her up. The others were just as tangled up with cursed Eltheneaen soldiers. A Nightcloak lunged at Urien with a knife. He evaded two attacks and then caught the Nightcloak's arm. He pointed the knife away from his body, then pulled the Nightcloak forward and kicked his knee, breaking it. The Nightcloak fell, and Urien brought his knee up into the Nightcloak's elbow. The knife fell from his hand.

He held the Nightcloak's arms to the side as Delyth, Tesni, Aeronwen, Cadfan, and Dysan joined him. Tesni leaned down and began to remove the curse. As she did so, more cursed soldiers moved in and attacked them. A heavily armored woman swung her sword at Dysan. He managed to dodge and then swung his axe down, hitting the woman's hand and knocking her sword loose. Dysan kicked the sword away and moved behind her and wrapped his arms around her. She struggled to get free of Dysan's grip. Aeronwen moved in front of the woman and held her hand up. Two cursed Ascalons attacked on each side. Cadfan and Delyth blocked their attacks.

The woman thrashed against Dysan as Aeronwen slowly removed small puffs of purplish-black smoke from her. Cadfan and Delyth were forced to push their opponents backward.

Tesni removed a huge chunk of smoke from the cursed Nightcloak. He fidgeted violently. Tesni removed more smoke, and the purplish-black lines that ran up to his eyes were pulled from his face. He then lay on the ground, confused and breathing heavily. Aeronwen removed the curse from the woman.

Dysan ran over to assist Delyth. The Ascalon hit her in the leg, which threw her off balance. The Ascalon prepared to thrust his lance into Delyth. Dysan caught the lance and tackled the Ascalon, dropping both of their weapons.

The cursed Ascalon rolled and began to punch at Dysan wrathfully. One hit caused his nose to spew blood over his face. He managed to bring his hands up to protect his face as the Ascalon punched at him violently. Delyth hit the Ascalon in the face with the blunt end of her lance, which threw him off of Dysan. Tesni joined in. Delyth threw herself onto the Ascalon while Tesni began to remove the curse. The Ascalon thrashed against her and threw her to the ground. As Delyth rose to her knees, the Ascalon grabbed her throat. She gasped as the air was cut off from her lungs.

Dysan rose to his knees and locked his hand around the Ascalon's. He pulled back with great force and managed to pull the Ascalon's hand off of her throat but only a few inches away. Tesni moved behind the Ascalon and held her hand to him. She removed a few small puffs of smoke as Dysan struggled to keep the hand away from Delyth. She then removed all of the curse, but it appeared to take great effort. The Ascalon came to his senses.

Tesni dropped to one knee, breathing heavily. Aeronwen had removed the curse from the Ascalon whom Cadfan had been fighting. Dysan grabbed his axe, and they all regrouped. As they did, several waves of blue energy hit the walls of the fort. Parts of the wall shattered. Several transport drills broke through the ground in front of the moat.

Alexander and his friends followed the hordes of troops headed toward the stairway. The only ones who did not move were those on the remaining cannons and those providing support for them. Alexander and his friends descended. They were now outside at the bottom of the fort and took defensive positions behind a wooden barricade. Shields were generated over the area. Alexander did not believe he had the energy to generate any. He was still recovering from earlier and the previous day. A barrage of spells and arrows collided into the shields on each side. Some shields dispersed into particles, and soldiers behind them were killed. Arrows collided into the wooden barricade that Alexander and his friends were behind.

He rose over the barricade and launched a *Faer Xaen* toward a group of enemies spilling through the hole in the wall. It was deflected by an enemy magic user. Several *Faer* spells were shot toward him. He quickly ducked behind the barricade and heard the spells hiss over his head. Some of them hit the barricade, and it caught on fire. Alexander and an Illustratum threw *Vandua* spells over the barricade. The water put the fire out with a hiss. The Illustratum created a new shield in front of them.

Camilla removed an arrow and flint from her pocket. She struck it a few times. The sparks fell over the tip of the arrow, and it caught fire. She rose over the wall and launched her arrow. The arrow sailed through the air and landed near the feet of the enemy troops. The grass below them caught fire, and thick smoke began to appear around and in front of them. The Xythuu troops, in a frenzy, moved away, coughing the smoke out of their lungs. Alexander leaned over the wall and launched multiple *Fulmenooo Xaen* and *Faer Xaen* spells.

The Xythuu troops moved into a formation and generated three-layer shields in front of and to the sides of them and charged forward once again. The Xythuu forces got close enough to launch javelins at the barricade. More shields were destroyed, and javelins hissed over the area. Some collided into the barricade, and some whizzed over Alexander's head. One hit the chest of a man next to Cadfan. Some Eltheneaen spells destroyed the Xythuu forces' shields. Delyth hurled a javelin into a Xythuu soldier, and Aeronwen and Tesni launched *Linwae Xon* spells, which collided into the enemy units.

The enemies who did not fall to the ground then smashed through the barricade. Alexander and his friends fought them off to the best of their abilities, pushing through the exhaustion.

Just as they had overcome the small group of enemies, an enormous surge of Xythuu forces made their way through the gaping hole in the fort wall. A bombardment of spells and arrows were exchanged. The battle waged on around them, and both sides suffered losses.

More blue energy crashed through the wall. A horn sounded three times in succession and then repeated. A barrage of fire spells destroyed the shield in front of Alexander and set the barricade on fire. Alexander, his friends, and the other soldiers scrambled away from the barricade. Arrows were hurled at them as they did so. Alexander launched a *Faer Xaen* with a *Vintae Xel*. The thick beam of whirling wind combined with the fire and spread the flames in a fierce rotation. Both spells hit the Xythuu forces. They caught fire with screams of agony.

Alexander continued the *Vintae Xel* spell and moved it back and forth. Tesni and Aeronwen released *Linwae Xel* spells at the group as well. The beams of white light tore through the Xythuu forces as the flames spread. Camilla shot an arrow directly into the head of a Xythuu archer.

Alexander stopped his *Vintae Xel* spell, and he and the others hurried toward the gate to the city. Eltheneaen troops were retreating from all sides as the Xythuu forces advanced behind them. They were near the gate when a barrage of *Faer Xaen* and *Fulmenooo Xaen* spells crashed into the stone wall by the gate. Alexander, his friends, and other soldiers ran through the entranceway as rocks began to fall. The rocks collapsed to the ground just as they had made their way through. The force of the crash sent Alexander and his friends tumbling.

Alexander lay still for a few seconds, then looked around. Camilla was next to him, while the others were a few feet to his right. He slowly pushed himself up, coughing as he did so. The others began to do the same. He was relieved that they were unharmed. More Eltheneaen soldiers poured through the entranceway, which was only partially covered by the rocks that had fallen over it.

More *Ruunae* spells fell on the stone wall. The barrage of fire and lightning bolts began taking out Eltheneaen artillery along the top of the wall. Hordes of Xythuu soldiers stormed through the entrance with an endless onslaught of magic coming from them and toward them. Holes were created where the stone walls had shattered. Xythuu forces poured through them. Alexander launched spells at the advancing forces, but they were deflected. Alexander overheard someone say a full retreat had been ordered and that they were to leave the city. This was confirmed when the beacon activated and shot its glow into the sky.

Alexander and his friends followed the fleeing masses of soldiers. A horn sounded, and somebody yelled out, "Escape plan C!" They hurried down a road and under a stone overhang. The soldiers there had already opened a secret entranceway that led to a set of stairs. Shouts instructed them to hurry and that the doors would be open for only three minutes. Alexander and his friends ran down the wooden stairs as explosions rang in their ears.

Chapter 15

Alexander and his friends followed the hordes of soldiers down six flights of stairs. The air was stuffy, but some fresh air filtered in from shafts connected to the ground level. They walked down a long corridor for ten minutes. Then everyone was instructed to stop so the wounded could be tended to. Many soldiers still had horrible wounds. Alexander and his friends sat on the dirt. Cadfan leaned against the wall as Aeronwen took a closer look at his face. She had closed up the wound, so she determined that he would not need stitches. Urien stared at Cadfan with a look of anguish. Cadfan caught his gaze, and Urien glanced away hurriedly. Alexander thought he saw guilt in his expression.

Tesni and Aeronwen were using their Lapideases to scan for injuries.

"No broken bones, amazingly," Tesni announced. "Just a few bruises. They should heal up within a week. I advise everyone to rest if possible."

Cadfan adjusted and then spoke. "Not trying to bring us down, but that's realistically assuming that we are not found down here. Then we can rest."

An order was given that everyone should keep moving, so they all rose and continued. Alexander assumed the path would lead to one of the many escape tunnels. After twenty more minutes of stumbling along, they arrived in a large rectangular opening.

"Gather round, everyone," said a male voice from the center of the crowd.

Alexander and the others moved forward behind a row of soldiers. Alexander looked closer at the man who had spoken. He was middle aged and had short gray hair. The lines on his shoulder marked him as a lieutenant marshal.

"As you all so very well know," the man continued, "the Kingdom of Xythuu has started a war with our country. There are other underground groups of survivors just like us. We know of reports from Ilgeth and Jylinae that both have fallen. Port Ivory as well. Now Fort Ydaeriin is among them. I honestly never expected to see any one of those places in the hands of an enemy. So far from our intel, we have gathered that one reason is because the Xythuu Army has weapons that we do not. It is unknown how or where they got them, but it puts them at an advantage. We also have not found any evidence of their motives. More than likely for resources, as most major conflicts are. Secondly, the army is large. We have no knowledge of the outer and central cities. Our plan of action now is to recover from these wounds and take back those cities. In order to do that, we will use these underground tunnels to our advantage. They were built for emergencies. There should be enough supplies down here to sustain us for three months. Our first action is to reconnect with the other survivors and use guerilla tactics to retake our city from the hands of the Xythuu Army, who wishes to see their flag flying over it!" Great passion carried in his voice.

Hours later, a makeshift camp was set up. There were sleeping furs spread out, with fires lit around the edges of the camp. Alexander lay on his fur, wondering if they would get a break from the Xythuu Army. He then drifted off to sleep.

* * *

Alexander woke to a noise in the middle of the night. Some of his friends stirred as well. In the light created by the fires of lamps around them, Alexander could see two soldiers, each carrying bodies over their shoulders. They were carrying Xythuu soldiers. A few moments later, soldiers were waking everyone as quietly as possible. Urien nudged Dysan, who was still sound asleep. Cadfan awoke and rubbed his eyes.

"Wha . . . what's all the commotion for?" he asked tiredly. Alexander and the others packed up their belongings and followed the hordes of people making their way farther down the tunnel. They took a right and proceeded another ten feet before taking a left and then another hard right.

Alexander knew that the Xythuu soldiers had most likely been sent down for reconnaissance and had been captured. They were likely relocating in case suspicions were raised when the spies did not return from their mission. They entered another open chamber stocked with pottery barrels and crates lining the walls. They set up a camp quickly. There were only small lamps lit, which made it difficult to see.

"Finally," grumbled Cadfan as he laid his sleeping fur on the ground and crawled into it. Alexander laid his fur down. He wrapped the warm fur around him and drifted back into sleep.

While he slept, moments from the earlier battle flashed through his mind. He saw the hordes of cavalry with Lieutenant Lydennan crashing into the Xythuu forces. He saw smoke and flames rising as his body filled with fear. He jerked awake. He sat up, sweat running down his face. He looked around. Some morning light filled the room from the small air shafts that connected to the surface. The room was also illuminated from candles embedded in the wall. The smell of cooking food wafted into his nose. His friends awoke now.

Cadfan grumbled. "Somebody bring me coffee," he said in a half-asleep voice with his head still facedown.

"Come get your own coffee like the rest of us," Aeronwen told him. He rose now, still half-asleep. "Let me take a look at your face first, though."

"Can't that wait until after I get my coffee and food?"

"It will only take a second," she said chidingly as she looked at the wound over his face. "It's healing up. It will leave a scar, though. Can you follow my finger?" She moved her finger in front of Cadfan's eye.

He followed it with a dull look on his face.

"How is your vision?" she asked. "I don't think you had any damage since it's only next to your eye, but I want to be sure," she said.

"Perfect. There are no dark spots or blurs in my vision," he answered.

"That's good. It's a miracle that you can actually see. Two inches to your left, and you would have lost this eye."

Urien glanced at Cadfan with a discerning look on his face. "Cadfan, how did you get that wound?" Urien asked. Cadfan hesitated for only a second.

"An enemy managed to knock me down and bring his lance down over my face," he stated.

Urien looked at him blankly. "Are you sure that's how it happened? I remember the army was in chaos. I don't remember anything from there afterward. My consciousness returned, and you already had the wound."

"You got knocked out by the same enemy. That's how I got it—because I ran to help you," Cadfan said. Urien looked away. Afterward, they had all gotten their food and were sitting in a group, enjoying the nourishment. Cadfan sipped on his coffee, and a small smile crossed his face. Dysan was eating heartily. Urien ate a few bites but still had a worried look on his face. Alexander stared at Urien nervously. His friend was usually calm, but he knew Urien would be particularly hard on himself.

While everyone was eating, the marshal made his way into the center of the room and began to speak. "Good morning, everyone. I want to inform you all that Xythuu forces are still looking for us. Last night four enemies attempted to gain access into our tunnels. We captured them before they could leave and are attempting to gather information on why they started this conflict, why they are here, what further plans they have, and where they have attained their new technology. With that said, it's only a matter of time before our enemies realize that their spies have not returned and will likely send more forces down here, which would either compromise us or force us to continually move. I realize that many of you are civilians and will do my absolute best to protect you all. I just do not know a safe place for us to stop," he stated. "I have already sent out a unit to Ilgeth to see their progress; however, I may also have to consider asking another country for aid. The most likely choice would be to see if Ciimerii will accept refugees and offer aid. Hyybeth may also be willing to do the same, but it makes it difficult to send a group of ships when both Ilgeth and Port Ivory have been destroyed and captured. I will send a message to Ciimerii and Hyybeth. However, I may have to risk sending a group of soldiers in order to do so." With that, he dismissed everyone to their business.

It was right after lunch when sounds of people shouting down one of the other tunnels filled the space. More enemies had infiltrated the area, and fighting had broken out. Alexander and his friends had just finished eating their lunches when the incident took place. A few of the enemies had been killed and the others captured and knocked unconscious. The soldiers on guard duty informed the marshal, who then ordered further evacuation. Alexander and his friends rolled their sleeping furs, strapped them on their backs, and moved once more. They proceeded down a very long corridor. This one was much darker than the others they had traveled through.

In the darkness in front of Alexander, Urien quickly glanced at Cadfan and then looked away. Cadfan noticed the gesture.

"Urien, what's wrong? I can feel the tension radiating off of you," Tesni said as they continued down the corridor.

"I've just got a few things on my mind," he stated. He took a larger step forward and put a little distance between himself, Cadfan, and Tesni. Afterward, their march down the corridor was marked by silence. An hour later, they made a right turn and continued for another twenty minutes.

They came to a stop when instructed. It was still quite dark. Alexander could see only a few feet in front of him. He heard the heaving of a door being opened. They shuffled through the doorway, which led into a set of descending stairs. Alexander took careful steps to avoid falling into or stepping on someone in the darkness. They descended for fifteen minutes before making their way through another doorway. Alexander entered a room filled with glowing candles. He thought it to be quite beautiful. They were instructed to set up camp again here.

Later in the evening, Alexander and his friends were approached by a soldier who informed them that they would have guard duty the following day. Lamps were lit, and pots of food were set above them.

Despite what had happened, Alexander felt a small comfort in the space. He knew it may not last long, so he was grateful for the comfort. They would more than likely be involved in taking the city back, which would probably put comfort to rest. He and his friends gathered near a lamp and began to eat. They all stared blankly at the flame in the lamp before them.

Alexander knew what they were all thinking. His thoughts turned toward his mother, wondering what had become of her. The very thought filled him with dread. He knew the others were thinking the same. Alexander pushed the thought aside and managed to smile to himself as he looked at his friends next to him. He knew they were all in pain. However, he was grateful to have his friends next to him. Having them around managed to dull the pain, and he was sure his friends felt the same thing too.

Chapter 16

Alexander and the others awoke and began their day. As breakfast was being administered, there was an announcement that no Xythuu forces had tried to infiltrate the tunnels the night before. Alexander and his friends sat around a pot of food being cooked over a small fire.

"How long do you think we will be down here?" Dysan asked.

"Hopefully, it won't be too long," Delyth answered.

"That depends on how long it would take for our armies to fight back. We lost a considerable amount of people. An effective guerilla campaign could take months to beat their forces, do damage, and take back the city," Alexander stated.

"I'm also sure we will not be down here the whole time," Camilla added. "More than likely, we will be participating in the attacks."

"I just miss the sun and the air. Even though we have small shafts which allow air and light in, it's not the same as being outside in it," Dysan said.

"So in other words," Cadfan said with a smirk, "we may be down here until we become like moles. We'll go blind and rely on our sense of smell to navigate." Everyone laughed a little, except for Urien.

"Come on, Urien. Laugh a little. You seem more distant than usual," Cadfan said.

Urien looked to the side and fidgeted.

"What's wrong?" Cadfan asked with a serious tone now. "You're never this withdrawn or transparent, which means something is wrong. Seriously wrong, because I have never seen you like this. Even after you saw our fathers die, you remained calm and were not like this at all."

Urien looked him in the eye now. "Cadfan, what happened to your eye?"

"I told you already. I got hit by an enemy who managed to land a blow on me. That's how battle and war go," Cadfan stated matter-of-factly.

"Then tell me something, Cadfan," Urien said. "I have no recollection of being knocked unconscious. I remember curses being launched on our area, and the next instant, Eltheneaen troops were fighting each other. After that, I remember being hit by one, but everything after that feels blank. Then I woke up, so to say, near you and Tesni. You had a horrible wound on your face, and I had a knife in my hand, which means I did that to you! None of you told me either!" he exclaimed, glancing around at his friends.

Cadfan's expression softened, and the others looked at Urien with guilt and sympathy. Alexander swallowed uncomfortably. Maybe lying had not been the right choice. But the truth had seemed more painful.

"You're right, Urien," Cadfan said in a low voice. "You were hit by a curse, which made you try to attack us. They succeeded, but it was not your fault. I told them not to say a word to you because I knew you would take it this way. I didn't want you to feel anger and hate toward yourself for what happened to me, because I knew you would." Cadfan sighed as Urien stood and left in a rush. Tesni followed him.

* * *

Tesni caught up to Urien in a corner of the chamber.

"Urien, stop," she said gently. "This wasn't your fault."

He turned and looked into her brown eyes. Her bangs hung over eyes, which stared at Urien intently.

"Tesni, I feel like this was my fault. I hurt Cadfan and had no control. I never wanted that to happen. I don't want to hurt any of my friends or get them killed," Urien said, almost choking on the words.

"Urien, this was not your fault. It was dark magic," she said. "Don't blame yourself. None of us like to see you like this." She laid a hand on his arm, but she removed it after a few brief seconds.

Urien looked at her. He knew she was just being herself and trying to comfort everyone. Yet he still felt like something was eating away at him. "I'll try not to dwell on it, Tesni," he said as they made their way back to the others. When they had rejoined the group, Urien looked at all of his friends. "I'm sorry, my friends, that I have acted this way. I promise I won't let anything bring me down again. I also promise that I will protect all of you, even if it means death itself."

* * *

Alexander and his friends were eating lunch in a hurry to prepare for their guard duty. Alexander finished the chicken he had grabbed and made his way back to their sleeping area. He slipped his armor plate over the red woolen shirt he had put on. He was wearing a pair of black cotton pants, which he had also grabbed from a supply barrel. He held out his left arm and snapped his vambrace onto it. He then did the same to his right arm. He stood, took in a breath, exhaled, and then walked to the center of the underground chamber.

The others joined him seconds later as well as some other soldiers. The current shift leader explained their duties and then divided them up. Alexander was paired with Dysan. They would be patrolling the center area along with Aeronwen and Tesni.

* * *

Alexander and Dysan had been on patrol for two hours. Mostly they had just watched as people were eating, sewing, or washing clothes or dishes. Alexander was bored. *Maybe the marshal will devise a plan of attack today*, he thought. As soon as the thought crossed his mind, a meeting was called for all soldiers to meet at the marshal's tent. There were only a few tents that had been stored underground, grabbed, and pitched during the evacuation. Alexander had expected a bit more humility of a high-ranking official. *Guess not everyone that is important is equal,* he thought. Apparently, the marshal was not worried about security, because all the soldiers were there, including the ones who had been patrolling the exits from the chamber.

Cadfan grunted dissatisfaction upon his arrival. "I hope this is info that says we will be attacking soon. This guard duty shit is boring as hell," he said.

"You realize this is the same stuff our fathers did when they weren't tasked with anything, right?" Urien asked him.

"Shut up," Cadfan said flatly.

"I agree with Cadfan," Alexander said to Camilla, who had moved next to him. She laughed.

The marshal then walked out of his tent, and someone shouted an order. Everyone snapped their heels together.

"Resume positions, everyone," he said. They relaxed. There were hundreds of soldiers, possibly up to six hundred, gathered around. Alexander was still amazed at the size of the underground chambers.

The marshal stood in front of his tent and spoke. "I've gathered you all here to inform you of a few things. Starting tonight, we will be conducting guerrilla strikes against the Xythuu forces." Cadfan's face twisted into a grin. The marshal continued. "We will be assembling groups and attacking key areas of the city after our intelligence reports come back. I have also sent word to Ciimerii to request transport and refuge for our people. When I have more information, I will notify everyone with an update. That is all. You are dismissed." He turned back to his tent.

Alexander and Dysan began patrolling around the tents once again.

"Hopefully we can start taking back the city," Alexander said.

"Yes, I hope so too," Dysan said. "I'd like to see more than small slips of sunlight shining from an air hole."

The rest of the night, Alexander and Dysan slowly patrolled their area. They were near the end of their shift and had already completed four complete patrol laps. Alexander's body and mind were growing tired. He was bored and tried to keep his mind focused on what he was doing. The last twenty minutes of their shift went by in what seemed like an eternity to Alexander. He looked to his left to see two armored soldiers coming his way and breathed out a sigh of relief. They told him and Dysan that they were relieved of duty.

Alexander and Dysan broke off in the direction the other soldiers had come from. They made their way to their sleeping area. Alexander gratefully removed his armor and gently placed it next to his bag. While he snapped off his vambraces, Cadfan, Urien, Tesni, Aeronwen, Delyth, and Camilla joined them and began the same process. He flopped into his sleeping fur, and Camilla lay near him while the others were gathered around. Alexander looked into her green eyes before falling into a deep sleep.

While asleep, Alexander relived the moments of the battles he had been in thus far. He watched as the walls of Jylinae were attacked with ballistae and magic. He and his friends were inside the town center now, and he could see the Xythuu soldiers attacking Jylinae troops. Lances whizzed past his head while he shot a spell at a Xythuu soldier. Now they were outside the city. He turned and saw the smoke rising over his home.

Everything blurred around him; then he was in Port Ivory. They were behind the walls, holding off the Xythuu forces. The enemy broke through, and he observed an exchange of spells flying from both sides.

Everything blurred again, and this time, he was transported to the battle of Fort Ydaeriin. He was on the tower again and watched the cavalries collide into each other. The next instant, he saw Marshal Holstead's head being shot off by a ballista bolt. The tower crashed to the ground now, with Alexander inside. He made his way out of the smoke-and-flame-filled tower to see Xythuu forces bursting through the wooden barricade. In that moment, he heard two distinct female voices screaming. One belonged to his mother. The other was Camilla's.

Everything went black, and all sounds came to an abrupt stop. He shot up, his eyes wide and his breathing heavy. He turned to see Camilla still lying next to him. She was sound asleep. He exhaled a deep sigh of relief and lay back down.

Before he fell asleep, his thoughts went to his mother. He remembered one day as a kid when he had fallen off of his rope-and-board swing in his backyard and skinned his knee badly. He could recall his mother cleaning and bandaging it. He had been five years old when that had happened, but it was still so vivid. Tears slowly ran down his face as he wondered what had happened to her and drifted back to sleep.

* * *

Alexander woke to the noise of people hustling about in the tunnels. Alexander and his friends sat up as people moved around them. A guard on duty told them that the marshal had ordered a meeting. Alexander yawned and rubbed his eyes.

Cadfan sat up, still mostly asleep, with his reddish-brown hair sticking up. "It's too early for this," he said groggily.

Dysan helped him up, and Aeronwen smoothed down his hair. They hurried to the center of the tunnel opening, where a large crowd had already gathered around the marshal's tent. The marshal was outside, his arms crossed.

The marshal appeared eager. "My countrymen, I have good news to report to all of you. We sent out a letter to Ciimerii some time ago. This morning, our hawk returned with news. First, Ciimerii will not be sending any aid to us," he said. Cadfan snorted. "They say it is not their war. Strategically speaking, I believe it is because Xythuu is next to them and may try an invasion if that is their plan. However, I must respect their right to neutrality. With that being said, they did agree to take in civilian refugees." The crowd let loose a small cheer. "I will be putting tasking teams together to escort you. However, they did issue a term to the agreement that military escorts will go no farther than Lein. This may be a lengthy process, though, as well. I will only send two groups at one time. I need our forces to start the guerilla campaign. I will be reviewing my team, and if possible, we will send the first group tonight. However, a warning with this. These tunnels go to five miles outside the city. It should help avoid detection. Once I send a group off, though, you will be without any assistance. Talk to me later if anyone wants to volunteer for it. My final decision will be at dinner." With that, he dismissed everyone.

* * *

Later in the day, Alexander and the others were sitting on their sleeping furs, eating their lunch. Cadfan and Dysan were arguing about which of the two would be legends. Alexander cleared his throat and looked up from his food.

"There's something I want to talk to you all about," Alexander said.

"What is it?" Cadfan asked.

"Would any of you be willing to volunteer for the escort job?"

Cadfan, Dysan, and Urien all appeared taken aback.

"I didn't expect that," Cadfan said. "Why are you asking?"

"I believe that helping our people get to safety takes priority over us getting pulled further into the war. I believe that the eight of us, in particular, lack the experience to help fight and take back the city," Alexander explained.

Urien let out a small breath and then spoke. "I do agree with you on lacking experience, but we won't build it any other way. I believe our best chance is to stay together as much as possible."

Alexander looked at him. "I agree too. We need to stay together, but I feel we should help these people, and then if the situation allows, we can return and help take back the city."

Cadfan stared at the ground as he pondered the idea. "It would get me out of these tunnels," he said, trailing off.

"Let's vote on it, then," Dysan said. "All in favor?" he asked. Alexander, Camilla, Dysan, Cadfan, Aeronwen, and Tesni raised their hands. "That means that Urien and Delyth oppose. Six to two. We are decided," Dysan said.

"I do agree with helping our people, but I believe we should focus on the city and country," Delyth said. "But I will go with you all."

"This is how war goes," Camilla said. "Sometimes you must discuss and make decisions such as these."

* * *

Alexander and his friends had just finished eating their dinner and were standing around the marshal's tent in the center of the underground room. Other people began to gather to hear the information he was passing along. After a few brief moments, the marshal walked out of his tent. He looked out at the people before him.

"My troops and fellow citizens, tonight I speak to you about the task of protection. I am sending a group of people to Ciimerii. This campaign will be long and difficult. We will not retake this city overnight. The potential for civilian casualties is high, something I wish to avoid if at all possible. I ask if any among you are willing to volunteer to escort a group of people from our tunnels to the city of Lein, Ciimerii. I have already chosen some of the members I will send. That being said, I will also take volunteers at this moment. Is there anybody who wishes to volunteer for this task?" he asked.

Alexander took a step forward. Camilla followed him. They moved through the crowd as people made room for them.

"Sir, I wish to volunteer," he said resolutely.

"Myself as well, sir," Camilla said.

Dysan and Cadfan followed suit and then were joined by Aeronwen, Urien, Tesni, and Delyth.

"We wish to as well, sir," Dysan said. The marshal looked at them for a moment, as if to measure their capabilities.

"Very well," the marshal said. "After my briefing, stay here, and I will introduce you to who will be in charge of you. I have had my executive officers gather up a list of names of everyone here. Now I know it seems unfair, but I have decided that the best possible way would be to send out a small number of groups or families by going down the list alphabetically. I can only send a small number of people to help avoid detection and to help defend this area as well as begin the campaign to retake the city. I apologize if this causes any inconvenience to you, but I will get you all to safety. I will ready a list of names of refugees and escorts," the marshal said.

A younger man with short brown hair and a small scar beside his left eye stepped forward.

"My executive, Captain Elwin, will give you the details. That is all I have for now," the marshal said as he turned away. There was a snapping of heels as he went into his tent. Alexander and his friends made their way up to the captain to discuss their journey.

"Sir, what information do you have for us?" Alexander asked.

"Meet me here at nine o'clock," Captain Elwin said. "Pack lightly. Bring clothes for a few days and sleeping materials. I will arrange for all of the food we will need for the journey. Wear some comfortable shoes too. We will be moving as much as possible tonight. That's all for now." Alexander and the others turned and made their way to their sleeping area.

Alexander and his friends gathered all their belongings and organized them into baskets. They sat and waited another hour to depart. There was silence among them. Alexander knew there was risk involved in their mission, but they would be exposed to risk either way. He felt it was what he should do. He believed it to be his duty to help the civilians, his countrymen, who had been caught in the middle of a developing war. He was grateful that his friends had agreed to volunteer with him. It would not be easy, but he was willing to escort and protect his people.

He lifted his eyes up from the ground now. His friends all held the same focused expressions. He cleared his throat, breaking the silence.

"Thank you, my friends," he said. They looked up now, seeming slightly startled. A brief moment of silence passed.

Cadfan then spoke. "For what?" he asked. "We're supposed to stick together. That's how this friendship works."

"Yeah, we are doing our duties as friends," Dysan said.

"Would we not do so?" Aeronwen asked.

Alexander flashed a thankful smile. Tesni placed her hand out in front of them. They each placed their hand over hers. She did not say anything. They just held their hands there for a minute in silence. Appearing content, she lowered her hand.

They all began to talk among themselves. Camilla turned her head toward Alexander. Alexander noticed and met her gaze. There were just a few inches of space between them. Her eyes seemed a deeper shade of green to him right now.

"What?" he asked with a laugh.

"You have a big heart," she said gently. "You're risking your life to protect and escort people you don't even know." She laid her head on his shoulder, and they joined hands. "I know your father would be proud," she said softly. "I'm proud of you."

* * *

The next hour passed, and Alexander and his friends waited at the location Captain Elwin had told them about. Each of them had a basket with their clothes and sleeping materials strapped to their back. A group of twenty people, each of them carrying a basket as well, waited with them. Twelve more soldiers, including Captain Elwin, joined them. Among them were two Illustratum, two Nightcloaks, two Vivicanterns, two Dynamis, and a Lepides. The captain was armored in leather, had a scarf draped over his neck, and carried a sword at his side and a small shield on his arm. He motioned for everyone to gather around him.

"We will be taking a tunnel not far from here. We should only be in there for an hour or two depending on how fast we move. From the exit, we will need to cover two more miles at least. When we are outside of the town, I will reform the group to better suit our tactical needs. It's going to be a long night, so be ready," he said. He then handed everyone folded parchments with the seal of the Eltheneaen Army, an eagle looking down keenly in blue wax. "These documents state our reason for entering their country, and Lein has been fully informed. I hope nothing happens to any of us, but if we get separated or killed, I would like the primary mission to be continued. But that also does not mean I will let any of you die, separate, or get captured," Captain Elwin stated.

With that, they followed the captain to the tunnel entrance. The guards let them pass and wished them luck. They were now outside of the chamber in which they had taken refuge and were crowding into the tunnel that would lead them out of the city.

Half an hour passed. They walked in silence during the journey. It was dark in the tunnel, with the exception of a few small glowing candles on the wall and some carried by members of the party. The path had contained many turns. This time they turned left and proceeded down a hallway so narrow that only two people could walk side by side. Alexander and Camilla walked together, with civilians in front of and behind them. Alexander could faintly make out a door at the end of the tunnel. Captain Elwin led the group to it. A coded lock hung in front of the door. He leaned over, entered the code, and heaved the door open.

Everyone crowded into the dark tunnel. Captain Elwin then closed the tunnel door behind them and made his way back up to the front of the group. Stale air wafted into Alexander's nose. The tunnel seemed as though it had not been used in some time. It still had the air shafts like everywhere else in the tunnel, but it seemed they were not as effective as the other shafts.

I would hate to end up locked in here, Alexander thought as they filed down the tunnel. They traveled for another two hours and were signaled that a ten-minute break would be given. Alexander sat on the ground. He wished for the fresh air that awaited them at the end of the tunnel. For the moment, fresh water would suffice.

Camilla and the others joined him, lifting their water canisters to their mouths.

"How do moles do this?" Cadfan asked. "I want air. And more than just dim lighting."

Urien looked at him blankly. "It's not so bad."

"Yeah, that's because you are trained in conditions like this," Cadfan stated. "Be honest, Urien. Did they use magic on you during your training to turn you into a mole?"

"They did," Urien said sarcastically.

After a short amount of time, they came to the end of the tunnel. Captain Elwin approached the door. He ordered all lights out, plunging the group into darkness. He then pulled on the door with slight force, and the door opened halfway. A handful of soldiers walked through the opening, followed by some of the citizens. Alexander and his friends stepped out.

The cool night air hit Alexander's skin and filled his nose. He looked up at the sky to find it filled with stars but absent of a moon. The starlight illuminated the area slightly. The rest of the citizens then came out, followed by Captain Elwin. He motioned for everyone to gather around him.

"That was just the first part of our journey. We should be about five miles outside of the city," he said lowly. "We still have a long journey ahead. Tonight the goal is to cover more ground. It should be close to midnight. We're going to move for about four more hours and rest then. Be advised—the intelligence we have gathered shows that there could still be enemy activity within this area. Be alert to everything." He motioned for them to continue.

They moved faster now than they had in the tunnel. Alexander looked up at the stars while they walked. It had been a while since he had seen them. He had not been outside since the fall of Fort Ydaeriin.

After about twenty minutes, they began to slow down. Many of the citizens were starting to tire. Captain Elwin ordered for a break, even though he appeared extremely reluctant. A group of soldiers and the captain encircled the area while the others were allowed to rest. The soldiers would switch positions in ten minutes.

Alexander and his friends were among those allowed to rest. They sat in a half circle.

"I guess now that we have a chance to talk," Cadfan said quietly, "how is everyone?"

Dysan took the chance to grab some jerky from his bag and began to eat.

"You've got the right idea, Dysan," Cadfan said. "I'm hungry."

"While we have the time," Alexander said, "I would like to bring all of your attention to something. It was mentioned as being after midnight, which technically means"—he gestured to Camilla next to him—"it's Camilla's nineteenth birthday." They all clapped softly.

Cadfan gave Camilla a piece of jerky. "Here. Happy birthday," he said.

"Happy birthday, Camilla," Tesni stated.

"Make a wish," Delyth said.

Camilla smiled. "Thank you. Glad I could experience this . . . ," she said, trailing off.

They all now rotated while the second group of soldiers took their breaks. Alexander and Dysan stood to one side while Tesni and Camilla were facing north, Aeronwen and Urien were facing south, and Delyth and Cadfan were paired with an Illustratum on the other side. Alexander looked around. He realized that he was more aware of his surroundings than he had been when he had first become an apprentice months ago. He could hear the leaves rustle as they blew in the gentle, cool wind. Dysan seemed to be the same way. He would keenly look at the area around him. Alexander knew it had to be the experience of combat, something that was generally unheard of while being an apprentice. He knew that there were many adults who had passed their apprenticeships and had never actually experienced combat due to Eltheneae not being in a state of war in years. Many had experienced raids from bandits or pirates but not true war. He knew, as bad as it was, that it gave him and his friends an edge. The rest of the soldiers finished eating, and everyone got up, returned to their formation, and continued on their way once more.

Hours passed as they covered considerable ground. They stopped for breaks three other times. During the last break, Alexander did wish that they could stop for the night. Soreness shot up and down his legs, and his feet were throbbing. The others seemed to be fighting off the same exhaustion.

He glanced up at the sky. From what he could tell, the sun would most likely be rising in a few hours. The flat ground provided no protection against the now-colder night. A breeze had kicked up within the past few hours, which brought even more chill to the air.

After another minute of trekking over the rocky, slightly grassy terrain, Alexander spotted a tree surrounded by a few bushes. They hurried over to it.

"We'll make camp here for tonight," Captain Elwin said. "We will rest for a few hours." He began to divide up the watch shifts. Alexander and his friends were given the last watch assignment. Alexander let out a small breath of relief.

Captain Elwin instructed that no fire would be lit, so everyone rolled out their sleeping furs. Alexander rolled out his next to Camilla's. The rest of his friends surrounded him, providing a cluster of warmth. He crawled inside his and instantly appreciated its heat. Camilla crawled into hers next to him. He was comforted by her presence and grateful to still have her with him. His eyes then shut, and he fell instantly to sleep.

* * *

Alexander was awoken by another guard. He crawled out of his sleeping fur. His hair covered his eyes, but he could see the sunlight as it just barely broke over the horizon. He reached into his basket and draped a thick brown robe over his white one and tied it shut. The robe kept him warmer than his white one and provided more protection from the cold morning air. He smoothed his hair and blinked a few times to try to wake up.

The other guard had informed him that they were going to be on guard duty for three hours to let the others get some sleep. His friends had risen, too, and looked just as tired as Alexander felt. Cadfan, in particular, seemed grumpy as usual because the no-fire order still remained in effect, so he was unable to make any coffee. He grumbled as they were divided into groups of two and three by the soldier in charge.

Alexander was paired with Urien and posted on the far right of their campsite, about six feet away from the tree. Camilla and Tesni were at the other side of the formation about twenty feet away, with Delyth, Dysan, and an Illustratum at the southern end. Aeronwen, Cadfan, a Dynami, and a Vivicantern were at the northern side, forming a small square around the campsite. Four other soldiers were tasked with patrolling the surrounding area. The civilians were still sleeping. Alexander looked at them with dull eyes. Instead of saying a complaint out loud, he decided to talk to Urien.

"Urien," Alexander said solemnly.

Urien turned his head slightly. "Yes, Alexander?"

Alexander was silent briefly as he tried to figure out how to ask what was on his mind. He then took in a breath and proceeded. "How are you holding up?"

Urien was silent. His face was pale, and his eyes looked hollow. "You would be referring to the event in Jylinae? About my father's death?"

Alexander nodded.

"I'm doing about as well as anybody who has had such an atrocity befall them would be doing," Urien stated. "It's like trying to climb a mountain and being stuck on a ledge, reaching up only to fall down again." His voice shook slightly, but then it returned to its normal calmness by the end.

"I'm sorry," Alexander said. "Truly. I don't know the full experience that you have faced, but I do know the feeling of losing a parent. I felt the same way when the soldiers came to my door to deliver the news of my father. It seemed like it couldn't be true, but my mind kept repeating it over and over again. It's pure agony."

Urien looked at him. "It's more agony not knowing if my mother was spared the same fate. And Maria too. I think about her with every passing hour every day. Where is she? What happened to her? Will I ever see her again? I think that for both of them. My mind is always on Lancet too. It's my fault he died. That's why this must end as quickly as possible," Urien said with a solemn resolve in his voice.

Alexander looked at Camilla at the other side of the campsite.

* * *

Tesni glanced at Camilla, her eyes bright and a beaming smile on her face. "So, Camilla," she said, "you're nineteen now."

Camilla smiled. "Yes, I am," she said.

"It's like you're on a bridge to adulthood," she said cheerfully.

Camilla laughed. "What are you talking about, Tesni? You're extra cheerful this morning too."

"Oh, I was just thinking about how one of my friends is growing up," Tesni said.

"Well, yeah. We all do," Camilla said as they paced slowly.

"You're a young adult. You could get a house soon. Be a Bowman in a garrison. Live your own life. Or you could be living with someone else. Could be married." Tesni winked.

Camilla coughed. "It's a bit early for that, right?"

"Not really." Tesni shrugged nonchalantly. "You only have a short life, " she said sweetly. "Isn't that all the more reason to do so?"

"You have a point, but if I am to engage in a marriage, I would prefer it not to be during a time of chaos and anguish. And traveling across the country could have been the way life was supposed to go, but that seems like a distant dream right now. Besides, why are you asking me this?" Camilla asked.

Tesni's face shifted from a smile to a solemn stare. "I just thought that we could talk about normal things. Take our minds off of reality."

* * *

The hours passed. Alexander rubbed the back of his shoulder. They had a few more minutes before they would be moving on. He ran his hand through his hair and took in a breath. He could feel the coolness of the air, but the warmth of the sun was also creeping up the back of his head. The sun had been up now for about three hours.

The day ahead is going to be long, he thought to himself. They still had more ground to cover and would not be reaching the river border until the end of the next day. The other escorts were now rising, moving quickly for bathroom uses, handwashing, arming, and eating. Within a few minutes, they were ready to go, and Captain Elwin ordered the march to continue.

The terrain was starting to get rougher, with uneven ground, loose rocks, and small hills and cliffs that hung in the distance. They began to pick up the pace. The loose gravel crunched beneath their feet as they moved over the land. Alexander looked at Urien next to him, who seemed to traverse over the jagged ground with little effort. Alexander darted his eyes to Camilla, who also seemed to be moving quickly without a struggle.

Eventually the pace began to slow as most of the civilians began to tire. Even though most of them would not admit it, they needed to stop to rest. Captain Elwin ordered a stop after close to nine hours of traveling.

The escorts gathered around for the guard shift assignments. This time Alexander and the others were split between two shifts. Alexander, Tesni, Urien, and Dysan would be taking a middle night shift, while the others would be doing the last shift.

After being dismissed, Alexander and his friends laid out their furs and began to eat jerky and down it with water. There was little talking. They were all exhausted from the journey so far. After a few minutes, they had eaten their food and began to settle into their furs.

"Good night, everyone," Tesni said wearily. "Get enough sleep before your shifts."

Alexander crawled into his fur. The ground was rough beneath him. He put up his arm and laid his head on it. The right side of his now slightly longer hair fell over his arm, and he closed his eyes and fell asleep.

* * *

Smoke and dust filled the air, and the sound of stone walls shattering and the anguished screams of people being harmed filled the air. The smell of burning flesh and stone wafted into his nose. A barrage of fire-balls blasted against green shields that dissipated like dust in the wind upon their destruction.

Upon the white stone walls that were now blackened with soot stood a young boy in a green robe and his friends, fighting amid the many members of defense forces. Alexander now saw the battlefield clearly before him—and every sound was amplified. He could see the Xythuu Army in front of Jylinae, attacking with spells, arrows, and cannon blasts. He heard people screaming near him, and it sent chills down his spine. The next moment, he was on a stairwell in the center courtyard, and an arrow whizzed past his head. His heart pumped so ferociously within his chest he thought it might break through his flesh and fall to the ground.

He was then in Port Ivory in the castle walls, making his way down the stairwell into the courtyard when the stone roof and floor of the level above crashed to pieces around him, taking off the arm of the governor who was with them. The sight faded, and the sounds turned into distant murmurs. He was then awoken by the sounds of shuffling around him and a small, gentle, smooth hand placed on his face.

Alexander awoke with a gasp and with sweat dripping down his face.

"Alexander. Calm down. It's okay," Camilla said from a few feet away.

He sighed in relief.

"Mine feel real sometimes," Camilla whispered. "The nightmares feel like being back in the real moment."

Alexander looked up at the sky. It was clear with a few sparse, long dark-purple clouds. The stars shone brilliantly above him. It was a wondrous, beautiful sight. The cold night air brushed against his nose. As he lay there, he wondered if it was possibly the last time he would see the stars above him. He did not know what the next day would bring, which terrified him. He had also survived so much up to this point. What had become of his homeland? Was it nothing more than ash and dust and filled with the smoke and flames of war? What had become of the people of the capital of his nation? Where was his mother? Was she held in chains? The stars above him dimmed as he closed his eyes, and his exhausted mind went blank, as it could not find the answers.

* * *

He was awoken a few hours later. He fidgeted and rose slowly, his body aching. He donned his chest armor and vambraces, wrapped his satchel around him, and prepared for his shift. He and Dysan were paired in a corner for their patrol. Dysan yawned wearily. Alexander seemed unable to focus on anything. His mind was filled with thoughts and memories of his mother. He thought of how she had held him in her arms while they had both sobbed after receiving the news of his father's death. He remembered how she would always bake cookies and let him roll the dough and place it on sheets. He recalled her voice, so kind and calm. When he was younger, she used to sing to him, even more so after his father's death—in a way to comfort him as well as herself. She had done that often for the first year or so.

Alexander felt tears well up behind his eyes and then slide down his face. They felt cold in the night air. He looked up into the sky. *I'm going to find you,* he thought. *I'm going to find you, Mom. I'm going to get stronger, find you, and I'm going to make this right. No matter what it takes.* The rest of his guard shift went by in a blur. The next team rotated in. He made his way to his fur, removed his armor and placed it in his bag, and then crawled into his fur. He drifted back to sleep.

* * *

Alexander felt a nudge. He rolled slightly but did not push himself upward. He was nudged again, and a voice next to him said, "Come on. It's time to get up."

Alexander looked with fuzzy eyes, waiting for them to adjust. He then saw Camilla, kneeling next to him with her bow in hand and her white robe and armor draped over her. Alexander sat up. It was still dark around him. He estimated that the sun would be rising within the next twenty minutes.

"We have to leave in ten minutes," Camilla said to him. He rolled out of his furs and quickly strapped on his leather chest armor over his robe. He then strapped his father's cloak to his side, pinned by his satchel. He snapped his vambraces on his wrists and then reached for some jerky from his basket. He downed some water and made his way behind a tree. He returned to his basket and hoisted it over his shoulders.

Everyone else started to rise and ready up for the day. Within five minutes, everyone had gathered in the center of the campsite for the briefing.

"We are making our way to a border fort today," Captain Elwin said. He gestured to all the civilians. "From that point, Ciimerii troops will be joining us on our way to Lein. They have agreed that all refugees can have harbor until we have liberated our country. Xythuu committed an act of war, and our military operations over the country have declared that we are at war. We lost communications with other parts of the country shortly after the invasion of Jylinae, but I know there are units still operating. With that being said, this briefing is to inform everyone here to be cautious. We have been in slightly flat terrain with a mixed abundance of vegetation. The area between here and the border is filled with high cliffs that will line our pathway. This is an area known for bandits. We also cannot rule out the possibility of Xythuu activity. Let's get moving now."

As they followed the path, tall cliffs began to tower above them. The sun had just started to break over the horizon, filling the area with morning light. Alexander looked cautiously over the cliffs for any signs of movement. They arrived at a narrow bend and squeezed through it slowly, in groups of four or five people. Alexander and Camilla went through, with three civilians behind them. Alexander took in a breath, feeling overcrowded in the small space. He made his way through and saw more cliffs rising above him on both sides. Looking at them made him uneasy. He felt like a rabbit waiting to get picked off by a voracious hawk. After everyone had passed through the bend, they continued their journey.

They traveled another twenty minutes over slightly rough sloping ground. They took another turn and made their way to a downward slope. "Be very careful here," Captain Elwin instructed. "It's a steep slope, and we will have to go down carefully in small groups. The border fort is just below us."

Captain Elwin looked up to the sky. Alexander followed his gaze and saw smoke climbing into the sky.

"That looks like our luck," Cadfan said.

Captain Elwin instructed the civilians and the escorts to stay in place. He then crouched at the edge of the slope. Alexander and his friends followed suit. He slid next to Captain Elwin.

"What are you doing here?" the captain asked in a whisper.

"I had to see for myself," Alexander said, and then his voice trailed off. His friends had crawled next to him.

"Can't anything just go the way we want for once?" Cadfan mumbled.

"I guess not," Dysan answered.

They peered below and saw a stone bridge stretching over a river, leading to a fort two stories high. In front of the border fort stood an encampment with a multitude of tents and soldiers surrounding the area. The source of the smoke was a small fire next to the border fort. The black flag of Xythuu flew high above the encampment.

Chapter 17

Captain Elwin, Alexander, and the others slowly crawled back below the ridgeline. After they had crawled about ten feet, they rose.

"Well, this certainly changes things," Elwin said in a sardonic tone. He rubbed his chin.

"So now what do we do?" Cadfan asked. "They'll see us from down there."

From their position, they could see two other bridges leading over to the fort. They were relatively empty in terms of the number of tents strung up in front of them.

Elwin walked back farther and motioned for everyone to gather around him, civilians included. He looked around, especially at the people they were escorting. "So unfortunately, there is a Xythuu encampment just below us. That means we have to think of a new way to the fort. I may have a plan, but this will take longer," he said. He turned to the two Nightcloaks. "I think we will have to take those other bridges. I want each of you to make your way over to the other bridges and see if there is still anyone there. I have not seen anyone yet, so we need to know what they are doing. Until we have that information, we will just have to wait. I want to have sentries posted just barely over the ridge. Anyone who has long-range capabilities, so magic users or bow users. Everyone else, just sit tight."

The Nightcloaks huddled together to plan which route they would take.

"Wait," Aeronwen said. "Shouldn't you take someone who can at least heal you if you get hurt?"

"That's noble, but no," one of the Nightcloaks responded. "Magic can heal things quicker, but we can still take care of ourselves."

"They're right," Elwin said. "We can't move like they can. And we would just slow them down. Believe me; I would like to go with them to heal them myself if need be, especially since I have known them so long, but they need to do this alone."

Aeronwen sighed, and the Nightcloaks began scouting out the area.

An hour passed, and neither of the Nightcloaks had returned. Alexander and Camilla had just been relieved of their watch on the ridge, and the two Illustratum had taken over. The others were sitting in a circle, drawing stuff in the sand with small twigs they had found. They made a game of guessing what they were drawing. Urien held a twig and drew a multitude of circles.

Cadfan had his chin in his hand with a blank expression on his face. "I'm so bored," he said as Alexander and Camilla came to join them. "Hey look, our friends have come to join us in our boredom."

"Just try to focus your mind on something," Aeronwen said.

Alexander looked over to where Elwin was sitting. One of the Nightcloaks returned just then and hurried straight for Elwin. After they had spoken for a moment, Elwin motioned for everyone to gather around him.

"So some new intel just came in—thank you for that," Elwin said, turning his head to the Nightcloak and then back to the crowd around him. "There is a small tunnel south of here; however, the bad news is that it ends halfway between here and the fort and goes topside fifty feet to the side of where the Xythuu encampment now sits. Currently, there is no direct route that we can take. When my other Nightcloak arrives, I will formulate a plan with the additional intel. For now, stay vigilant. We will still rotate turns on the ridge and not rest. We had a break, but it's now time to remain vigilant, so everyone who is escorting, stay on your feet for the next two hours." Elwin crossed his arms and furrowed his brow. Everyone else dispersed not far from him in small groups.

* * *

Their two hours were now almost up. It was just past midday, and the other Nightcloak had yet to return. Alexander munched on some jerky. He knew they would have to formulate a plan soon, or they would most likely have to head back to Fort Ydaeriin. They had brought just enough food for over a week, meaning they had about four days left.

"Do you think he made it?" Cadfan asked. The others looked up, seeming slightly distracted by their own thoughts. "I know that Nightcloaks are well trained, but that's a lot of ground to cover and a lot of people to avoid."

"How do we know he didn't get killed or captured?" Dysan asked, fidgeting.

"We just have to trust he has made it over by now and that none of that happened," Aeronwen said.

"Neither of those have happened," Urien said. "If they had, they would have sounded alarms."

"They probably would have sent search teams and would have surely found us too," said Delyth.

"I don't understand why they would not have any sentries or patrols up here, though," Alexander said.

"They would be able to see anyone from down there, though," Dysan remarked.

"I agree. Why not control this area too?" Camilla said.

"Maybe they are getting cocky." Cadfan shrugged.

"Or it could be that their encampment is only temporary and they need every unit ready to mobilize. Possibly into Ciimerii," Tesni stated. Understanding dawned for Alexander.

"They intend to violate Ciimerii's neutrality and invade them too," Alexander said.

"Isn't an army outside your border already violating neutrality?" Cadfan asked.

"In some ways, yes," Dysan said, "but they have not yet crossed over the border, so it hasn't fully. It shows hostile intent but does not directly violate the neutrality."

Alexander made his way to Captain Elwin.

"Sir," Alexander said as he approached the captain.

Elwin looked over at him blankly. "Yes, what is it?"

"I have reason to believe the Xythuu Army may be considering an invasion of Ciimerii," he said.

"Yes, that thought occurred to me," Elwin stated. "It's the only valid reason to have an army encamped outside their border." Captain Elwin rubbed his head. At that moment, Alexander heard swift footsteps behind him. The other Nightcloak had returned.

"Any news to report?" Elwin asked him as he approached. Elwin also motioned for everyone to gather around him. Alexander's friends crowded up behind them.

"Ciimerii still has units there. They reported no Xythuu forces have crossed the river border, yet they have sent a message to their leaders stating the Xythuu Army is at their borders and that they would need reinforcements. It could reasonably take a few days for the message to be received and the armies to come from Lein," the Nightcloak said. "There is some good news, though. There is a tunnel that goes directly to the border. The only downfalls are that it is only narrow enough for two people to move through at a time and there are roughly ten feet of open area between the end and the actual border of Ciimerii."

Elwin rubbed his chin. "Well then, I have what I need to take action," he said. The sun had just set, and the glow of torches below the ridge illuminated the cliffs of the area—but not enough to where the Eltheneaen encampment could be seen. The Nightcloak then told Elwin some additional information.

Captain Elwin spent a few minutes formulating a plan. He rubbed his chin again as everyone gathered around. "We are about to embark to the tunnel. I have been informed that it is just a few minutes away but is quite long. The Ciimerii guard has given us permission to enter and escort you to Lein if need be. This news means there is the possibility of separation. If we come under attack and get overrun or separated, everyone keep the civilians moving toward the fort. The Ciimerii guard has readied stables for us. If we are engaged, I will also shoot a *Linwae Vael* into the sky and shape it into an eagle. This will signal the urgency to get to the fort. Once there, you are to wait a period of ten minutes. If the ten-minute time is reached while we are under attack, all units at the stables will leave immediately. I understand this seems controversial, but our mission is to escort you to Lein," he said. A few citizens assured him that they would trust his judgement.

He motioned to a Dynami and a Lepides. They were each carrying an extra basket, which they dropped to the ground and opened. They pulled out cloaks. Each was made of tan-brown cloth that had brown smudges across them and leather spheres resembling rocks sewn onto them. Some were small in size, and others were larger. The Dynami opened one gently. Alexander could see that once they were open, they had irregularly shaped edges. He could also see a small patch, the green flag of Eltheneae with its three vertical white lines on it, sewn to the garments' left shoulders. There were also three buttons down the middle of the cloak. It had two coattails: one in front and one in the back. Toward the bottom of the front were three more buttonholes.

"These will help with warmth and also help us blend in. There is one for everyone here. Put them on, and we will move out once everyone is ready," Elwin instructed.

Alexander and his friends moved toward the baskets. As with the other escorts, they let all the citizens garner their cloaks first and then grabbed theirs. Alexander picked up his basket. He quickly removed his satchel and placed his father's worn cloak next to it. He draped the new cloak over himself. He placed his father's cloak in his satchel with his Lapideases, then strapped the basket to his back. Alexander looked down at the cloak. On the inside, there were loop straps with a few adjustable buttonholes. The new cloak draped down to his ankles.

He slipped his legs into the straps and buttoned them. Everyone around him had placed their baskets on their backs over the cloaks. This would make emergency removal easier.

"What are the straps for?" Dysan asked.

"They're to help the cloaks stay closer to your body to aid in warmth and to blend the silhouette of the cloak," Urien said.

"Did you ever get anything like this during your training?"

"Yeah, we tried all sorts of stuff."

Captain Elwin had now gotten into his cloak. Everyone else, including the children who had come along, were now in their cloaks.

"Lead the way," Elwin said to the Nightcloak, who proceeded to the left of their location. They passed a few pieces of the tunnel that had collapsed an indeterminable time ago. Afterward, they traversed under a few overhangs. Captain Elwin organized them into a tactical formation. He had himself and the leading Nightcloak take the lead, with two citizens behind them. He continued this formation, alternating escorts and civilians, with an Illustratum and Lepides at the very back. The Nightcloak then squeezed into the narrow entrance of the tunnel, making it look almost effortless. Captain Elwin followed. Some of the children went through next, being quite brave in manner despite the situation.

Alexander and Camilla then squeezed through. As he entered, Alexander took in a deep breath. He and Camilla were inside the tunnel. It was a grim sight. There was a faint amount of light from a lamp held in the Nightcloak's hand. The rest was darkness, and what could be seen was just dust and rocks on the walls and ground. Alexander had barely enough space between his basket and the wall. The tunnel dripped with trickles of water.

"Comfy, isn't it?" Camilla asked.

"Could be worse," Alexander said. *Let's hope we aren't in here too long,* he thought. They moved forward so that the next people could come in. Alexander and Camilla were followed by two more citizens, and then Cadfan and Aeronwen squeezed in. Cadfan's sword hit against the stone as Aeronwen stood next to him.

"This is going to be annoying," Cadfan said. "Are we even going to be able to move without our weapons banging against the wall and making noise?"

"Guess there is only one way to find out," Aeronwen said. There was more shuffling forward as more people crowded in. Alexander wondered how many times they would have to go underground. He looked at Camilla. Her face contorted into a frown. He could tell she was thinking the same thing. That she wanted to hurry up and get this over with. After a few minutes, the rest had finally joined them in the cave. There was another fire lighting the middle of the formation and one close to the back.

Captain Elwin then addressed them. "Everyone stay close, and we will get this over with as soon as possible," he said in a hushed tone. "Also, from here on out, all communication is in low tones or silence. We don't want to give away our location. I know space is small, so do your best to carry your weapons without them hitting the walls, but avoid making a hazard. I have arranged a space of healers in this formation. You have myself up at the front, responsible for the first seven rows; and then another at the eighth, responsible for the next seven; one at the sixteenth row; one at the twentieth; and one toward the rear. Let's move out now," he instructed, and the Nightcloak took a step forward to lead them through.

They shuffled along slowly. Alexander took one step at a time at the pace of the crowd. He felt confined inside the tunnel as he breathed in the mix of fresh and stale air. Camilla seemed to sense his discomfort.

"This won't be long," she whispered.

Alexander hoped she was right. They continued for some time, mostly on a smooth trail. They slowed as the lead Nightcloak whispered that there was a roughly foot-wide gap in front of them. He also said that he had tested it in his previous recon and estimated that it also dropped about eleven feet down. He and Elwin carefully crossed it. They then proceeded to lead the others over it. Some citizens had a difficult time crossing, especially the front ones who had children. A few more minutes passed, and Alexander and Camilla moved only about three feet.

Alexander took in a breath and tried to ease the tension he was starting to feel. He inhaled stale air as he imagined finishing his apprenticeship completely and receiving his Illustratum badge and his certificate. This seemed to help, as he was unaware of what was happening.

Camilla nudged him. He did not respond. She nudged him again.

"Anytime would be nice, Alexander," Cadfan quietly screeched from two rows behind them.

Alexander shook his head and then proceeded forward with Camilla. They got to the gap that the Nightcloak had mentioned. Alexander peered down but could see nothing but darkness past the first three feet.

"I'll go first," he said. He wanted to do so in case Camilla needed any help. Rocks crumbled as he put his feet closer to the edge. He braced his right arm against the cold stone. He breathed in slightly and then exhaled as he lifted a leg across. He stepped over easily and grimaced as his hand passed over something slimy.

He then turned and prepared for Camilla to cross. She breathed in and took a step over. As her foot hit the other side, the edge crumbled, and she slipped.

"Camilla!" Alexander exclaimed as he jumped forward and reached out his right arm. She caught it in her right hand and then dragged Alexander forward. Her left hand caught a groove in the wall. Alexander's shoulder hung at the edge and dug into it as Camilla dangled. Then the young couple in front of Alexander dropped and began to pull him back while he lifted Camilla up. Alexander heaved as his arms strained. He was pulled backward inch by inch. After a few moments, he tugged Camilla all the way up, and the others pulled them both away from the crevice. More of the rock crumbled beneath them, effectively widening the gap. They quickly stumbled forward as the rock crumbled just inches behind them. They all gasped for air, and Camilla winced as she held her left hand. Alexander looked down at it. In the light provided, he noticed that the rock had cut through the leather of Camilla's glove and sliced her hand.

"Is everyone all right?" Elwin asked.

"Yes sir," Camilla answered, "but I have cut my hand really badly." Alexander could see the blood pouring down from her hand.

A Vivicantern who had been farther ahead of them squeezed her way to them and held out her hand. A white pulsing light radiated from it. Slowly, the wound on Camilla's hand began to heal until it had disappeared.

"What about the gap? How much broke away?" Elwin asked.

Camilla turned and looked at it. "At least three feet wider," she observed.

Alexander could hear Elwin ask the front Nightcloak if there were any other routes. He said the route was only a single direct line to the exit.

"Here's what we are going to do," Elwin said. "Get a rope, throw it across, and stake it to the ground with knives. Everyone on the side that has crossed will also hold the rope, and then after everyone is done, we will cut what we can and keep it." A rope from the back of the line was passed to the front. A knife was stabbed into the ground to keep the rope in place. The rope was then thrown across the gap, and five rows of people, including Alexander and Camilla, grabbed hold of it. They took large steps backward until the rope was taut and there was enough room for three more sets of people to cross.

The rest of the people began to shinny across the rope. Aeronwen's turn came, and she clung tightly to the rope. She turned upside down and wrapped her legs around the rope and slowly made her way across. Once she had crossed, everyone took another step back to make space. Cadfan seemed eager to make his way across and wrapped himself around the rope as well. His sword hung at his side awkwardly as he inched across. Once his feet were above the ground, he slid and dropped to the other side. He then took hold of the rope as the next set of people crossed.

Everyone took another step backward. Tesni was next. She stared at the rope in front of her with a bewildered look.

"Tesni, are you okay?" Urien asked.

"Just nervous," she said, still gazing at the rope. She then changed her focus to Urien. "Can you help me?"

Urien nodded. Tesni placed her lance on the ground and moved to the rope, then grabbed hold. Urien removed a smaller rope from his bag and tied it around Tesni and then tied it to himself. He stayed planted on the ground as she began to weave across the rope.

"Now just slowly move forward one arm's length at a time," Urien said.

Tesni inhaled loudly and moved her arm forward and began to pull herself across. The rope was still held taut. She pulled herself farther, shaking visibly.

"You're doing good," Urien instructed from behind. She pulled once more, inching little by little. She had proceeded halfway across the rope. She forcefully expelled some air and then continued. She pulled herself near to the edge, but her legs slipped from the rope. Tesni now dangled, holding with only her hands. The force of it pulled Urien slightly. He then eased his way onto the rope and made his way over to her.

Urien inched forward and dropped his left arm under the rope to provide support for her flailing limbs. Tesni's feet kicked in the air, getting no stabilization. She finally managed to lift them up and over Urien's arm. Tesni scurried across the rest of the rope, with Urien following right behind. She made it to the end and swung herself backward onto the ground. Urien lifted his left arm back to the rope and then dexterously pulled himself across and swung to the ground. Tesni was still breathing heavily.

"Thank you, Urien," she said.

One of the people behind them threw her lance across. She caught it and laid it on the ground next to her feet. The others took a step back now. Some people at the front were now no longer holding the rope. She and Urien took hold of the rope as the next individuals crossed. A father crossed with one of his children clinging to the rope above him. They made their way across in a matter of minutes. The mother and other child then followed. Dysan was now standing at the front of the rope, gazing across the gap.

"Come on, Dysan," Cadfan muttered from the other side.

"Delyth, you go first," he said.

"Are you sure?" she asked.

"Yes," he said. "I'm gonna be pretty heavy on this thing. I don't want to snap it. If I did, I would want all of my friends to cross first." She placed her lance on the ground and pulled herself to the rope. She quickly wormed across, making her way to the end.

Dysan sheathed his axe in a strap on his back and then tossed Delyth's lance across. She caught it in one hand and placed it on the ground. She took hold of the rope as Dysan began to latch on to it.

Dysan heaved his legs over the rope. More tension was placed on the rope as it lowered with the weight. Dysan slowly pulled himself across. He exhaled forcefully as he proceeded to the halfway mark at two feet. He then lost partial grip of the rope as one leg fell completely off. He still inched his way forward, but then the other one fell off. Not bothering to lift his legs back up, Dysan swung his right arm to the side and pulled his way along the rope. He then did the same with his left and pulled himself farther. He repeated this action three more times and then pulled himself up to solid ground at the end.

He took hold of the rope, and more people made their way across. After ten more minutes of people heaving with the effort of holding the rope, everyone had made it across. The rope was quickly detached and returned to a basket.

"I'm glad that's over with," Cadfan said. Alexander agreed with him as he shook out the tension in his arms.

They continued down the tunnel for fifteen more minutes. Alexander wished for the task to be done with. He was starting to feel annoyed with the time they had spent in tunnels underground. The Nightcloak at the front informed them quietly that they were nearing the end. After a few more seconds of shuffling along, Alexander felt something odd. He stopped in place, as did Camilla next to him. This caused everyone behind them to stop, which irritated some people.

"Camilla, do you feel that?" he asked.

She looked around for a moment. "Yeah, actually. I feel a faint breeze of cold air to the left."

"Come on, you two. Keep moving," Cadfan said in an annoyed but hushed tone. Alexander reluctantly pressed forward. He could not help but feel uneasy. They inched forward, but then Urien and Tesni stopped at the same spot. There was more commotion from behind.

Alexander turned to look behind him. Suddenly, to Urien's left, some movement occurred, and it appeared that the stone wall was pushed out. Two Xythuu soldiers made their way through. They appeared startled when they saw Urien and Tesni. Urien lunged forward. He instantly pressed his knife through the neck of one and pinned him to the wall. The man's blood spewed over his face.

"Intrude—" the second soldier began to say as she attempted to attack Urien, but Tesni hit her over the head with her lance. The woman fell, unconscious. Urien felt along the wall that they had popped out of. Upon looking closely, Alexander thought he could see fake rocks of various shades adorning it.

"What's going on?" Elwin asked from the front of the formation.

"Sir, we have an issue. There is another tunnel here. It was camouflaged as part of the wall. We just encountered Xythuu forces," Urien said quietly. Elwin turned to his Nightcloak, who said he had not noticed it as he had been exploring. They sped into a trot and hurried down the tunnel. Captain Elwin held up his right hand. A blue light shone from it, and he began to rapidly administer a blessing. The blessing etched across the tunnel and reached every member. Alexander, while running, pulled up the robe on his arm and watched the Onglikae runic script for the *Perae Cuutein* and *Anae Luma* blessings appear in a glowing blue until they dulled. Alexander saw one on Camilla's arm as well. He was amazed that Elwin had the magical prowess to apply this to everyone. They ran for a few minutes, and then Alexander saw the people in the front step out of a dimly lit hole. As he got closer, he could feel the cold night air flowing from the hole.

He made his way out of the hole and followed the others who had taken position behind many large rocks just outside of the tunnel. Cadfan, Aeronwen, Urien, Tesni, Dysan, and Delyth took position next to him and Camilla as the final people at the back of the formation filed out. Alexander peeked over the side of the rock. To his left, he could see the border fort, with a cannon at each corner. There were about thirty Ciimerii guards on or within it. To his right, he saw the stone bridge over the river they had just passed under. There stood a formation of Xythuu soldiers. He could hear shouting too.

A voice belonging to a Xythuu man then spoke. It was a booming, thick, powerful male voice from where the Xythuu forces stood. The man demanded that the guard hand over the fort with no fight. He promised they would all be treated with dignity and respect as their prisoners. Alexander wondered if that was true. Why had they not just attacked the fort?

After a moment of pondering, he then moved behind the rock and told his friends, "If they are asking for the fort to be surrendered, that means they want to keep it intact," he said.

"Which means they may have motives to move more people through here," Urien said.

"That means this is now a direct violation of their neutrality," Dysan said with some disgust in his voice.

"I don't like this," Cadfan whispered. "Something doesn't feel right."

"They didn't do this in Jylinae," Delyth said. "Why do it here?"

Alexander peered back over the rock. A voice shouted that they would not hand over the fort.

"I think they plan to invade Ciimerii," he whispered.

Within the next instant, spikes with thick chains were launched at the top corners of the fort. They smashed into the walls around the cannons. Next he heard the loud sound of the cannons firing down upon the Xythuu forces. He saw a wall of Xythuu units rush forward.

Alexander bolted from his position to his right. He looked up as shields were generated over the cannons and a few arrows fired from the fort. Camilla charged after him.

"Hey, wait!" Captain Elwin exclaimed behind her.

Alexander grabbed a Lapideas in his right hand. He launched a beam of electricity at an advancing formation of Xythuu troops. The beam crashed over many of the soldiers, blasting off limbs in the process. Alexander held it for a few moments and moved it across the open ground between them.

Camilla slid next to him in a crouch and nocked an arrow in her bow. She quickly pulled a box of matches from her pocket and removed one, then tossed the box to the ground in front of her. The remaining Xythuu forces were still stunned from a surprise attack from the side. Camilla struck the match just at the tip of her arrow and pulled the string back, with the flames just a few inches from her bow. She then fired it toward the Xythuu forces. It hit a target, engulfing the person in flames. His terror-filled voice echoed across the open ground and bounced off the cliff walls around them. Captain Elwin then rushed out and removed an iron stick from his side. He extended it and unrolled a small Eltheneaen flag attached to it, then waved it in the air.

Captain Elwin then created three shields to the sides and front of the location where they stood. Each shield was comprised of four layers. Alexander was once more impressed with Elwin's prowess. Alexander saw the main formation of Xythuu troops surge toward the fort, with their magic users generating shields. A detachment charged toward his location while chains were shot from the main formation to the cannons at the top of the fort.

Spells of fire and lightning came crashing toward Alexander's location. He launched another *Fulmenooo Xel* at the advancing forces. An enemy, however, moved toward it and blocked it with his hand. He deflected it into the ground.

Tesni launched a *Linwae Xon*. The two Eltheneaen Illustratum launched *Faer Xaen* spells while two more *Linwae Xon*s were fired from the Vivicantern. The dispersing light spells crashed into some of the moving Xythuu forces, taking out a few units, while the other spells were deflected to the ground around them.

The Xythuu soldiers launched a flurry of spells. They collided with the shields in front of the rocks that Tesni, Urien, Aeronwen, Cadfan, Dysan, and Delyth were using for cover. Alexander launched another *Fulmenooo Xel.* The yellow beam of lightning fired at the Xythuu forces. It hit a few and then was dispersed by an enemy.

Alexander attempted to charge another, but his Lapideas had now turned a dull yellow-gray color. More spells began to barrage the shield in front of him. Camilla shot an arrow, which hit the head of a moving Xythuu target. The Xythuu forces were now close to twenty feet away.

Blue lightning crackled around Alexander's hands and then formed into a four-foot-tall ball. Alexander launched the *Fulmenooo Xaen* at the forces. It collided into some of them, and he charged and launched another. It hit near the ground, toppling some of the forces and blasting the area with shards of rock and severed limbs. The smell of sweat, metal, blood, and charred flesh filled the air and then wafted into Alexander's nose from the gentle wind that was blowing.

At this moment, the Xythuu horde breached the shields. Elwin charged and stabbed his sword into one. Tesni thrust her lance from behind the rock, and it collided with a Xythuu soldier. The Xythuu forces broke their formation slightly. A Xythuu soldier knocked Aeronwen to the ground and raised his sword. Cadfan blocked the soldier's downward strike and grabbed hold of the man's wrist and spun him around. They exchanged blows, each blocking the other's attacks.

Dysan and Delyth were each fighting soldiers using lances. Delyth kicked one back and thrust a lance at her. The soldiers and the other Xythuu forces around them had blessings etched into their arms. Delyth's lance collided into the stomach of the soldier's armor but did not pierce through. The Xythuu soldier then thrust her lance toward Delyth. It tore through her camouflaged cloak but just grazed her armor underneath. Urien charged forward while reaching into a pocket. He removed a small wound chain. He swung it a few times and wrapped it around the soldier.

Alexander looked around him. He breathed heavily, and his vision narrowed as his eyes darted everywhere. He saw Dysan had been pushed slightly away from them and was exchanging blows with a soldier while the rest of the Eltheneaen units were engaging the other Xythuu forces.

Alexander's eyes now locked on Urien as his body suddenly froze. Urien wrapped a chain around the soldier's arms. Urien struggled to hold the chain as the soldier thrashed about. Tesni had finished off an enemy and darted toward Urien. Urien pulled the chain and brought the enemy forcefully down to her knees. Tesni held out her hand and began to remove the blessing from the soldier. Blue particles lifted off the Xythuu soldier. Alexander turned and launched a *Faer* toward some enemies. The fire landed near one. His head swiveled to his left, and his eyes locked on Cadfan.

Cadfan was still exchanging blows with a Xythuu soldier. He blocked his opponent's sword three times, then ducked as it swept over his head. He quickly stepped forward, turned, and swung his sword up. It hit his opponent under his chin but did no visible damage. His opponent swung his sword down. Cadfan sidestepped and grabbed his arm. He attempted to pull it up and snap it, but the blessing that had been applied to the soldier protected him. Cadfan brought his sword into the Xythuu man's face through the openings in his helmet. It scratched his skin a few times, like a sword against a rock. The Xythuu soldier thrust his sword hilt into Cadfan's face.

Alexander started deflecting spells that had been launched his way while he still focused on Cadfan. The strike to the face knocked Cadfan back. The Xythuu soldier then brought his sword across Cadfan's cheek. It hit hard but did not cut him. The soldier stepped forward and swung his sword. It passed just inches from Cadfan's face. The soldier then reached his leg under Cadfan's and used his arm to toss Cadfan to the side. Cadfan rolled a few times. He used his arm to bring himself to a kneeling position. Alexander deflected a spell and saw a Xythuu soldier dash forward in a blur and reappear in front of Cadfan, swinging his sword at Cadfan's head. Cadfan managed to take a step to the side and thrust his sword. It hit his opponent's sword, knocked it from his hand, and sent it skidding across the rough, rocky ground.

The soldier attempted to dash for it, but Cadfan jumped onto him before he could go far. Cadfan swung the man around, knocking the soldier's helmet off. He then brought the man's head down into his knee. It did little damage. He brought it down again more forcefully. This time, a few blue particles dispersed from the impact. He brought the man's head into his knee again, and more particles dispersed from the soldier. The next time, there was a loud crack, and blood dripped from the man's nose. The force sent the man wrenching free from Cadfan's grip. He stood limply with blood pouring from his face. The soldier then fell face-down to the ground beneath him. Cadfan sighed and rejoined the rest of the group. Alexander also breathed a sigh of relief. His eyes then focused on those around him.

Tesni was still in the process of removing a blessing from an enemy. Dysan was fighting another enemy, the same one from earlier. Dysan swung his axe downward. The Xythuu soldier deflected the attack and then thrust his lance at Dysan, grazing the side of Dysan's armor and tearing his cloak open. Meanwhile, a *Faer* spell crashed into Alexander's armor. It knocked him down. He hit the ground hard and heard the sizzle of his armor. He quickly cast a *Vandua* spell over it. He looked under his armor and saw no damage.

He looked back at Dysan. The Xythuu soldier Dysan was fighting launched a *Linwae Xon*. The dispersing spell of light hit Dysan four times—two to his chest, one to his leg, and one to his right shoulder. The spell knocked Dysan back and to the ground. The front of Dysan's cloak had been blasted open from the spell, exposing his armor. Both of his blessings had disappeared. He lay on the ground, wincing in pain. His right shoulder was bleeding.

Alexander started heaving himself into a crouch, ignoring his own pain.

Cadfan hurried to Dysan, crashing right into the approaching Xythuu soldier. They hit the ground hard, and he slid away from the Xythuu soldier. Cadfan lay face down. He pushed himself up as blue particles dispersed from his arm. The force from the impact had destroyed his *Perae Cuutein* blessing, but his *Anae Luma* still remained. The soldier also had blue particles dispersing from his body.

* * *

The enemy Tesni had been engaging with knocked Tesni to the ground and tried to punch her. Tesni pulled her foe to the ground with her. She placed her hand against the head of the Xythuu soldier and removed the blessing that had been placed on her. The soldier then punched Tesni's face. Due to the *Perae Cuutein* blessing she had received, this did barely any damage. Tesni could hear the bones in the soldier's hand snap. Tesni kicked the soldier off her, thinking it was odd that her opponent showed no reaction to the intense pain she must have just experienced.

Tesni and the soldier both stood. Her foe extended a lance and charged toward Tesni. Tesni sidestepped, grabbed hold of the lance, and spun her opponent. The soldier's helmet flew off. Delyth prepared to charge the enemy. Tesni let loose a gasp of astonishment.

"Delyth, don't! She's Eltheneaen!" Tesni exclaimed. Delyth stopped her charge just six feet away from the soldier.

Now that the helmet had been knocked off, the soldier's hair fell down her shoulders in two slightly dirty long blonde braids. Tesni could see the face of the person in front of her. She had pale skin and a small birthmark under her right eye. Her eyes, though, showed the purplish-black coloring in and around them that indicated she was cursed. Tesni was in disbelief. Before her stood her friend from her apprenticeship training, Christina.

Christina charged at Tesni with a dull, vehement stare that showed she had no memory of who Tesni was. Christina thrust her lance forward. Tesni pushed it aside with her own lance, being careful to not hit Christina. Christina's lance was deflected, but she swung at Tesni again. Tesni's lance collided with her friend's lance once more. Christina then forcefully knocked Tesni's lance to the ground and kicked her back.

Tesni landed hard with a roll. Christina began to move forward. Delyth quickly extracted a compressed lance from her side. She pressed the top of it, and it sprang into full-length form. She removed a rope from the basket on her back and tied it around the end of the lance. She then threw the lance forward in Christina's direction while holding on to the end of the rope. The lance landed in front of Christina, who had sprung toward Tesni, and she crashed over the rope.

Tesni sprang on top of Christina, holding her lance in her right hand and her left hand to Christina's face. She frantically screamed to Christina that this was not her and that she was being controlled. She screamed at her to fight the curse. Tesni's hand glowed with blue light as she began to attempt the curse removal. Christina thrashed about screaming while puffs of black-purple smoke came off her face. She butted her head into Tesni's three times and then threw her to the side. Blood oozed down Christina's face between her eyes as blue particles dispersed around Tesni. Christina's hands then went tight around Tesni's throat from behind.

Tesni could feel the force of her friend's grip. She tried frantically to get air in through her nose but could not get any. She held her left hand to Christina's face. Tesni's hand once again glowed with blue light. Christina screamed as more smoke drifted from her face. Tesni could see the black leaving her eyes and the familiar blue appearing. Delyth then charged into Christina and smashed the blunt end of her lance into Christina's side, just enough to slow her.

The force caused Christina to release her grip on Tesni's throat. Delyth took Christina to the ground as blue particles drifted away from Delyth's body, indicating that one or both of her blessings were now gone. Tesni bent over to the ground, gasping for air and feeling the intense pain in her neck slowly ebb away.

Delyth dropped her lance as she and Christina began to wrestle on the ground. Christina punched Delyth, landing three direct blows to Delyth's nose, causing it to bleed. Christina then reached for a collapsed lance on her side and extended it. Delyth extended one as well, and the lances crashed into each other.

They exchanged two quick fierce blows before Christina knocked Delyth's lance out of her hand. The lance crashed into the rough, rocky terrain beneath her, and Christina's lance slashed the side of Delyth's leg. The lance cut through Delyth's cloak and thigh guard strap. Her leg began to bleed, and she pressed her hand on the wound. Tesni launched a *Linwae* at Christina. The small blast of white-colored light magic hit Christina in the leg, causing a loss of balance.

Tesni darted toward Christina and launched another *Linwae* at her. This one hit Christina's hand and knocked the lance out of her grip. Christina lunged at Tesni as she drew near. Tesni hit the ground hard, with Christina atop her violently thrashing at Tesni's face. The blows loosened Tesni's hair while she attempted to block her face with her left arm. She felt something wet at the front of her cloak. Tesni's hand glowed blue once more. Two more puffs of smoke were removed from Christina as she continued to thrash at Tesni.

Christina grabbed Tesni's left hand and smashed it into the ground. Tesni felt a sharp pain in her wrist. Her left eye had been partially cut from Christina's fists as well as her forehead and chin. She then brought her face into Christina's, feeling the break of Christina's nose. Tesni did not want to seriously hurt her friend but was met with an unrelenting effort from Christina.

Tesni then lightly kicked Christina off of her and saw the blood at the lower part of Christina's torso. Tesni's heart felt like a stone in her chest as she realized that Christina had landed on her lance moments before. She looked toward Delyth, who was lying on the ground using a chunk of ripped cloak wrapped around her arm to try to stop some bleeding from a cut she had sustained. Christina was about five feet away from Delyth, on her hands and knees, breathing heavily from the bleeding and the force of Tesni's kick. Tears began to run down Tesni's cheeks. For a brief moment, she felt as though time slowed as the impossible choice before her tore her heart to pieces.

Tesni pushed herself upward with her right arm and bolted to Delyth. She covered the ground between them quickly and slid next to Delyth.

"It's okay, Delyth," Tesni said frantically. She held her right hand to Delyth's wound. Her hand glowed white. The wound slowly closed bit by bit. A few more agonizing moments went by. The wound had closed from a large cut to a small scrape.

"Tesni, look out!" Delyth shrieked as Christina charged toward them. Delyth shoved Tesni to the side, and Christina crashed into Delyth.

Tesni screamed at Christina, telling her to take control. Christina hit Delyth's face as Tesni rushed toward them. Delyth pushed Christina upward. Christina then looked at Tesni, and for the first time, she seemed surprised.

"Tes . . . Tesni!" she exclaimed with a choked voice. "You're alive?"

Tesni stopped in her tracks. "Yes, Christina. You're cursed. You need to take full control. You're also heavily bleeding. I need to heal you," she said as she inched closer to Christina.

Delyth held up her left hand and winced slightly. She now stood in front of Christina.

Christina looked relieved and scared at the same time. "I remember Jylinae being attacked. I was near my house as Xythuu troops moved in," she said with tears starting to stream down her face. "The evacuations had been ordered. They defeated all of us in the area and captured us. Then they took control of me. I fought to get away, but I wasn't strong enough. They repeatedly cursed me and controlled me. They made me attack a set of villages south of Jylinae."

Delyth gave Tesni a wary look, indicating for her to hurry. Tesni moved closer to Christina now. She held both of her hands to Christina. They glowed white, and she began to heal Christina. The pain in Tesni's left hand was still present, but she ignored it as she began to remove the curse once more. Puffs of black-and-purple smoke drifted from Christina's face.

At that moment, Christina began to scream as the curse took control of her once more. She lunged toward Tesni. Both went tumbling to the ground. Christina lashed vigorously at Tesni. Tesni took a few hits to the face and placed both of her hands on Christina's face. They shone with blue light once more. Christina screamed as the smoke was pulled from her face. She then fell onto Tesni. Tesni lifted Christina up, rolled to the side, and held Christina in her arms. Tesni could see the blue fully return to Christina's eyes.

Delyth stumbled over. She tore a piece of Christina's robe and wrapped her hands in it. She then placed her hands firmly on Christina's lower torso, where the blood was coming from.

Tesni held her left hand to the wound and began the healing.

"Tesni," Christina said with heavy breathing. "Don't. I don't have much left."

Tesni kept healing.

"If you find my sister, tell her . . . tell her . . . I'm sorry. And . . . that I love her. Please tell her," Christina said.

Tesni looked at her while still healing. "No. You're gonna tell her whatever you want. Because you're not going anywhere," Tesni said gently yet frantically while tears poured from her eyes.

"Tesni," Christina said weakly, "you were a good friend." Her voice went quiet.

Tesni looked at Christina with disbelief. "No!" Tesni exclaimed in a choked voice. "Christina!" she screamed. Tesni placed her head on Christina's forehead, still crying vigorously.

* * *

There was still an intense exchange of spells and arrows between the smaller Ciimerii-Eltheneaen forces and the Xythuu forces. Cadfan was vigorously fighting a different soldier, exchanging blow after blow.

Aeronwen had made her way to Dysan. She told him to be still, with the intentions of healing his shoulder, but he ignored her and bolted from the ground with his axe in hand.

He is so damn stubborn, she thought.

He charged toward a soldier with a huge bellow escaping from his lungs. The Xythuu soldier stood his ground with an arrogant posture and launched a *Linwae Xon* toward Dysan. It crashed near his leg, knocking him to the ground and sending shards of stone smashing against Dysan's leg armor.

Aeronwen launched a *Linwae Xon* from each hand. The white bursts of light magic flew at the Xythuu soldier. She then launched a *Linwae Xon* into the air above the soldier. He raised his left arm, with a small bronze shield attached to it. The bursts of magic struck it, doing little damage. Aeronwen held her hands toward the *Linwae Xon* above the Xythuu soldier and brought it downward and tore it to many smaller pieces.

The soldier generated a small shield above him, so the bursts of light crashed into it. Cadfan then darted at the man. He moved in a blur and slammed into the man, his sword colliding with the man's shoulder. They fell onto the ground with a roll.

Aeronwen rushed over to Cadfan. She asked if he was hurt. He murmured a *no*, trying to rise. The Xythuu soldier then stood. He thrust his lance at Aeronwen. It barely cut against the tops of her gloves on her forearm. The lance made a scratching sound as it scraped across the vambraces over her gloves. Aeronwen could feel sweat trickling down most of her body. Her limbs felt extremely heavy.

The soldier thrust again, and she generated a shield to block it. The force of the blow destroyed the shield and knocked her to the ground. The Xythuu soldier thrust once more, colliding with the bronze-plated leather pad on her left shoulder. He swiped to the side. Aeronwen quickly ducked, hearing the heavy whoosh of the lance over her head.

Cadfan sprang up again and lunged at the soldier. His sword pierced through a gap in the armor between his arm and shoulder. The Xythuu soldier grunted as Cadfan's sword wedged into his skin.

Dysan then charged again and swung his axe downward. The soldier stepped and spun away from Cadfan's sword. He lifted his shield to Dysan's axe, which absorbed the blow. While doing so, he brought his lance across Cadfan's lower leg. It cut across it and sent him to the ground.

Dysan swung his axe once more. The Xythuu soldier deflected with his lance. Dysan hooked the lance, and they both struggled to maintain balance as they attempted to force the other to the ground.

Aeronwen crawled to Cadfan. She placed her right hand near his leg, and her hand glowed with white light. She prepared a spell. At that moment, she saw the Lapideas in her left hand turn a dull gray.

She was unable to change it out while healing the wound on Cadfan's leg. She charged a spell in her hand, using her own Essence. She aimed at the Xythuu soldier, who was still locked in a power struggle with Dysan, but then lowered her hand, realizing she might hit Dysan. The Xythuu soldier and Dysan spun. The Xythuu soldier kicked Dysan's knee and launched a *Linwae Xon* directly at him. The spell shattered parts of his chest armor and knocked him to the ground. He landed just a few feet in front of Aeronwen and Cadfan. He groaned in pain.

In addition to his already bleeding arm, Aeronwen could see more wounds. One on his chest and one on his right leg. Aeronwen launched a *Linwae Xon* at the soldier. He blocked it with his shield. The Xythuu soldier retaliated with a *Linwae Xon*. Small bits of the spell crashed into the ground near her and Cadfan. One hit Cadfan's right shoulder, and one hit Aeronwen in the leg. She cried out in pain.

At that moment, one of the Eltheneaen Oracles thrust his lance toward the Xythuu soldier. The Xythuu soldier blocked with his own lance and shoved him backward. He shot a *Linwae Xon*. The Eltheneaen Oracle deflected the medium ball of white-colored light magic and raised his left hand. Green particles dispersed from his shield in many clumps.

The Xythuu soldier thrust his lance at the Eltheneaen Oracle. He caught it in his hand, just a few inches from his hip. Aeronwen had finished most of Cadfan's healing. She brought both her hands together. White light charged in them, making a small ball around her hands. She then launched a *Linwae Xon* at the Xythuu soldier. The beam of light collided with his legs, slowly tearing away cloth and armor and then completely destroying his legs and sending his body crashing to the ground. She stopped the spell and then generated a healing field around Dysan, letting the magic gradually heal his wounds. Dysan healed as Tesni, with a tearstained face, and Delyth made their way over.

* * *

Alexander stood behind a shield as a few spells thudded into it. A ball of fire smashed the top of the fort, showering the area around it with rubble. The cannon still remained and fired on the enemy forces. Two spells slammed into the ground in front of Alexander and Camilla.

Elwin ordered for everyone to regroup and move to the fort. Alexander generated a few shields around himself. Aeronwen assisted Cadfan up while Tesni and Delyth did the same with Dysan, heaving as they lifted him. Urien joined them.

A small blast of fire hurled toward them. Aeronwen raised her left hand and generated a long green shield to the sides of them. The spell crashed into the shield.

Cadfan muttered to Aeronwen that he did not need her to carry him. They ran from their location behind the shield to an open stretch of land.

Elwin generated another three-layer shield in front of Alexander and the other units around them. He then generated a long one connecting to the rocks where the other escorts were protecting the civilians. Aeronwen generated another shield to her side. A *Faer Xaen* struck it, followed by multiple sparks of lightning. This destroyed the shield. A *Fulmenooo Xaen* hurtled toward her. She deflected the ball of crackling lightning, then launched a *Linwae Xaen*. One crashed into Xythuu forces at high speed along with spells and cannon fire from the fort.

A *Faer Xaen* barreled toward Aeronwen. Cadfan immediately pulled her close and jumped forward, taking her with him. The fire spell struck the ground just a few feet away from them as they rolled in the dirt. It would have hit her leg, possibly severing it. Cadfan yanked her up and pulled her behind the shield. Tesni generated a shield to the side so she, Urien, Delyth, and Dysan were hidden behind it. Spells destroyed it as they moved behind the shield that Elwin had generated.

Alexander and Camilla began to escort civilians along the length of the shields, toward the fort. The others followed shortly. They had covered about half the ground as the shields were getting battered and destroyed. Alexander tripped over a stone and tumbled to the ground. A sharp pain stung his knees and legs. Camilla knelt down and began to pull him up by his arm. They rose and began to run once more. Spells of fire and lightning smashed into the shield several feet to their left and destroyed it. This time they both tripped.

Alexander looked to where the Xythuu forces were and saw them launching objects from small siege weapons. They hit in various locations among the Eltheneaen units. One hit a shield above Elwin and turned it into particles.

Alexander crawled to Camilla. A glass jar landed two feet away from them.

Pink dust spewed from it and then blew toward him. He attempted to cover his mouth but did not manage in time. It entered his lungs. He pulled Camilla up, and they continued toward the fort. He held his hand to the side and tried to fire a spell but to no avail.

More spells whizzed past them and hit the ground behind them as they moved. The blast from a *Faer Xaen* knocked them to the ground. Another hurled toward them and crashed into the ground a few feet in front of them. The spell shattered the ground into pieces. A small chunk of the ground hurled toward Alexander. It scraped across the top of his left eye, making him cry out in pain. Blood began to pour from it. Camilla rose and started shrieking. He pushed himself up, grabbed her, and continued to run.

Another spell of fire blazed behind him as they ran. The force of it flung him a few feet forward. He fell hard to the ground, groaning in pain. He felt something warm near his legs. He looked down and noticed that the spell had caught the bottom part of his robe on fire. Camilla pulled a dagger from her forearm glove and tore into the robe. She ripped the bottom part off.

Camilla rummaged through her basket and removed a bandage and wrapped it above his eye. A fire spell struck the top of the basket, setting it ablaze. She quickly threw it to the ground and pulled him up and into a run.

They and the others regrouped behind various shields that were being bombarded. They still had about twenty more feet to cover. Alexander looked up about thirty feet and could see spells of fire and lightning forming. In the distance, he spotted the Xythuu soldiers who were forming the spells above. A massive four-layer shield then appeared across the sky above them. Elwin was holding his hand up.

Alexander turned to the Xythuu forces and watched a *Linwae Ruunae* bombard the enemies. The spells of light along with the artillery from the forts did some damage to the Xythuu forces. As Alexander's group continued to the fort, a ball of fire crashed down on its edge, sending rocks flying.

As they arrived at the fort, the sounds of fighting filled Alexander's ears. He heard spells colliding into shields and destroying parts of the fort. He also heard the groans of pain from people. It was deafening.

A bearded and balding man clad in gray armor with yellow robes approached them. Over the roar, he said he was the fort commander and that the carriages had been prepared for them. He wanted them to make it to Lein so the news of the Xythuu invasion could be reported.

Alexander noticed a look of apprehension on Elwin's face. He obviously wanted to stay and assist in the fighting, but even with the combined force of the Ciimerii guard and the Eltheneaen escorts, they did not have the numbers the Xythuu encampment did. Their primary objective was to escort their own citizens, which had been an agreement between their two countries. They also, however, could not go back the direction they had come without surely being killed or captured or leading the Xythuu forces to their hiding location.

Alexander looked up. He could see clearly out of his right eye, but his left was slightly worse. He saw nothing of the sun. The smoke around them had blocked all of its light, and some ashes had begun to fall.

The fighting outside the fort increased in noise. A formation of Xythuu forces charged toward the fort as spells and artillery fire collided into their shields. Alexander then saw a familiar blue energy fire from the front of the formation. A shield at the top of the fort was destroyed, and the energy melted through part of the cannon. More were fired, and one hit the arm of the man at the cannon. The energy completely severed the man's arm as he fell to the edge of the fort. Alexander could see the man hanging at the edge, twenty feet above him.

Cadfan looked across the battlefield. Alexander knew what he was looking at because it caught his eye too. At the front of the formation, he saw the commander who had led the Xythuu forces during the invasion of Jylinae. He stopped and fired more energy blasts from his lance as the forces around him continued to charge for the fort.

Cadfan immediately bolted for the front door of the fort. Dysan wrapped his arms around Cadfan, preventing him from moving as he squirmed about.

"Let me go!" Cadfan shrieked.

"What the hell do you think you're doing?" Dysan asked him.

Cadfan slipped out from his arms and again dashed to the door. Dysan grabbed hold of him once more. He slipped off his right gauntlet and then uppercut Cadfan on his chin. The hard impact knocked Cadfan unconscious. Dysan caught Cadfan as he fell and dragged him back to the group.

Elwin ordered all his forces to the carriages. The Ciimerii guard commander ordered two of his Ascalons to go with them to the capital and explain the situation.

Dysan hefted Cadfan over his shoulder. There were eight carriages, each with four horses. Each also had a large covered wooden wagon that could fit roughly twelve people. They made their way to one, which already had two Illustratum in it. Urien climbed up and assisted Dysan with Cadfan, and they all sat wearily on the wooden benches. The civilians were spread out among the carriages with either Ciimerii escorts or Eltheneaen escorts.

A signal was given to the drivers, who then urged their horses on. Alexander sat back against the wall of the wagon and looked at the fort as it grew smaller in his vision. The sound of horse hooves beating down on the dirt was all he heard now. He touched the blood on his face—most of it was dry—as he looked on at the fort. He felt he was abandoning this unit in a time of need. A sense of hopelessness began festering inside him.

Chapter 18

The heavy galloping of hooves pounding against the road and the rapid turning of metal wheels created quite a racket. Alexander leaned back against the wall of the wagon, with Camilla next to him. He felt hollow thinking of the scene he had just witnessed. Camilla said nothing but was obviously feeling the same.

The ride was a long and somber one. They rode fast along the road, stopping for nothing. After a bit of time, the horses slowed to a trot. Close to two hours had passed. The carriage then stopped completely. The riders informed them that they had covered approximately twenty-one miles. They were going to take a short rest and continue on.

Most of those who could heal within the Eltheneaen group were doing their best to tend to the wounded. Aeronwen and Tesni were out of Essence but were still assisting with non-magical practices. The Vivicanterns who were with them, and Captain Elwin still had small amounts of Essence left and were healing people.

Cadfan stumbled out of the wagon and made a beeline straight for Dysan, who was casually stretching. Alexander tensed.

Cadfan shoved Dysan hard.

"Calm down!" Dysan demanded.

"Calm down? That was the killer of my father, and you stopped me!" Cadfan screamed.

"Yeah, I stopped you from recklessly charging to your death! How stupid can you be?" Dysan yelled back. "Quit being selfish! You're not the only person here who is suffering!"

Cadfan raised his hand. Urien and Alexander quickly moved in between them. The other escorts nearby braced themselves as well.

"Cadfan, I am sick of hearing this!" Dysan continued. "What would you know," he muttered as Urien pulled him away.

Cadfan walked away, his shoulders slumped.

"Let him go. He needs to cool off," Alexander said. Everyone went back to what they had been doing, and Captain Elwin pulled Cadfan to the side—to deliver a stern lecture, Alexander assumed. Elwin finished his discussion with Cadfan and returned to tending the wounded. Cadfan made his way back to the wagon he had come from.

Tesni and Aeronwen were seated in the center of the camp, wrapping people's wounds. Tesni winced as she moved her arm.

"What happened to your arm?" Elwin asked Tesni.

"My arm . . ." She paused, her voice cracking. "My arm was pinned by an enemy."

"Let me see it," he said. Tesni rose and moved a few feet and sat to the left of Elwin. She removed her vambrace and held her left arm out. He took hold of it gently. She winced. He placed a finger on the top of her arm. A white pulse glowed from it, and Alexander could briefly see the blood vessels, tendons, ligaments, and bones along her limb.

"There's the issue," Elwin said. "There is a slight tear in the tendon." A white light then shone from his hand, and small waves generated into her arm. "This should speed up the healing process, but you still need to cool it whenever possible."

A Vivicantern was tending to Alexander's face wound. Alexander watched Elwin while he performed healing magic on Tesni. He was still amazed at Elwin's magical prowess. They had endured a very long battle, and Elwin still had Essence left. Alexander had had a small amount left by the time he had been hit with blocking dust, and he had none now. He wondered if his own prowess would increase to match Elwin's.

The Vivicantern said he had just used what was left of his Essence. He informed Alexander that the wound was partially closed. The rest would need to heal normally. He also informed Alexander that there was a good chance he would develop a scar. Alexander thanked the Vivicantern, who then left.

Moments later, Alexander gathered around the others. Each of them had a cup and a bowl of chicken that they were consuming quickly. Two bigger bowls lay on the ground, filled with water. Cadfan finished his lunch and used one of the water bowls to rinse his materials. He then removed his basket from his back and placed his clean bowl in it. He stood and slung the basket onto his back.

Alexander and the others stared at him, waiting for him to speak up.

"I'm sorry, Dysan. I'm sorry to all of you. I shouldn't be acting this way, and not to any of you," he apologized. "I just keep seeing this over and over again. The constant death. And then I see the person responsible, and it reminds me more. Reminds me that I'll never see my father again. It also makes me feel powerless, constantly reminding me that I am not strong enough."

"We're all feeling that way, Cadfan," Delyth reminded him.

Alexander sat still. He was physically and mentally exhausted but still found his mind drifting to the events he had endured so far. To his home of Jylinae. He had so many memories there. Memories of his childhood with his father and mother. Memories of his basic schooling. Memories of when he had met his friends. Memories of his affinity determination and apprenticeship training. Now that home was gone, consumed in the malice of neighborly aggression. And that same aggression continued to relentlessly pursue them. He knew inside some change would have to occur. As these thoughts assaulted him, his weary mind could barely keep up. Everyone had gathered all their supplies now and were prepared to move once more.

* * *

It was late afternoon, and the trot of the horses picked up to a heavy gallop. The noise of hoofbeats created a constant rhythm in Alexander's mind as he stared blankly at the floor of his carriage. Camilla was with him as well as two Eltheneaen Lepides and eight citizens.

He stared at the carriage floor for some time, not fully aware of his surroundings. He felt Camilla nudge his shoulder. A bit startled, he looked up into her green eyes. Her gaze conveyed a mix of concern and exhaustion.

"Hey, how are you feeling?" she asked.

He drew in a deep breath and held it in his lungs for a few brief moments. He exhaled slowly. "Not good. I'm weary," he said softly. "What's left of the place we used to know? I feel like there is nothing but smoke and ash everywhere. When will this end? Camilla, you just turned nineteen a few days ago. How many people our age have experienced what we have? Who decides things like that?"

She peered at him in silence for a moment before speaking. "I'm sure in the past there have been plenty of people who have experienced the same thing we are," she said softly. "I don't know who would decide this fate for anyone, but there is one thing I know." He looked in her eyes, and there was a resolution within them.

"What is that?" he asked.

"New life springs from the ashes," she said. "We will keep fighting, and we will take back our home, no matter the cost. Our fathers were warriors, and we carry their blood in our veins."

He pondered and wondered what his father would have done and felt. Alexander still felt uncertainty and hoped he could live up to his father's legacy.

* * *

The horses had been trotting for hours. Alexander had drifted to sleep a few times but had been awoken by a Lepides, who had reminded him that he was still part of the unit in charge of protecting the citizens who had come with them. He was annoyed at their dutifulness. He just wanted to rest his eyes before arriving in Lein. He then told himself that he had volunteered for all of this.

They stopped after a few hours to quickly eat. Some of the carriages held pots of horse feed and water, which the horses gratefully consumed. Alexander and his friends were outside their carriages, stretching their legs.

They gathered in a circle. The other units were dispersed in similar formations. They were in a clearing next to the road that had short tufts of yellow grass and a slightly rocky terrain. There were shrubs and small trees scattered all around.

Alexander looked at the horizon. The sun hung just above with an orange glow.

"How much farther do we have to go?" Dysan asked, rubbing his shoulder.

"Probably only another few hours," Urien estimated. A cold wind blew across the clearing. They were all still wearing the thick cloaks they had been given. Alexander was glad to have them. In just a month, the temperatures would become much colder. That cloak with the white Eltheneaen robes underneath kept him mostly warm. They all had some form of damage to their thick outer cloaks, though, which would need to be mended soon.

There was then an order to move out once more, so they all returned to the carriages.

They trotted along the road again for a few more hours. It was dark by the time the horses came to a stop. They were told the horses were taking a quick break. Everyone stepped out of the carriages to stretch. The sound of horses gulping down water dominated the otherwise silent scene. Dysan, Delyth, two other escorts, and the citizens they were guarding climbed into a carriage.

The others followed suit, and then the carriages were loaded up. Alexander and Camilla were instructed by one of the Eltheneae Illustratum to load into a cart. Cadfan and Aeronwen loaded into it with them, along with two groups of civilians.

They sat there for a few more minutes while the other carriages were loaded up and the remaining traces of their presence were covered. Alexander and Camilla sat in the back with the civilians while Aeronwen and Cadfan sat in the front. The cover above them helped keep in warmth. Alexander felt the carriage pull forward. The rhythm of hoofbeats once again resumed.

A young man and woman sat next to Alexander and Camilla. They had a young son, about three years old, who was lying atop his mother's lap. Alexander, with weary eyes, looked at the boy. The mother was stroking her son's face. The father then looked up and shifted his gaze to Alexander. Alexander averted his stare and then glanced around at his friends.

"I wonder why they started this war," Alexander pondered aloud.

"It sounds like they just want control," Cadfan suggested. "They even were at the border of Ciimerii."

"He's right," Aeronwen added. "Their presence there was a violation of Ciimerii neutrality, but when they initiated the attack, they took it one step further. What goals could they possibly have involving Ciimerii?"

"Like I said," Cadfan insisted, "I think they just want control. During the last wars, they pushed into Kilnaveth and held it for some time before we took it back."

"Those wars were centuries ago, though," Alexander pointed out. "What motive could they have here?"

"Do you think some of the other cities are still fighting?" Camilla asked.

"I would imagine that they are. We're technically part of one based in Fort Ydaeriin," Aeronwen stated.

"Yeah, but now we have to take a different route back there—if we are even going back," Cadfan commented. The talk dulled into a quietness until there was nothing but the sound of the hooves and wooden wheels striking the road underneath.

Alexander was bored. He leaned back against the carriage wall, his eyes heavy. He tried to keep his mind occupied but kept coming up short. Even though he was not supposed to, he began to nod off, his head slowly drooping to the side. He could still hear the sounds of hooves against the ground. This only helped to lull Alexander further asleep. His hearing dimmed considerably. When the carriage came to a stop, the abrupt motion woke him from his slumber and he sat up straight.

"What's going on?" he asked.

"Not sure," replied Camilla as she turned her head to the entrance of the carriage.

"Why didn't you wake me up?" Alexander asked, slightly groggy.

"You haven't been asleep that long," Camilla said. "Besides, you looked exhausted. We all are, so I thought I would let you enjoy a few minutes."

"I'm grateful for that, but I could still get in some trouble. You too," he said to her. Cadfan stuck his head outside the carriage's cloth covering. Alexander looked at him.

"Cadfan, what do you see?" he asked.

"Nothing but nature behind us," Cadfan said.

"Do you think we're there?" Aeronwen asked. At that moment, the covering was pulled to the side, and the two Ciimerii guards who had sat at the front of the carriage stood there.

"We're all stopping briefly. We've been authorized a fifteen-minute stop," one of them said. Cadfan hopped out of the carriage and stretched his legs. Aeronwen followed and did the same. The civilians made their way to the end of the carriage, and Alexander and Camilla crawled out after them.

Alexander and Camilla slid to the ground. Alexander's legs ached as he stood up. The air held a mild chill, and a small breeze wafted past him. They were on a set of rolling hills covered with yellow-tinted grass. Around the area were sets of trees, their leaves turning orange and dropping to the ground. He saw a small pot with a fire under it some twenty feet away. The other units were gathered around it, including Dysan, Urien, Delyth, and Tesni, who were all looking at something off to their left.

"Let's go get some food and water," Alexander suggested. As they ambled over to the gathering of people, Alexander saw something in his peripheral. He stopped in place to look at what was before him.

At the bottom of the hills, Alexander spotted two long stone walls wrapping around a cluster of buildings. He and the others then continued forward until they were by the fire with Urien, Dysan, Delyth, and Tesni. They all stared at the stone buildings below them. Alexander saw towers at each corner of the wall. Flags flew above all the towers. The flags had a large yellow circle on the left side with thin orange lines coming from the top and bottom of the circle. Four smaller circles were to the right of the larger circle.

A smile slid across Alexander's face, and a look of awe spread over those of his friends. The city of Lein lay before them on flat ground with small sloping hills just outside the city. Farms surrounded the city. The sun was just beginning to break over the horizon and cast a vermillion glow on the sprawling towers and buildings of Lein.

www.ingramcontent.com/pod-product-compliance
Lightning Source LLC
Chambersburg PA
CBHW070536260626
47161CB00002B/406